Passion, Pain

&

Perseverance

Monica Harper
and
Adonica Williams

We dedicate this book to those who are excited about life, love, and inexpressible joy.
We've learned that the journey of growth takes prayer, perseverance, and plenty of passion.

-Monica and Adonica

"When you hear the word passion many definitions come to mind. Some think about fruit. Some think about love, but after tonight, none of you in this building will be able to say the word passion without thinking about the people on this stage right now. Together, these women took passion to an entirely new level. They developed a passion group and turned their love for humanity into something more meaningful than they ever imagined. It has been my honor and privilege to be in the presence of such successful, prominent, and genuinely good-hearted people. And now the moment we have all been waiting for. I would like to present this check for five hundred thousand dollars to the Excel in Spite of Scholarship Fund," Dr. Elaine Morris proudly announced.

Applause roared from everyone in the ballroom. The six women standing on the stage could barely contain their emotions. They had all been through so much together in order to get where they were at this very moment. It just proved the saying that hard work plus dedication breeds success.

Gabby smiled at Sha'Miracle. Sha'Miracle squeezed her hand and smiled back. Madison was trying her best not to cry, while Egypt couldn't keep her tear ducts dry. Hazel-Ann beamed with pride and gave Charity a tight hug. These six women had barely known each other when they first embarked on this great adventure that was the passion group, and now they were exactly where they wanted to be—accomplished.

Sha'Miracle spoke first. "It has been a pleasure to work with such dedicated and phenomenal women. I would like to thank all of the sponsors for taking a chance on us and believing in our dream." Sha'Miracle passed the microphone to Gabby.

Gabby was overwhelmed with emotions. "Thank you to everyone involved in making our dream a reality." She turned and faced the women on the stage. "I want to thank everyone on this stage as well. You all never gave up on me and saw this project through to the end." Gabby's voice began to crack. "You all could have walked away so many times, but you didn't; you stayed with me, and for that, I will forever be grateful."

Hazel-Ann took the microphone away from Gabby and rubbed her back. "We are all so grateful for the vision and the work. Now so many students, who otherwise would not be able to, can attend college. This feels amazing. The journey was rough, but anything that comes too easily won't be appreciated as much, and we wholeheartedly appreciate everything that has come forth."

Madison spoke next. "I am so humbled to be a part of such great humanity. These women have become my best friends. Together we have made things possible that I never could have imagined. I love you all."

Egypt was still crying but managed a "Thank you, everyone" through her sniffles.

Charity spoke next. "This is truly a blessing. Proverbs 22:6 says, 'Train up a child in the way he should go, and when he is old, he will not depart from it.' I am just elated that I could be a vessel in training up children. It is because of the generosity of the sponsors and all of you here that bought tickets that we are able to provide this service to these children. On this day, I know the Lord is pleased, for we have all done a great work in his name."

Charity turned to look at all the ladies. "Ladies, I am pleased to let you all know that you have earned another star on your crowns that the father in heaven has especially for you. I love you all." They all smiled. They could always count on Charity to give them just a little bit of Jesus, even when it was redundant. Charity passed the microphone back down until it reached Dr. Morris.

Dr. Morris and Sha'Miracle hugged each other for what seemed like forever. Dr. Morris whispered, "I love you, and I'm so very proud to call you my daughter," in Sha'Miracle's ear. The ladies then smiled for what seemed like a million flashes from photographers and exited the stage.

Back at the head table, Egypt finally spoke. "This is just too much for me. I'm so happy and so sad all at the same time. I do love you all, and I'm blessed to have a bond with all of you. I never want to lose any of your friendships. Please don't let this be the end of our bond."

The ladies all crowded around Egypt and gave her hugs and kisses.

"Can you imagine that just a year ago we came up with this idea, and now it has manifested full circle?" asked Gabby.

"I can't believe how different we all are and were able to actually work together and make this happen," Sha'Miracle added.

"Well I knew from the beginning that I would have to pray long and hard, as well as fast every week, to whip y'all heathens into shape," Charity teased.

All the ladies laughed. A year ago, they would have been bothered by her comment, but they had gotten to know Charity and made the choice to accept her just the way she was.

"I'm just glad I got to know you all and finally was able to let go and just be me," Madison said.

"I won't say this hasn't been a crazy ride, but I will say I'm glad I was riding with you girls," Hazel-Ann told them.

"I'll just be glad when you all stop reminiscing and drink a little champagne, so we can get this party started," Lucas said. "I'm ready to dance."

"Oh hush, you crazy man. Let us have our moment," Charity chastised.

"I still remember that weekend like it was yesterday. It was the most eventful weekend of my entire life. Look how far we've come," Sha'Miracle stated.

"And it's only going to get better," Sha'Miracle's husband said and kissed her neck.

"Get a room," teased Gabby

"I know, right," Egypt added.

"Gabby, is that Reece?" Madison asked.

Gabby looked over to her right. Sure enough, it was Reece.

"What's he doing here?" Hay asked.

"I don't know, but I'm going to pretend like I don't see him. This is our night, girls. Let's enjoy it," Gabby said, raising her glass to toast.

Everyone at the table laughed, sipped champagne, and went on the dance floor. They had all grown so much since the Friday that started it all. What started out as the day before the weekend ended up changing their lives forever.

One generation shall praise thy works to another, and shall declare thy mighty acts. (Psalm 145:4)

Sha'Miracle

"Get up; get up, and get moving. Good morning to all my favorite listeners living in 'The City Beautiful.' Looks like a cooler, sunny day for Central Florida. The highs will hit the lower-to-mid fifties, and by sundown, expect the lows to fall near forty degrees. This is Linda J. reporting from your secret-charm station, WRAP 96.3 FM, where your secret is always safe with us."

Yeah, right, Linda J. couldn't keep a secret if her life depended on it. She is the mouth of the South. If you want all of Orlando and the other surrounding cities in Florida to know your business, then you should tell Linda J.

I wish I could lie in this bed forever. I hate cold weather. I don't even have any shoes to put on. Wait, I do have those ridiculous running shoes my mother bought me last Christmas. I picked up a little weight during and after college, so sue me. Sha'Miracle Morris is not running anywhere. Although, if I don't hurry up and get dressed, I might be running late for work.

"Welcome to Subway; how can I help you this fine morning?" Trevor announced.

"Where is Bobby?" I said, reading his name tag.

"He is having car trouble, so I'm taking his place until he gets here," Trevor stated while he looked at me in amusement.

"Bobby knows exactly how to fix my sub. I'm trying to eat healthier these days, so let me get your Italian BMT on wheat," I replied.

"May I suggest the Veggie Delite sub?" Trevor recommended.

"No, you may not! Do I look like I'm on Jared's journey to you? What you can do is fix the sub I asked for and put a little hurry up on it!" I said with as much sarcasm as I could.

"Sorry, I just thought the Veggie Delite would be a healthier choice — my bad," Trevor said with a huge smile on his face.

"At least you got that right; it was definitely your bad," I said with a frown.

"I see you have on a William J. Clinton Middle School jacket. Do you work over at Clinton Middle?"

"Can you put the mayonnaise on the bread first, before you put the meat on the bread?" I said as I pointed at the bread.

"No problem. Is this enough mayo?" Trevor asked, looking up at me.

"No, I need you to add some more mayonnaise, and put it on both sides of the bread."

"Are you sure? That seems like a lot of mayonnaise."

"The only thing that I am sure of is that you are almost on my nerves," I said to him, rolling my eyes.

"I got your cheese. Would you like this toasted?"

"No, for fear it might have me in this place even longer."

"OK, tell me your favorite veggies," Trevor said, smiling. Was he flirting with me?

"Let me get some lettuce…No, that's too much lettuce; take some off. I need banana peppers, cucumbers, a few onions, and tomatoes. I don't want the ugly tomatoes from last week either."

"Is that it?" Trevor asked.

"I would like a little salt and pepper and oil. Thank you."

"You are so very welcome."

"Are you sure that was oil you just put on my sub?" I asked.

"It is an oil and vinegar blend," Trevor stated cautiously.

"I didn't ask you for a blend," I barked.

"I'm sure you won't be able to taste it over the enormous amount of mayo already on the sub."

"What did you say?" I cut my eye at him. Who did he think he was talking to?

"I didn't say anything. Is there anything else I can do to complete your order?" Trevor questioned.

"Bobby always puts my pickles in a little cup on the side," I said.

"Pickles in a small cup, I think I can handle that," replied Trevor.

"Good morning, Sha'Miracle," Bobby said.

"Bobby, I'm so glad you made it in to work. Please take this money, so I can try to get to work on time. I don't think that the new guy is going to work out. He talks too much, and he is just way too slow. Just look at the line of people all frowned up behind me."

"I'm sorry about the delay. Do you have to pick up Gabby this morning?" Bobby asked.

"I forgot my cell phone in the car. She has probably called me a thousand times by now. I have to go; hope to see only *you* tomorrow, Bobby!"

"Have a good one," Bobby said while laughing.

"I will," I said.

"Open the door!" I yelled. Every morning it's the same thing. I get them up for school, and then they drag. I swear, sometimes I think I never should have had children. I have four teenagers, all stairsteps, all in high school. The boys are worse than the girls.

"Chill, Ma! I'm almost done," cried Marlin.

"I'm gonna be late. I hate when Miracle blows her horn and I'm not ready."

"I know; I know. Here you are, my queen," Marlin says, opening the bathroom door with the sweetest smile on his face. I couldn't help but smile back at him. No matter how mad they made me, one flash of their perfectly white teeth and I melted. That was my problem. They were all as sweet and charming as their father.

Marlin had just gotten back from an East Coast college tour two weeks ago and was excited about attending college at Legacy University. I myself preferred Wise University, but either way, I was glad he wanted to attend an HBCU (historically black college and university).

I would have to come up with money to send him. My wheels were already turning, and after a little bit of research, I decided to create a passion group. I coerced Miracle into just about everything I did, so I knew she would be on board.

When I walked downstairs, I expected to find everyone sitting at the table, eating the breakfast I had prepared. Instead, the four pack was all over the place.

"Hey! Why isn't anyone eating?" I asked.

"I'm finished," said Jade.

"Me too," replied Mark.

"I'll eat at school," Jalyssa said.

"I don't have time now," Marlin cried.

"Oh well. Does everybody have everything they need? The bus will be here soon."

"Yes, Ma," they all cried chorally.

I asked the same question every morning. They all knew me like a book. As they were walking out the door, everybody said their good lucks. But my dear, sweet Mark kissed me on the cheek and said, "If they don't hire you, they're crazy." It made me smile. I loved the four pack. They knew I was nervous about my job interview.

For all my children knew, I had been at the same 411 call center for five years and longed for a change. So today I was going to the sister company and interviewing for the supervisor's position. This would allow me to display my skills and train the new hires. Plus, it would be more money.

Well, at least that was what I told them. The truth was I had been unemployed for six months now. I lost my job at the call center because I was always late. But, hey, it wasn't my fault. I didn't have transportation. My car had been giving me some problems, and I spent a lot of money getting it fixed.

Well, the money had to come from somewhere, so I took it from the car payment. I mean, surely they would understand, right? Wrong! They came and got my car in the middle of the night two days after I got it running again. I was pissed! I called the car people and gave them a piece of my mind and hung up on them. They'd know next time not to mess with me.

Well, after that, I was depending on people to give me rides to work, because I was *not* catching the bus. But when I started to be late all the time, they had to let me go. I didn't have the heart to tell my children, so I kept it from them. All they knew was they were never hungry, the lights were always on, and we keep a place to stay. What they didn't know was I got food stamps, an unemployment check, and my *D*-boy boyfriend, Reece, kept me paid. Whenever he served, he always looked out for his girl.

When my children went to school, I was mostly in the house, but sometimes I hung out with the boys on the block. I knew a lot of them from school, and they were all nice. Plus, they always made sure I was taken care of, because they loved my children.

But this morning, I was going to another call center to try to begin again. I loved getting money from Reece, and the boys on the block always looked out, but I felt like I wanted more, like I wanted money to call mine. My children were almost grown, and I would be all alone soon. I needed to make sure I would be OK.

Miracle was on her way. I wasn't in the mood to hear her complain about waiting on me, so I made sure I was ready. That's the number one rule when you don't have your own car; you have to be ready when the horn blows.

Today she was going to let me take her to work and borrow her car for my interview. I was glad she didn't get off until later on in the day, because I had some errands to run when I finished. I needed to get Reece's clothes out from the cleaners and go to the spa to get a bikini wax. He was coming over later on tonight, and he loved when I had that Mohawk downstairs. He said everything tasted better. I made sure I kept up with it, because it drove the both of us wild.

Reece and I had been together for about six years now. It was rumored that he was messing with some girl on the other side of town, but that wasn't my business. As long as he took care of me, there were no problems.

Beep, beep. I jumped, and my thoughts were interrupted. I walked outside, locked the door behind me, and got inside the car.

"How is my favorite Miracle doing this morning?" I said with the biggest smile on my face.

Miracle rolled her eyes at me and said, "Girl."

All her juicy stories started with that one word. I knew this was gonna be a good one. I sat up erect and listened attentively.

Hazel-Ann Dawson was dreading getting out of the bed. She had been partying late last night with her friends and regretted it now that it was time to go to work. Hazel-Ann, known to everyone as "Hay," was a juvenile-probation officer for Orange County and currently had twelve children on her case load. Six were boys, and six were girls.

Linda J. had awakened her from her deep and peaceful slumber with the morning gossip. Hay wanted Linda J. to be quiet. She wanted the radio to stop. She wanted absolute peace and tranquility, but she could not, for the life of her, muster up enough strength to hit the snooze button. She heard Linda J. say, "This is Linda J. reporting from your secret-charm station, WRAP 96.3 FM, where your secret is always safe with us." With that, Hay chuckled. Linda J. was the biggest joke. She couldn't keep a secret even if it was her own.

"Welp," Hay said. "I'm up."

Hay went to her closet and took down her uniform. She absolutely loved her job. She thought that she had done quite well for herself to only be twenty-eight years old. She had graduated from Wise University six years ago when she had just turned twenty-two. She was always a driven individual. She never needed anyone to motivate her, because she had a desire to be great ever since she knew what greatness was.

Hay had been named after her great-grandmother, her mom's grandma. Her mother was a single parent who raised her and her sister all by herself. Her mom didn't struggle financially, and she taught Hay and her sister, Patrice, good manners and self-respect. She was a really good mom.

When Hay turned fourteen years old, her mother turned all financial affairs over to her. She taught Hay how to read the bills when they came in, write the checks, balance the checkbooks, and make sure the bills were paid. Hay thought this was fun at first, then it started to get difficult. She resented her mother for a few years, for forcing her to grow up so fast, but when she went to college, she thanked her mom for it. Hay was able to help her roommates out. She couldn't believe how unskilled they were in the smallest of things. Like really, who couldn't balance a checkbook?

What Hay's mom always lacked was a man. Hay never saw one come, and she never saw one go. Her mother had never even expressed the desire to have one. For this reason, combined with taking care of the household, Hay became the man of the house. She wasn't like most lesbians, who always had "feelings" or had been "trapped inside the wrong body." She simply enjoyed being the provider for her mom and sister, and as she grew older, she became attracted only to women. She had never had a boyfriend before, because she was all the man she needed.

Her best friend from college had a little boy, and Hay was his godmother. He was a four-year-old named Luke. Hay treated Luke like he was her own son. He even had his own room at her three-bedroom, two-bathroom, two-car-garage home in Central Florida.

"Yes! That's my jam!" said Hay. "You can be *my* naughty girl." Hay loved Beyoncé. She was one of Hay's favorite artists.

"This is just what I need to get me in the mood. I gotta go to the middle school today, and those little crumb snatchers always make me earn my coins."

Hay gathered her clothes and took a shower. Just as she was getting out, she heard her phone ring. There was no way to get it in time, so she decided to call whoever it was back when she got dressed. Hay brushed her teeth, applied lotion to her body, splashed on her Kenneth Cole Black cologne, and put her shoulder-length dreadlocks in a ponytail. She had just gotten an edge yesterday at the barbershop and was looking as handsome as ever.

Hay thanked God for waking her up for another day and then picked up her cell phone and keys. She meant to see who had called her first, but her fingers sort of reverted to Facebook whenever she picked up her phone. As she touched the icon and opened the app, she saw that she had one notification. It was from Charity, inviting her to a passion group.

Hay thought to herself, a passion group? What the hell is that? She clicked on the page but was given very little information—just a date and time.

"If I didn't know exactly who Charity was, I would have thought this was spam," Hay said to herself. "And why is Charity inviting me to something? We haven't spoken in years."

Just then, her phone rang again. It was a number she didn't recognize. She answered it.

"Dawson."

"Hello, may I speak with Hazel-Ann?" the voice on the other end said.

"Who, may I ask, is speaking?" Hay asked.

"This is Charity Love. Remember me?"

"Yes, I remember you. How are you?"

"I'm blessed and highly favored. And yourself?"

"I'm fine."

Hay was ready to cut the extraneous small talk. What did she want? Since Hay had never been the tongue-biting type, she decided to speed this nonsense up.

"Charity, what is the reason for your call? And how did you get my number anyway?"

"I got your number from your page on Facebook."

What?! Hay thought. She had to change her settings as soon as she ended this conversation.

"Anyway, the reason for my calling," Charity continued, "is to include you on this blessed venture that I am about to embark upon. I have been invited to a passion group and wanted to know if you would join me."

"What is a passion group? Is it like a Passion Party?" Hay asked.

"Oh, heavens, no!" Charity gasped.

"Well?" an agitated Hay said.

"It's where people of common interests get together and do something good for mankind," Charity explained.

Hay was always down for helping people. Suddenly she was less agitated and more intrigued. "OK, what's the cause?"

"The group will develop a scholarship fund of some sort. Would you bless us with your presence?" questioned Charity.

"Sure, I'll get the information off the Facebook page."

"OK, Hazel-Ann."

"Please, call me Hay."

"If you insist…*Hay*," Charity said awkwardly, "I'll talk to you later. Have a blessed and glorious day, because Jesus loves you, and so do I."

Hay grimaced. "Um…hmm, bye-bye now."

Hay pressed the red End key on her phone five times, just to take out her frustration. Why was this girl so extra? "Hallelujah now; bless the Lord now; praise the Lamb now" — Ugh!

"I love that nice Jesus just as much as the next man, but a walking Bible, it's too aggravating. I *would* like to see what this group would be about though. Oh yeah, that reminds me…"

Hay went to her settings on her Facebook page and made her phone number read (000) 000-0000. She chuckled to herself. "Next time Jesus *himself* is gonna have to call."

Hay locked her door, got into her all-black Lincoln MKX, and turned on Linda J. It was just what she needed after her sermon with Reverend Charity this morning.

Hay was on her way to the office and then off to William J. Clinton Middle School to see her favorite juvenile, a sixteen-year-old eighth-grade girl named Sashay.

Charity

"Hay..." Charity said to herself. "Now why would she go and mess up a perfectly good name by calling herself the food that the horses eat?" She shook her head. "Young people these days."

Charity was a thirty-four-year-old divorcée. She had been married for ten years when her husband came home one day and said that he wasn't happy. She had been listening to him gripe for months, but when she suggested counseling, he refused. She didn't know what else she could do, so she just ignored him and prayed about the situation. After all, prayer changes things.

She and her husband, Sam, had met on the campus of Wise University some fifteen years ago. He was a nerdy computer-science major, and she was a music major. All she wanted to do was sing. She sang while she walked; she even sang while she talked. Her friends often had to stop her from doing that.

She had been walking to choir practice, singing "The Center of My Joy" — the original version, not the Ruben Studdard one — when Sam touched her arm. She'd turned around and seen the most hideous thing she'd ever laid her eyes on. She couldn't believe the nerve of this ugly stump touching her soft, cashmere skin.

"Yes?" Charity had said.

"Um, excuse me. I...I don't know how to say this, but I've been watching you for a while now and finally had the courage to just say hello," a nervous Sam had replied.

"Well, hello," Charity had replied.

"My name is Sam, Samuel Love. What's your name?"

"Nice to meet you, Sam. I'm Charity."

"Well, Charity, can I walk you to the choir room?"

"Sure, I don't see why not."

Together, they had walked to the choir room. They talked every day after that, and when they graduated, they got married. Sam wasn't a very attractive man, but he made up for it in so many other areas. He was charming, polite, very sweet and thoughtful, and he worshipped the ground Charity walked on.

Charity always wanted children, but Sam did not. He was always so career driven that he never thought he would have the time. As the years went on, Charity's desire to have children died down also. Instead she poured herself into pleasing her Lord and Savior Jesus Christ all day of every day. She walked, talked, and ate righteousness. She needed it like she needed air. She believed that the more she sought God, the more blessed her life would be, and, thus, the happier she would be.

During her marriage, she figured God had already blessed her with a loving husband. He respected her; he never strayed and became unfaithful; he was a good provider and Charity's support system. The thing that bugged Charity, though, was that he always wanted to go somewhere and do something. He had to understand that she didn't want to travel the world all the time. She just wanted to work hard, shop sometimes, and work in her local church. She was on so many different boards that if she missed a Sunday, things were likely to fall apart. They argued countless times about that. Charity had even suggested that he travel with his friends, but he didn't want to. He only wanted to go with her. She thought he was a bit clingy, but it wasn't anything that Charity couldn't handle.

Sam was an executive engineer for Microsoft. He was the one who tested the Office software and saw to it that there were no glitches. He made seven figures and was very generous. For this reason, Charity didn't have to work. She did, however, have a job. She wanted something to do that she would love doing every day, so she became a teacher. She taught chorus at a local high school. She loved what she did. It gave her a sense of purpose in an otherwise chaotic world.

Each paycheck she earned went directly into her pocket. Sam paid all the bills and gave her a healthy weekly allowance. Sometimes, she would even forget that she had gotten paid, until she checked her account to buy something. She mainly spent her money on things for her church. She made sure the youth in the church had everything they needed. From Black History Month in February all the way to Christmas in December, Charity was sponsoring the children in the church. She bought whatever they needed for each of the programs. She and Sam sponsored back-to-school backpacks every year in the fall. Each child at the church received a backpack filled with school supplies. It always made her feel good when she worked with the youth president. Money was never an object.

This particular day, when Sam came home and said he wasn't happy, Charity's heart dropped. She didn't know why she felt this way, because he had said it all the time, but something in her spirit told her this was different. She tried to ignore the feeling, because she ignored Sam all the time, but the Holy Spirit told her to probe. So she asked Sam what the problem was.

"I'm not happy," Sam reiterated.

"Could you be more specific?" Charity said curiously.

"I want out. This relationship has run its course, and I'm done," Sam blurted out.

"What!" Charity exclaimed. "You can't be serious. I mean, look at how long we've been together. Look at the empire we've built. Look at us!"

Sam looked perplexed. "Us? Empire? Huh? We're married, yes. We've been together for a long time, yes. But what do we do? NOTHING! I want a wife who wants me. I want to travel with you. I want to go out with you. The movies, comedy shows, concerts, long weekends — miss church for crying out loud."

Charity could not believe what she was hearing. *Miss church*? Was he out of his mind? "Sam, you know that I can't do that. It is because of the Lord's mercy that we are not consumed."

"Cut the crap, Charity. This is exactly what I mean. You didn't marry Jesus...you married Sam! Sam wants to feel like he's wanted, enjoyed, celebrated. I don't get that at all from you."

"Is there someone else?" Charity asked.

"No, there's not. I just want to break free from this relationship, because for years I've been trying to *live* and you're comfortable just *existing*. I know that I cannot change you, so I must change me. And the change begins with me leaving you. You can have the house and half of everything I possess. I would like for this to be as painless as possible. I love you; I really do. I've loved you since the day we met, but I love myself even more. I've gotten me a house, and I will be moving out tomorrow. The lawyer will serve you with divorce papers, and as long as you agree and sign, we will never have to set foot in a courthouse." With that, Sam kissed Charity on the forehead and left.

Charity was speechless. She didn't know what she had done wrong. Sam was out of his mind if he thought she was going to skip out on church to travel this sinful world. Movies? Comedy shows? Concerts? What good, clean Christian woman would be caught dabbling in all that worldly filth? Not her. So she had no choice but to oblige his request. It was obvious she wouldn't be able to keep him here. She loved him, but she loved the Lord even more. He sent Sam, and he would send another man, if that's what he wanted her to have. She was not making any changes.

Charity logged onto Google while she was on her break. The phone call with Hay had taken up more time than she thought it would. She typed "passion group" into the search engine. The first thing that popped up was Oprah Winfrey's page.

Better is the end of a thing than the beginning thereof;
and the patient in spirit is better than the proud in spirit.
(Ecclesiastes 7:8)

"Avery, do you realize that we have been waiting in the car for over fifteen minutes? You need to hurry up so that the children are not late for school," I said.

"Madison, do *you* realize that we wouldn't be having this conversation if you had listened to me and taken your car to the dealership to be fixed instead of taking it to the 'shade-tree man.' I don't understand how a woman carrying an eighteen-hundred-dollar Gucci bag will trust her car to a dude working on cars in his mother's yard," Avery responded.

"Noah is not a shade-tree mechanic; you know he gave up his garage to be at home to help out their sick mother." Avery could be so judgmental at times. That was one of my pet peeves when it came to him.

"I know that's the lie that you and Europe want people to believe. She just wants you to give her brother money so that she doesn't have to do it," Avery said.

"My friend's name is Egypt! Why do you always have to call her by the wrong name?" I yelled.

"Europe, Egypt, whatever! People shouldn't name their children after continents!"

"Daddy, Egypt is a country in Africa, not a continent," my daughter Mikayla said sweetly.

"Mikayla, what did Daddy tell you about being in adult conversations?" Avery said while eyeing her through the rearview mirror.

"I know, Daddy, but Mommy says that it is our civic duty to share knowledge everywhere we go, so that the world is not consumed with ignorant people." My baby girl made me so proud.

"Maddie, why do you tell her to say things like that?" Avery was so livid at this point that I thought I actually saw a small vein pop out of his forehead.

"What? The world is filled with ignorant people," I replied.

"Yeah, you are one of them," Avery said as he pointed a finger at me.

"Daddy, A. J. wants you to turn the radio up," Mikayla screeched. "Mommy, it's Taylor Swift! Turn it up some more, pppllleeeaaassee!"

"Who touched my radio? Never touch a black man's radio! I listen to Linda J. every morning. Kids, you can learn a lot about your heritage by listening to 96.3 FM," Avery said proudly.

"I beg to differ. That R&B and hip-hip station is far from being beneficial to anyone," I insisted.

"It is called hip-hop, baby. All right, kids, have a great day," Avery stated while pulling up to the front of the school.

"A. J. and Mikayla, Miss Egypt will be here in this very spot on time. I will not tolerate tardiness from either of you. You know how important it is to be punctual?" I said to my children.

"Yes, Mother," the children said in agreement.

"A. J., today is another day to be great. Aye, dawg, I'll pick you up from football practice," Avery said.

Avery and Avery Junior have this two-minute handshake that I feel is completely and utterly ridiculous. It is a complete waste of time and just stifles the uniqueness of a good, firm handshake.

I need to make sure that Egypt remembers that today is her turn to take Mikayla and Asia to their ballet lesson and drop A. J. off at the football field. It is counterproductive for me to take time out of my busy schedule to make a calendar of events if Egypt is not going to adhere to the schedule.

"Madison, make sure you call Master P. back today. She has called the house, dry cleaners, and my cell phone. Holler if you hear me," Avery joked.

"Avery, that is almost funny but not quite. Why do I have to be the one to call Auntie Pearl?" I whined.

"You look so cute when you frown up like that. You got me thinking about doing something dirty to you. You know you like it dirty."

"Hence that is why we own several dry-cleaning businesses," I said, rolling my eyes.

"Maddie, you just couldn't say something back to me dirty? See, that's why you have to call Ms. Pearl back. Since you can't talk dirty, you can do the dirty work," Avery said with a huge grin on his face.

In my mind, I kept repeating the words, *the dirty work*. I had to get up, get the kids up, and start breakfast. I had to make sure that everyone had everything that they needed in order to have a successful and productive day. I took the kids to school and came back home to get the house in order.

I was not Superwoman, nor was I a stupid woman. I secretly hired a maid to come and help out around the house. Tina, from Keep It Kleen Maid Service, had saved my life on many occasions. She was usually late, but I trusted her to keep my secret safe, so I had to put up with her punctuality issues just to keep the house clean and soul food on the table.

I had promised Avery I would learn to make some sort of cobbler or that God-awful potato salad, but I didn't have time. I had to go to the cleaners and make sure the employees were completing their daily tasks. I was constantly going back and forth to the bank. I handled all the customer complaints. I handled anything and everything that Avery did not.

I wasn't happy about going into business at first. Anytime you own your own business, there is a lot of risk involved. Avery had a degree in business. He was making a six-figure salary when he quit his job, emptied out our savings account, and borrowed against his retirement fund. We sacrificed a lot those first couple of years, and I would do it all over again, because I was head over heels in love with this man. I would do anything to please him, even if that meant never seeing my mother and father again.

Avery and I are from a small town in Florida. I guess you could say we were from opposite sides of the track. When you live in a small town, everybody knows everybody, and I would see Avery from time to time. He was two years older than me.

I must have been about fourteen the first time Avery Clark knocked on our door. He was very intelligent and articulate. It didn't take him long to convince my father that he would do a better job on our lawn than that kid from down the street. Avery was a real go-getter.

Countless Saturdays, I would watch Avery from my window. He never wore a shirt while he mowed the lawn. He was an athlete. His body was chiseled and sculpted in all the right places. I was confused and terrified of my feelings for him. I wanted to touch him, and I wanted him to touch me.

One Saturday I convinced myself that I was going to say something to him. I got up before the sun was up. I took so much time getting ready. I looked perfect. I was so caught up in my hair and makeup that I didn't notice that it had started to rain. It rained all that day. I was so distraught. The next day I told my mother that I had hurt my leg playing softball and I wanted to stay home, instead of going with her and my father to church. On that Sunday, with my hair wild all over my head and no makeup on, Avery Clark knocked on our door.

"Hey, Madison, is Mr. Alcott home?"

"Um...um...um, no, he's not. Can I do you? I mean, can I do something for you?"

"Tell him I would be happy to reschedule the lawn service for maybe later on in the week," Avery said, looking at me strangely.

"I will let him know. Maybe I can call you and tell you what he said," I said as I tried to fix my hair.

"Are you asking me for my number?"

"You know, just to talk business. You can write it on this paper." I gave Avery a sticky note.

I called Avery that night, and I have talked to him almost every night since that day.

News travels fast in a small town. I knew my father would kill me if he knew I was dating a black guy. John Alcott would have no part of an interracial relationship. He believed that black people were great to be friends with but when it was time to have a family, we should all stick with our own kind. I was so in love that I didn't care. Avery wasn't my first sexual partner, but I had decided that he would be my last.

When my father got wind of my relationship with Avery, he was furious. He threatened to take everything away. He started with the door to my room. I had no privacy. I couldn't go anywhere by myself. He would show up to all my school functions. So, in order to see Avery, I started skipping school.

Avery was a senior in high school. It got to the point where our grades were starting to suffer. He was not going to get into Legacy University if his grades started to slip. However, I didn't even get a chance to figure out what to do about our relationship, because my father showed up to the school and withdrew me.

I didn't even pack my room before I was sitting in Orlando, with new house, new school, no Avery. My father claimed he got a job promotion, which put us in Orlando. I started to rebel after that. I cut my hair. I pierced my belly button and got one of the five tattoos that I have today. My father insisted that I get a job and stop the ridiculous and immature behavior. I knew he was right. Avery was in college. He was probably going to meet some black girl with a big butt and forget all about me. So I got a job at Wet-N-Wild. I started eating healthier, working out, and saving my money.

I had some really good times at Wet-N-Wild; this was where I met Sha'Miracle Morris. She was beautiful. She had one of those bodies to die for. She was a cheerleader, so she was always smiling. Miracle and I hit off immediately. We were inseparable. People at the job used to call us Salt and Pepper. We loved it, because we thought it was after the rap duo, but very early on, we learned it was because she was black and I was white. She taught me so much about nightclubs, alcohol, and things you should and should not say to black people. I taught her everything I knew about designer shoes, handbags, and money.

"Madison, did you hear anything I just said? What are you thinking about?" Avery said, snapping me back from my daydream.

"I'm sorry, Avery; I was thinking about Miracle. I've called her several times this morning, and she hasn't called me back yet. She knows I hate when she doesn't answer the phone."

"I have to meet with Lucas about some repairs needed in the cleaners," he continued, ignoring my comment. As soon as I heard "Lucas," I immediately went into business mode.

"Avery, don't go overboard. Lucas can talk you into buying things we may not necessarily need."

"Maddie, I got this. We are only as good as the product we put out. We can't give people clothes that are not our signature clean. So whatever it costs to get this thing right, that's what we got to do."

Taylor Swift's "I Knew You Were Trouble" began to sing from my purse. I picked up my phone and swiped across Egypt's face.

"Hello, Egypt, how are you?" I said to my friend on the other end.

"Oh, you just gonna pick the phone up and start talking to Africa while I'm talking to you? Damn, you just gonna ignore me." Avery pouted. He was so cute when he pouted.

"I told Avery that you would pick me up from the cleaners and give me a ride over to your mother's house. We are almost there…OK, I will see you in a few minutes." I ended the phone conversation.

"Avery, hurry up. Egypt is already at the cleaners waiting," I said. "Avery, do you hear me?"

"Madison, who are you talking to?" Avery calmly replied.

"I'm talking to you; your name is Avery, right?" I said in the most sarcastic tone I could.

"You can't be talking to me, because I am no longer talking to you," he said, staring straight ahead.

"What? Did I miss something? Avery Clark, please do not start this right now!" He was upset. I couldn't stand it when he was mad at me. I had to think fast.

"All right, let me tell you something in your ear." Avery was a sucker for kisses on his neck and ear. So I pressed my lips super close to his ear and started whispering. "Tonight, Daddy, I'm going to do that thing you like."

"That...that...thing that I like?" He lit up.

"All night," I whispered seductively.

"I'm going to hold you to that, Mrs. Clark."

"You can hold whatever you like."

"I love you, Maddie."

"I love you more. I'll call you later," I said as we pulled up to the cleaners.

Egypt rolled the window down on her red Aston Martin V8 Vantage Roadster. She smiled as she removed her Jimmy Choo sunglasses, but her smiled quickly turned into a grimace when she saw Avery.

"Good morning, Nefertiti!" Avery said with a smirk on his face.

"Hey, Stank, I see we got jokes this morning," Egypt said.

"Let your brother know if Madison's car is not ready today, he's gonna have to see me. I don't think he wants to do that," Avery threatened.

"Whatever, Avery, we are not twelve anymore!"

"You just tell him what I said," Avery snapped.

"I'm sorry, Egypt. Sometimes Avery can be very adamant about getting things done," I said.

"No apologies needed, and besides, Avery is the least of my worries," Egypt said as she sped off.

"Egypt, can you please turn that music down?" I yelled.

"Madison, you know how I feel about Lil Wayne!" Egypt exclaimed with such enthusiasm.

"'*I don't want your gonorrhea!*' Wow, these are powerful lyrics. Egypt, are you serious? What kind of rational adult sings about a sexually transmitted disease?" I shrieked.

"Lil Wayne is a lyrical genius. You have to listen to words to really understand what he means, white girl. He is rapping not singing," Egypt said proudly.

"I'd rather not listen. If you want me in this car, you'd better find something on that radio that we both can agree on. My stomach is hurting listening to this nauseating music," I replied.

"Fine, what about 96.3 FM? I know you listen to that with Avery," Egypt stated.

"I guess it will have to do; anything but rap," I sighed.

It didn't surprise me that Egypt would be zooming around town in her fancy car with explicit rap music blaring out of it. She was the complete opposite of predictable. When I first met Egypt, she was a sophomore in high school. Miracle had needed a ride to work one Saturday and called me to pick her up from Egypt's house. Miracle told me that Egypt's brother was becoming a really good mechanic, and she agreed to tutor Egypt in geometry in exchange for her brother repairing her car. I remembered Egypt's mother telling us that the only class Egypt was passing was chemistry. I thought that it was odd, considering how difficult chemistry could be.

One day the three of us were at the mall, debating if we should buy one-hundred-dollar sneakers, when Egypt declared that she already had two pairs of the exact same shoe. Miracle and I said at the same time, "Stop lying!" Egypt was very determined to prove us wrong. When we got back to her house, sure enough, she had two pairs of one-hundred-dollar Nikes. So, of course, we accused her of stealing the shoes. Egypt just laughed, and before we could blink our eyes, she presented the receipts. Our mouths dropped open.

"Egypt, where the hell did you get money from to buy those shoes?" Miracle had yelled.

"Damn, girl, do you want my mother to hear you?" Egypt sulked.

"I'm interested; what did you have to do to get those shoes?" I asked.

"I didn't have to do much; I just *pretend* like I like him," Egypt lied.

"Egypt, those dirty sophomore boys at Kennedy don't have money like that," Miracle alleged.

"I know that. I don't have time for boys," Egypt announced.

"Damn, girl, so what's the four one one?" I cried.

"Miracle, do you know Mr. Brown?" Egypt asked.

"Mr. Brown, the damn chemistry teacher?" Miracle asked.

"Well, that explains why she is passing chemistry," I interjected.

"Yes, I know Busted-Up Brown. Egypt, he has got to be thirty something. That is just yucky on so many levels," Miracle stated while rolling her eyes to the ceiling.

"He's only twenty-six. He gave me the money for the shoes. But the both of you have to promise to keep this information a secret," Egypt pleaded.

"I don't know what to say," Miracle stated.

"Here, let's use this pin to prick our fingers until they bleed, and then we should make a blood pact," Egypt stated excitedly.

"I'm not getting AIDS just to keep your dumb secret!" I exclaimed.

"Forget it. I'm not doing anything wrong, just some harmless flirting, and if I can get a few things in return, so be it," Egypt proclaimed.

Egypt and I agreed that Miracle was such a worrywart. Miracle wanted no part of Egypt's new relationship. I, however, thought that it was very mature of her to be dating a teacher. I wanted to know every detail of their escapades, so I started hanging out with her more and more.

Her brother, Noah, wasn't around much, but when he was home, you knew it, because there would be a houseful of people. I felt really comfortable at Egypt's house, except when Gavin Upshaw came over. It was like he had me under some sort of spell. I had never met a man, black or white, for that matter, quite like him. He knew exactly what to say to get me to do exactly what he wanted.

Gavin was training to be a boxer, so he was in excellent shape. I thought it would be fun and healthy to start working out with him. I started to spend too much time with him and less time with Egypt. Then, one day, Miracle called me on the phone, screaming in hysterics.

"Miracle, what's wrong?" I asked.

"It's Egypt; there's been a freak accident!" Miracle yelled.

"Miracle, you need to calm down! What happened to Egypt?" I said impatiently.

"She was in the chemistry lab at school, and somehow a chemical splashed in her face!" Miracle screamed.

"Oh my God, which hospital is she at?" I said with sheer panic in my voice.

"She's in County General. Hurry up," Miracle yelled and hung up the phone.

Egypt

I turned to 96.3 and let the music play. Madison was
one of my favorite people in the world, but when it came to
Lil Wayne, she'd better watch out. I had a full day of fun
planned out for Madison and me. We were going to get
manicures and pedicures then go shopping at the mall,
followed by lunch. I was living the good life — no children, no
rules, just pure freedom. My mother was always hounding me
about going to medical school, but that was her dream, not
mine.

There was a time my mother was afraid of whether I
would live or die. I was in high school and dating one of the
finest teachers there. We were in love, and he said he was
going to marry me as soon as I graduated. I was only a
sophomore then, but I could put it down in the bedroom
better than a grown woman.

Ever since I was young I have always had a thing for
older men. My therapist said it was because my father wasn't
around. But I wasn't going to give him any credit for the way I
turned out. He had left my mother for some young girl when
my brother and I were in elementary school, and he never
came back. He married her and had two children from her, a

boy first then a girl — just like with my mom, except he never married her.

The worst part about this dysfunctional-ass issue was that we all lived in Orlando. We lived on the west side of town, and he lived on the east side of town, but the same 407 area code. I resented my father for what he did to us. The way I felt, if he was on fire and I had a glass of water, I sure wouldn't be thirsty.

So when I met Mr. Brown in high school and he showed me interest, I naturally gravitated toward him. He was always telling me how beautiful I was, how smart I was, and, of course, how mature I was. We started dating but no one was supposed to know. He said that people weren't mature enough to accept the kind of love we had. What we had was special — well, until he tried to mix things up and I had a terrible accident as a result.

The day before the accident, I was not thinking clearly. I had been calling Brown for days. He hadn't returned any of my phone calls. We even had a substitute in chemistry class. At first I was worried. How could he go three days without talking to his baby girl? When Brown finally surfaced on day four and he wasn't wearing a cast of some sort, I was furious.

As I walked down the hall, trying to keep my composure, I noticed that skank, Mahogany, was talking to Brown and leaning in closely. It looks like she is pushing up on my man, I thought to myself. Did this ninth-grade trick have on the same shoes Brown bought for me the other day?

"Mahogany, I need to speak with Mr. Brown about an important assignment; can you excuse us?" I said with such disdain in my voice.

"Bye, Mr. Brown. Thanks for everything." Mahogany whispered.

"Why haven't you returned my calls?" I complained.

"Baby girl, you smell real good this morning," Brown whispered so seductively.

"How good?" I asked, my anger starting to fade.

"Good enough to eat," Brown replied.

The look in Brown's eyes started to affect me in a weird way. I was so confused. I finally said, "We need to talk!"

"I got something to talk to you about, but you have to promise to be a big girl. Can you be a big girl for Daddy?" Brown asked.

"Yes, of course. What is it?" I asked anxiously.

"Tonight I want you to come over with Mahogany. She can learn a lot from you. I want to know what it's like to enjoy the both of you," Brown announced.

"Brown, what we have is special; you said so yourself," I answered in a confused tone.

"Egypt, listen, what we shared has run its course. You're starting to bore me. I need more. Do you want Daddy to be happy?" Brown asked.

"I'm not sharing. Look at me; I don't have to!" I exclaimed.

"Egypt, come over with Mahogany tonight, or it's over. What you won't do, five others will," Brown stated and then walked off.

Over? This is far from over. I thought. I decided that I wanted Brown to pay. He hurt me, and now I wanted to hurt him. If I couldn't have Brown, then no one else could. I needed a plan, and it had to be a good one.

I went into Brown's room just before seventh period started. "Brown, I don't want this to end; can we talk after school? Please meet me in the chemistry lab," I said.

He agreed. I went into the lab with the full intention of flooding it. I knew if I mixed something with carbon dioxide that would do the trick. I only needed a little bit, and then I could run out of there. I had to do all of this before Brown showed up. That way he could take the rap for destroying the lab, and then he would surely be fired.

The only thing I had learned in chemistry class was that H_2O was water, and that's about it, but if I put carbon dioxide in it, that would make the mess even bigger. The chemicals were locked up, but I knew exactly where he kept the key. I had seen it many times when we were locked in the lab together, making love.

I grabbed two containers. One container read "carbon dioxide" and the other "hydrogen." I wanted to make a really big mess, so I decided on two chemicals. I placed a bucket in the sink. I turned the water on, and once the bucket filled halfway, I added the carbon dioxide; next I added the hydrogen.

What happened next I can only speculate on, because when I woke up, I was lying in a hospital bed. Dr. Nicholas explained to me that a female teacher found me unconscious in the chemistry lab and immediately began rescue breathing and CPR. She saved my life.

I had suffered third-degree burns to the entire right side of my face. My ear had been melted down, and my eardrum was toast. I couldn't hear a thing out of my right ear. I was going to need surgery.

First, I needed to have a skin graft. My mother, with all her infinite wisdom, suggested to the surgeon that he take the skin from my buttocks to replace the missing skin from my face. I would never forgive her for that. What was wrong with using the skin from my inner thigh? I would have never allowed a doctor near my butt.

In order for me to have a full recovery, I would need rehabilitation by qualified physical and occupational therapists. Oh, and not to mention a damn mental-health counselor because my mother was sure that I would develop post-traumatic stress disorder. I lay in that hospital bed for three weeks, hoping that I would die. I thought that my face would never be the same. I went from one doctor's appointment to another. I refused to see or talk to any of my friends.

One night I overheard my mother telling my brother that my medical expenses were mounting and that the insurance was not covering everything that I needed. I was mixed with emotions. I hated Brown, and I hated myself.

It had been about three months before someone from the school board contacted me about my recollection of the events on the day of the accident. My brother suggested that I say absolutely nothing without an attorney. I didn't have money for any attorney. My brother had been saving his money so that he could start his own business. He gave me the money I needed to hire the most notorious attorney in Orlando.

Attorney Klein was ruthless. Once I told him about the affair I was having with Brown, backed up by nude photos, a sex tape, and hotel receipts, he agreed to take my case. Attorney Klein proved Brown to be a manipulating and negligent sex offender who preyed on innocent, young, and naïve little girls. I was awarded 46 million dollars from the county school board, and I never heard from Brown again.

Sha'Miracle

"Girl, let me tell you about Subway. There was a dude there this morning getting on my last nerve," I said.

"Where was Bobby?" Gabby questioned.

"He was having car trouble this morning, so ole boy was there to open for Bobby. He was questioning my order, acting like it was all that to do the sub the way I wanted it. He even went as far as to make a suggestion of an entirely different sub," I shouted.

"Shut up!" Gabby yelled.

"I know, right! What kind of foolishness is that?" I said.

"What kind of sub did he suggest?" Gabby asked.

"A damn Veggie Delite!" I roared.

"Miracle, shut up!" Gabby said while laughing hysterically.

"Gabby, I cannot make this up!" I alleged.

"Was he cute?" Gabby asked.

"Gabby, are you serious right now?" I asked.

"I'm just saying, Miracle; I'll entertain a lil foolishness if that face and body is right," Gabby stated while winking her eye.

"I wasn't even looking at him like that. Let me see; I need one more sandwich-making brother in my life like a hole in the head," I said, feeling irritated.

"Everybody can't go into the NFL," Gabby claimed.

"Gabby, do not bring him up! My morning is already off to such a dismal start. I really don't have room in my life for one more conversation about my ex," I declared.

"Miracle, why are there always so many police cars at this school? For someone with a master's degree, why do you work at Ghetto Middle?"

Here we go again, I thought. I could hardly wait to see what this was about. "Gabby, are you ready for the interview? Do you remember what I told you?"

"Miracle, I promise if you start quoting some junk to me that you heard Oprah say, I will scream like someone is after me!" snapped Gabby.

"I wish a paycheck was after you. Gabby, just remember to be authentic. I've got a good feeling about this interview. I'll call you later, because depending on this situation, I may not get off on time," I stated sadly.

"Good morning, Ms. Morris. The administrative team is waiting for you, along with the school resource officer, in the conference room near Dr. Beacon's office," Mrs. Higgins, the school secretary, announced as I walked into the building.

"What exactly am I walking into, Mrs. Higgins?" I questioned.

Mrs. Higgins replied, "Let's just say we are all very *blessed* to be working here."

"Hello, Dr. B., what can I do to help?" I asked, still unaware of the matter at hand.

"Did you happen to see the news last night?" Dr. Beacon inquired.

"No, sorry, I went to bed early. What's going on?"

"I think you should sit down for this. Yesterday, around six o'clock, Blessed Douglas was seen leaving the Florida Mall while driving the bus that belongs to the Superior Tour Bus Company."

"Excuse me! Blessed Douglas, the eighth grader in my anger-management group?" I gasped.

"I'm afraid so," Dr. Beacon continued. "He allegedly got into the driver's seat of the bus and then proceeded to take the bus full of Spanish-speaking tourists back to their hotel on International Drive."

For a split second, I was in a trance. I could not believe what I was hearing.

"I'm going to need anything and everything you have on him. Someone from the sheriff's department is going to be interviewing all of his teachers, counselors, and peers. We need to try to keep this huge distraction to a minimum for Blessed and our students' sake," Dr. Beacon concluded.

I left his office and hurried to my own. There is never a dull moment at Clinton.

"Hey, *Hey*, Hay," Thomas said as Hay walked through the doors of the juvenile-detention office.

"Good morning, crazy boy," replied Hay. Robert Thomas was ten years older than Hay and made it his business to greet her like Dwayne on *What's Happening* every time he saw her. "What's new?" Hay asked.

"Not much. Oh, but you did get another kid this morning," Thomas said, handing over a file folder.

"What? Another one? Boy, I'm telling you, they trying to get the butter from the duck these days. Run me the particulars," Hay said.

"Blessed Ahmad Douglas, sixteen years old, eighth-grade boy at William J. Clinton Middle."

"So his initials are BAD? Poor fellow didn't have a chance. But why did I get him?"

"He was mine before, but that was only because of truancy issues. Now he's graduated to crime. Plus, he goes to the same school as little miss hot-wire, Sashay."

"Don't talk about my kids, Thomas." Hay smirked. "Besides, at least I don't have little miss sticky fingers; but it wasn't me; he touched me, but he didn't; pathological; lying-behind Angel."

"That was way harsh, Hay," Thomas said sadly, imitating Cher from the movie *Clueless*.

"You and these movie quotes, I swear," Hay said. "I'll catch up with you later."

Hay walked into her office, sat down at her computer, and logged on. The first thing she did was check her e-mail. There was a message of high importance with the subject "New Client." She opened the message and read it thoroughly. As she read the case, her jaw dropped. Blessed Douglas had been wanted for stealing a bus and endangering the lives of over twenty people. Really? A bus? That was absolutely absurd. Apparently he had noticed the key inside the bus at the mall and went in and sat in the driver's seat. No sooner than he had sat down, people started loading the bus. He drove the people, who were tourists, to their hotel and unloaded the bus.

"You've got to be kidding me," Hay said to herself. "Never a dull moment when you're dealing with crimikids." Crimikids was what Hay and Thomas called them; children who were also criminals. Sure, they loved them and wanted what was best for them, but it was what it was, and they were what they were.

Hay would have to wait until Blessed was arrested, processed, and released from the juvenile-detention center before she could monitor him at school. What she could do now was interview his teachers, peers, and counselors, and she could speak with the S.A.F.E. coordinator, Sha'Miracle Morris.

Ms. Morris was very helpful and worked well with Hay. She was also very attractive. If Hay thought she was into women, she would have made a pass at her. Hay loved herself some thick girls, and that Ms. Morris was thicker than a Snickers.

"Hay." Thomas peeked his head inside the door. "I'm taking lunch orders; you getting anything?"

"Already? What y'all ordering?"

"Wings."

"Nah, I'll pass." They ordered wings every week; sure the wings were off glass, but dang, could a sister get a salad or something? "I'll pick something up while I'm in the field."

"OK."

"Thomas, wait."

"What up?"

"This little boy stole a bus and drove tourists from the mall to their hotel."

"You're lying!" Thomas gasped then released a laugh.

"I can't make this up. Look at the story."

"Nah, I believe you, fam. That's crazy. These kids should have been breast-fed. That formula done messed them all up. A bus? I'm done!" Thomas laughed as he walked away.

Hay gathered her things and walked to her patrol car. That was another good thing about her job. She didn't have to drive her SUV around all day. The state had cars for them to take care of state business. As she pulled up to Clinton Middle, she noticed that there were two patrol cars already there. She walked inside the front office and was greeted by Mrs. Higgins, the school secretary.

"Good morning, Officer Dawson," Mrs. Higgins said with an unusually large smile on her face.

"Good morning," Hay replied. "Is Sashay in school today?"

"Let me check," Mrs. Higgins responded, her smile never leaving her face. What was up with her? She clicked her mouse a few times then finally spoke. "The morning attendance says she's absent today."

Figures, Hay thought. Sashay missed a lot of days in school, because her mother had a newborn and no baby-sitter. Hay took out her clipboard, scribbled something down on a Post-it, and placed her clipboard back under her arm.

"Well, I received a new client today, Blessed Douglas. I need to interview his teachers and some of the students. Is Ms. Morris available to assist me?"

"Ms. Morris is in with Dr. Beacon. I'll let her know you're waiting."

"Thank you," Hay said as she took a seat in the front-office lounge.

I went back to my office and gathered the file I had on Blessed. The phone had been ringing off the hook, but the principal was waiting for me. I glanced over at the caller ID. It was my aunt Pearl's name and number. Odd. I had to see what it was she needed that was so urgent.

"Hello, good morning, Auntie Pearl."

"Well damn! I could get Barack on the phone faster than I could you. And he is the leader of the free world, the POTUS," Auntie Pearl rambled

"*POTUS*? What is that?" I asked.

"The *president of the United States*," replied Pearl. "Don't you look at the news at all?"

"Auntie, it's been on my heart to call you," I explained.

"Well, it wasn't on ya hands, 'cause you ain't picked up the phone to call me yet," Auntie Pearl snapped.

"I'm so busy this morning; can I call you back?" I asked.

"Wait a minute, Sha'Miracle; don't throw me off the phone! I'm calling to find out about the badass lil boy over there at Clinton. The news folks say that y'all don't know where he at. I suggest they try looking for him at the damn Saint Bernard bus station. Lord knows those sorry-ass drivers falling asleep at the wheel could probably use some help from the youth, and don't get me started on how old those damn buses are. Hell, those must be the same buses Rosa Parks refused to give up her seat on," Auntie Pearl babbled.

As I sat there listening to my aunt go on and on, I started to realize why someone would get on a bus full of Spanish-speaking people and drive off. I would do the same thing right now to escape this ridiculous conversation.

"Auntie, I really need to get back to work. I can't discuss anything with you about that student."

"Damn, Miracle, last time I checked you were a damn counselor not an FBI agent! The news folk say that the child is sixteen. What the hell is a sixteen-year-old child doing at Clinton? You know his parents are deceased and he's living with his grandmother?"

I sighed out of sheer frustration. Auntie Pearl must have picked up on my body language through the phone.

"Miracle, we can talk about the lil boy later, when you bring me a few things from the store. You know what? Never mind, I'll call Lila. She is always at the damn store in your car anyway," said Auntie Pearl.

"Auntie, I don't know anyone name Lila."

"That damn girl, with all those kids, who ain't working."

"Do you mean Gabby?"

"I call her Lila, Lie-la. All she do is tell one lie after another lie."

"What do you mean she is at the store in my car all the time? Gabby is looking for a job!" I practically yelled in the phone.

"Lila ain't looking for no job. Honey, they will find the weapons of mass destruction before Lila find a job." Auntie Pearl laughed.

"Auntie, I will be over there when I get off today. Love you, bye."

"OK, honey, I'll talk at you later, love you."

Can I just please rewind this day and start it over? I need an Advil cocktail real bad right about now. I cannot wait to talk to Gabby. If she has been playing me, I will delete her from every part of my life.

Focus, focus, Miracle. Did Blessed say anything over the past few days that will indicate where he is?

"Bobby, I'm about to take off," Trevor said.

"Man, I really appreciate you coming from the other side of town to open the store and get things going for me this morning," Bobby stated.

"Hey, time is money. I've been looking over your financial reports. This store is doing really well. I know I don't tell you this enough, little bro, but I'm proud of you. Making you a store manager has proven to be a very good decision. I know you have great customer service. What's up with that one chick who only wanted you to make her sub?" Trevor asked.

"Who are you talking about?" Bobby questioned.

"The chick that was kind of thick, she was about to leave just as you got here this morning," Trevor said while making hand gestures.

"Oh, oh, you are talking about Miracle," Bobby said with a grin.

"No, what's her real name, not her stripper name?" Trevor laughed.

"Trevor, her real name is Sha'Miracle. She is in here a lot. You should be nice to her. Not only does she spend a great deal of her own money in here, but she arranged to have several panther pride nights at this very location, and Clinton's PTA sponsored subs for clubs, which generated a ton of revenue. I was thinking maybe we could do something to show our appreciation for the faculty and staff at Clinton Middle."

"That is not a bad idea, Bobby. Of course we should do something for Clinton. I got an e-mail the other day about becoming a partner in education. I have a friend who works for the school board. This brother is always talking about different community-outreach programs. I could do something good for the community, and maybe, by some miracle, Miss Miracle can do something good for me." Trevor winked at Bobby.

"Wait a minute, Trevor. Whatever happened to don't mix business with pleasure?"

"Bobby, now you want to listen to me? I told you not to get involved with what's her name, Ebony, or was it Jet?"

"Her name is Essence, and she is usually pretty stable, when she is on her meds," Bobby said, annoyed.

"Well, Bobby, you didn't listen to me then, and I'm not listening to you now."

"Trevor, I've really gotten to know Miracle over the past year, and she has been through a lot. I don't think she is interested in dating right now."

"Bobby, every single woman is interested in dating right now. And besides, she is not married; I checked her hand."

"So, she was engaged to Gerald Hall," Bobby announced.

"Gerald '*Do It All*' Hall, the Pro Bowler that plays for the Saints?" Trevor exclaimed.

"Miracle and Gerald both went to Legacy University. I don't know the whole story, but my dawg Avery is married to this white chick that claims to be good friends with Miracle. She said that right before Gerald went into the draft, he ended the engagement with Miracle. Miracle supposedly was so depressed that she tried to commit suicide," Bobby reported sadly.

"The feisty young lady I saw this morning would not try to kill herself over some dude, Pro Bowler or not. I just didn't get that kind of vibe from her this morning. This young lady seemed to be very strong, independent, and very sure of herself. I'm intrigued, which doesn't happen to me often. I have a few minutes this afternoon; maybe I'll stop by Clinton to see if Miracle enjoyed the sub," Trevor said with a mischievous smile.

Charity

There was a knock at the door. Charity turned to see who was interrupting her time. She saw that is was Fallon. Fallon was a sixteen-year-old junior that sang alto in her choir. She was a very intelligent young lady who was going places. Wise University and Legacy University were both observing her and wanted her in their concert choirs. Charity liked Fallon. She was a joy to have around. She always did as she was asked and was never disrespectful. She came from a good home. Her mother worked two jobs to support her and her younger brother.

"Excuse me, Ms. Love; I need to talk to you. I have a problem, and I'm really scared," Fallon said.

"Well, go ahead and tell me what's on your mind, sweetheart," Charity replied.

"Ms. Love, I'm pregnant."

"Pregnant? What do you mean pregnant? After all the hard work your mom has done, this is how you repay her? By getting pregnant from one of these little nappy-headed boys?" Charity scolded.

Fallon began to sob. She was so sorry. She never meant to get pregnant. Blessed told her that they didn't have to use condoms, because they were monogamous and he would always pull out. It had been foolproof for over a year now. She couldn't understand what happened this time.

She was scared, confused, and mad at herself all at the same time. She wanted to get an abortion, but what if she was carrying something great? She wanted to kill herself, but she also wanted to live. She wished every day, since she found out three months ago, that she could rewind the time, go back, and not invite Blessed over that day. She prayed every day that she would miscarry or her period would somehow miraculously appear and make everything OK.

Blessed was ecstatic about the baby, but her mom was going to kill her when she found out. Fallon's plan was to keep the pregnancy a secret as long as she possibly could. That was all she had right now.

Fallon and Blessed had been dating for two years now. He was so sweet and kind. He was also severely misunderstood. Blessed didn't have parents. They were both dead. He had lived with his grandmother since he was three years old.

His grandmother had him spoiled rotten. She did everything for him. She washed and ironed his clothes; she cooked and fixed his plate, and she didn't even make him wash dishes. She let him go and come as he pleased. Whenever he got into trouble, he didn't care, because his Nay-Nay was always there, taking his side. In her eyes, he could do no wrong.

For this reason, she treated Fallon the same way. They had sex in her house plenty of times, and Fallon was sure Nay-Nay knew it, but she pretended like she didn't know what was going on. She would always be so nice and kind to Fallon, and she sent little toys and books and crayons home for Fallon's ten-year-old brother, Farrell.

Fallon's mother knew she was dating Blessed but had no idea she was sexually active. The deal was Fallon and Blessed could be boyfriend and girlfriend as long as there was no hanky-panky. If she started to have sex, the deal was off. Fallon's mother, Farrah, was a no-nonsense parent. She wanted her children to go far in life. She pushed Fallon beyond her potential and challenged her every day.

This was arduous for Fallon, but she had become a straight-*A* student because of it. She was also a member of the marching band, the concert choir, the National Honor Society, and Future Educators of America, and she worked alongside the athletic director at the basketball games. She appreciated her mother, but her mom was so hard to live with. It was for this reason that Fallon threw herself into school and consumed the rest of her time with extracurricular activities. The less time she was at home, the less time she had to wait on her mom hand and foot, do all the chores, and take care of her brother. She had been overwhelmed since the day she started middle school, and it hadn't stopped yet.

"Ms. Love, I'm coming to see you because I have no one else to turn to. I know you're disappointed in me but not more than I am in myself," Fallon said through her sobs.

"I just don't know, Fallon. I thought so highly of you. I am disappointed. You are a top student. Now you'll have to drop out of school to support a baby."

"Drop out? Who said anything about dropping out? I don't plan on dropping out at all. You know my motto: Fallon Jenkins is nobody's failure. I just need a little guidance from you, because I trust you the most," Fallon cried.

"I suggest we call your mother and see what she says," Charity replied

Fallon was speechless. She loved Ms. Love so much. Ms. Love was always so full of good, positive words. If Fallon had known Ms. Love would make her feel like a complete fool, she never would have confided in her. But now that the secret was out, Fallon was sure it would be a matter of minutes before her mom was notified.

"Ms. Love, forget it. Forget I said anything. I'll just have to handle this on my own. All I ask is that you please not say anything to anyone," Fallon pleaded.

"I won't breathe a word to a soul. But I hope you learn a valuable lesson in all of this."

"Yes, ma'am, I did. Be careful who you look up to," Fallon murmured.

"Excuse me? That's the lesson you learned? You should have learned that you should keep having babies reserved for that precious thing called marriage. Having babies out of wedlock is surely a sin. You will pay for what you have done. But what I do want is for you to do what's best for you and your unborn child."

Charity was concerned about Fallon's well-being. She really was. But she had an eerie way of showing it. Charity couldn't let this teenager think that what she had done was inexcusable, but what she knew from the past was that almost every girl that had gotten pregnant in high school never finished. They ended up dropping out, trying to get a job but could not, and then ended up on the welfare system for years to come. She didn't want that for Fallon, but that was exactly what was about to happen.

"Thank you for listening, Ms. Love. I'll see you in practice after school," Fallon said.

"Ms. Love is out of her mind if she thinks I'm gonna drop out." Fallon talked to herself as she walked to class. "My GPA is a perfect four point. There's no way I'm doing anything but being successful."

Fallon had thought that talking to Ms. Love would help her feel better. She didn't get the feeling of comfort she had desired; she did, however, get the push that she needed to keep moving. Fallon Jenkins was *nobody's* failure. She had to develop a plan and soon. Right now, she couldn't trust Ms. Love to keep her secret. The way she was feeling, she couldn't trust anyone. She had to call Blessed, and they had to meet up and talk. It was time they acted like adults — parents — and devised a game plan for their future.

Just then Fallon's cell phone rang. She looked at the screen and smiled. It was her world, her love, her boo; it was Blessed. She answered with the same greeting she always had.

"Princess Douglas speaking."

"Boo, I need you," Blessed said quietly.

"Boo, what's wrong?" Fallon worriedly replied.

"I messed up. I messed up big time. I think the police are looking for me. Matter of fact, I'm sure they are," Blessed said while punching the door.

Fallon's heart stopped beating. She, too, was now terrified. "Boo, what did you do?"

"OK, you know how I want to be a bus driver when I grow up?"

"Yes," Fallon said. It was all he ever talked about.

"Well, I was at the mall yesterday, and I saw the keys inside of a bus, and I got in and drove it."

"Blessed Ahmad Douglas!"

"Boo, please don't be mad. When I got in the driver's seat, people started getting on. Nobody spoke English, so I looked at the clipboard, and it said to take them to this hotel on *I*-Drive. So I took them all, dropped them off, and drove away."

Fallon couldn't believe what she was hearing. Part of her wanted to laugh, because she just knew he was joking. She was waiting for him to yell, "SIKE," any minute now. But he didn't. Instead he kept talking.

"I drove the bus to the Saint Bernard station after I was done, because I had gotten the gas off my chest, and then I walked home."

Having gas on your chest was an expression they used for someone who really wanted to drive. Blessed always had gas on his damn chest.

If he keeps this up, I won't have to worry about a baby; I'll miscarry from sheer stress, thought Fallon.

"Blessed, how do you know they're looking for you?"

"Because the police called my grandma and told her what was going on, and then they came by and asked if I was here, and she said no. She told me they would only be able to take me over her dead body, and she already took all her pills for the day, so she ain't dying no time soon," Blessed explained.

"Is your grandma mad?" Fallon asked.

"No, she's not mad. I told her they were lying on me and I didn't do anything like that."

"So you lied to Nay-Nay?"

"I had to."

"No, you didn't. She'd stick up for you even if you were guilty. You go to her room right now and confess. She'll protect you. I'll be over after school," Fallon instructed.

"OK, boo. I will. Hey, how's my son?"

Fallon blushed. "He's fine."

"OK, you don't be carrying no heavy books now. I'll see you later."

"OK."

"Fallon?"

"Yes, Blessed?"

"I love you."

"I love you, too." Fallon pressed the End key on the phone and started to cry. Lately she had been a big bag of emotions. She had felt happy, sad, scared, and pissed, all in under three minutes. This boy had stolen her heart two years ago and still had it. She would have to go and help him when she got out of school. Yeah, she and he would make excellent teen parents.

Charity shook her head in disbelief. Her beautiful, wonderful Fallon, caught up by sin. She never would have thought that Fallon would be so irresponsible, so, so stupid. Charity's disappointment overshadowed the more important issue — Fallon needed her. She needed to have someone that she could talk to.

Charity realized that she probably had blown any chance of having Fallon trust her, because she reacted the way she did. But she would just have to explain to her that it was because she loved her. She didn't mean to be so harsh, but the fact of the matter was Fallon had committed a sin. Now she would have to pay for it for the rest of her life.

Class was due to begin in two minutes. Charity prepared for her last period of the day and then choir rehearsal. They were studying jazz music, and she couldn't wait for the students to sight-read the new pieces she had picked out. She couldn't get Fallon out of her mind, but as soon as the bell rang, she reshifted her focus, said a quick prayer for Fallon and for herself, and then greeted her students at the door.

And I pray, that your love may abound yet more and more in knowledge and in all judgment... (Philippians 1:9)

Sha' Miracle

I gathered the file on Blessed and skimmed through it. Our last session had gone well, but there was something about Blessed's demeanor that had me perturbed. He kept insisting that he was fine, but he seemed very distant and curt when it came time to reply in dialogue. I didn't think much of it then, but now that he had committed this absurd crime, maybe his attitude was a foreshadowing of today's events.

I tapped lightly on Dr. Beacon's door.

"Come in," Dr. Beacon replied.

"Sorry it took me so long to get back here, but I feel that it was important to reread the documentation from our last session. In my opinion, Blessed was very anxious and preoccupied with an issue. The only thing that he would admit to was the need for money. I asked him what he needed the money for, but he wouldn't say. He was very evasive about the subject," I explained.

"OK, Miss Morris. I trust that you will keep me informed on any new information you might receive. I also would like for you to use all the resources you have to keep this situation as serene as possible, in order for our students to maintain a productive learning environment," Dr. Beacon stated.

"I would like to meet with each grade-level guidance counselor today to map out a strategic plan for the students directly affected by this situation," I said.

"Whatever you wish to do, you have my support, one hundred percent."

"Thank you," I said and turned to leave his office. I stopped by the teacher mailboxes to check in, because with all the fuss, I had forgotten to do so, and the last thing I needed was an e-mail from Mrs. Higgins saying that per my professional contract, I was to sign in and out daily. After I placed a check mark in the box next to my name, Mrs. Higgins came around the corner.

"Oh, I see you're out of your meeting with Dr. Beacon," Mrs. Higgins said.

"Yes, I just left the office," I replied.

"OK, well, Officer Dawson is in the front, waiting for you. She says she needs to speak with you about Blessed A. Douglas."

I rolled my eyes. Blessed, Blessed, Blessed, this was all I had been hearing since I walked onto this campus this morning. I hadn't even eaten breakfast, which just happened to be my favorite meal. I wanted to leave the school and start the day over; that way I could prepare in advance for all of this nonstop going. Instead, I exhaled, smiled sweetly, and said, "Yes, ma'am. I'm coming right now."

When I walked outside of the office, Officer Dawson stood up. "Good morning, Officer Dawson, or should I say good afternoon? How are you?"

"I'm doing well, thank you, and yourself?"

"Ask me tomorrow," I said, and we both laughed. "I have arranged for us to meet with two of Blessed's teachers in the conference room. They should be coming down any minute now. We can go on back and get set up, if you'd like."

"That sounds good," Dawson said.

We talked while we walked to the conference room.

"I was wondering if there was any background information you could give me about Douglas?" Dawson asked.

By this time, we were both seated and Dawson had booted up her laptop.

"Well," I started. "He lost both of his parents within a month of each other when he was seven years old. His father died in April, and his mother died in May. He never received counseling, because his grandmother refused the services.

"He has been battling with behavior issues ever since that traumatic time in his life. In his student-profile folder, there is documentation from conferences where his grandmother was very defensive and supported his erratic behavior. He repeated the third grade, due to low performance on the state standardized test, and also the fifth grade, due to chronic absenteeism. It was later discovered that if Blessed wasn't suspended, he was simply at home."

I stopped talking, because Ms. Rood and Mr. Smart had now entered the room. Dawson had been typing the entire time I was talking. She hadn't asked any questions as of yet.

"Good morning, good morning, good morning," Mr. Smart said as fast as he could. He always greeted everyone with three very hurried "good mornings." It was so redundant, but we all just ignored him. It wasn't even morning anyway. It was twelve thirty for crying out loud.

"Hello," Ms. Rood said in a high-pitched, sarcastic tone.

"Good afternoon," I said. "This is Officer Dawson. She is the juvenile-probation officer for Blessed Douglas. We have asked you here to give input on Blessed's academic and behavior performance."

"What happened to Officer Thomas?" Ms. Rood interjected.

"Mr. Douglas was transferred to me," Dawson replied.

"OK, I can see that, but that's not what I asked," said Ms. Rood. "I've already submitted this information before, and now you're telling me I have to do it all over again just because you're new?"

"Previously he was with Thomas due to truancy issues. Now he's involved in a criminal investigation," Dawson explained.

"That's surprising," Ms. Rood huffed facetiously.

"If you don't mind my asking, what kind of criminal investigation?" Mr. Smart asked.

"An investigation involving grand theft auto and driving without a license," Dawson answered.

"Wait a minute. That's the student who stole the bus from the mall? Get the hell outta here." Ms. Rood laughed. "That boy done lost his freaking mind. I always knew the elevator didn't go all the way to the penthouse."

Dawson's jaw dropped. I had to redirect this conversation. Ms. Rood was completely out of control. "Officer Dawson, do you have questions that you would like to ask these two teachers?" I asked.

"Yes, let's move this along, because this is my planning time. I only get five seconds to myself, and y'all are taking up three," Ms. Rood said to the both of us.

Dawson cleared her throat and began. "First off, how is his relationship with his peers in class?"

Mr. Smart responded first. "I don't have any problems with him. When he's here in school, he'll most likely go to sleep, and I just don't bother with him. I was taught that if students are tired, they can't learn, so I let him get his rest. When the assignments are due, I just give him a packet and have him turn it in before I submit the grades. He has a hundred percent in my class right now."

Dawson typed as Mr. Smart talked. "What subject do you teach?" Dawson questioned without looking up.

"Intensive math," he responded proudly. "It's my job to make sure they have the skills they need to perform well on the state test. I can show you his grades right here." Mr. Smart opened his case to his touch-screen tablet and started to swipe. He swiped for about thirty seconds before he finally asked for Ms. Rood to open up his e-mail for him.

She looked at him from the corner of her eye, sighed heavily, and then said, "Why should I? Grades are online, not in your e-mail. Really, Smart?"

If Mr. Smart wasn't as dark as night, his face would have turned red. He snapped back quickly, "All this technology, you know? It's always something new." He let out a nervous chuckle and said he would bring work samples back later.

Ms. Rood began to speak next. "Well, he does nothing in my reading class. All he does is talk and play around. He is not serious about anything. I think they should just get rid of him. Send him to an alternative school or, better yet, find him a job. God knows he's old enough. He's spoiled rotten by that grandma, so it's useless to call home. She condones everything that he does, disruptive behavior included. She even had the nerve to blame me for his low test scores and the zeros he got on his homework. What was I supposed to do? Do the homework for him? Well, according to Ms. Granny, I was. All I want to say to Blessed is, 'I like a lot of ice in my ice tea,' when I come through the drive-through; and 'Make sure my fries are hot,'" Ms. Rood said while chuckling.

"Ms. Rood, are you quite finished?" I asked with an intentionally upset tone. I thought she would have picked up on it, but she didn't.

"Yep," she replied. "And I have to go. Glad I could help. Toodles," Ms. Rood walked out of the room.

I thought Mr. Smart would have followed, but he stayed behind.

"Miracle, I mean, Miss Morris, is there anything else you need me to do? Anything at all?" Smart asked as he stared me directly in my eyes.

"No, that will be all. Officer Dawson, do you have everything you need?" I asked as I opened the door.

"Yes I do," Dawson replied.

"Are you sure, Miss Morris?" Mr. Smart said slowly. "I mean anything at all. I'm your man."

Ugh, the thought of him doing anything for me threw me into utter disgust. Mr. Smart, with his extra charcoal fingers, too-tight jeans, sneakers that were always dirty, yellow coffee- and cigarette-stained teeth and lips, and, let's not forget, the receding hairline that comfortably started in the exact middle of his head — he couldn't leave that conference room fast enough to suit my taste.

"Officer Dawson, if you have everything you need, I'm going to get back to my office and finally properly start my day," I said.

"Well, I would like to speak to some of his friends, if that's possible," requested Dawson.

"I'm afraid that's not possible. Most of these students here are all younger than Blessed. He doesn't have any friends per se. He just goes with the flow. However, he does have a girlfriend who is the same age as he is. She's a junior at John F. Kennedy High School."

"What's her name?" asked Dawson.

"Fallon."

"Fallon what?"

"He never said her last name. He always called her by his last name, because he said they were going to get married when they turned eighteen. I know the counselor there, so let me make a call and let her know that you will be coming there. I'm sure she won't mind helping you out. Will you be going today?"

"Yes, as soon as I leave here. Sashay isn't in school, and I need to go ahead and put this file together," Dawson replied.

"Sashay is absent again? Poor thing. She just may be baby-sitting again," I huffed while shaking my head.

"I'm sure she is. I'll get back to her after I have gotten more information on the current situation with Mr. Douglas. Miss Morris, once again, always a pleasure. I'll be in touch. Oh yeah, you better watch out for Mr. Smart; I think he's sweet on you," Dawson joked.

"I almost threw up just then, Dawson. Don't play. Mr. Smart better keep on moving. I'll call you with anything new I get."

"Good day," Dawson said and walked out of the office, out the front door, and to her car. I went back to my office and looked up the number to call Raven Thompson, the eleventh-grade counselor at John F. Kennedy High School.

I pulled up to the company. I repeated my mantra. "I am an asset. I am unique, and I am qualified." I then said a small prayer. I really, really, needed this job. I got out of the car, straightened my clothes out, took one last glance in the mirror, and snapped my finger in the air. I was fierce, and if I didn't get the job, they were crazy.

I walked straight up to the desk. I held my head up high and put the biggest smile of confidence I had deep down inside onto my face. "Hello," I said. "I have an appointment for the call-operator position."

"Your name?" the receptionist said.

"Gabrielle Sweeny," I responded.

"You've been checked in, Ms. Sweeny. Please have a seat. Someone will be with you shortly."

I sat down and observed my surroundings. There were five other people dressed up and waiting, just like me. I really hoped we weren't all going after the same job.

Suddenly, my palms began to sweat. They did that whenever I was nervous. I usually kept a handkerchief with me, but in the excitement of actually getting an interview, I completely forgot it. I rubbed my hands on my pleated skirt. Then I held them down by my side. "Lord," I prayed. "You know I really need this. I'm trying to be a good example and make an honest living for my children. I have one child about to graduate this year and every year after for the next three. Please find it in your plan to bless me with this job. Amen." With that, I breathed a sigh of relief.

My business degree from WU hadn't gotten me far. What was I thinking, majoring in business? I should have majored in education, but then again—no. I had four children at home that got on my nerves; I wasn't about to deal with a group all day and then go home to the four pack.

I sat there for what must have been forty-five minutes before they finally called my name. I had scrolled down my Facebook news feed, looked at some inspirational quotes on Twitter, tweeted a few things myself, and seen the latest pictures on Instagram. I did anything to keep myself busy while I nervously waited. I had just placed my phone back inside my handbag when my name was called by the receptionist.

I stood up, and she ushered me through the doors and into a conference room. I tried to contain myself when I walked into the room; however, I was more petrified than anything. I'd been thinking that it would be one person interviewing me, but instead it was a panel of five people.

I sat down, smiled, and said, "Good day."

No one replied; instead everyone gave a serious nod. Each person had one question for me. I answered each question as intelligently as I could. I may be ghetto, but one thing I had learned was how to turn it on and off. They asked if I had any questions, and I said no. Then, as I stood, so did they. They all shook my hand, one by one, and told me they would be in touch. Yeah right, I thought, and I walked out.

No sooner than I had walked out of their conference room, my cell phone buzzed with an e-mail. It was from them—odd. I opened it up and saw the dreaded five words, "We regret to inform you…" I was devastated. Another failed interview.

I placed my phone back into my purse and began to walk out the door. Halfway to the car, my phone buzzed again. This time it was from an unknown number. I answered, hoping it was another company about another interview.

"Hello," I said, trying to disguise my recent disappointment.

"Hello, may I please speak with Ms. Sweeny?"

"This is she."

"Ms. Sweeny, this is Dan Morton; we just met a few minutes ago in your interview."

"Oh, yes." I couldn't believe they were calling when they had already turned me down. Did they think this was funny? Hell, I got the message already; I didn't need it rubbed in.

"I received your e-mail, Mr. Morton; how may I assist you?" I said.

"Well, that's what I wanted to speak with you about. You are overqualified for the position in which you applied, but I do, however, want to offer you a higher position," he explained.

"A higher position?" I questioned.

"Yes," he continued. "Your resume is impressive, and you interviewed above and beyond all of the other candidates. I believe that you would definitely be an asset to this company. I would like for you to be team lead."

"What does that job entail?" I asked.

"As team lead you will be responsible for training all of the new hires on our company software. Is that something you think you would be interested in?"

"Of course," I said excitedly.

"I was hoping to reach you before you got too far away from the building. That way you could come on in and fill out the necessary paper work to get started. You can start on Monday. All we need is a drug screening and your W-4 form, and we'll be ready to go. Thank you so much, Ms. Sweeny, and welcome to the team."

"Thank you, Mr. Morton. I'll see you in a few," I said.

A drug test? Shit. I'd started smoking casually with Reece and the guys since I was laid off from my last job. It had been so long that I completely forgot that companies did drug tests. Oh well, I would just have to get Jalyssa to do it for me. It wasn't like this would be her first time. She'd done it for one of her friends before; surely she would help me out. I just hoped she didn't blab her big-ass mouth to nobody about it. I picked up my phone to call Reece.

"Speak," he said when he answered the phone.

"Bae, guess what?"

"What up?"

"I got the job."

"Oh yeah?"

"Yep."

"OK then, that's what's up. When you start?"

"Monday, but the only thing about it is I have to do a drug test."

"That ain't no problem, right? I mean, ain't your piss clean?" he asked.

"Um, no. Don't you remember this past weekend?"

"Oh yeah, my fault. Well, what you gonna do, bae?"

"I was thinking I would have Jalyssa do it for me."

"You sure? You know Jalyssa love to run her mouth," he said in a concerned tone.

"Yeah, I'm sure. She's the only one with enough sense to pull it off. I would have one of the boys do it, but what if they come back and tell me something's wrong with my prostate?"

We both laughed.

"Well, OK, baby, if you think you can pull it off then do that shit then." He paused for a second then continued. "Oh yeah, you got my clothes already?"

"Naw, I came here first. I'm on my way to the cleaners now."

"Cool, meet me round to Noah's; I gotta meet up with Gavin."

"Bae," I whined. "You know I don't want to go over there. Every time I go to that house that high-priced ho Egypt be there, and you know she can't stand me."

"Aww, baby, she's just jealous, because you're better than her. Don't let her steal your joy. Meet me over there. I got a big congratulations hug waiting for you."

"Yeah, you're right. Everybody can't be as fly as the Gab. A hug huh? A special one?"

"The kind that makes you melt in my arms," he flirted.

"You drive a hard bargain, sir. And I do mean hard, but I'll be there," I said.

"Cool, love you, bae," he said.

"I love you too," I said. We hung up, and I went back inside the building. To hell with Egypt. I was the new team lead.

"Look, Madison, that's Gavin's car," Egypt broadcasted.

"Not many Land Rovers have those outrageous twenty-inch rims," I said rudely.

"I don't see Noah's car, Madison. We might have to wait a few minutes," Egypt replied.

Nothing was ever easy for me. I just wanted to get in my freaking car and drive off without any crazy banter from Gavin. I felt my heartbeat quicken, and I could feel sweat starting to develop on my nose, which I really hated.

I quickly looked inside my handbag and got out my MAC cosmetic bag. I started to apply some Viva Glam Nicki 2 Lip glass. My Chanel sunglasses were on top of my head. I took them down and wiped them off with a small cloth and then put them over my eyes. I brushed my hair so that it laid perfectly down my back. By this time I was calm and looking great.

"Miss Thang, what are you over there doing?" Egypt laughed.

"Nothing, it's been a while since I've seen your mother; that's all," I lied.

"Right, my mother cares how you look, Madison," Egypt joked.

Gavin looked amazing. He was wearing a Jordan sweat suit. Of course he had on the shoes to match. He was under the hood of his car. I thought to myself, please let me make it in this house without being seen by him. No such luck, thanks to big mouth.

"What's up, Gavin? I haven't seen you in a minute," Egypt called out.

"Well, I'll be damned, if it isn't Ebony and Ivory. What's up, ladies?" Gavin replied.

"I had to give Madison a ride over here to get her car. Where is Noah?" Egypt asked.

"He needed to get a part for that car over there. He should be back shortly," Gavin stated while staring at me the entire time he spoke.

"Come here, Cotton; I can't get a hug?" Gavin asked while reaching out for me.

"My name is Madison, and I'll pass on the hug," I responded.

"Oh, it's like that? You're probably scared that George will find out that you were in my arms again." Gavin laughed.

"Who is George?" Egypt asked.

"Cotton married George Jefferson. How many cleaners y'all got now, three or four?" Gavin teased.

"Damn, Gavin, that's cold. Let me give y'all a minute to converse. You know Madison is going to cuss you out about her precious Avery," Egypt responded, walking into the house.

I was so damn mad at that point that I had already made up my mind to just walk off and not entertain such foolishness. I turned to walk off, and Gavin grabbed my arm. My handbag landed on the ground. We both bent down to pick it up. His face was close to mine, and I could smell his aftershave. Damn, he always smelled good.

"Gavin, you can be a real ass when you want to be," I said irritably.

"Girl, you better give me a damn hug. I'm checking you out. You look good, Cotton," Gavin said with a huge smile on his face.

He had perfect, straight white teeth. His hair was perfectly groomed on his face. His lips, his lips…damn! He pulled me real close and hugged me so tight.

"Madison, is it still soft like cotton? If I put my hand under your dress right now, I bet your panties are wet. So wet that, right now, you want to take them off and give them to me," Gavin voiced his suspicions.

"Cut it out, Gavin; let me go!" I insisted, breaking free from his hold.

"I'll let you go if you let me give you a big kiss on the lips," Gavin assured me.

I started to lean back. I didn't like the affect he was having on me.

"Where you going? I got you. Stop leaning back. You know which lips I'm talking about?" Gavin smirked.

Suddenly Celine Dion started roaring from my handbag; "Because You Loved Me" was playing so loudly. I grabbed my phone and saw my husband's face. I jerked away from Gavin with all my strength.

"Avery, Avery, yes, baby, what's up?" I said nervously.

"Madison, I need to talk to you about what I discussed with Lucas. I invited him over for dinner tonight. I told him about your famous homemade buttermilk fried chicken and cornmeal waffles with strawberry-cider syrup," Avery bragged.

"Tonight, Avery? I have so much to do already," I said.

"Maddie, I need you. When I drop the ball on the goal line, what are you supposed to do?" Avery asked.

"I'm supposed to pick the ball up and run it into the end zone," I huffed.

"Touchdown!" Avery shouted.

"Avery, I really don't—" I tried to speak quickly.

"I'll see you later at home, bye, baby," Avery interrupted.

My mind started racing a mile a minute. I didn't normally cook on Fridays. What was I saying; I didn't normally cook at all. We generally took the kids out to eat at their favorite restaurant on Fridays.

Damn it, I needed Tina. What was I going to do if I couldn't get her to come over on such short notice? I started hyperventilating. It was cool outside, but I was sweating. I frantically started going through my contact list in my phone.

"Hey, Madison, sorry I kept you waiting," Noah said.

"Oh, goodness, Noah, you startled me. What was wrong with my Cadi.?" I asked.

"You had a crack in your radiator, nothing too serious. I replaced the radiator, and I did an oil change on it," Noah explained.

"Thanks, Noah, how much do I owe you?" I questioned.

I followed Noah into the house. I went into the room that Noah called his office and watched him print out a work order. I gave him a check for the amount of the expenses, with a tip, of course, and then proceeded to the dining room. Egypt and her mother were sitting at the dining-room table.

"Hi, Butterfly, you're looking well today," I said.

"Hey, Madden, honey. Thank you so much for bringing me lunch the other day. I really enjoyed it. That was the best smothered shrimp over grits that I have ever had. What did you put in that gravy?" Butterfly asked.

"Huh...um...um...I...um," I stuttered. "I will e-mail the recipe to Egypt," I fibbed.

"OK, baby, I'm proud of you for trying to serve food that you probably wouldn't be eating if you hadn't married a black man," Butterfly stated.

I wanted to crawl under the table. I needed to get out of this house immediately. I told Egypt to walk me out. I needed to have a rain check on our shopping plans. When I looked out the window, I saw Miracle's car.

When I pulled up to Noah's house, I saw a lot of cars, one of which was the Aston Martin that belonged to Miss Hotshot Egypt. I didn't want to get out of the car without Reece being there, so I called him to make sure he was inside. He answered the phone and said that he was pulling in now. Thank God.

He pulled up on the side of me and flashed that award-winning smile. I rolled the window down, smiled, and rolled it back up. Then I got out of the car to get my hug. As soon as I stepped out of the car, people started flowing from the house.

"Hey you," I said to Reece.

"Hey yourself, Miss Team Lead. Come here, and give me some of that sweetness."

I walked over to him and placed my arms around his neck. He hugged me tightly and, to my surprise, picked me up and spun me around. When he put me down, we engaged in a passionate kiss. God, I loved this man. When I opened my eyes from the kiss, Gavin, Madison, and Butterfly were clapping.

"Bravo, bravo," they teased.

"Trashy," exclaimed Egypt.

"Oh, hi, everybody," I said. "Guess whose interview went quite well?"

"Congratulations," said Madison. Madison was such a sweetheart.

"Well, ain't God good!" shouted Butterfly. "When do you start?"

"Monday," I replied.

"Well, that gives you an entire weekend to get high and drunk with nowhere to be the next day," Egypt said.

"Excuse me, ma'am? Would you mind repeating yourself?" I said, walking toward her.

"You heard me. By the way, it must be nice to drive around in a luxury vehicle. Too bad you gotta give it back in an hour. Hmm, pity," Egypt teased.

"An hour…a month…either way we both have to return our vehicles. Isn't your Aston Martin a lease?" I scowled back.

"Your point?" Egypt asked.

"That ain't your car either, so I suggest you come down off your high horse pronto, Miss Girl."

"Ladies, ladies," Gavin interrupted. "Why make war when we could all make love?"

Gavin is such a whore, I thought. I'm sorry, I mean sex addict. You know there's a difference. He'd hump anything that would stay still long enough.

I walked over and hugged Madison and complimented her on her lovely outfit and pretty hair. Then I hugged Butterfly and apologized for getting ugly in her yard. She laughed and said she didn't mind, because she had been praying that Egypt and I would get along one day. Today just wasn't the day.

Reece came and touched my hand. "You got that for me?"

"Oh, yeah, I almost forgot. It's in the trunk." I handed him the keys.

He got his dry cleaning out of the trunk of Sha'Miracle's car and brought the keys back to me. We kissed again, and he said he would see me later. Then he walked inside the house to talk with Gavin. There was no way I was staying here any longer than I had to, so I said my good-byes and started toward the car.

"You're leaving so soon?" Madison said, catching up to me.

"Yeah, I need to run a couple more errands before I pick Miracle up from work."

"Tell that lady to call me. I've been trying to call her all day long," Madison said as she placed both hands on her hips.

"Funny thing, when I dropped her off at work this morning there were police cars at her school. You know she's the S.A.F.E. coordinator, so they call on her for everything. She's probably extremely busy today. But I will most certainly deliver the message," I said.

"Gabby, don't let Egypt get to you. She's really a sweetheart once you get to know her," Madison explained.

"It just seems like she has unexplained disdain for me, and I don't know why," I responded.

"I know, but she's just been through a lot. Promise me you'll give her a chance," Madison pleaded.

"How can I turn you down for anything, Maddie? I'll try." We hugged and I left.

I drove and thought and thought and drove. I had so many things going through my mind. I wanted to smoke so badly, but that's what got me in the position I was in now, so instead I chewed a piece of gum.

The four pack should be home by now, and I had to have a talk with Jalyssa. I wondered if she had said anything to her teacher about the passion group.

I had been doing some research on the Internet to see how I could get money for my children for college. I stumbled upon Oprah's site and got stuck. Oprah always did that to me. It was like I got into a trance when I read anything she was involved with. She had a page that explained how to start a passion group.

When I looked at it, it seemed pretty straightforward; it said to "do what you love." That was easy. I loved my children, and I needed money. So I researched some more. The quickest way to get money — well, legally anyway — would be to write a grant. I already knew how to do that. So I thought I could start a passion group to write one. The grant would allow me to receive money to start a scholarship fund. Bingo, Gabby. See? I thought. My business degree did me some good after all.

I had created an event to meet at Miracle's house on Sunday to organize the group. I had invited Jalyssa's teacher Mrs. Love because we had spoken from time to time, we were Facebook friends, and I thought she would be an asset to the group. All I needed was about six people, and we could make this happen.

I would tell Miracle about it this afternoon. She probably wouldn't mind. She had the most beautiful home. It was very large, and she was the only one who lived there. She had a split-level, four-bedroom, two-and-a-half-bathroom home with a loft. She had a three-car garage and an enormous backyard that sat just next to the lake. Even though she didn't swim anymore, she had a screened-in pool with a Jacuzzi and a separate patio area. Miracle's home was the bomb.

My cell phone rang. I looked to see who it was. Jalyssa's pretty face was on the screen. "Hello," I answered.

"Hey, Ma. I was wondering if I could go to Blessed's house today with Fallon," she asked.

"How long will you be gone?" I asked.

"I don't know. She just asked me to come with her. She said she doesn't want to go by herself."

"Well, don't stay gone too long; you know it's your night to do the dishes."

"Aw man," she whined. "OK."

"Eight o'clock, Jalyssa. Don't play."

"Yes, ma'am," said Jalyssa.

"Oh yeah, guess what?" I said excitedly.

"What?"

"I got the job. But not the one I applied for, an even bigger one."

"Yea! I'm so happy for you. Now can I get fifty dollars to go to the mall tomorrow?"

"Um, no," I said.

"Well, it was worth a try. See you later."

"Bye," I said.

Fallon and Jalyssa were best friends. Fallon's mom was very strict on her, and she often escaped to my house with Jalyssa, because I was a little bit more lenient. Hell, I was never there anyway. There was just too much going on in the world for me to sit at home with them all the time. Besides, Reece's two little boys had to be baby-sat when he had them. My children were the ones who did it.

Blessed was Fallon's boyfriend. He was a troubled little boy, but Fallon loved the ground he walked on. Whatever was going on, Jalyssa would tell me later. That loquacious child couldn't hold water. If I hadn't pushed her out myself, I would have thought she belonged to DJ Linda J.

No sooner than I ended my phone call, the phone rang again. This time it was Miracle's aunt Pearl. Oh Lord. She always had something smart to say, but I figured I'd answer before she called Miracle and made some story up about me.

"Hello."

"Hey, you still got Miracle car?"

"Well hello, Auntie Pearl. How are you today? Me? I'm just fine. I even got a new job today," I said sarcastically. How was she going to start off asking questions? This lady was too boorish for me.

"Mmm hmm, yeah right, sure you did. Like I said, you still got my niece car?" she replied uninterestedly.

"Why, yes, ma'am, I do. Is there something I can help you with?" I said in the kindest voice I had. Now I was just trying to piss her off.

"Yeah, you can come get me and take me to the store. Matter of fact, never mind, you probably already up there anyway, so just pick some stuff up for me," Pearl said.

"Well, I'm actually not at the store right now, but I will be more than happy to stop for you."

"I'm so sure you would. You got something to write with, Lila?"

"Lila?" I asked.

"Chile, you know your name. You got a pen?" she asked again.

"Yes, ma'am. Go ahead when you're ready."

Pearl rambled off what I thought was a million items, which really turned out to only be nine. I wrote them down and headed to the store to pick those items up. I didn't ask if I would be reimbursed, because I knew she would say something slick about me driving Miracle's car, and I didn't feel like listening to her loose lips. I wouldn't be using cash anyway. I still had some stamps left on my card for the month.

I sold my food stamps at the beginning of every month. I had bills to pay and children to take care of. Tina and her cousin Trina were my top buyers. They were good to me too. Sometimes I needed the money before the stamps hit my card, so I would get the money from one of them and let them hold the card until the stamps became available. When I didn't have a car to drive, Tina would get some stuff for me from the grocery store.

It was a good hustle I had. I sold the stamps at half value. I didn't know what I was going to do once I reported my income. I had to report it, because the government did not play about those food stamps.

I looked inside my wallet and didn't see my card. "Damn, I forgot I already gave the card to Trina to shop for the passion-group brunch on Sunday. Looks like I will be using cash after all. Oh well, there goes Miracle's gas money."

I wouldn't have enough time to get to Pearl then get to Miracle, so I chose to go get Miracle first. I hoped she had some juicy gossip about the police cars at her job when I got there.

Madison

I left Butterfly's house like a NASCAR driver in the Daytona 500. I was in a serious hurry. I needed to talk to Tina badly.

Tina had told me on many occasions that she was a woman on the go. She only had one son, and he didn't live with her. Every month she would be on some new occupational adventure. One month she wanted to pursue a career as a makeup artist, then an event planner, next a security guard. I encouraged her to really think about a culinary career. Tina was very talented in the kitchen. When she wasn't on her cell phone, she made amazing dishes in no time at all. She was probably out right now, trying to sign up for some class at the Vo-Tech.

I needed coffee to help me think. I pulled into a Starbucks. I ordered a zucchini, walnut muffin and a white-chocolate mocha Frappuccino with two Splendas, minus the whipped cream. I then pulled out my phone, scrolled through the contacts, and found Tina's name. The phone rang for what seemed to be an eternity. To my surprise, she answered the phone. Wherever she was, there was so much noise I could barely hear her.

"Hello, Tina, this is Madison Clark," I stated.

"Hold on, Mrs. Clark, for a minute," Tina shouted back into the phone.

"Tina, Tina, please listen to me. This is super important; I really need your help," I said, desperately trying to get her attention.

"I can't talk to you right now; I'm gonna have to call you back. If you don't hear from me within the hour, it's because I'm in jail," Tina screamed.

"Wait, Tina, what's going on? Where are you?" I asked.

"I'm at the hair salon downtown! I told this chick to do my hair like this lady in this magazine," Tina said.

She then told me the most ridiculous story I'd ever heard. Tina had told the stylist that her hair didn't look anything like the picture she provided the stylist with. She refused to pay the stylist. Since the stylist would not do Tina's hair over, Tina got up and walked out. Just as she was about to leave the salon, the stylist dumped a bucket of water on her head.

"This trick is going to pay me for this weave. Either I'm going to get my money out her pocket or out her ass!" Tina demanded.

I didn't know if I should laugh or cry. How in the world was I going to convince this lunatic to leave the salon and meet me at my house?

"Tina, I need you to listen to me. I have a very lucrative offer for you," I said excitedly.

"Lucrative, lu…what?" Tina asked.

"Lucrative, I mean rewarding. I can give you enough money to make your hair troubles go away for a while," I replied.

"I use one hundred percent Peruvian Remy. It can get very expensive, depending on the length of the bundle," Tina said.

"One hundred percent human hair, no problem — if you are available to come over to the house today and cook chicken and waffles, I would be so grateful," I declared.

"Ms. Clark, I can help you out. You must be in a real jam. Do you have all the ingredients I need at the house already?" Tina asked.

"No, I'm afraid I don't. Do you mind going to the store? I will pay you for your time and effort. How much do you need for the store?" I inquired.

Tina started to do pretend math in her head. I agreed to give her the money for the food, her time, her gas, and a very hefty convenience fee. I told Tina I had to go because I still had errands to run. I stressed to her that I would be home in an hour and she could pick the money up then. If I pulled this off, it would be a miracle. Speaking of a miracle, I needed to invite Sha'Miracle over tonight for dinner. She would know how to help me stay calm.

Hay was on her way to Kennedy High School. She had to speak with Ms. Raven Thompson about Fallon. Blessed was one mysterious young man. No one knew where he was, and no one had any useful information about him. His teachers both seemed like they hadn't taken the time to get to know him, let alone help him. His life seemed textbook: parents dead, grandparent spoiled him, he acted out. What Hay had to do was sit him down and have a heart-to-heart counselor-type conversation with him. But first, she had to get to him.

Hay walked inside Kennedy and asked the front-desk clerk if she could speak to Ms. Thompson. The receptionist, a Vietnamese woman who spoke very little English, had to be asked the same question three times by Hay.

"Missy Tomsum?" the clerk said.

"Yes, Ms. Thompson," Hay replied.

"Oh, OK. Let me see if she available, OK?"

"OK, no problem," Hay said. The clerk dialed a number on the phone and asked for Ms. Thompson. She hung up the phone, looked at Hay, and smiled.

"OK, she wait por you in brack office, OK?"

"Thank you so much," Hay said back.

Hay walked to the back conference room where Ms. Thompson was waiting. They said their hellos, and Hay sat down.

"Thank you so much for meeting with me on such short notice, but I have to find out some information, and time is of the essence," Hay started. "I have been assigned to Mr. Blessed Douglas, and as of right now, I am gathering information from the people he is connected to."

"I don't believe we have a Blessed Douglas enrolled at this school. Are you sure this is the correct location?" Ms. Thompson replied.

"No, Mr. Douglas is not a student here at the high school, but his girlfriend is. Her name is Fallon. I don't have a last name. She's a junior here. I was hoping that I could speak with her. This way I could gain some insight on Mr. Douglas."

"I know Fallon. Fallon Jenkins. She's one of our top students. But as for her boyfriend, couldn't you just talk to him?" Ms. Thompson questioned.

"I'm afraid that's not possible at this point, because Mr. Douglas is still at large."

"At large? You mean he's committed a crime and he hasn't been caught?" said Ms. Thompson, now noticeably nervous.

"Yes, ma'am. I'm not at liberty to divulge the details of his case, but it's a matter of public record if you watched the news last night," Hay hinted.

"News, news, news," Ms. Thompson said to herself. "Oh, yes, I remember now. You mean to tell me that's the student who stole the tourist bus yesterday?"

"I'm afraid so, ma'am."

"Officer Dawson, I will be more than happy to help in any way I can. Let me call Fallon right now." Ms. Thompson got out of her seat, left the office, and returned a minute later. "She should be right down."

"Thank you," Hay said. No sooner than Hay had thanked Ms. Thompson, Fallon walked in the door.

"Hello," she said.

"Hello, Fallon, sweetheart," Ms. Thompson spoke back. "This is Officer Dawson. She has a few questions about your boyfriend, Blessed. Have a seat."

Fallon froze. She wanted to sit as she was asked, but her feet were glued to the floor. Her heart began to beat so hard that she thought the two women could see her chest throbbing. The police were here at her school. Why did Blessed have to call her just an hour before? Now she had to pretend like she knew nothing, when, in fact, she knew everything. She slowly sat down and tried her best to play it cool.

Hay started asking questions. "How long have you known Mr. Douglas?"

This was easy, Fallon thought. "About six years," she answered.

"How long have you two been a couple?" Hay continued.

"Two years," Fallon replied proudly.

Hay noticed the huge smile that crossed Fallon's face when she answered the question about their relationship. So she decided to probe.

"Tell me, Fallon. What kind of boyfriend is he to you?" Hay asked.

Fallon became more relaxed. She could talk about Blessed all day and all night. She still got butterflies in her stomach whenever she thought of the two of them together. Blessed made her so happy. She just wished he would calm down.

He would have to calm down soon, because they now had a baby on the way. Fallon wondered what they would have, a boy or a girl. Fallon wanted a boy. She would name him after his father, and they would call him B. J.

"Fallon. Fallon!" Hay yelled and clapped her hands.

This broke Fallon from her trance. She sat up and tried to concentrate. "Blessed is the sweetest guy I know," Fallon began. "He's kind, thoughtful, and treats me like I'm the only one in the world that matters to him. He loves me and says that we're gonna get married and grow old together."

Hay typed on her computer as Fallon spoke. Fallon's head was so far up in the clouds for this little boy that it was unbelievable.

"When was the last time you spoke to him?" Hay asked.

"Yesterday morning," Fallon said quickly.

"I see. So you haven't spoken to him all day long today?"

"No, ma'am."

"So how do you feel about that? Not speaking to the love of your life for almost two whole days?"

"I mean, it's cool. Our school schedules are different, so we'll talk to each other later," Fallon said.

"Speaking of school schedules, how does it make you feel that you and Blessed are the same age and three grades apart?"

"I don't really care. Blessed is smart; he just has issues with getting up for school. That's why he got left back those times."

Fallon was beginning to get upset. How dare this lady, who knew nothing about Blessed, come in and attack him like that? She had no right to judge. Fallon had had enough of this, so she decided she would cut this short. "Are there any more questions? I have to go before they dismiss the bus riders."

"That's all for now. May I contact you if I have any more questions?" Hay said, handing Fallon her card.

"Sure," Fallon said, taking the card. Fallon got up to walk out. She had opened the door and had one foot out when Hay called her name.

"Fallon, honey?" Hay called to her.

Fallon didn't even bother to turn around. "Yes, ma'am?" Fallon said, rolling her eyes.

"When's the baby due?" Hay asked.

Fallon turned around, and her eyes were as wide as the moon. "How...how did you know?" she asked Hay.

"I didn't, but you just told me," Hay answered.

"What made you ask me that?" Fallon said, sitting back down.

"I don't know. I just got a feeling that it was more than just puppy love you had for Blessed. There is something connecting you to him too strongly for you to defend him like you did. That, and the fact that your nose is super wide and swollen. Your face is also very clear and bright. Even though it's only my first time meeting you, you have a pregnancy glow. Oh yeah, and your frame is too small for your stomach to be that round. That jacket isn't hiding anything, at least not from me."

Fallon dropped her head into her arms on the table and once again began to cry. If she couldn't hide her pregnancy from a complete stranger, how was she going to hide it from her mom?

Hay could sense the hurt through this child's sobs. They were tears of fear and disappointment. These weren't just regular tears. She asked Ms. Thompson, who had been quietly observing all this time, if she could step out of the room for just a second. Ms. Thompson said that she would, but she had to stand right outside and leave the door open, for student-safety purposes.

"Talk to me, Fallon. I know we just met, but it seems like you're holding a lot in," Hay said to Fallon.

"Officer Dawson, I'm scared. My mom is going to kill me. I have a 4.0 G.P.A., and all I want to do is go to college and get out of my mom's house. Blessed is the best thing that ever happened to me, but, Officer Dawson, why can't he just be good? Why can't he go to school, not get in trouble, and be good?"

Hay was speechless. Her heart went out to this baby. All she could do was rub her back and say, "It's going to be OK."

"No, it's not," Fallon cried. "How am I supposed to raise a baby? My chorus teacher, Ms. Love, said that I would have to drop out of school and get on welfare. She didn't make me feel any better when I confided in her, but maybe she's right. Blessed is in big trouble now, because if he wasn't, you wouldn't be here, and there's a chance that I might have to raise this baby all by myself."

Hay heard everything she said, but what stood out the most was when she said her chorus teacher was Ms. Love. Charity was a teacher here? And she told the girl she would have to drop out? What a prude.

Hay sensed something special in Fallon. Fallon was too young to be this stressed out. She had already snatched Hay's heart, and that wasn't on Hay's agenda.

Hay held Fallon's chin and tilted it back so that they were eye to eye. Then she spoke in the most caring voice that she could. "Fallon, listen to me, and listen to me clearly. You are amazing. You are very strong, and you will be very successful. Things are hard right now, but they will all work out for you in the end. As long as you stay focused, all of your dreams will come true. And if you need me for anything, and I do mean anything, you use that card; do you hear me?"

Fallon tried to stop crying, but she couldn't. This was the nicest thing anyone had ever said to her. Officer Dawson had called her amazing. Fallon's feelings went from sadness to joy in that split second. All the things she thought she might have heard from Ms. Love, who had known Fallon for three years now, instead came from the police officer who had only known her for three minutes.

"Thank you, Officer Dawson. Thank you so much," Fallon said, wiping her eyes and regaining her composure. Fallon spoke again. "Officer Dawson?"

"Yes?"

"If I tell you where Blessed is, do you promise to take good care of him?"

"I promise, sweetheart," Hay said.

"He's at home. His grandmother will tell you he's not there, but he is."

"Thank you, Fallon. You just saved Blessed's life."

"Another thing, Officer Dawson," Fallon said nervously.

"What's that?"

"Could you wait until I go and visit him first? I'm going there right after school."

"I'll tell you what. Why don't you give me a call when you finish your visit? That way I can brief my team, and we'll know just what to do to keep everything safe."

"OK. Thank you so much, Officer Dawson."

"You're welcome. Now take care of yourself," Hay said.

Fallon smiled and walked out of the door.

Hay shook her head. That had to be the most emotional interview ever. Fallon had so much going for herself. She seemed like a great kid. And Charity worked here at this school. The world was just too small.

Hay thought she'd better leave before Charity saw her there. She didn't feel like being ministered to by the Holy Ghost any more today.

Hay drove back to her office, finished up some notes, and updated some other cases while she waited for Fallon to call. This little girl had better not be playing her. But if Fallon hadn't called by seven o'clock, Hay would be moving forward.

Fallon caught up with Jalyssa just after everyone was dismissed. The two of them had always met out front next to the flagpole. Today was no different. Fallon asked where Jade was. She always followed Jalyssa around wherever she went. Sometimes Jalyssa didn't mind, and sometimes it aggravated her. Fallon loved Jade. She was like a little sister to her, and she knew Jade looked up to the two of them.

"Jade said she had a project to do for world history, so she couldn't hang out with us today," Jalyssa told Fallon.

"Oh. OK. Are you ready?"

"Fallon, dawg, you're acting kind of crazy. And your entire face is swollen. Have you been crying?" Jalyssa asked.

"Um..." Fallon had never lied to her best friend. "Yeah, but only because I was scared. The police came up here and questioned me about Blessed."

"Police?" Jalyssa asked curiously. "Juice me, please!"

Fallon exhaled. She knew she would have to tell Jalyssa everything, so as they walked to the stop and waited for the city bus, Fallon explained everything.

"OK. First of all, Blessed took a tour bus for a joyride yesterday at the mall, and now he's wanted. When he sat in the seat, people started to get on the bus, and he ended up driving them to their hotel then ditching the bus. The police came here to question me, because they're looking for him."

Jalyssa didn't speak. She wasn't the judgmental type. She would simply gather all the information and somehow, in her head, try to process a solution. Fallon loved that about her.

Fallon continued, "So now we're going to his house to see how we can help him get out of this mess. And second, I'm pregnant."

"Pregnant?" Jalyssa repeated.

"Yes, three months," Fallon said.

For some reason, Fallon felt a lot better now that she had gotten all of that off of her chest.

"Who knows you're pregnant? I know good and hell well not Farrah ass."

Fallon burst into laughter. It was the first time she had laughed all day long. "How do you know my mom doesn't know?"

"Um, you're still standing on two feet. If Farrah knew, you wouldn't be alive right now to tell the story. But don't worry about her right now. One crisis at a time. You've got six more months to figure out what to do about the baby. Right now, let's attack Blessed, 'the Bootlegged Bus Driver.'" Jalyssa laughed.

Fallon absolutely loved Jalyssa. This was who she should have been talking to all along. She had way more sense than any of the adults Fallon knew.

"How do you even know I'm keeping the baby?" Fallon asked Jalyssa.

"Fallon, please," Jalyssa exclaimed, rolling her eyes. "Number one, you wouldn't kill anything living, and letter *B*, that child belongs to Blessed. You know Blessed is right under God in your world. Y'all really think y'all are Jay-Z and Beyoncé. Well, it's time to ride to the very end, Bonnie."

"Bonnie?"

"Yep, Bonnie and Clyde. Blessed done got himself in some mess, and I know you're not gonna leave him hanging, so let's see just how far you're willing to go to save your man."

The bus pulled up. Both girls got on and found a seat together. Jalyssa squeezed Fallon in the biggest bear hug she could. "I can't wait until my god baby gets here. My mom is gonna be so happy. I'm gonna ask her if we can go shopping tomorrow for the baby."

"Jalyssa, no!" Fallon exclaimed.

"What?" Jalyssa said back, puzzled.

"You can't tell anybody. Not even Gabby."

"So you're swearing me to secrecy? You know that's going to be hard for me," Jalyssa stated.

"Yes, Jalyssa, sworn to secrecy. As a matter of fact, give me your hand."

"Fallon, no!"

"Jalyssa, yes. Give it to me."

The two girls interlocked pinkie fingers. They had pinkie sworn the biggest of their secrets since they were ten years old. A pinkie swear was the most serious of the swears. Without it, Jalyssa could still tell people's business but just tell others, "Don't say anything," but a pinkie swear was like swearing on a stack of Bibles.

Damn, thought Jalyssa. Fallon had brought out the pinkies.

When they arrived at Blessed's house, Nay-Nay was sitting outside on the porch. She squinted her eyes through her bifocal lenses and smiled.

"Hey, sugars," Nay-Nay said to the girls.

"Hey, Nay-Nay," Jalyssa said. "What'd you cook?"

"I got some barbeque pig's feet in there. The macaroni and cheese is in the oven, and the green beans are on the stove. Go on in there and help yourself."

Jalyssa was starving. She had skipped the nasty breakfast her mom called cooking; she hardly ever ate school lunch, because it always gave her the runs, and when Fallon asked her to go to Blessed's house, she knew that Nay-Nay would have a full-course meal fixed, so she skipped lunch today.

Jalyssa went into the house, washed her hands, and went to the kitchen. Fallon was still outside with Nay-Nay.

Nay-Nay spoke first. "You know them polices been by here, looking for my baby. Talking 'bout he stole a bus. Can you believe that? A bus. My Blessed ain't done no such thing. I don't know why they out to get him so. If it ain't the school folks, it's the law. I wish they would all just leave him be." Tears filled Nay-Nay's eyes.

Fallon placed her arm around Nay-Nay and laid her head on Nay-Nay's shoulder. Nay-Nay was a fancy old lady. She always smelled so good. She only purchased the finest perfumes and never went a day without getting fully dressed, knee-high stockings and all, just to sit on the porch. Fallon wished that none of this was happening. Nay-Nay was too sweet to have to endure all Blessed was putting her through.

For the next five minutes, neither of them said a word. Then Fallon said, "Nay-Nay, I have to go and talk to Blessed."

"He's in his room, baby. Go head on, and talk to him. And make sure before you leave, you get that bag of grapes and cookies I got laid out for Farrell. Make sure you take it to him, so he can have a snack."

"Yes, ma'am, I will, and thank you," Fallon said.

"Mmm hmm," was all Nay-Nay said back.

Fallon went inside the house and knocked on Blessed's room door.

"Who is it?" Blessed whispered.

"It's Princess Douglas," Fallon whispered back.

Blessed flung the door open, snatched Fallon inside, and slammed the door back and locked it. He was so happy to see her. He hugged her and didn't let her go. Tears ran down his face.

Blessed knew that he had messed up. He had messed up big time. Nay-Nay couldn't bail him out of this one. He was gonna go to jail. He didn't want to be like those brothers who got locked up and their babies never knew them while growing up. He wanted to be there every day for his baby. He was gonna teach him how to be a good man. But how would he do that from a prison yard?

"Boo," Fallon said. "What are you going to do?"

"I don't know; I don't know; I don't know," Blessed said, pounding his fist against his forehead.

"We have to think of something, quick," Fallon told him. She wouldn't tell him that she had ratted on him to Officer Dawson. She always wanted him to know that she was his ride-or-die chick.

"Maybe you should turn yourself in. Plead guilty, and maybe cut a deal with the state," Fallon suggested.

"What? Never that! I'm sixteen now. They'll try me as an adult for sure," Blessed said.

Jalyssa knocked on the door. Blessed looked at Fallon and said, "Who the hell is that? Who's with you? Are you a narc, Fallon?"

"Blessed, you're paranoid. That's just Jalyssa. She came here with me. Let her in; maybe she can help us."

"So you already told Mouth of the South my business. Damn, Fallon!"

"Blessed, we need help. I can't do this by myself and neither can you," Fallon exclaimed.

Fallon opened the door, and Jalyssa walked in. "Blessed, what's up, bro?"

"Man, sis, you already know. But what you don't know is I'm not trying go to no jailhouse. Did you hear the charges they got on me?" Blessed asked.

"I don't watch the news, but I pulled it up on my tablet when I was eating just now. Dawg, you're the talk of the city right now," Jalyssa said.

"Man, they've been playing it on the news every ten minutes, all day long. All I've been doing is pacing back and forth, trying to plot my next move. You got any ideas, Jalyssa?" Blessed asked while holding his hands together in a prayer position.

Jalyssa thought for a moment. "Reece," she said. "Call Reece. He'll know what to do."

Blessed could have kicked himself for not thinking of that sooner. Reece was like an uncle to him. He made sure Blessed's pockets stayed fat every week.

Reece was Ms. Gabby's boyfriend. He was well respected in the hood. He and Gavin ran the block. All Blessed had to do was ask Reece what he should do. Blessed picked up the phone and dialed Reece's number.

"Speak," answered Reece.

"Hey, Unc. What's up? It's Blessed."

"Nephew, what it do?" Reece asked.

"I need your help." Blessed sniffed, fighting back tears.

"For sure. What you need?" Reece listened attentively.

"I don't know, man. I'm wanted by the cops for stealing a bus. Nay-Nay has been fighting off anyone who comes looking for me, but I don't know how much longer I can hide."

"Stealing a bus? Oh, that was you on the news? Man, they got the hounds out looking for you. The first thing you need to do is dump that cell phone. They got tracking systems on those things. Second thing, meet me at the store at six thirty tonight. I'll have everything for you then."

"Ten four, Unc. I'll be there."

Blessed hung the phone up and told the girls what Reece had said. Jalyssa suggested that Blessed pack an overnight bag. Chances were Reece was going to get him a hotel room for a few days.

"I'm coming with you," Fallon blurted out.

"Have you completely lost your mind, Fallon?" Jalyssa asked. "How will you explain this to Farrah?"

Fallon hadn't given her mom or her brother a thought. She spent so much time being forced to think about them that, for once in her life, she only thought about herself.

"I'll text her. Then I won't answer until I'm ready to face the music," Fallon said.

Jalyssa said to Fallon, "What about when she calls me?"

"You haven't seen me," snapped Fallon.

"But my mom knows I'm with you right now," Jalyssa responded.

"Well, tell her you left me at Blessed's house. Nay-Nay will cover for me," Fallon said matter-of-factly.

"OK. Cool," Jalyssa said.

After they gathered clothes for Blessed, they were on their way out the door. It was already five forty-five.

"Wait," Jalyssa yelled. "What about clothes for you, Fallon?"

"I hadn't thought about that," Fallon replied.

"Don't worry," Blessed interjected. "I'll ask Reece for some money so you can get some new clothes."

The three of them packed Blessed up and prepared to leave. They only had a few minutes to make their move. Jalyssa went to catch the bus home. She hugged and kissed both Fallon and Blessed. Reece would handle things from here.

I made the phone call to Raven Thompson. She was her usual cheerful self. She agreed to help Officer Dawson with her investigation. I quickly got up out of my seat and turned the lights off in my office. The only light in the room was coming from my computer monitor. The phone was still constantly ringing, but if I wanted to eat, I would have to ignore the phone. I took the sub out of my minifridge and prepared to finally eat it. Over the PA system, I heard that damn Higgins's voice.

"Miss Morris, are you in your office?" Mrs. Higgins questioned.

"Yes, Mrs. Higgins, what do you need?" I said with tons of resentment in my tone.

"You have a visitor in the front office. Can I just send him to your office?" Mrs. Higgins asked.

Is this damn lady for real? I thought. Why not send twenty more people to this office. I don't need to eat; I can just live off satisfying her every request. Father God in heaven, please help me to be patient with whoever this is; I'm so hungry.

When I got downstairs, I noticed that my shoe was untied. I quickly bent down to tie my shoe when I noticed that behind me was that arrogant jerk from the Subway. When will this nightmare end, I thought to myself. If this man is a parent to one of the students here at Clinton Middle, I will call Gabby to stick a fork in me, because I will be well done!

"Wow, I hadn't realized Subway delivered?" I said with a smirk.

"Hello, Miracle, I was in the neighborhood, and I hoped we could talk for a minute," Trevor stated.

"Well, it just so happens that I am extremely busy today, so I'm sure someone in the guidance department would be happy to set you up for a parent conference," I said.

"A parent conference? No, I'm single with no kids," Trevor replied.

"What can I do for you?" I asked, suddenly kind of interested.

"I own the Subway that you frequently visit, and I was hoping to become a partner in education," Trevor announced.

I was very confused by this entire conversation. He was giving me way too much information at once. He owned the Subway. He wanted to be a partner in education. This day would go down in the books. No one was going to believe this story.

"You seem to know my name pretty well, but I don't know yours," I said.

"My name is Trevor. I mean, my name is Trevor Goodman," he said proudly.

Wait a damn minute, I thought. Did he just say Trevor Good-Man? I don't have time for this foolishness. I turned around to look for Ashton Kutcher, because I was definitely being punk'd!

"Well, Mr. Goodman, we would appreciate your help here at Clinton Middle. If you wait here, I will go to my office and get you a flyer for a community fair that we are having here just before the holidays. This is the perfect time of the year for the community to show their support for underprivileged teens," I said.

I smiled and walked away. As luck would have it, I bumped into Mr. Smart coming out of the main office. I picked up speed, before he had a chance to stutter through whatever nonsense he was going to say. I heard him say that stupid good-morning greeting to Trevor.

"Trevor, dawg, what's up? You're looking like new money!" Mr. Smart managed to get out of his mouth without too much stammering.

"Damn, Isaac, you look…well…let's just say that you are still keeping it one hundred," Trevor joked.

"Yeah, man, you know I got these women 'round here going HAM over me," Mr. Smart lied.

"Oh yeah, I can believe that!" Trevor said, swallowing a giggle.

"I got my eyes on Miracle. She wants me, but she's playing had to get," Mr. Smart said with that look of determination in his eyes.

"How much do you know about her, Isaac?" Trevor questioned.

"Man, look, Miracle was so fine in high school, we nicknamed her Miracle Whip! She had Gerald Hall walking around the school in a daze. You can't be *p*-whipped; you got to whip that—" Mr. Smart almost confirmed.

Mr. Smart's conversation was cut short by my presence. I gave him the look of death. He quickly did an about-face and left the area. I knew these two dummies were *not* having a conversation about me. I didn't know them, and they didn't know me.

I would deal with Mr. Smart later. First, I needed to get rid of Trevor. I was just about to hand him a few papers when his phone started to ring. He put one finger up in my face, as to suggest for me to wait a minute. I was very close to setting the papers on the counter and walking off, but if his wife was on the phone, I wanted to hear that. Single? Yeah right.

"I will be there in about thirty minutes. I will call Lucas and see if he can come over and look at the oven. Don't worry, Mia," Trevor said.

"Mr. Goodman, here is the flyer I promised," I said with no enthusiasm in my tone.

"Mr. Goodman, so formal, please call me Trevor. That was one of my employees calling. I have to go and fix a crisis in one of my other restaurants on the east side of town. It was a pleasure to officially meet you, and I look forward to working with you," Trevor flirted.

"Have a good day, Mr. Goodman." I smiled and walked away.

I had been so busy all day that I just realized I never took my cell phone out of my bag. As soon as I reached for it, I saw Madison's face.

"Hey, chick, what's up?" I asked.

"Do not 'hey, chick,' me; what the hell have you been doing all day?" Madison barked.

"You wouldn't believe me if I told you," I said.

"Miracle, I need you to come over for dinner tonight," Madison stated with such desperation in her voice.

"Madison, I would love to, but after the day I've had, I want to take a hot shower, eat my sub, and go to BED!" I exclaimed.

"Sha'Mircle, when I drop the ball on the half-court line, what are you supposed to do with it?" Madison asked.

"I'm pretty sure that's not how that saying is supposed to go. You need to pick up your ball and maybe do a lay-up with it or do a chest pass to someone else on your team." I laughed.

"Miracle, please come over. Avery waited till the last minute to tell me that he has invited a couple of business associates over to the house for dinner. I need you there for moral support. I'm not sure how this night is going to turn out," Madison whined.

"OK, OK, count on me through thick and thin," I replied.

"That's my Miracle; I'll see you at seven thirty sharp. I'm going to invite Egypt over as well. You should bring Gabby with you. I want to try to help those two get along better."

Madison responded so contently. I laughed as I ended the call with Madison. I hoped Gabby was already outside. I was more than ready to go. I'd send her a quick text message.

By the time Gabby picked me up from school, I was completely brain-dead. I had so many thoughts running through my head at once. I got into the passenger side of my own car and just sat there with my hands covering my face.

"Miracle, are you all right?" Gabby asked.

"No, Gabby, I'm not all right," I replied dryly.

"I tried calling you a couple of times today. I figured you were busy. I have terrific news!" Gabby exclaimed.

"I could use some good news. What happened with your interview?" I questioned.

"Nothing really, the job I applied for I was overly qualified for that position, so I didn't get the job. However, as it turns out, I am qualified to be the new team lead!" Gabby yelled.

"Gabby, you need to slow down. Why do you think the crossing guards are there?" I asked with a frown on my face.

"Miracle, the man is walking a grown lady across the street. That is so stupid. If she can't make it across the street by herself by now, shame on her," Gabby replied.

"Is that what you are going to tell the police when you are arrested for a vehicular homicide? I'm going to tell the police that you kidnapped me and stole my car," I joked.

"Did you hear what I said about the job?" Gabby asked in an irritated tone.

"Gabrielle Sweeny, I was about to congratulate you before you scared me to death. I guess you'll be missed at the store!" I said sarcastically.

"What do you mean? Are you insinuating something?" Gabby asked.

"I'm not insinuating nothing; I'm telling you how it *I S* is! Auntie Pearl said that you were not always job hunting every time you borrowed my car," I said.

"Did Pearl also tell you about the many different errands I had to do for her? We have to go by her house now to drop off some groceries," Gabby stated.

Oh, God no, I thought. I forgot I'd told Auntie Pearl that I would stop by her house when I got off.

As Gabby zoomed to my aunt's house, she told me about her day. She saw Avery at the cleaners when she picked up Reece's clothes. She also saw Madison and Egypt at Butterfly's house. She told me that she and Egypt had got into it for the one hundredth time. I was trying to focus in on what she was saying, but my mind was on Blessed and, oddly enough, Trevor.

"Miracle, we need a plan. We need to get in and out of this house as quickly as possible," Gabby said.

"You don't have to tell me that; I actually worked today. I'm exhausted." I sighed.

Gabby had purchased enough groceries that we both had bags in our hands. We agreed to tell Auntie Pearl that we were on our way to Kennedy High to pick up Mark from band practice. I knew that we were doomed when Auntie Ruby opened the door. If you thought Auntie Pearl was bad enough, try being in the room with her and her identical twin, Ruby. Auntie Ruby was a sweet, very religious lady. You were not going to get by her without a good dose of encouragement and a word from God.

"Bless God, come on in here. You girls are looking well; I can see God's favor all over you. We missed you at church last Sunday. You know the Bible tells us that we need to meet together as believers and to encourage one another. What better place to do that than in God's house, amen?" Auntie Ruby preached.

"Amen!" Gabby and I said in agreement.

"Gloria asked the church to pray for little Gerald as he starts rehabilitation to repair his torn ACL," Auntie Ruby stated.

"It's about damn time y'all got here. I'm glad ice cream wasn't on my list. Y'all got all this technology, but black folk still haven't mastered the art of the *hurry up*! Go on; sit down, Ruby, and let the girls put the groceries up," Auntie Pearl insisted.

"Did I hear you right, Auntie Ruby? Gerald is injured?" I asked.

"Damn, Miracle, don't you watch the ESPN? It was breaking news last week. The local news even interrupted my damn soap operas, talking about little Gerald. Gloria said that he would be here one day next week. I'm going to bake a sweet-potato pie and take it out to Gloria's house. You know Gerald bought her a beautiful home out there in Lake Nona," Auntie Pearl said with such conviction.

"I guess I hadn't heard that, or maybe it slipped my mind," I said in a confused tone.

"Miracle, what did I tell you about walking around with an empty head? Use your head, girl, for more than just a hat rack, and for you to have such beautiful hair…why do you keep it in a damn ponytail all the time?" Auntie Pearl questioned.

"Pearl stop nagging the girl! Would y'all like something to eat?" Auntie Ruby asked.

"Yes, thank you," Gabby said.

"What are you doing?" I whispered to Gabby.

"We can't stay, Auntie; plus Madison invited us over for dinner tonight," I blurted out quickly.

"Child, please, Manhattan invited y'all over for dinner? I don't know why; she ain't cooking nothing. Y'all can stop by a soul-food restaurant by yourselves." Auntie Pearl laughed.

"So what do you think about Gerald being in Orlando next week?" Gabby whispered.

"I don't really care. It is really funny to hear my aunts call him 'little' Gerald when he's a six-foot seven-inch two-hundred-and-sixty-five-pound tight end." I laughed.

"Your aunt is a trip. We both know that Madison wouldn't lie to Avery about taking some silly cooking lessons, right?" Gabby asked.

Gabby and I exchanged strange looks at one another. As far as we knew, Madison had been going to a cooking class for a while now. She was so proud of everything that she had learned. She even e-mailed me a couple of recipes.

Auntie Ruby insisted that we take several plastic containers of food with us. She wanted to make sure Gabby's children got something to eat, because Auntie Pearl insinuated that they only ate ramen noodles and that they rarely got a home-cooked meal.

Once in the car, I explained to Gabby the short version of my day.

"So, the kid who stole the bus…what is his name?" Gabby asked.

"His name is Blessed. I've told you different things about him before, but I just never mentioned his name," I said while looking straight ahead.

"Repeat that; the kid's name is Blessed?" Gabby asked.

"I know, yes, he has an unusual name, but then some people think that about me," I said sadly.

"Miracle, I need to tell you something. I know Blessed. My children are friends with Blessed. I need to call Jalyssa right now," Gabby said nervously.

I pulled over into a gas station so that Gabby could talk to her daughter and I could get an energy drink. I hoped the kids knew where Blessed was hiding out so that I could help him. For some reason I was starting to feel like I had let him down in some way. I knew what it was like to want to run and hide out.

The thought of Gerald being in Orlando was a bit unsettling to say the least. I had managed to bury my feelings for him deep down inside me. It took me a long time to get here, and I wasn't about to turn back now.

"I talked to Dr. Morris about providing you with a letter of recommendation for that medical school in Maryland," Butterfly said angrily.

"Ma, why does every conversation with you start off with me going back to school?" I asked.

"Egypt, you are doing nothing with your life. There is more to life than just shopping, hair, and nails. Put that money you have left to good use. You did so well in college. I know you would make a fine doctor," Butterfly demanded.

"I don't want to go to school, so just drop it. You wanted me to start volunteering, and I'm doing that. I'm at Kennedy High and Clinton Middle at least three or four days out the week, working with the S.A.F.E. coordinators. I get to talk to teens with anger issues and behavior problems, as well as those who are survivors of sexual abuse. Not once have you said anything about that, or are you still pretending that it didn't happen to me? I'm proud of the relationships that I have built with those girls. Did Dr. Morris tell you that she hasn't spoken to Miracle in two weeks? She should be more concerned about that than writing a letter on my behalf," I replied.

"Egypt, I'm very proud of you. I just don't want to see you running around town without some real purpose. I'm not going to be here forever, and before I close my eyes for the last time and go to meet my maker, I would like to see you with a husband, children, and a blossoming career," Butterfly stated while wiping tears from her eyes.

My mother was very dramatic. I wasn't going to let her bully me into doing one more thing. From the time I got my settlement money, she had been on my back about how I should spend it. She was holding the purse strings until I turned eighteen. She made stupid investments and gave a lot of the money away.

My mother found out about my relationship with Brown in court. We have never had a real conversation about what went on with me and Brown. She said the money was evil, because an evil thing had taken place.

I had been in a couple of relationships in college, some with men and some with women. I just couldn't trust anyone. No one was going to hurt me again. My therapist said that I should start a journal. I have found writing to be more therapeutic than having different sexual partners or abusing alcohol and prescription drugs. For the last couple of months, I have been trying to figure out who will win my heart, Trevor or Hazel-Ann.

I hugged my mother and headed for the door. When I got outside, my brother and Gavin were having what looked to be a heated conversation. Gavin has a huge tattoo that starts from his wrist and goes all the way up to his elbow, and it reads, "*MADISON*." Madison had left in such a huff, and I needed to talk to her.

"Good-bye, big brother; I'll see you at the kids' game tomorrow," I stated.

"Egypt, are you going to be able to do that for me?" Noah asked.

"Noah, we will discuss that later," I said with a frown. "Gavin, your girlfriend doesn't say anything about that huge tattoo? It's painful, but you can have it removed," I said.

"Egypt, you are forever worried about the wrong thing. Run along, little girl, and find you some business. This tattoo is not going anywhere and neither is Madison," Gavin said as he pulled his shirt sleeve down.

I definitely needed to talk to Madison about Gavin, and I needed to do some soul-searching of my own. I didn't want to hurt Trevor or Hay, but I knew in the end someone was going to be hurt. I was going to have to make a decision soon. May the best man or woman win.

Madison

I had a list of things to do before Avery called and threw a monkey wrench into my plans. I called Tina only to find out that she had to go home first and change out of her wet clothes before she headed to the store. I decided to go home, toss back a shot of vodka, and wait for Tina. I needed to know if Avery was still at the cleaners. When I located my cell phone, it was ringing. Oh Lord, it was Pearl. I had forgotten to call her back. I'd better think of something good.

"Hello, Aunt Pearl, how are you doing today?"

"Maddie, I done called every number on this here card y'all gave me. I'm glad you finally decided to answer your phone. I got my blouse back the other day, and one of my damn buttons is cracked. Now Ms. Pearl don't buy nothing cheap. I need my blouse fixed so that I can wear it to church on Sunday."

"Aunt Pearl, I am so apologetic about this unforeseen incident. I will personally stop by your house tomorrow and pick that blouse up and have it repaired."

"Well I appreciate that, honey. Now this is the third button y'all done cracked. You need to tell that husband of yours not to press down so damn hard on my clothing. There is history in this garment."

"Yes, Aunt Pearl, Avery is very much aware that this is the blouse that you wore on August 28, 1963, for the historic March on Washington," I said, rolling my eyes.

"I was a freedom fighter. Now I'm just a fighter. Make sure you tell jarhead Avery what I said; you hear me?" OK, I'll talk at you later. I heard you were cooking tonight."

"I am preparing my famous homemade buttermilk fried chicken and cornmeal waffles with strawberry-cider syrup. Would you like me to bring you some supper?" I asked as cheerfully as I could.

"Madison, listen to me; Avery didn't marry you because you were a chef. He married you because he loves you and them kids. You hear me? All right, now I got to go. I can't miss the news fooled up with you. And black folks don't eat no damn supper; we eats dinner when we can. I can't eat no damn fried anything; you're trying to kill me. My damn pressure would be so high —"

"Hello, hello, Aunt Pearl?"

Just like that, she hung up. I quickly poured another shot of vodka. Did Aunt Pearl know my secret? Should I keep this charade up? It was times like this when I really missed my mother. I tried so hard not to. I wanted to hate her for not being there for me all these years.

I started to think back on the time when I told my parents that Avery had asked me to marry him. This was supposed to be the happiest time of my life. Surely my mother and father would let bygones be bygones, but instead my father insisted that my mother pack everything I owned and box it up. When I say everything, I mean everything, from old report cards and things I made for them in ceramics to my baby photos. They sent my things to Mr. and Mrs. Clark's house without a return address. It was as if I was dead to them. So to keep my children from asking too many questions about my parents, I told them that my parents died in a terrible plane crash.

Before I knew it, I must have dozed off, because the sound of the doorbell woke me up. Finally Tina was here with bags and bags of stuff. What I didn't know was that Avery was at the cleaners, talking to our neighbor Charity.

"OK now, Avery. Do you think you can have those robes all done by Tuesday? The choir recital is next Friday, and I cannot afford any mishaps. I love you and Madison to death, but something is always going wrong when I bring my stuff here," Charity stated.

Avery shook his head up and down and smiled the tightest, fakest smile he could. Charity was at the cleaners. She was the most ridiculous person Avery knew. She complained about everything everyone else did while she always remained perfect.

"Don't worry, Charity. I will handle this job personally. Sixty choir robes in three days is a piece of cake," Avery said, still smiling.

"Maybe you can have your sister help you out," Charity said.

"Sister?" Avery asked.

"Yeah, your sister. She's always with your wife, always in and out of your home. Every now and then I wave at her, and she'll wave back. I figure she has to be *your* sister, because let's face it, she looks nothing like your blond-haired, blue-eyed wife."

"Charity, what are you talking about? I don't have a sister. Who is at my house?" Avery's ears were getting hot. Was Charity just yanking his balls, or was she serious about a woman at his house? Avery wondered.

"Come to think of it, Avery, she could *not* be your sister, because she's never there when you are."

"Seriously, Charity? Make up your mind. Is she my sister or isn't she?"

"Well, darling, I have no idea at this point. Maybe you should talk to that sweet, busy wife of yours. I just know the spirit led me to bring this up. And you know me; I don't go against the spirit. But do me a favor, when you talk to Madison about it, don't let her know that you heard it from me. I don't want to be labeled a gossip. You know that gossiping is not of God."

Avery couldn't take it anymore. He was tired of trying to get answers from Charity, and since she had brought "the Lord" into it, that was his cue to end this.

"Well, thank you for the information. I'll call you when your robes are ready," Avery said, feeling irritated.

"Thank you, sugar. You be blessed now, you hear," Charity said while pointing at the ceiling.

"Later," Avery replied.

Avery was surely upset, Charity thought. But then again, everything happens for a reason, so whoever the black lady was at his house, he would surely find out.

The highlight of Charity's life was work. When that was over, she was awfully lonely. She wondered what she would cook for herself to eat tonight. Going out to eat alone had become the norm, until people started to whisper. Then she began to stay inside. Maybe she would invite Jalyssa's mother out for dinner. Charity knew she would have to pay for her, but at this point, she didn't mind. What she longed for more than anything was companionship. If she had at least one child, she wouldn't be so lonely.

As Charity drove down her street, she saw Avery's alleged "sister." This time she would do more than wave her hand. She let down her window and said, "Hey there."

"Hello," the lady replied.

"What's your name?"

"Excuse me?" the "sister" said.

"My name is Charity, and you are…"

"I'm Tina."

"Are you Avery's sister?" Charity asked.

Tina began to grow nervous. She and Madison had been able to keep their secret for quite some time now. This nosey-assed lady was doing the most.

"Yes, I'm his sister," Tina replied.

"Well how come I never see you when Avery is home?"

Was she serious? How dare she be audacious enough to pry like this? If the ho wanted a story, a story was what her nosey ass was gonna get.

"Avery and I don't get along. You see my mom is still kind of pissed, because he's a sellout. He didn't marry a sister. So since I still get along with my mom, Avery doesn't mess with us. He thinks he's too good for us black folk. So I sneak around here when he's not here, so I can see my niece and nephew," Tina lied.

Charity was more perplexed than ever now. Avery had said he didn't have a sister. So he was lying, because he really had disowned his family. Now *that* was top-flight sin. He didn't have to lie to her like that. If she didn't need his services so badly, she'd drive right back up to that cleaners and get her robes. Liars would definitely not inherit the kingdom of God.

Charity spoke back to Tina. "Well that sure is a shame. If you ever need anything, I live right here across the street. I'm praying for the reuniting of your family. Be blessed now."

Tina said, "Yes, ma'am. Thank you so much. It's hard, because I love my brother, but you know we have to keep living. You be blessed too."

Tina turned around and walked swiftly to the door. When Madison opened the door, Tina burst into laughter.

Charity pulled into her garage and let the door down. She was still contemplating calling Gabby when her phone rang. It was Sam. She hadn't heard from Sam in at least two years. When they divorced, he completely stopped talking to her, and she did the same. She wondered what he wanted after all those years of separation. It didn't matter; he had left her, and the Lord hadn't sent her another man in years. She picked up the phone and said hello.

"Charity," Sam spoke.

Charity's heart dropped. She instantly melted. She had forgotten how beautiful he made her feel when he said her name.

She took a deep breath then replied with a strong, "Sam."

"How are you?" he asked.

"I'm blessed in the Lord and highly favored by God. And yourself?"

"I'm well. The reason for my calling is simply to say hello and see how you were doing. Now that I know, I'll let you go."

Charity didn't want him to go. She wanted him to stay on the phone with her. She wanted to ask him how he was doing. How was the job? Did he have any children? She wanted to see if he wanted to go to dinner. But Charity was on a horse too high to get down from.

As much as she wanted Sam, needed Sam, right now, she let her pride once again get in the way. She said to him, "OK. Thank you for calling."

"It's my pleasure. Take care," Sam said.

"Be blessed," Charity replied. Then she hung up.

Sam had taken too much of Charity's time just then. She needed to resift her focus. She walked over to the window and peeked out.

Tina and Madison were bringing groceries back and forth from the car to the house. It looked like they were getting ready for a big dinner.

"It's so nice that Avery's sister helps out the way she does," Charity said to herself.

Just then, a light bulb in Charity's head went off. Now would be the perfect time to call Avery and tell him to come home. That way he could finally see his sister and know that Charity was not making this up.

Charity picked up the receiver on her house phone and dialed the number for Clark Dry Cleaners.

Faithful are the wounds of a friend, but the kisses of an enemy are deceitful. (Proverbs 27:6)

I couldn't believe that Blessed was in that kind of trouble. I had to get in touch with Jalyssa as quickly as I could. I had already called her cell phone three times and got her voice mail. I dialed a fourth time. This time she answered.

"Hello," Jalyssa answered.

"What the hell are you doing? I've been calling you for thirty minutes straight," I yelled.

"I'm sorry, Ma. My phone was on silent," Jalyssa said back nervously.

"Yeah, fucking, right!" I said back. Jalyssa was a big liar. I knew she was trying to avoid me. She probably was doing something she had no business doing.

"Tell me what's going on with Blessed."

"What do you mean?" said Jalyssa, playing dumb.

"You know damn well what I mean. I know Fallon told you what was going on. Now you need to tell me." I was getting annoyed with Jalyssa.

"OK, I'll tell you. But first you need to calm down," Jalyssa reprimanded.

She was right. I did need to calm down. I was so antsy for information that I got upset when she didn't answer. But one thing I knew about my baby was that she would give me the juice. All of it. With no problem.

"OK, I'm calm. Now talk," I demanded.

"Blessed stole a bus yesterday, and now the police are looking for him," she started. "Nay-Nay won't let the police search her house, and the police came to school today and questioned Fallon."

"What? So what is he going to do?" I questioned.

"He called Reece, and Reece told him to get rid of his phone and meet him at the store at six thirty. Fallon went with him, but she doesn't want Farrah to know yet. So you can't tell on her, Ma," Jalyssa said.

"Well where are you?" I asked, looking at my watch.

"I'm on my way home. Jade called me and said she was there by herself with the boys," Jalyssa answered.

"The boys are there? What's today? Oh yeah. Well, I don't know what's there for them to eat. Just give them some cereal until I get home," I told her. Reece's two boys were at the house already. Their moms didn't waste any time.

"What are we gonna eat tonight?" Jalyssa asked.

"If you went to Nay-Nay's then you should already be full. Miracle's aunt Ruby sent some food home for the rest of y'all. And where is Marlin?" My thoughts were going a mile a minute.

"I don't know. I guess at Sade's house. You know he stays booed up," Jalyssa said.

Sade and Marlin had been together for about a year. It was a wonder I wasn't already a grandma with all the sex they had.

"OK, well, I'm on my way up to the store, so just make sure everything is good until I get there."

"Man, Ma, how long you gonna be up there? I don't have no kids, and I don't even feel like watching those two bad-behind little boys. They're always talking about what their mama says this and what their mama says that. And tell me again why they all live in the same house anyway? Just weird," Jalyssa complained.

"Hell, I don't know. I can't stand neither one of them. I bet you they be pushing up on Reece when he takes the boys home. But I can't worry about that right now. Just hold it down. I shouldn't be there long," I replied.

"OK," Jalyssa said.

I ended the phone call and went back to the car.

"What did she say?" asked Miracle.

"She said that Blessed had gotten in touch with Reece and is supposed to meet him at the store at six thirty," I replied.

Miracle looked at her watch. "That was over half an hour ago."

"I know. Don't take me home; just drop me and Mark off at the store," I requested.

"You sure you don't want me to take Mark home?" Miracle asked.

"No, he can just stay up here with me," I said.

"OK then, please let me know the minute you find out something," Miracle responded.

We rode to the store in complete silence. I was scared for Blessed. I was scared for Fallon. Nay-Nay was out of her mind for spoiling that boy the way she did. Now look at this mess. I knew that Reece would tell me everything. I just hoped the police hadn't found him yet.

As we pulled up to the store, I thanked Miracle for letting me use her car, and Mark and I got out. We found Reece on the side of the store. He had just finished a deal with some man and turned and saw my face. He walked over and kissed me on the cheek.

"What's up, beautiful?" he asked me. Then he turned to Mark. "Hey, Mark. How was school?"

"Good," Mark answered.

"Where is Blessed?" I asked, wasting no time.

"Oh, you know about that?"

"Duh, Reece, everybody in the city knows about that. Jalyssa told me he called you and you told him to meet you up here."

"That damn Jalyssa. Them lip just too loose." Reece laughed.

"Well where is he?" I asked again.

"I got him a rental under a fake name and put him up at the hotel for the weekend. I contacted my homeboys in Georgia, and by Monday, he'll be in Atlanta. New identity, new job, new car and apartment—he's good. You know I take care of mine," Reece explained.

"What about Nay-Nay?" I asked.

"As soon as he gets settled in, he'll call her, and she'll know everything. One thing about ole girl is she's a ride or die. She'll do time herself before snitching on Blessed," Reece responded.

Relieved that Reece had worked everything out for Blessed, I picked up the phone and called Miracle. She didn't answer, so I left everything on her voice mail. I knew I could trust Miracle, so the voice mail was no problem.

While I was leaving the voice mail, Reece's phone rang. I saw him look at it, silence it, and then put it in his back pocket. I had been down this road way too many times with him. I knew it was probably some chick, but I was at the point where I wasn't arguing about it anymore. Whether I fussed or not, he was going to do what he wanted. Just as long as he kept me and mine straight, and none of those chicks stepped to me, I was good.

We stood at the store for another two hours. It was kind of boring for a Friday night. Mark had complained about being hungry, so I sent him inside for a hot sausage, chips, and a peach soda. I didn't have any money, and Trina had my food-stamp card, so I just put it on my tab.

"Miss Crystal said your tab is up to forty dollars and you can't credit no more until you pay it," Mark said when he came out of the store.

"She'll be OK. I'll pay it when I get the money," I told him.

Reece had heard me. I was in trouble. He hated when I charged stuff at the store; he said it made him look like less of a man, because his lady wasn't supposed to be broke.

"What the hell I told you 'bout that, Gabby?" he fussed.

"Man, calm down; it's OK," I assured him.

"Like hell it is. What I look like with a wad of cash in my pocket and my lady out here poor-mouthing?" Reece said.

I couldn't respond. I just looked at him and rolled my eyes.

Reece gave Mark a hundred-dollar bill. "Go in there and pay the bill, little man, and tell Crystal I said credit the rest to your mama's account. That way she'll already have credit."

Mark did as he was told. I went over to Reece and laid my head on his chest. He put his arms around me. He was such a softie. "I'm sorry," I said.

"It's OK," he responded and kissed the top of my head.

This was the reason why I worried about no other women — well, except his two baby mamas.

I was on time to pick the kids up from school. Madison Clark, aka *Father Time*, would be happy to know that I cut my lunch plans short with Trevor in order to be punctual. He was not happy either. I told him I would make it up to him tomorrow.

When the kids got into the car, I couldn't help but laugh to myself. A. J. had his Beats by Dre headphones on, totally ignoring the girls. The girls, however, didn't seem to mind much, because they were busy texting on their cell phones.

"Hello, Triple Threat!" I said.

"Auntie E., can we please go get something to eat?" Asia asked.

"Let me guess, Planet Smoothie?" I said with a grin.

"Yes!" the girls yelled.

I was a little worried that the girls didn't eat enough, but even at their age, they were well aware of how important it was to stay thin. I didn't want them to grow up and develop body-image issues just for the sake of ballet. Madison swore that the girls were at a healthy weight, but Madison herself seemed a little thin as of lately. We all got smoothies, and I dropped A. J. off at the football field for practice first.

"Thank you, Miss Egypt, for the ride; my dad will pick me up," A. J. announced while pulling the headphones down off his head.

"You are so welcome, Prince Avery," I said with a smile.

A. J. blushed and made a hand gesture at the girls and jogged off. As much as I couldn't stand Avery Clark Sr., his children were beautiful, and he was an awesome dad.

Avery and Madison were both athletes in college. I guess that's why they kept the kids in every extracurricular thing you could name. I spent so much time with *"Triple Threat,"* I really never thought of having my own children. Hell, Noah's baby mama had enough kids for me and her. Asia was the oldest of six.

Asia's mother, Candice, insisted on being called Candy. I made it a point to never call her that. When I tell you I hated to go over to Candice's house, I hated it! I had never been to a house where dirty clothes were everywhere. There were even dirty clothes in the kitchen. She treated Asia like a friend, baby-sitter, and meal ticket.

It was the weekend, so once I dropped the girls off for their ballet lesson, I headed over to Candice's dungeon to get Asia's clothes for the weekend. I had made the mistake of promising Noah that I would talk to Candice about relinquishing her parental rights to Noah and his soon-to-be bride.

"Hey, little boy, is your mama home?" I asked.

"She not home; she is next door getting her hair braided," he whined.

I parked the car, against my better judgment, and proceeded to knock on the door next to Candice's house. I was already annoyed. I couldn't talk about Asia in front of her neighbor, so I would have to table that conversation for later.

"What's up, E.? Girl, you need to give me that leather jacket!" Pebbles stated.

"Tell Candice I need to holler at her for a minute," I said dryly.

"Come on in the back; Candy's hair is almost finished," Pebbles said while grabbing my arm.

Pebbles guided me to the back of the house, which she had conveniently turned into something very similar to a hair salon. Candice and three other young ladies were sitting there, watching the news.

"Girl, these damn kids are out of control," Candice stated while high-fiving with one of the other ladies.

"They have been talking about this middle-school kid who stole a bus full of tourists all day. I don't see what the problem is; hell, he took they ass where they needed to be." Pebbles laughed.

"I want to know where he at? If there is a reward, I'll go look for his ass. They are trying to charge him with grand theft auto and driving without a license," Candice said.

"He better hope that they don't charge him as an adult. Little boys don't need to be in jail with grown men. That's not a good look," Pebbles said.

"Candice, do you have Asia's bag packed?" I asked, trying not to sound irritated, because I truly was.

"I thought I would have had time to wash clothes today, but my hair is taking longer than I expected," Candice said without much remorse.

"I guess that means no on the bag?" I said.

"Look, Egypt, don't come around here trying to start nothing with me. Tell your tired-ass brother to go out and buy Asia something to wear for the weekend. Damn, it's not like he can't afford it," Candice said as she snapped her fingers.

"You know how we can avoid all of this? You can let Asia go live permanently with Noah. Then he can pack a bag and *you* can see Asia on the weekend," I said.

"You and your brother can stop singing that song. You think I don't know that trick pregnant. I see her trash ass on Facebook, talking about how happy she is to be having a boy. I don't care if she is having ten boys; my baby money better not decrease by one cent, and I'm done talking. Close door!" Candice made a hand gesture like she had just slammed the door in my face.

Everybody in the room started laughing. Whenever Candice was finished talking, she would always say, "*Close door*." I started to reach across Pebbles to punch her right in her face. But if I would have hit her, I probably would have ended up fighting everybody in that room. I just told her that she needed to think about what I said.

When I got outside, there were three children sitting on my car. I had never seen a child's nose run for three years straight until now. I didn't even know what his name was. The kids all called him Little Brother. Little Brother had had a cold, I guess, since the day he was born. He was outside without a jacket on; his face was covered in what looked to be a mixture of dirt and mucus.

"Get y'all butts off my car, and go in the house somewhere!" I said.

"Auntie E., can you give us some money to go to the candy lady?" Little Brother managed to get out between coughs.

"If I give you this money, do you promise to share with your sisters and brothers?" I asked.

"No! They don't share with me," Little Brother stated.

I gave him twenty dollars and drove off. Candice was such an unfit, sorry excuse for a mother. She needed a little wake-up call, and I was just the one to give it to her. I was going to see if she closed the door on the Department of Children and Families, I thought while dialing Noah's number.

"Thank you for calling Clark Dry Cleaners, where we clean and press better than rest," Avery answered.

"Avery, it's Charity. You need to come home right now. Your sister is at your home as we speak," Charity said quickly.

"Charity, I told you before, I'm an only child," Avery huffed. Charity needed to give this up.

"You may be an only child, but I spoke to this woman personally, and she told me what happened between you and your family," Charity said matter-of-factly.

By now, Avery's curiosity was thoroughly piqued. He didn't know who was at his house, and he knew for a fact that he was the only child his parents had, but he wasn't about to try and explain any of this to God the Father Almighty. Right now he had to get to his house and see what was going on.

"Umm, OK, thanks for the heads up, Charity," Avery said.

"You're most welcome. Now can I get a twenty-percent discount on my robes for this information?"

Avery roared with laughter. "Only in your holy dreams, missionary."

Charity was insulted. "There is no need to get fresh, Avery. I just asked a simple question. Don't bring the Lord in this. Christ is nothing to play with. Good day, sir." She hung up the phone.

Charity was shocked and appalled. She couldn't believe Avery had the audacity to mock her Lord and Savior, and all she was trying to do was help.

"In the name of JESUS! Whoo!" Charity exhaled.

Charity went back to the window and peeked out again. She didn't see either woman anymore, but Tina's car was still there, so she assumed she was inside with Madison. Charity went to the refrigerator and got a bottle of water. All this ministering and helping the needy had dehydrated her tremendously.

Charity heard Avery's car alarm chirp, and she ran back to the window. Avery got out of the car and shut the door. He walked up to his door and went inside. He couldn't have been in the house for more than five minutes before he stormed back outside. The children were getting their stuff out of the trunk when he told them to get back inside.

Charity rushed out of her front door before Avery could pull off.

"Hi, Ms. Charity," A. J. said with a huge smile.

"Hi, sweethearts," Charity replied.

Mikayla, who was listening to music on her iPod, didn't say anything back; she just waved.

"Well, Avery, what's the problem?" Charity inquired.

"Oh nothing. I forgot the children were supposed to be staying at my mom's tonight, because we're having a dinner party," Avery lied.

Charity was puzzled. "So you do talk to your mom? Well Tina said that your family was estranged."

"We're not, and as a matter of fact, we're closer than ever. The lady in the house is not my sister, but she's a family friend," Avery told Charity while getting inside the car.

"My Lord, my Lord, I am so confused. Why did she say she was your sister? Why didn't you know who I was talking about?"

"Charity, I would love to sit here and explain everything to you, David, Daniel, *and* Judah, but I have to get to my parents' house before dinner," Avery said as he started the ignition.

"Well OK, Avery. I'll see you later. Be blessed. Bye children."

None of this made any sense to Charity. She was determined to figure this out. Avery said that they were having a dinner party. Perhaps she would bake a cake and take it over. You can never have enough desserts. She could bake a nice buttermilk pound cake in a few minutes. For now, she went back inside her house and watched the window.

Make it your goal to live a quiet life, minding your own business and working with your hands, just as we instructed you before. Then people who are not Christians will respect the way you live. (Thessalonians 4:11-12)

The doorbell woke me up with such a fright. My head was starting to hurt, and when I passed by the mirrors near the front door, I got a good look at myself. My mascara was no longer on my eyelashes; it was stained on my eyes and cheeks. I looked as bad as I felt. I opened the door to find Tina struggling to hold several bags.

"I got a story to tell you! Damn, you look terrible. Is everything all right?" Tina asked.

"I'm fine, Tina; please let me help you with that."

"Madison, have no fear, because Lady T. is here! I was able to go to a wholesale store, so that you could get more and pay less." Tina hoped to lighten up the mood.

"I can't thank you enough for your help, Tina. Let's get everything out of the car and into the house," I said with a sigh.

"Madison, you look as if you have been crying. Are the children OK? Do you want to talk about it?"

"Tina, everything is great," I lied. "I know I usually don't help out in the kitchen, but because we have so much to do in such a short period of time, I hope that I can be of help to you and not a nuisance."

Tina and I must have walked back and forth from her car to the house a hundred times, carrying bags and bags of stuff. I was so happy she remembered to purchase fresh-cut flowers. She knew me so well. I loved to make flower arrangements with lilies and roses.

These lilies were red and white. They were beautiful. The red roses complemented the lilies so well. There were enough flowers for the dining and living rooms.

One year for my birthday, Miracle gave me the most beautiful Baccarat spiral vases from Neiman Marcus. She had such good taste and an eye for home decorating. I put the flowers in the vases and headed for the kitchen.

Tina decided that I should start working on the strawberry-cider syrup. I washed tons of strawberries and cut them in half. I was not quite sure as to how to use the food processor, but I didn't want to disturb Tina from cleaning shrimp. So I started putting the strawberries in the processor, along with white sugar, cornstarch, cinnamon, lemon juice, and, lastly, the butter.

I was starting to feel a little sluggish. Why on earth did I drink that vodka? I thought. I can do this; I just need to focus. Here goes nothing. I turned it on. I hit the pulse button. I walked over to the refrigerator to get bottled water, and then all hell broke loose.

I started screaming as suddenly everything in the food processor was coming out of the top of it. I dropped my water down on the floor. It started creating a huge puddle on the floor. I was becoming more and more covered in strawberry mush. Tina came over to help me, but she slipped and fell down onto to the floor, because of the water. She managed to get up and unplug the food processor. She was wet and covered in strawberry mush, and so was I. We looked so ridiculous that I just started laughing uncontrollably. Tina started to laugh along with me.

"You see this? This is why I avoid the kitchen!" I managed to say through my laughter.

"I can't believe I need to change my clothes again," Tina said while still laughing.

"Oh my goodness, Tina, do you have extra clothes in your car?

"I don't think so. This is crazy. I definitely cannot fit anything that you own, Madison."

"You can wear one of my husband's shirts while I put your things in the washer. Come on; let's get cleaned up and try this again," I said while still laughing.

For the next hour, Tina and I worked really hard to clean up the mess and get all the prep work done. I found a Legacy University T-shirt for Tina to wear, and I just decided on a sports bra and boy shorts. Tina decided that we should have a small garden salad with Cajun shrimp to start off the dinner. So I started working on the salad. Surely I wouldn't mess that up. I thought if I turned the music on in the kitchen, it would help to ease the burden of having to *be* in the kitchen. So, of course, Tina wanted to listen to 96.3 FM.

"You got to turn that up. This is my jam!" Tina yelled.

"Oh, I know this song; we did this song before at a karaoke bar," I said excitedly.

"Come home late; it seems you barely beat the sun. Tapping my shoulder, thinking you gon' get you some!" Tina and I yelled Sunshine Anderson's lyrics together with our arms intertwined.

"Madison, what the hell is going on?" Avery said with such rage in his tone.

"Avery, um, what are you doing home?" I said, scared out of my mind.

"Answer my question, and turn that damn music down!" he yelled.

"Avery! That is not the way to speak to me in front of a guest," I said.

"A guest? Have you lost your mind? Who the hell is this? Oh, I forgot, the neighbor said that she is my sister. My sister who is always at my house when I'm not at home, and to think, all this time I thought I was an only child!"

"Avery, we need to speak in private. I can explain everything."

"What do you want to say to me now, Madison, that you couldn't say to me months ago? Maybe you want to tell me that your lover stops by the house from time to time when I'm out trying to make a success of our dry-cleaning businesses."

"Lover? Avery, wait a minute. You got this all wrong. Tina and I are not lovers. I pay for her services. That's not what I meant to say." I sounded confused and foolish.

"You're paying her? I can't believe this! Madison, there is not enough time to call this damn dinner party off! I'm going to take the kids to my parents' house for tonight. Get rid of her. We'll talk when I get back."

With those words, Avery walked out of the house and slammed the door. My heart broke into a million pieces. How was I going to explain to Avery that I was not sleeping with Tina but that she was the person doing the cooking and the cleaning for the past couple of years?

I started sobbing hysterically. I'm not an emotional person. It really takes a lot to rattle me, but on a scale of one to ten, ten being the worst thing that could happen to a person, this event was about a nine. I knew I needed to focus on finishing the dinner, but my heart ached. The look on Avery's face was not one I was accustomed to seeing.

Tina being my lover was laughable. Well, I guess it would be laughable one day. Today, at this moment, nothing was funny. My pride wouldn't let me cry one more tear. I was pissed that Avery would just leave the house without allowing me to explain myself.

For the next forty-five minutes, Tina and I worked in silence. When all the food was prepared and the kitchen was cleaned up, Tina and I sat down to the kitchen island. I put two shot glasses on the table with the same vodka I was drinking out of earlier.

"Madison, I've never been married, so I'm not going to pretend to be a relationship expert, but I do know what it is like to be so giving of yourself that at the end of the day, you feel as if you are running on empty."

"Tina, there was a time in my life when I would laugh at my married friends who referred to themselves as their husbands' *better halves*.' Why would anyone refer to themselves as a half of something? I'm not half of anything. I am a whole person; well, I used to be."

The truth was I hadn't felt like a whole person in quite some time. There were bits and pieces of me in my marriage, family, businesses, and friendships. I didn't know what to do. I missed my parents more and more with each passing year, and sometimes I thought I secretly resented Avery for maintaining a loving relationship with his parents.

I wondered what my parents would say to me about the mess I had made of my life. Knowing my father, he would lecture me about my time-management skills or lack thereof. As I thought of my parents, tears started to roll down my face. I took two more shots of vodka and then escorted Tina to a guest bedroom so that she could get dressed. I took a shower and got dressed. When I heard Tina call my name, I assumed she was ready to leave.

"Tina, thanks for being a friend to me. Here is the money I owe you. I'm truly sorry for all the drama I involved you in," I said while giving her a hug.

"Madison, with everything that went on today, I forgot to tell you that I ran into your nosey-ass neighbor. Look, she is looking out the window right now."

"Who? Her? She is harmless. She is the only person I know that listens to gospel music during the weekdays. As long as she's got King Jesus, she don't need nobody else, as she has told me on many occasions." I put my hands together as if to pray.

"I told her that I was Avery's sister and the reason I came over when Avery was not at home was because our family disowned him for marrying you. You know some people are kind of funny about that interracial thing," Tina said with a slight smile.

"That Jesus freak is the reason that Avery came home early?" I said.

"I know I shouldn't have said that to her; it's just that she rubbed me the wrong way," Tina replied.

"Don't worry; I got a trick for her. I will call you soon, and thanks again," I said as we approached Tina's car.

"Damn, the trunk was not closed all the way. I think my battery might be dead. Can you give me a jump?" Tina asked.

The entire time Tina and I worked on her car, Charity watched us outside of her window. Tina's car would not start. I didn't know what else to do but to call Noah. He said he would come right over. Tina wanted to leave before Avery got back, but as fate would have it, Tina would be staying for dinner.

Hay rushed back to the office to transfer her notes to Blessed's permanent file.

"What happened?" Thomas asked.

"Way too much to tell," Hay replied exhaustedly.

"That much, huh? Well you need any help?"

"No, thanks, I've got it," Hay answered.

"OK, well, I'm gone for the day. See you on Monday." Thomas waved and left Hay's office.

Hay looked at the clock. It was almost eight in the evening. She hadn't heard from Fallon at all. Hay knew she shouldn't have trusted the teenager. She should have gone to the house directly when she left Kennedy High School. Hay figured it was time to make a move. She phoned her colleagues at the sheriff's office and gave them the information Fallon had told her. They said they could be over there in less than an hour. By nine o'clock, SWAT would be at Blessed's door.

Ring, Ring. Hay's personal cell phone went off. She looked at it and saw the name Egypt. Hay grimaced. She really didn't feel like talking to Egypt right now, but if she didn't answer, Egypt would swear she was cheating on her. She answered the call.

"Hello," said Hay dryly.

"Hey," replied Egypt.

"Yeah," Hay said back.

"What are you doing?" Egypt asked.

"I'm working right now. I have a new case, and it's taking me longer than I expected to wrap it up. What's up, Egypt?" Hay asked, sounding annoyed.

"Nothing. How was your day?" Egypt asked.

"Are you serious?" Hay asked. "I just told you what was going on. Egypt, can I freaking help you?"

"Well damn, bae, you don't have to be so mean. I was just trying to be nice to your ass," Egypt barked back. Egypt's head was spinning from the confrontation from Noah's ghetto baby mama. All she wanted was to tell Hay what was going on, but she was being a total ass.

"Well thank you. Can I call you back later?" Hay said calmly.

"What are you doing that's so important that you can't talk to me right now?" Egypt asked. She really needed to be talked to sweetly right now. She needed her precious Hay. Instead she got some other creature.

"I'm working, Egypt!" Hay yelled. She was 100 percent aggravated now.

"Well are you coming over tonight? Maybe we can go out to dinner and have a nightcap?" Egypt asked, steadily trying to sweeten the conversation.

"Egypt, baby, I can't do this right now. I'm extremely busy with work. I don't know what time I'll be finished, so I don't want to commit to anything right now."

"That's your problem right there. You don't want to commit. I bet you got some ho you messing with; that's why you ain't got no time for me. To hell with you, Hazel-Ann. You good." Egypt roared and hung up the phone. She tried her best, but Hay had her head so far up her ass her dreds probably reeked of shit. All Egypt needed was a few minutes, and the woman she loved couldn't even give her that.

Hay looked at the phone in amazement for a few seconds and then burst into an incessant laughter. Egypt's ass was cuckoo for Cocoa Puffs. They had just gone clubbing together last night. Shoot, it was Egypt's fault Hay had stayed out so late. She didn't have a job to go to the next day, but Hay did.

Hay's phone rang again. It was Egypt. Hay wasn't falling for that trick again; she sent the call to voice mail. As soon as it stopped ringing, it rang again — Egypt. Hay sent the call to voice mail again. Egypt called Hay's phone seven more times before Hay finally powered her cell phone off. Hay had to focus.

Hay shut everything down in the office and started on her way to Blessed's house. She was hoping she could beat SWAT there, so there could be very little attention drawn. Hay grabbed her belongings and hopped inside of her SUV. Although she was still on duty, she didn't want to come back to the office if she didn't have to.

Inside the car, Hay turned her cell phone back on. Once it booted all the way up, she saw that she had ten text messages from Egypt. Egypt was so dramatic. She and Hay had been seeing each other on and off for about a year.

Hay knew she wanted women, but Egypt was still trying to figure out her sexuality. She had been with both men and women. She would leave Hay for a guy, and then when he treated her badly, she reverted back to Hay. For the last two and a half months, Egypt and Hay had been going strong; however, Hay didn't want to make their relationship official until Egypt had proved to her that she could stay faithful for over ninety days.

Hay didn't even bother to read the messages, because she would go soft and either text back or call. That was not what she needed right now. Right now, what Hay needed was to focus.

Hay pulled up to the side of Blessed's house. There was an old lady sitting on the porch, swatting mosquitoes.

"Good evening, ma'am," Hay started. "Is this the home of Blessed Douglas?"

"It sure is," the woman replied without so much as looking up at Hay.

"My name is Officer Hazel-Ann Dawson. I'm the officer assigned to Blessed's recent case. Is he at home?"

"Well I'm Blessed's grandmother. You can just call me Nay-Nay. Blessed is not here," Nay-Nay said, still looking away from Hay.

"Not here, huh?" Hay said. Fallon had already told her that Nay-Nay would say just that. Hay was prepared. "Well, Nay-Nay, do you mind if I look around?"

"Yes, ma'am, I do mind. You see, this here is my home, and unless you got some paper work that forces my hand, you will NOT be permitted to enter," Nay-Nay snapped, this time looking Hay directly in the eyes.

Hay tried to reason with her. "Ma'am, your grandson is wanted for stealing a bus. I'm trying to help him."

"Please." Nay-Nay chuckled. "You ain't trying to help him no more than I'm trying to help you. Who you think you fooling, child? Besides, I already told you, Blessed...is...not...here. Now you just go on about your business, and have yourself a good evening."

Before Hay could respond, she saw Nay-Nay's eyes widen as she jumped up and stood in front of her front door. Hay turned and saw four black vans pull up, and twenty SWAT members poured out and surrounded the house.

One officer came up to Nay-Nay and showed her a warrant to search her home and a warrant for Blessed's arrest.

Nay-Nay closed her eyes and recited the twenty-third Psalm. She opened her eyes and started talking to Hay.

"My grandson is a good boy. He ain't hurt nobody by driving that bus. All this here is uncalled for."

Nay-Nay looked at the officers. "Y'all can search all you want and sit out here all night if you want to. What you ain't gonna do is find Blessed here. So go ahead. Set up your little 'spring' operation. Let me know when you finish, so I can lock up and watch the news." She walked off her porch and pulled Hay by the arm.

"Now listen here, Miss Officer Ann. If you truly want to help my Blessed, I'll tell you where he is. If you're fibbing, then I ain't saying shit," Nay-Nay said, crossing her arms.

Hay was stunned. "If I can get to him before these guys do and talk to him, I can help him out. I'll make sure he has the best defense lawyer and gets the best deal with the state. I could probably get him no jail time and only probation."

That sounded like music to Nay-Nay's ears. "No jail time? No lie?"

"Yes, ma'am, I'll do my absolute best."

"He's up at the Corner Store. He went to meet someone up there. He left here about an hour ago."

"What's the name of the store, ma'am?" Hay asked as she wrote on a small pad.

"It's called, the 'Corner Store,'" Nay-Nay replied, rolling her eyes. She had just told the girl the Corner Store. Was she slow or something?

"Where is it located?" Hay asked.

"On the corner of Military and Church Street," Nay-Nay said.

"Thank you. I'll do my best to return him to you safely."

"God bless you, Miss Officer Ann. Now what do you suppose I do about your cousins here?" Nay-Nay said, pointing to the SWAT team.

Hay chuckled. "Don't worry about them. I'll handle it." Hay walked up to the commanding officer and told him that Blessed really wasn't there and that they could reconvene their search tomorrow.

The commanding officer called the team, and they all loaded up back into the vans. With everything that was going on, Hay didn't realize that so many people were standing outside. She scanned the faces to see if she could recognize any, but she could not. She did, however, spot an Aston Martin a few cars back. Hay couldn't believe that Egypt was here. She walked over to her car and exploded.

"Egypt, what the fuck? What are you doing here? You don't know anyone over here! What are you thinking?"

"You wouldn't answer your phone or text me back, so I came to your job to talk to you. Then I just followed you here. Baby, I just want to talk to you," Egypt cried out, her eyes quickly becoming glossy with tears.

Hay had seen Egypt act this way too many times before. Whenever Egypt didn't get her way, she cried. It had worked with so many people for so many years that she thought it was acceptable. Hay had fallen for it herself in the past but not today. Egypt's behavior was completely unacceptable.

"You crazy, deranged, psycho! Who the hell follows someone just to talk? I told you I was working. I'll talk to you later. Get your crazy ass on up outta here, before I have one of these guys take you to the mental ward."

"But, baby, I—" Egypt pleaded.

Hay cut her off. "Bye, Egypt!"

Egypt looked at Hay with her sad puppy-dog eyes. Hay started to feel sorry for her but quickly snapped back. She turned around, got into her truck, and left. She couldn't deal with Egypt and her issues right now. She had to go to the dumb, dumb, Corner Store.

Sha' Miracle

If I changed my clothes one more time, I was not going to the Clarks' house. I was seriously considering having a breast reduction. I was almost sold on the idea, until the great neurosurgeon Dr. Morris told me that the surgeon would have to remove my nipples to get the fat out of my breasts.

"Why have cosmetic surgery for an issue that can be solved with simple exercise?" were the exact words my mother used. It didn't matter what kind of ailment I had, my mother would always recommend exercise and diet. I bet if I called her and said that I had been in a horrific car accident, she would tell me that the accident could have been avoided had I simply exercised and ate less.

The more weight I gained, the more strained our relationship became — not that our mother-daughter relationship was so great to begin with. If my father didn't guilt trip me into coming over to the house on Sundays, my mother probably wouldn't see me from one month to the next. I decided to put thoughts of my judgmental mother out of my head for now and focus on looking my best.

I decided on a simple black DKNY dress with a deep *V* cut, with black Coach Boots and silver Coach Accessories. My aunt would be pleased to know that I rolled my hair using my super-jumbo rollers. I couldn't believe it only took two minutes for the rollers to heat up. I probably should use these more often.

My hair, with a little oil, looked nice. I spent the next thirty minutes applying my makeup. I put on my short leather jacket, set the alarm on the house, and got into my car. My cell phone was dead. I reached for my car charger, but it wasn't in the car. I laughed to myself. My Auntie Ruby would tell me to stop what I was doing and pray.

"Lord, I know this day is just a test. I know I have to trust in you at all times. Please guide my steps and help me to keep my emotions intact." I decided to ride without any music playing. The garage door went up, and I was finally on my way to the dinner.

As I drove down the street, I started thinking about Gabby. I hoped Gabby had convinced Blessed to turn himself in. For some reason, Gabby doing the right thing left me feeling perturbed. We argued all the time about her spending so much time with Reece instead of being with her children. I thought to myself about a time when Gabby was mad at me.

"Miracle, would you go to a Lamaze coach who didn't have any children?" Gabby had asked.

"If the person was certified to teach the class, yes, I would. It shouldn't matter that the person doesn't have any children," I said.

"See, that's where you are wrong. Why the hell would you listen to someone telling you how to have a baby, if they haven't experienced it for themselves? Life is the best teacher," Gabby yelled.

"Gabby that is ridiculous. I don't have to smoke cigarettes with four thousand different chemicals in them to be able to teach people about the harmful effects of smoking," I yelled back.

"You just don't get it. Don't try to tell me about parenting my children when you're not a parent. You keep reading those stupid psychology books, but there is nothing like raising four children all by yourself," Gabby said, sounding annoyed.

"I may not be a parent, but you know what I have plenty of life experience in? The absent-mother syndrome. You spend more time with Reece and his damn kids than you spend with your own," I said.

"I have to go. Reece is at the door," Gabby snapped.

Honk, honk. Egypt blowing her horn at me stopped my thoughts of Gabby. I rolled down my window to talk to her.

"Hey, Egypt, how are you?" I asked.

"I'm not in a good mood; I just told Noah to apologize to Madison for me. I can't be around anyone right now," Egypt confirmed.

"Egypt, call me later if you want to talk. Is everything all right with Butterfly?"

"You know how my mother is; she is all right I guess. She has been talking to the good doctor lately. She wants me to go to Johns Hopkins University," Egypt said sadly.

"I guess you don't want to do that, but maybe a change of scenery could be good for you," I suggested.

"Right now all I want is a hot shower and a glass of Moscato d'Asti," Egypt exclaimed.

"That sounds real good; I'll talk to you later," I said and pulled off.

Why in the world was Noah working on a car in Madison's yard? Thanks to Gavin, Noah was not one of Avery's favorite people. I couldn't wait to hear this story. I parked my car. I talked to Noah for just a few minutes before I headed into the house to find Madison. I found Madison in the kitchen. I would simply charge my phone with Mikayla's phone charger.

"Hey, lady, do you need help with anything?" I asked.

"Sha'Miracle, look at you! I love that dress. Why didn't you wear your red boots and red accessories?" Madison questioned as she hugged me tightly.

"Madison, don't start with me! You are lucky I'm here," I scolded.

"I have everything ready. I want you to meet someone. Miracle, this is Tina. She is a good friend of ours," Madison said.

"Hello," I said, feeling puzzled.

"I'm going to go outside and see how my car situation is coming along," Tina said dryly.

"Madison, where are the kids?" I asked.

"Avery took them to his precious parents' house to spend the night," Madison said sarcastically.

"His precious parents? Never mind, I need a cell phone charger right now," I said.

"Follow me into Mikayla's room. I need to tell you something," Madison whispered.

"Have you been drinking? What the hell is going on over here?" I demanded.

Madison was about to tell me something when Avery entered into the room and announced that the guests had all showed up. I connected my cell phone to the charger and headed out of the room, determined to seek some answers to the bizarre things that I had already witnessed. When I got into the dining room, I stopped dead in my tracks.

"Miracle, this is Lucas, Bobby, Trevor, Attorney Brooks, and the others you already know," Avery stated.

"Good evening," I managed to say as best I could without revealing my sudden impulse to run out of the house.

I sat down at the end of the table near Tina, Noah, and Charity. The conversation was pretty light over dinner. Everyone complimented Madison time and time again on how good the food was. Charity ate about three bowls of fruit at dessert.

"This is some tangy fruit," Charity said.

"Thank you," said Madison, smiling.

"Maybe next time you should get some fruit that's actually in season. This fruit smells funny," said Charity.

"Charity, are you insinuating that my wife chose bad fruit?" Avery asked.

"I'm not insinuating anything. I'm telling you straight out something's wrong with the way it smells and tastes."

"So why do you keep eating it?" Madison asked.

"Because the chicken was so greasy I need something healthy to soak up the cholesterol," Charity snapped.

Madison and Avery looked at each other and quickly looked away.

"So, Avery, how is it that you and Tina are acquainted with each other again?" Charity asked.

Tina quickly interjected, "Charity, we have already had this conversation. Why don't you help me clear the table?"

"Clear the table, huh? Sure, I'll help you." Charity looked at the people at the dinner table. "Excuse me, everyone. I'm going to help clear the table." She walked into the kitchen without a single dish in her hand.

I observed Avery and Madison at the dinner table. They seemed very different. Their moves were cold and calculated. They didn't even say much to each other.

After dinner, Tina and I, along with Charity, started cleaning up, so that Madison could be a part of the business discussion.

"Tina, you really know your way around this kitchen," I said.

"Why wouldn't she? She is over here all the time!" Charity said as she almost dropped two glasses.

"Look, Charity, I promised Madison that I wouldn't say anything to you, but don't push your luck," Tina said.

"Don't push my luck?" Charity laughed. "Who do you think you are talking to?" Charity said as she reached for Tina.

"Charity, no!" I grabbed Charity to keep her from falling. "Are you OK?" I said.

"You're no sister of Avery's. He tried to say you were a family friend, but I don't think that's true either. I think you trying to push up on that man's wife!" Charity said. "It's an abomination, I tell you. And just plain, old sick."

"Why are you so worried about what's going on in the Clarks' house?" Tina had her hand in Charity's face now. "Did you enjoy the fruit, tramp? I soaked the fruit in orange liqueur!" Tina laughed.

Charity gasped. "No thieves, nor the greedy, nor drunkards, nor revilers, nor swindlers will inherit the kingdom of God; First Corinthians 6:10. What have you done to me?"

"No one likes an angry drunk; why don't you go home and sleep it off?" Tina suggested.

"Tina, please make some coffee. I'm gonna try to calm her down on the patio. Maybe the coffee and the fresh air will help her sober up," I said, walking Charity outside.

"Hey, Avery told me to come in here and get some beers," Lucas said.

"Lucifer, I see you haven't changed much. What is this so-called business you need to talk to Avery and Madison about?" Tina questioned.

"Look, Tina, I think that it would be in the best interest of everybody if we just pretended not to know each other. Really, you don't know me," Lucas said angrily.

"I don't know you? I wish I could forget your garbage-ass face! How do you forget the person who ruined your life? How do you forget the person who introduced you to cocaine without even telling you?" Tina yelled.

"Tina, keep your damn voice down. I'm a changed man. I've been clean for years, and I have a legitimate business." Lucas reached in his pocket for a business card.

"Tina, is the coffee ready for Charity?" I asked, walking back into the kitchen.

Both Tina and Lucas looked at me like they had seen a ghost. I heard their entire conversation. I didn't know what to think. Why would Madison and Avery have such shady characters in their home? I was more confused now than I was an hour and a half ago. I needed some answers, and I was not leaving this house until I got some.

"Is everything all right? Maybe I can help your friend. Coffee never helped me when I felt a hangover coming on. She needs plenty of water. The water will help her to quickly get rid of the alcohol in her system," Lucas said.

Tina gave the water to Lucas, and I walked him halfway in the direction of the patio. As I turned around and got closer to the kitchen, I could hear Trevor's voice.

"What's up, Miracle?" Trevor said with a slight grin.

"I don't know; why don't you tell me, stalker?" I said.

"Stalker? I'm here on business. I will admit that the night did seem to get better once I saw you. You look beautiful," Trevor said while he walked toward me.

"Thank you. Do you also own a dry cleaner?" I questioned.

"No, I just opened up a brand-new Subway in the same plaza as Clark Dry Cleaners," Trevor said as he moved a curl of hair out of my face.

"I didn't really see it before, but you and Bobby have a slight resemblance."

"I know that's pretty common with brothers. However, I work out while Bobby is usually eating chips and subs," Trevor said as he lifted up his shirt to show me his abs.

"Damn, whatever you doing in the gym, it's working!" Tina said.

"Did you enjoy the sub?" Trevor asked with a grin.

"Funny you should ask. I never ate it." I laughed.

"I wish I could talk to you alone. Let me take you to the Blue Martini Lounge for one drink. I'm good people; my brother will vouch for me," Trevor whispered in my ear.

"I really would like a caramel-apple martini," I said.

"That smile on your face is doing something to me. Is that a yes?" Trevor asked.

"Yes, but first I have to talk to Madison for a minute," I said, and then I turned to walk away.

"I'm sorry to interrupt your meeting, but I really need to speak with Madison before I leave," I said.

"Miracle, do you have to leave right now?" Madison questioned me as we walked out of the room.

"Madison, what's going on with you and Avery? You guys are behaving so strangely tonight. And don't get me started on the strange characters in this house. How is Tina a good friend if this is my first time seeing her? I am completely baffled," I said.

"I can't even think right now. Avery just agreed to add delivery to the many services we already provide at the cleaners," Madison stated angrily.

"Madison, if you don't agree with what Avery is doing, you need to speak up. You are not a silent partner; you own half the business." I felt the need to remind her of that.

"I have to go to your Aunt Pearl's house tomorrow to pick up her stupid blouse. Can you meet me over there tomorrow? I will explain everything then," Madison said miserably.

"Fine, I guess this can wait until tomorrow. Call me," I said.

"I promise, no worries. Go home, and get some sleep."

"I'm on my way to have drinks with Trevor. So *you* go and get some sleep." I laughed.

I went in Mikayla's room and got my cell phone. By the time I made my way back to the front of the house, Trevor was standing there with my jacket in his hands. The more I looked at him, the more I realized he was so damn cute.

"Aye, man, thanks for having me over tonight. Your crib is tight," Bobby stated.

"Aye, dawg, anytime you need anything, just hit me up," Avery replied. "It was good to meet you, Trevor, and I think that advertising together is going to be beneficial for both of us and cost-effective," Avery said.

"Miracle, are you ready?" Trevor asked as he handed me my jacket.

"Sha'Miracle, you will be at your godson's game tomorrow, cheering loud, like you did for Gerald back in the day," Avery said with a smirk.

"I heard about what happened to Gerald. They're going to miss him in the play-offs," Bobby said excitedly.

"I know, but despite everything that has happened, he is in good spirits. I saw him earlier today. He'll be back on his feet in no time; because that's the kind of person he is, resilient! Isn't that right, *my Miracle*?" Avery looked at me like I was consorting with the enemy.

"Good night, Avery," I said as I got real close to Trevor so that he could help me into my jacket. I smiled at Trevor and whispered thank you in his ear. I turned around and winked my eye at Avery and walked out the door with Trevor behind me.

"I'm sorry about that. Avery and Gerald are best friends. I'm over it; I guess Avery is still holding on to the past," I said as we walked to my car.

"I'm not tripping on that. I can tell he is protective of you. *'My Miracle,'* is that what Gerald used to call you?" Trevor asked as he grabbed my hands.

"I'm my dad's miracle, no one else's. Gerald didn't appreciate my love, end of story," I said.

"Damn, what a fool. I've been thinking about you all day. I want to know you, Miracle Morris, inside and out. Can I do that? Say yes; I want to hear you say 'yes, Trevor,'" Trevor teased.

"Yes, Trevor," I said with a big smile on my face.

"I'm going to keep you smiling," Trevor said.

I needed to get some clothes for my niece. I got on the highway and headed toward Altamonte Springs. Deja Voo is a clothing store that my friend Deja Ward owns. This really cute boutique caters to toddlers and teens. I called her and asked if she would stay open a little while longer, so I could purchase a few things. I was happy to see Deja. Talking to her while I shopped really helped to take my mind off things.

When I got back to my mother's house, Asia was already asleep. I explained to Noah that I was going to send an anonymous phone message to the Department of Children of Families about Candice.

"Egypt, what do you hope to gain by getting Candy investigated? You are so vindictive," Noah said as he paced the floor.

"What do I hope to gain? I'm trying to help your dumb ass!" I yelled.

"If those white folks get involved, the children could be placed in a foster home," Noah replied.

"So?! At least they would be in a clean home, where people actually cared that they are alive and well. And once they contact you about Asia, you can get her and raise her right," I said as I jumped out of my seat.

"She does care about those kids. She is doing the best she can under the circumstances," Noah responded.

"Noah, can you explain to me why Little Brother's nose is always filled with snot, even in the summertime? Oh and let's see, two more things I want to know, why is Too'Precious named Too'Precious? And why are all of her outfits two sizes too big? One guess, she is wearing Asia's old clothes," I said as I fell back into my seat.

"Before you got that money, Miss High and Mighty, we were struggling to make ends meet, because we were a one-income household. Dr. Morris gave you clothes that used to belong to Miracle all the time growing up. Y'all women like to walk around here like a man is optional instead of necessary!" Noah said.

"Hell, men *are* optional! You can't depend on them for shit; as soon as you need something, anything, they're gone. Just like Daddy, just like Brown," I said.

"Egypt, I'm still here. I will always be here for you. There are plenty of men out there that love and respect women that first love and respect themselves," Noah said as he walked off.

"What's going on in here?" Butterfly asked.

"Nothing, Ma, I was just leaving. Make sure Asia is dressed and ready in the morning, because she has to cheer."

As I turned to leave my mother's house, I picked up my cell phone to call Trevor. His cell phone was going straight to his voice mail. I needed to get laid, but I guessed I would go home and take care of myself. I got home and decided to take a bubble bath. When I got out of the tub, I could hear my cell phone ringing. I answered it, smiling from ear to ear.

"Hello, beautiful, are you in the bed?" Trevor asked.

"Yes, waiting on you," I flirted.

"Oh yeah? Come open the door," Trevor said.

I went to the front door in nothing but a towel, which I ended up leaving near the door. We made love right there in the living room. To my surprise, he managed to remain erect during the entire time. I don't know what color the pill was he swallowed before he came over tonight, but I was eternally grateful. He was so patient and gentle. I had never been with a man that was so unselfish. He was the type of lover that would make sure that you were completely satisfied before he got his. He was a great kisser, I supposed from years of practice. I could really get used to this kind of treatment. I felt so comfortable and safe in his arms. I felt myself nodding off.

"Egypt, darling, can we take this party upstairs?" Trevor said wearily.

"Of course, come on. I'll set the clock for you so that you can get up in the morning," I said as I kissed him softly on his lips.

Madison

By the time Avery walked the last guest out, I was already in the shower. I purposely took my time washing my hair. When I came out of the bathroom, Avery was sitting on the edge of the bed. He seemed sad and worried. I was still angry, but I was not in the mood for a heated argument. I wanted to go to sleep, but I knew Avery wanted some answers from me. I started telling him a story about a high-school bake sale.

"I promised my coach and teammates that I would bake some cupcakes to sell in order to raise money for new softball equipment. I practically begged my mother to help me with the cupcakes. However, my father insisted that I finish my algebra homework first. By the time I finished my homework, I only had a few minutes to talk to my friends outside before the sun went down. I got in the house, washed up, and was ready to bake. My mother just shook her head at me and said she didn't feel like helping me. 'Madison, if you don't have the intellect to bake the cupcakes on your own, then simply buy some.' I was so mad at her. You can't bring store-bought goods to a bake sale. Did she notice the word *bake* in bake sale!

So I didn't have a choice. I went to the store and

bought a dozen cupcakes and placed them in the cutest cupcake holder I could find. I didn't want to let my teammates down. I sold all those cupcakes, but I didn't feel good about it. I felt like a fraud. I lied about baking those idiotic cupcakes, just like I lied to you about wanting to learn to cook some of your favorite childhood meals."

I knelt down in front of him and put my hands on his face. "I am so sorry. You have to forgive me. I know I let you down. Tina has been preparing our meals for a while. I hired her to cook and clean the house."

As I poured my heart out to Avery, he just sat there, very quietly. The silence in the room was deafening. I started crying. He couldn't trust me anymore. I was going to have to regain his trust.

"Baby, don't cry. I didn't know what to think when I walked in here this afternoon. I know I overreacted, but, Maddie; I was shocked and completely thrown off my game. You don't ever have to lie to me," Avery said, wiping tears from my face.

"Avery, I need some help. I can either do less at the cleaners and more around the house or vice versa. What should I do?" I said somberly.

"You should do what is best for our family. If Tina coming over and cooking and cleaning is helping our household run more efficiently, then keep that going. I know it's not easy loving me, but I'm not going to lose you over some food. I know that the businesses are thriving because of you and your smarts. Next time you hire somebody, just let Daddy know." Avery smiled for the first time tonight.

"I'm super smart; I was head of my class," I said as I started to untie my robe.

"I can believe that. It takes a big brain to do calculus," Avery said, watching me unzip his pants.

"Avery Clark, your children are not home, so it's OK to scream," I said.

"Madison Clark, I bet you'll scream before I do," Avery said.

Avery picked me up off the floor and placed me in the bed. I watched him undress. My heart was beating so fast I thought it might pop right out of my chest. He got on top me and started kissing me very slowly, as if to drive me crazy.

"Tell me what you want me to do," Avery said so seductively.

"I want to feel you inside of me right now. Avery, please don't tease me," I said as I scratched his back and neck.

"That's not what you want, not yet anyway. We said no more lies. Say it; tell me what you want." Avery was smiling as he was torturing me.

"Damn it, Avery, you know what I want! I want you to taste me," I said as I pushed his head between my thighs. Avery didn't need any help finding his way to my clitoris, but it felt so good guiding his head there.

"Are you sure this is what you want? I'm not going to stop until I hear my entire name, loud and clear," Avery said as he placed kisses on the inside of my thighs.

"I'm certain that's what I want and need." I closed my eyes and squeezed my pillow tight. "AVERY DEWAYNE CLARK SR.!" I yelled.

"I won!" Avery said as he started planting soft kisses on my stomach.

"You won round one; I'm ready for round two," I said, trying to regain my composure.

I was so glad when Avery finally fell asleep. I was exhausted. All I could think about was how grateful I was to be married to my best friend. I said a prayer and closed my eyes for some much-needed rest.

Reece, Mark, and I walked inside the door. We were just getting home, and the boys were already jumping from couch to couch.

"Hey! Get y'all little asses down and sit down somewhere. Y'all ain't with ya mammies right now," I screamed.

Both the boys ran to Reece and grabbed a leg.

"Daddy!" they said simultaneously.

"Hey! Fellas!" Reece replied with the widest smile.

I rolled my eyes and walked away. I didn't want to be bothered by these little boys. I had my own children, but they were a part of the Reece package.

"Mama, Miss Trina called, and she's pissed at you," Jalyssa said.

"What? Why?" I asked, puzzled.

"She said she went to the store with the card and there was only forty-six dollars on there."

"Couldn't be. I know I saved her a hundred dollars," I said.

"Well she said she was embarrassed when she got to the checkout and you're gonna have to make this right," Jalyssa said and walked off.

"Where are Jade and Marlin?" I asked Jalyssa.

"Jade's in the room, and Marlin still hasn't made it home yet," she replied.

"Mama, what's for dinner?" Mark asked. I had totally forgotten that he hadn't eaten dinner.

"Warm this food up from Aunt Ruby's house," I told him.

"What about me? What am I gonna eat?" Jade asked, appearing out of nowhere.

"You didn't eat either?" I asked.

"No, there was nothing in there except cereal, and I had to feed the boys that. Jalyssa ate at Nay-Nay's house, and I haven't seen Marlin since the last school bell rang today."

"Reece, you hungry?" I asked.

"Yeah, a little."

"Well I don't know what you're gonna eat, Jade. Reece and Mark got dibs on the plate from Aunt Ruby."

"I'm good, bae; let her and Mark share that food," Reece said. He was so thoughtful.

Jade's eyes widened then filled with tears. "Never mind, I'm not hungry."

I wasn't about to entertain her drama, so I just kept quiet and let her go back into the room. Jade was always playing victim.

The night was almost over, and I still hadn't heard from Miracle. It was OK. I would see her at the game tomorrow.

Saturdays were like a girls' day. Madison, Miracle, me, and Egypt met at the football field. A. J. played tackle football; Asia was a cheerleader, and Reece's two boys played flag football. Madison had the biggest, best tent and always brought lots of drinks for us. I had to support Reece's boys, not because I was their number-one fan—because I wasn't— but because I wanted Reece to know that I was there for him. The boys' mothers would occasionally come to a game, but the weekend was our time with them.

Marlin walked in the house and went straight toward his room. I got up and walked to the room behind him. I had every intention to yell at him for staying out so late, but he wasn't there. He was in the girls' room, talking to Jalyssa.

"I can't believe it. We've been using the pull-out method for all this time, and it always worked. I don't even remember the time she so-called said I didn't."

"Mama is going to flip when she finds out," Jalyssa said.

"I ain't worried about that. Sade has a plan. She's gonna get an apartment in her name, because she'll qualify, and I'll just move in with her."

"What about school?" Jade asked.

"I'll still go, but I need to get a job, so I can help pay bills."

"Why don't you ask Reece to help?" Jalyssa suggested.

"No, thanks. I'm more of a man than he'll ever be. You know he has a chick on the other side of town, Mama, and those two baby mamas. I'm going to handle my responsibility like a real man should."

Jade spoke, "Mama makes me sick. All she cares about is Reece and them bad-behind little boys."

"Don't worry about dinner, Jade. You know how she is. She doesn't mean to be so dumb," Jalyssa assured her.

"What about dinner?" Marlin asked.

"I didn't eat anything, because Mama wanted to make sure Reece ate first. He said he didn't want the food, and then she offers it to me. I am your child. Like really, Ma?" Jade explained.

Marlin fumed, "She does stuff like this all the time." He got up and left the room. He walked past me without so much as a word and walked out the door.

"It's always so much better when Reece isn't around. She notices us then," Jade said to Jalyssa.

"So you wanna make me seem like the bad guy, huh, Jade?" I asked, coming into the room.

Jade was stunned. She didn't know what to say. She covered her face and cried.

"You make me sick being so over-dramatic. You are the one who refused to eat, so whatever," I told her.

"But, Mama, you do little stuff like this all the time. It's like you put him and his kids before us, and we even have to help take care of them. They're not our kids. He isn't even our dad," Jalyssa said.

"Oh yeah? That's how y'all feel? Well fine then," I yelled and stormed out of the room.

Reece had been taking care of them and me for years now. I have always heard rumors about the girl on the other side of town, but I never cared. He always came home to me. Jalyssa and Jade were too young to understand how a relationship worked. They'd see when they got older.

Marlin walked back into the house with two pizzas. Pizza was Jade's favorite food. She ate all types of pizza. She didn't have a preference.

"Jade, come eat now," Marlin demanded.

Jade came out of the room and stood next to Marlin. Marlin hugged her and kissed her forehead.

"As long as you've got me, I've got you, understand?" he asked.

"Yes, Brother," Jade replied.

I smacked my teeth at them and went to my room. Reece had already rolled a fat blunt and smoked it and was passed out on the bed. I was so jealous because I wanted in on that good kush he had. He had recently upgraded to "high grade," and I heard it was that fire. Instead I had to defend myself against my own children.

I peeked my head outside my room door. "Jalyssa," I called.

"Yes, ma'am," she answered.

"Get the boys ready for bed, and make sure their stuff is laid out for tomorrow."

"OK," she responded.

I shut my door and took a shower. When I got out, I woke Reece up by sitting on his chest. There was no way I was going to let a fresh wax go to waste. And since I couldn't smoke, I had to relieve my stress some kind of way.

He opened his eyes and smiled. "My, my, what do we have here?"

"You tell me, kind sir."

"Damn eating dinner. I've been wanting to sample this since earlier today."

"Now's your chance. What are you going to do?"

Reece blew on me softly down low and caused the hairs on the back of my neck to stand up. I shivered as he continued to blow softly. He held me still. He hated when I moved too much, but I couldn't help it. I had to be patient, because what he was going to do would be well worth the wait. He kept blowing until juices spilled from inside of my body and trickled down his throat toward his chin. He lifted my body and sat me directly on his face.

Reece was an expert at working his tongue. Many times, I didn't even need sex after the foreplay. This, however, wasn't one of those nights. I needed to feel him tonight. I wanted him to take me and have his way. So badly I needed him to release inside of me and stay there, like he's done so many times before. I wanted to catch all his love with mine. Then we could shower together and finally fall asleep in each other's arms.

I felt my inner thighs tightening and my heart start beating faster. Right when I was about to climax, he flipped me over, tongue still inside, and my back was now on the bed. All of a sudden, he stopped.

As I opened my eyes to see what was happening, he laid back down on the bed.

"What are you doing?" I asked.

"I don't want you to cum" he explained.

"Why the hell not?" I pouted.

"Because you're on punishment," he said.

"Why?" I asked, confused as ever. My thighs were soaking wet from the combination of his saliva and my natural moisture.

"For running up the tab at the store. You've been a very bad girl, Gabrielle," Reece said seductively.

Tonight of all nights, he wanted to role-play. If I wanted my satisfaction though, I had to play along with him.

"I'm so, so, sorry. Can you ever forgive me, Reece?" I said in my naughty-girl voice.

"I don't know. You really made me feel like a chump," Reece replied, shaking his head and stroking his chin.

"I'll do anything to make it up to you," I pleaded.

"Anything?" he said while licking his lips.

"Anything," I repeated then placed his index finger in my mouth to suck.

"Lie back, and don't touch me. Whatever you do, don't touch me," Reece instructed.

"Yes, sir," I said obediently.

Reece picked up where he left off, and before long, I climaxed like I never have before. My head was even throbbing. I wanted to stroke him so badly but couldn't, due to the rules. I just knew that next he would part my legs, get in between, and get this party started, but he didn't. Instead, he got up, brushed his teeth, climbed into bed, and kissed me on my cheek.

"Ummm, that's it?" I asked.

"Yes," he replied. "As long as you're good, I'm good. I love you, good night."

My jaw dropped. Was he serious? I hopped out of the bed and stomped to the shower. All that heatedness and he didn't want to have sex? Was I just that good, or was he dipping his chocolate stick in someone else's "Fun Dip"?

I woke up to Avery looking for his lucky Legacy University visor. I told him to look for it in the laundry room and turn the light off. I'd known he would get up early so that he and A. J. could get haircuts before the game. I agreed to meet him at the football field later today.

I was so sore, but I didn't care, because it was a constant reminder of our lovemaking from the night before. I grabbed Avery's pillow just so I could smell his cologne. It was so intoxicating. The things that man did to me—I couldn't help but blush.

I decided I needed a hot bath. I was dressed and out the door in a reasonable amount of time and headed to Aunt Pearl's house. I knew not to eat breakfast, because Aunt Pearl would have a buffet of food already prepared.

I was in such good spirits on this Saturday morning. I really felt like Avery and I had weathered another storm. The storms had started as soon as we decided that we were going to be in a relationship. Avery would always say, "It's me and you against the world!" When fake friends went from being many to few, we weathered the storm. When imprudent stares from our neighbors became unnerving, we weathered the storm. When his uneducated home girls made derogatory comments about me on social-media sites, we weathered the storm. Last, but certainly not least, when my parents called it quits, together, we weathered the storm.

Aunt Ruby told me that God sends storms in your life so that you can have a genuine appreciation for the sunshine and always remember to praise him through every circumstance. It would have been so easy for Avery and me to just isolate ourselves from the world, but that was not the kind of people we were. We committed ourselves to the fact that society was not going to dictate our destiny. We were going to live our lives on our own terms.

I wanted Miracle to think of me as a person who was strong and true to my core values. I'd stressed to her the importance of being trustworthy, and yet I lied to her about the cooking classes. I needed to come clean with Miracle about last night. I was unsure of how she would react, but just like Avery, I needed her to forgive me for being deceitful.

There were several cars parked in front of Aunt Pearl's house. This was not surprising for a Saturday morning. I knocked on the door, expecting to see Miracle.

"Um, hello, Mr. Morris, what a pleasant surprise," I said.

"Good morning, Madison; how are you?" Mr. Morris responded as he opened the door wider.

"I'm wonderful. Thanks for asking. How are you and the dedicated doctor?" I asked.

"We can't complain. I'm on my way out to the football field. There is plenty of breakfast in there; please help yourself. The two troublemakers are still sitting at the dining-room table." Mr. Morris laughed as he walked out the door.

I couldn't help but think that for a man Mr. Morris's age, he was still very handsome and physically fit. As I rounded the corner, I could hear Aunt Pearl talking about world events. Miracle described her aunt as a person who knew a little bit about everything. I could certainly believe that to be true.

"What do you mean you didn't have a chance to watch the news?" Auntie Pearl complained. "You need to watch the news. How in the world can you go an entire day without watching the news? Hell, the news is on twenty-four hours a day."

"Why do I need to watch the news if you are going to tell me everything that happened on it?" Miracle asked.

"Don't wait on me to tell you nothing. If an amendment to the US Constitution ended slavery, how do you know that Congress is not voting today to create another amendment to bring slavery back? I'm not going to be the one to tell you about that, because I'll be busy packing so that Ruby can drop me off in Canada," Auntie Pearl said as she put dishes in the sink.

"Good morning! It smells really good in here," I said as I sat down in a seat next to Miracle.

"Madison, honey, don't be like this one. Pay attention to the news. There was a break-in at the barbershop in the same plaza as Clark Dry Cleaners on the west side of town. You know the Hook and Uppercuts Barbershop? The news folk interviewed one of the owners. His name is Gavin Upshaw. The other owner, Timothy Hook, was unavailable for comments," Auntie Pearl informed me.

"I do know both owners. I will see if I can get some more information on that. Was anybody hurt?" I questioned.

"I don't think anybody was around when the burglary happened. I think it was somebody those guys knew, because the robber only took the safe. Why would you leave the flat-screen televisions and other electronics behind?" Aunt Pearl wondered.

"Madison, I put your plate in the microwave. Let's go talk on the back porch," Miracle stated.

Once we were outside, Miracle started talking about her night. "Girl, last night I really enjoyed being with Trevor. We had a couple of drinks and really got to know one another. I'm not going to tell you how many skinny skanks passed by our table checking him out," Miracle said as she sipped on lemonade.

"Well, from a business standpoint, I can tell you he is very serious about his investments. He is very intelligent, and he provided us with some valuable marketing tips," I replied.

"I will have you know that Trevor Goodman attended one of the most prestigious colleges in New York, and his father owns fifty-one percent of the Goodman Building Corporation. Their family construction business, which started with his grandfather, is worth ninety million dollars to date," Miracle said excitedly.

"His last name is Goodman? Before we moved to Orlando, we used to live next door to Matt and Lindsay Goodman. Their family probably owned Trevor's family," I said without even thinking.

"Madison, you can't say shit like that!" Miracle said as she hit me on the arm.

"What? Is that something I'm not supposed to say?" I apologized and tried to hug Miracle.

"You remember that long list of things I told you to never say in front of black people? Please add that stupidness that just came out your mouth to the list," Miracle suggested.

"OK, OK! So Trevor is intelligent, sexy, and rich? Did you give him any? You are way past the acceptable mileage for an oil change and tune-up. Matter of fact, you need your tires rotated and—" I didn't get to finish teasing Miracle, because Aunt Pearl came outside on the porch.

"Honey, if you don't take care of your car, it will break down on you. Now your Uncle Earnest made sure my check-engine light never came on. When you got a man that will come home after working all day and still want to check under the hood of the car and make sure all the parts are oiled and fine-tuned, that man is a keeper. Lord, I miss that man," Aunt Pearl said as she looked toward the sky.

Miracle and I just laughed and laughed. Aunt Pearl never ceased to amaze me.

"Auntie, do you know what we are talking about?" Miracle laughed.

"Sex, Miracle, which you definitely need some of. It's just so much them damn toys can do for you. If you didn't give that young fellow any, be ready by the next date." Aunt Pearl laughed as she walked back in the house.

"Will there be a next date? You do realize that 'Do It All Hall' is in town? He had the nerve to tell Avery that you refuse to talk to him. Duh, I wouldn't talk to that creep either," I said as I studied Miracle's facial expressions.

"I think that Trevor is a very nice guy, but he can get any skinny young lady in this town to go out with him. I really don't see him wanting to go out with me anymore. As for Gerald, the reason I refuse to talk to him is because I simply don't have anything to say to him. He is another fool that can find some skinny simpleton to be at his every beck and call," Miracle stated without much feeling.

"Look, Miracle, I know Gerald hurt and embarrassed you. But I have watched you push away some really terrific guys over the years. I can tell you this, because I love you; you purposely sabotage your relationships, because I think you feel that it is better to hurt them before they hurt you. If you are not over Gerald, why are you refusing to talk to him?"

"For a person who majored in women's studies in college, whatever the hell that is, I guess you got me all figured out. Wow, Madison, I wish I had your great life. You have the great husband, the great kids, and successful businesses," Miracle said, fighting back tears.

"My great life? A few hours ago, I thought Avery was going to leave me for having an affair with Tina."

"You're having an affair with Tina? Have you lost your mind?" Miracle yelled.

"No! I'm not having an affair with Tina. I hired Tina to clean the house. Oh yeah and she has been the one preparing all the meals as well. Miracle, I never found the time to attend any cooking classes. I actually don't like to cook. I'm sorry for lying to you, and I hope I haven't compromised our friendship, because it means a lot to me," I said.

Miracle sat there for a moment with her hands over her mouth. She took her hair down out of her ponytail and started pulling on the ends of her hair. She seemed nervous or scared. Then, to my surprise, she started laughing. I put my hands in her hair to push her bangs out of her eyes.

"White girl, why are you around here fronting like you cooking full-course soul-food dinners? Madison, being you is tough enough. Why would you try to pretend to be Susie Homemaker? I'm disappointed that you didn't let me in on the hoax." Miracle laughed.

"I guess it is pretty funny. I'm sorry, Miracle. I didn't say anything to you because I knew you would have talked me out of hiring Tina; plus I wanted you to think that I had it all together.

"You know the way that you are acting right now about Gerald. You're not the first person to have her engagement called off," I replied.

"I ended the relationship with Gerald. I was so stressed out with graduating from Legacy U and preparing for graduate school that I turned to food for comfort. I figured out later that I was depressed and unhappy with my life. I put the weight on, and no matter what I did, I couldn't seem to lose the weight. I knew once Gerald went into the NFL draft, he would be surrounded by skinny women in every color, so I figured that I would hurt him before he hurt fat me. I guess you figured me out, SMART GIRL!"

"Miracle, you told us that Gerald called the wedding off! If you ended the relationship, why did you end up in the hospital?"

"I went to Miami to see this doctor about these so-called pills that would help me to lose weight quickly. I did start to lose the weight but at the expense of my kidneys. If it wasn't for my mother, I could have ended up as a dialysis patient or worse — dead. It scared me so bad I said I didn't want to ever hear another word about diet or weight loss," Miracle said as she covered her face.

"I can't believe you kept that from me all this time. Miracle, you are a beautiful young lady. That's really unfair, what you did to Gerald. He loved you unconditionally. Did he tell you that he had a problem with you gaining weight? You guys seemed very happy to me. You were planning a beautiful wedding."

"I tried talking to Gerald about how I was feeling, but he was gone a lot. He was visiting different NFL teams throughout the country. He really didn't have time to worry about my feelings. I just figured that he needed to start the next chapter of his life without me. And I needed to fully recover after I was connected to a kidney machine for almost two months," Miracle stated as she wiped tears from her eyes.

"So, what are you going to do? Are you going to talk to Gerald, since he is in town? Are you going to give Trevor a real chance to get to know you? He obviously doesn't care about your so-called weight gain," I asked.

I hugged Miracle for what seemed like an eternity. We both had secrets that could have potentially cost us the love that we deserved. I encouraged Miracle to embrace her body with the same vitality that she put into church, graduate school, and work. We decided to have one quick mimosa while Aunt Pearl wasn't looking.

I needed to drop Aunt Pearl's blouse off at the dry cleaners and head to the football field. Miracle said that she would catch up with me later but first she needed to make a phone call. I wondered if she was calling Gerald or Trevor.

The morning sun beaming through the window woke Hay up. She rolled over and kissed Luke on the forehead. He had his own room, his own toys, and his own bed, yet he insisted on sleeping with Hay each time he visited.

Yesterday had been such a busy and eventful day that Hay just laid in bed and replayed the events. As of this very moment, Blessed was still on the loose. Some kind of way, he had dragged Fallon with him, and now her mother was frantic.

When Hay had gone to the Corner Store, she was told that Reece had just left. Of course, no one knew how to get in touch with him or where he lived. Hay had hit a dead end. She gave word to her superiors and was waiting for the call to make her next move.

Egypt, the psycho femme, had not returned any of Hay's phone calls. Hay wanted to explain herself and make Egypt understand that she took her job seriously and needed to take care of business before embarking on any pleasure.

The mere fact that Egypt didn't answer her phone or return any phone calls made Hay suspicious. Egypt had a very bad reputation of cheating, and although they were working toward a solid relationship, Egypt still had to prove that she was being faithful, especially during a rough patch.

After hitting a dead end at the store, Hay called her best friend, Laiah, and told her to get Luke ready. Spending time with Luke was always the highlight of Hay's life. Today was Luke's flag-football game. Hay never missed a game. Laiah often did, because she worked on the weekends. It never bothered Luke that his mommy wasn't at the games; as long as he had his "Ma" there, he was happy.

Hay got up and took a shower. Then she checked her messages. She had one message. She hoped it was from Egypt, but it turned out it was from Charity. At first, Hay wasn't going to call her back, but she needed to talk to her about Fallon.

"This is the day that the Lord has made; we should rejoice and be glad in it. Please leave a detailed message at the tone, and I will surely return your phone call at my earliest convenience. Have a blessed day." Hay waited for the excessively long message to be over before leaving her message. Why did Charity have to be so over-the-top?

"Good morning, Charity; this is Hay. I was calling because I had some questions about a student you have. Her name is Fallon Jenkins. Please call me back when you get a chance. Thank you." Hay pressed the End button on the phone.

"Ma," Luke called.

"Hey, big man," Hay said back. She went over and picked him up out of the bed.

"What's today, Ma?" he asked.

"Saturday," Hay answered.

"You know what Saturday means?" Luke asked, looking wide-eyed into Hay's eyes.

The both of them shouted simultaneously, "FOOTBALL!"

Hay put Luke down and pretended like she was going to sack him. Luke faked right then ran around Hay's left side, out of the room. Luke ran all the way to the kitchen then yelled, "Touchdown!"

Hay said, "You're unstoppable, big man. They're not even ready for those swift feet. Let's get some breakfast. What do you want? Oh wait, let me guess...and pancakes?"

"Yep! You know it, Ma," Luke replied.

Luke ate pancakes every time he came over. He could eat them all day long. Hay spoiled Luke rotten and gave him anything he wanted, so she kept her pantry stocked with pancake mix.

Luke and Hay ate breakfast and got ready for the game. Hay had purchased Luke all Michael Jordan attire. He had a Jordan duffel bag, Jordan slides, a Jordan hat, and Jordan basketball shorts. Hay packed the cooler with water and Gatorade. Then she got the sandwiches and snacks for the team. Hay was a team mom, and it was her turn to feed the team after the game.

"Ma, I'm fitted, huh?" Luke said posing in front of Hay.

"They can't hold a candle to you, big man," Hay said, smiling.

"Will Mommy be at the game today?" Luke inquired.

"No, big man, Mommy had to work today," Hay answered.

"Well, too bad for her. She's gonna miss me pulling everybody's flag *and* the ten touchdowns I'm going to make," Luke announced proudly.

"*Ten* touchdowns, big man?"

"*Ten* touchdowns, Ma. Come on. I don't want to be late. The coach needs me," Luke said, pulling Hay's arm.

They got into the car, and Luke turned on his DVD player. He started the movie *Shrek* and ate some dry Froot Loops out of a ziplock bag.

Hay's cell phone rang. She looked at the Bose screen on her dashboard, hoping it would be Egypt. It was Laiah. Hay pressed the Answer button on her steering wheel and said, "Hello."

"Hey, you two," Laiah answered.

"Mommy!" Luke screamed.

"Hey, baby. Are you all ready for your game?" Laiah asked.

"I sure am. Ma made me pancakes, and now I'm feeling big and strong. It's too bad you have to work, because you're gonna miss the ten touchdowns I'm gonna make today."

"Ten touchdowns? Oh man. I hate that I'll miss it. You do well, and be a good boy for Ma, OK?" Laiah instructed.

"Yes, ma'am. Bye, Mommy," Luke answered.

"Bye, baby," Laiah said.

"So what's up, Muffin?" Hay asked Laiah.

"Nothing. Just wanted to call and check on Luke and see if Ms. Egypt called you back yet," Laiah said.

"Hold on. Let me put you in my Bluetooth," Hay said and switched the call from speaker to ear.

"Muffin?" Hay asked.

"Yeah, Pooh, I'm here."

"I still haven't heard from her. She didn't call me back last night, text, or leave a message. I'm hoping she'll be at the game today; that way we can talk."

"I don't know why you put up with Egypt's shit. There are so many women who would love to be with a stud like you," Laiah said.

"I know, Muffin; I know. But something is keeping me connected to her. She's really a good person; she's just been through a whole lot," Hay explained.

"You make up excuses for her all the time, Pooh. I just want to know when you'll finally realize that you're too good for her," Laiah argued.

Ugh, Laiah was getting on Hay's nerves. Just because she was all married and happy didn't mean she had to rush Hay's decision to cut Egypt off. "I really appreciate you, Muffin; I do, but I have to find my own way. Right now I'm in love with Egypt. That's just the way it is."

"Well, fine then. I'll back off. Take lots of pictures of my baby for me. Hopefully you'll see his dad there," Laiah said.

"Smooth Lucas will be there? He hasn't been to a game all season. Much too busy with his business, I assume," Hay said.

"I don't know, but be nice. He hasn't been to any games, but he does pick Luke up from school every day for me. Don't mess up my help with your input, Hazel-Ann."

Hay laughed loudly. Whenever they called each other by their real names, it was serious. "Hazel-Ann, huh? Well, yes, ma'am, Laiah Denise. I'll call you after the game."

"OK, tell Egypt I said grow up; I meant what's up," Laiah joked.

"Bye, Ugly," Hay said and pressed the End button on her Bluetooth.

Just as she ended the call with Laiah, Hay and Luke made it to the field. Hay had to hurry and get inside, because Luke's game would be starting in less than half an hour.

"Let's go, big man," Hay called to Luke.

"You need me to carry anything, Ma?" asked Luke.

"No, I got it. You go find your coach. I'll be inside in a minute," replied Hay.

Hay took everything out of the trunk and went inside. As soon as she walked in and started to set up her tent, she saw Egypt. Egypt was looking good enough to eat. She almost made Hay forget that she was mad at her. She was wearing six-inch heels with her toes out. Her feet were freshly manicured with French tips, which was what Hay preferred. Hay wanted to put Egypt's feet in her mouth and caress her toes with her tongue until Egypt begged her to stop. Toe sucking was Hay's specialty, and Egypt had the feet of an angel.

Egypt was wearing Daisy Duke shorts and a shirt that was cut long in the back but short in the front. The front was cut just long enough to show her belly piercing. She had on her million-dollar sunglasses and a sun hat with her long hair flowing down her back. Her caramel-brown skin glistened in the sunlight and Hay wanted to touch it. Hay finished setting up the tent but kept her eyes on Egypt. Luke snapped her out of her trance when he screamed, "Maaaaaa!!!!"

"Hey, hey, what's going on, big man?" Hay answered.

"I was calling you so you could see me. I'm the team captain today." Luke jumped up in Hay's arms and squeezed her neck.

"Really? You go, big man," Hay answered.

Hay spun Luke around, and as soon as she placed him back on the ground, he screamed again. "Daddy!"

"Hey, my man," Lucas replied. Luke ran back toward the field.

"What's up, Luke?" Hay said.

"What's up, Hay?" said Lucas.

"You want to sit under the tent with me? Luke's game is just about to start," Hay asked.

"Sure, but let me go and speak to my friends first," Lucas said, pointing to a tent a few feet down from Hay's tent. There had to be at least ten people down there. Egypt was one of them. Hay took a double take.

"Is that Sha'Miracle Morris down there?" Hay asked Lucas.

"Yeah, it is. Miracle is good friends with my homeboy's wife."

"Small world," Hay said.

"You're telling me," said Lucas.

"Tell Egypt I said come here when you go down there," Hay said to Lucas, pointing toward the tent.

"Sure thing, Hay. Be right back," Lucas said.

Hay watched Lucas walk to the tent. He gave out hugs to the women and fist pounds to the guys. He pulled Egypt to the side and said something to her. He pointed in Hay's direction. Egypt glanced, threw her head back in laughter, and turned her body completely away from Hay's direction. Lucas talked for a few more minutes then made his way back down to Hay's tent. To Hay's surprise, Egypt walked with him.

"I'm going to the concession stand. You want anything?" Lucas asked Hay.

"No, I'm good. Thanks," Hay replied, glaring at Egypt. "Hey, Egypt."

"Mmm hmm," was what Egypt replied, not even looking in Hay's direction.

"What's going on with you? Why didn't you return my phone calls? Are you OK?" Hay questioned.

"My, how the tables have turned. When I was blowing your tired ass up yesterday, you didn't have a second to spare. Now you want to know how *I'm* doing? Child, please. I'm good. I hope you are too, because this" — she pointed at Hay and moved her finger from Hay's head to her feet then back to her head again — "I haven't the time for."

"What the fuck?" Hay said. Hay was perturbed and vexed at the same time. "I'm trying to make sure you're OK, and this is what you choose to say to me? Egypt, baby, please, calm down, and think for a second," Hay pleaded.

"Oh, I thought all right. When you blew me off, I thought all night long. I thought about how selfish you are, how all you think about is your job, how you never have time for me, and how I really don't know if it's you or a very large dick I want. You forced me to think, Hay. And thought I did."

Hay couldn't believe what she was hearing. She made one last attempt to reconcile with Egypt. "Egypt, baby, listen. You know I've worked very hard to get where I am. You knew when you signed up for this that my job was very demanding. I'm usually always there for you, but the one time I can't be, you flip out on me. I'm not sitting on millions like you are; I have to get up every day and go get it. But if we can go somewhere after the game and talk, I promise I'll make last night up to you."

"Your sorry is a day too late. I'm good. I've got friends waiting on me. I didn't come out here to talk to you; I came to see my niece cheer. You have yourself a good one." With that, she turned around and walked off.

Hay felt heartbroken, but she would never show it. She was much too strong to let her emotions get the best of her. For the rest of the game, she focused on Luke. He pulled three flags and threw them in the air. He also ran one touchdown. Too bad he ran in the wrong direction and scored for the other team.

During the fourth quarter, the coach took him out to let someone else play, and when Hay looked over on the bench, Luke was fast asleep.

She tapped Lucas and said, "That's our baby."

Lucas laughed and replied, "Luke, the all-star football player."

Gabby

I hated Saturday mornings — especially when I had to play mommy to MyReece and TyReece. MyReece, who we called "My" was seven years old, and TyReece, whose nickname was "Ty" was six years old. Reece and I had gotten together right before Ty was born.

Every weekend, the boys had football. Reece wanted his boys to be well rounded. He signed them up every year. Their coaches picked them up and dropped them off from every practice; and somehow it was always me who ended up at the games. Usually I would drag one of my girls to the game with me, but after last night, I really didn't want to be around either one of them. So my sidekick Mark tagged along.

Reece and I held hands in the car. He was a hopeless romantic, and so was I. The three boys were in the back seat, singing along to some rap song that was playing. When we entered the football-field parking lot, instead of parking, Reece pulled up to the gate.

"You're not staying today?" I asked sadly.

"I can't stay, baby. I gotta go and make this drop and see who's coming up to the store," answered Reece.

Reece could see the disappointment in my face. He turned and looked out the window.

"Daddy, aren't you coming?" asked Ty.

"Yeah, you always miss me when coach puts me in," added My.

"Daddy will be here for the next game, boys. Y'all get on out there and represent like I know y'all can," Reece said.

"Please stay, Daddy. Please," My begged.

"Daddy, you always say next time; then when next time comes, you say next time again," Ty said, eyes watering.

"Now look, I have to go do some important things. I love you boys, but I can't be everywhere at once. Ms. Gabby is here. Aren't you happy for that?"

"Ms. Gabby is always here. Never you or Mommy," Ty huffed and hopped out of the car.

My got out behind him and slammed the door.

"MyReece!" Reece yelled.

"Leave them alone," I said. "I don't want them too upset before they play. I'll call you when we're ready. Come on, Mark."

I closed the car door and went over to the boys. "My and Ty, it's time to get your head in the game. My, I want three touchdowns. Ty, I want you to block like never before. Crushers on three, OK? One, two, three..."

"Crushers," we all yelled and high-fived each other.

We walked in, and I saw Madison's Macy's Thanksgiving-sized tent. I was so glad she already had everything set up. Nothing for me to do now but chill and watch the boys play.

"Hey, Gabby," Madison said.

"Hey, Madison. I see Coach Clark is already sweating in the sun. Speak to Ms. Madison, boys," I said.

"Hi, Ms. Madison," they said in unison.

"Boys, go find your coach. I'll be right here."

"OK." They ran off.

"Good morning, Mark. You're looking as handsome as ever," Madison said.

"Hi, Ms. Madison," replied Mark.

Just as I unfolded my chair and sat down, I saw Miracle walking up. I sprung out of my seat and walked swiftly toward her. I had to speak with her privately.

"Where the hell have you been?" I snapped.

"Good morning, Gabrielle. How are you today?"

"Gabrielle? Oh hell no! Give up the dirt. I call you and no answer. Then you don't call me back. Now you're calling me by my government name? What's going on?" I demanded

"Well, after the disastrous dinner party last night, I went out with Trevor," Miracle responded.

"Disaster? Trevor? Pause!" I stopped her. "I left you a message about Blessed. Did you get it?"

"Oh my goodness. I haven't checked my messages since I turned my phone back on this morning. Why didn't you text me?" Miracle asked.

"Because I left a damn voice mail. That shit was too much to text. Well anyway, Blessed got up with Reece yesterday evening, and Reece put him up in a hotel and got him a rental car. By Monday, Blessed and Fallon should be in Atlanta with a new identity, new job, and everything." I smiled.

"Why are you smiling, Gabby? That's the dumbest, most irresponsible thing I've ever heard. This child is only sixteen years old. What the hell does he need with a new identity? He needs to turn himself in, show remorse, and hope he has clemency with the courts. It's not like he killed somebody. Reece is as stupid as a sack of shit if he thought that was brilliant."

I was utterly offended. "Miracle, no, Reece fixed it. He handled everything. The objective is to keep Blessed out of jail."

"No, the objective is to keep Blessed safe. This isn't the way," Miracle said.

"Well, it's too late now. It's already done. I just thought you'd want to know," I said. I'd actually thought it was a good idea, until Miracle had said what she just said. Maybe sending Blessed and Fallon on the run wasn't a good idea. I just knew that Reece took care of his people.

"I just hope and pray that those babies remain safe. Honestly, Gabby, sometimes I think you slept through college and bought your degree, because you don't use your head at all," Miracle said.

"Are you done?" I asked.

"What?" questioned Miracle.

"When you're finished putting me down, I'd like to go watch the game. I was only trying to help. Damn, Miracle, everybody can't be as perfect as you," I told her.

"I'm sorry. I just let my emotions get the best of me. I really didn't mean to hurt your feelings. Do over?" Miracle asked.

I could never stay mad at Miracle for long. Whenever things got too heated and we didn't know how to recover, the words "do over" allowed us to shake everything off and start clean.

"Do over," I said to Miracle.

We hugged and walked over to Madison's tent.

"You really came for me, Miss Girl," I said to Miracle.

"Well you really did the *most*, little Miss Ride or Die," Miracle replied.

"Shut up," I said and pushed her. I glanced back to see if I saw the boys and saw Egypt coming up. "Oh Lord, here comes Miss America," I said to Miracle.

"Be nice, Gab," she replied.

"I'll try, but I make no promises," I assured her.

"Good morning, Miracle," Egypt said.

"Good morning, love. How are you?" replied Miracle.

"Just splendid. Hi, Madison. You're looking as lovely as ever," said Egypt, removing her sunglasses.

"Good morning, friend. That's a bad handbag you have there," Madison said, smiling.

Egypt then turned her attention toward me. She looked me from feet to head and back to feet then finally said, "Gabby."

I did the whore no favors and said, "Egypt," then turned my head away.

I thought for a second. This would be the perfect time to let everyone know about the passion group. I pushed my pride aside, put on the fakest smile I could, for Egypt's sake, then spoke.

"Hey, while I have you ladies all here, I wanted to invite you all to be a part of a passion group," I began.

"What's that?" inquired Madison.

"Well, it's when people get together and find something that they're passionate about and turn it into something big," I explained.

"OK, so what does that have to do with us?" Egypt asked.

"Well, everyone I invited is passionate in some way about children. Plus, since we're all college graduates, we know firsthand how important education is. However, funds tend to be limited for students who want to further their education. So my vision is for us to all get together and write a grant of some sort to start a scholarship foundation. That way we can send more students to Wise and Legacy."

"Impressive, Gabby," Miracle said.

"Yeah and I used my empty brain to think all of that up by myself," I said and stuck my tongue out playfully at her.

"Count me in," Miracle said.

"Me too," said Madison. "Anything to help students further their education I would love to be a part of."

"I'll do it too," Egypt said. "But let's make this clear; I'm in it strictly for the kids. I still think you're garbage."

"Egypt, please, if I'm garbage, you're the fucking Dumpster, but this is for us to build a legacy for our children, nieces, nephews, and kids who actually have no support. This is much bigger than your ego; although I never thought anything else could be," I said.

Egypt rolled her eyes at me, and I rolled mine right back. I really couldn't stand her uppity ass, but I needed her. She had a plethora of money left over from her lawsuit, even after all these years, and could possibly be a sponsor. I didn't want to deal with her, but for the sake of the passion group, I'd do it with a smile. OK, well, maybe not a smile. But I'd do it.

"So great, I'll see you all at Miracle's house tomorrow for brunch. Thanks so much, ladies; you all will not be disappointed."

"My house?" Miracle questioned.

"Oh yeah, thanks for volunteering your home for the meeting," I said, blowing her a kiss.

Miracle laughed at me. "OK then."

I had already e-mailed Charity and let her know the details, so everything was a go. The Gab had done it again.

When the alarm sounded, I woke Trevor up and went right back to sleep. A short time later, I woke up to the smell of coffee. I heard Trevor on his cell phone, but I couldn't make out what he was saying. Trevor needed to get up early for a business meeting, I guessed.

"Good morning. How did you sleep, sweetheart?" Trevor questioned as he pulled a beautifully wrapped box from behind his back.

"I slept like a baby. What's with the box, Mr. Goodman?" I asked as I pushed myself up from under the comforter, revealing my breasts.

"The other day when you cut our lunch date short, I decided to do something that you enjoy doing, shop." Trevor bent down and kissed me on my lips. Then he made his way down to my breast. His tongue made small circles around my nipple. He was sucking on the right nipple while he caressed my left breast. Once he started to nibble on my breasts, I felt the urge to pull him back in the bed with me.

"Wait, baby, don't you want to open your gift?" Trevor asked as he laughed.

"Don't start anything you can't finish," I said, reaching for the box.

I opened the box to find a Jimmy Choo handbag and shoes. I'd told Trevor about the new Jimmy Choo winter collection at Nordstrom, and he must have gotten these gorgeous items from there.

"Trevor, you spoil me rotten. I love my gift, but what is the occasion?"

"Do I need a reason? Egypt, I'm falling for you fast. You make me happy, and I want to do the same for you. Do I make you happy? Look me in my eyes and tell me."

"Big daddy, you make me very happy," I said.

"I have to go out of town for business today. I'll be back on Sunday. Why don't you come over to the house Sunday evening and let me cook something for you," Trevor said as he was just about to walk out the door.

I got in the shower and then dressed in all new clothes. I was definitely going to wear my new shoes with my new handbag. I was looking so good I had to compliment myself. These tired-ass tricks at this football game were not going to be ready for me.

Noah had left a message on my cell phone that said he was going out to the field early to help Mr. Morris set up the concession stand and that he would have Asia with him. I was glad of that, because that would give me more time to run some quick errands before I had to be at the field.

I had several messages on my phone, one of which was from Hay. I didn't even listen to it. She would probably be at the game today, and I was not in the mood to even talk about how she blew me off yesterday. If she loved that lil job that much, she could have it. It was going to take more than our usual make-up sex for her to get back in my good graces.

When I got to the football field, I looked for certain cars. It looked like the gang was all here. Yes, I was purposely a little late; I had to make a grand entrance. After all, they should be honored that I even showed up at all.

"Got damn, lil mama, let's go back to my crib and do something AMAZING!" Wall Street said, grabbing for my hand. "How long you gonna keep me on the bench?"

"Until you learn your position, keep me on your wish list!" I said, yanking my hand away.

"I'm saying, Egypt, I've been trying to get at you for the longest. What, I'm not old enough for you? My pockets aren't fat enough for you? Tell me what I got to do to get next to you," Wall Street cried.

"I got my starting five; when it's your turn, I'll let you know," I said with a smirk and walked off. I can't stand a thirsty man.

I have known Mike, also known as Wall Street, since we were in middle school. I have always known him to have on a suit and tie, even when the occasion didn't call for it. Once he started carrying a briefcase to school in the ninth grade, the nickname Wall Street just seemed fitting. He was way out of his league trying to get with me. I guess you couldn't blame a guy for trying.

On my way to Madison's tent, I must have passed fifty people trying to converse with me. Some of them wanted a handout. Some of them, for some crazy reason, felt like they were entitled to something from me. Of course, I couldn't be bothered with such commoners.

"Well if it isn't Cleopatra; I didn't get a chance to thank you for picking up the kids for us the other day. All jokes aside, Egypt, I really appreciate what you do for the kids," Avery said.

"It's my pleasure. I'm glad I could help," I said as I moved past Avery to sit next to Madison.

"All girls in? That's my cue to leave," Avery said, heading toward the sidelines.

"Egypt, you look great. What happened to you coming over for dinner last night?" Madison asked.

"Don't ask. I told Noah to tell you that I was in a bad mood. Did you save me something to eat? I love your chicken," I said.

"Yeah, Egypt, I'll tell you about that later," Madison said.

"Miracle, I saw sexy Scott Morris in the concession stand, still serving up the best popcorn in town," I said.

"I was going to tell Miracle that Scott could *get* it if things don't work out with me and Avery," Madison said, giggling.

"Everyone knows that I'm Scott's favorite," Gabby joked.

"Y'all gumps can get on a bench, because Scott Morris is in love with Elaine Morris for whatever reason," Miracle stated irritably.

"Oh you know the reason. Who knows your body better than your doctor?" I questioned while I laughed.

I was having a good time with my girls, until *she* walked up. We all stopped laughing at the same time and stared at Candice. She knew how to push my buttons, so I tried to remain calm, but if she knew what was good for her, she would make this visit short and sweet.

"What's up, everybody? I had to come over and see how the upper crust was doing today. I have some information to share with each of you," Candice said with a devilish look on her face.

"Madison, I wanted to give you a business card from my neighbor. Mikayla loves my hair, as she should, and she would like to get her hair braided. So please contact Pebbles as soon as possible, because she is very busy and can probably fit Mikayla in, since you are a friend of mine," Candice said.

"Um, thank you, Candy, but Mikayla is not getting her hair braided any time soon," Madison replied with an annoyed facial expression.

"Why not? Are you afraid she will look too black? You're probably one of those white girls that think that their black children are biracial, but, honey, when you decided to have children with a black man, you decided to have black children," Candice stated like she was some kind of authority on the issue.

"Excuse me! Mikayla is not getting her hair braided because I said so. Unlike you, I don't have the time to sit there and take a million braids loose," Madison replied.

"Candice, is this really necessary?" Miracle asked.

"Yes, Sha'Miracle, it is necessary. Just like it is necessary for Gerald to be back in town with a cute, petite Asian girl. My home boy works at the rehabilitation center that is helping Gerald to walk so that he can make it down the aisle for real this time." Candy laughed.

"Wait a minute, Candy; you are way out of bounds!" Gabby stood up and walked toward Candy.

"Gabby, please! I called your cell phone a couple of times last week. Of course, I didn't want you; I was looking for Reece. You didn't have to call me back, because he was not at your house anyway. He was across town at his girlfriend's house. You know, the place where he receives his mail?" Candy asked.

"Let me get her ass," I yelled as I started removing my earrings.

"Girl, who are you fooling? I'm safe with you as long as there are no chemicals around! I would hate to have to scuff you up out here at a damn Pop Warner football game in your new club outfit. Close door!" Candy laughed as she gave her notorious hand gesture.

Before I knew it, I was kicking my shoes off and knocking over my chair. If Noah had not showed up and separated us when he did, I was going to kick Candy's ass. She insulted my entire crew. I had put up with her crap long enough. I promised Asia I would be there for her, and I didn't want to let her down, but as soon as the game was over, I was leaving. Madison grabbed me and pleaded for me to calm down.

"Egypt, you have to think of Asia. She won't understand if you hurt her mother. You have to lead by example. You have to set a good example for Asia to follow," Miracle said.

"Candice is simply intolerable; forget about her. Come with me to the concession stand. I need to speak to someone," Madison said.

I walked with Madison to the concession stand, where we bumped right into Gavin and Little Gavin. I immediately turned around to look for Avery, but I didn't see him. I encouraged Madison to hurry up.

"Hey, Little G., how are you? You played a good game today," Madison commented.

"What's happening?" Gavin asked with a smile.

"I just wanted to know if you were alright after the robbery the other day," Madison said.

"I got my people on the street checking things out for me. It's nothing I can't handle. So you're concerned about me, huh?" Gavin smirked.

"How is Tim doing?" I asked.

"He's out of town on business. I'll bring him up to speed when I see him in a couple of days. I don't know when these cowards are going to realize that I play for keeps," Gavin alleged as he looked Madison up and down.

At that moment, Avery walked up and stood directly behind Madison. He put his arm around her waist and pulled her even closer to him. I started talking to Little Gavin in the hopes to keep things civil.

"What's up, A. C.? Your boys looked real good today. I heard that they are undefeated," Gavin said without blinking an eye.

"Yeah, you know how it is; if you're not in it to win, why even show up," Avery said as he looked down at his wedding band.

"You're right. I know all about winning," Gavin stated as he pulled up his sleeve so that his tattoo would show.

"OK, well, Gavin, let us know if you think we need to tighten up security measures as a whole at the plaza," Madison said and grabbed Avery's hand so that they could walk away together.

"That dude is a clown. I don't know what Madison is doing with him," Gavin said.

"The way you feel about Avery is the way I feel about that tramp Candice. There is nothing we can do about it, right?" I questioned.

"I'm not so sure about that," Gavin said and winked his eye.

Charity

Charity's head was throbbing. She couldn't believe she was drugged last night. All she wanted to do was have a nice dinner with her neighbors, and she ended up getting her fruit poisoned by "the woman."

Charity heard a door slam. She got scared. She jumped up and hid behind the door in her room. There was someone in her house. She remained quiet as the footsteps grew closer. Charity began to pray.

"Father God, please shield and protect me. Send your angels to encamp around me right now. Amen."

"Good morning," Lucas said, and Charity jumped.

Lucas dropped the tray with the hot coffee and two mugs. The glass shattered on the Italian-marble tiled floor.

"Oh my goodness; I'm so sorry. Did I scare you?" Lucas asked.

"Lucas?" Charity exclaimed. "I feel like such a fool. I forgot you were even here."

"It's OK," Lucas said, bending down to clean up the horrible mess.

"Here, let me help you," Charity insisted.

Together, they cleaned up the glass then mopped the floor. It was as good as new in less than twenty minutes.

"We make a great team," Lucas told Charity.

Charity smiled. "Yeah, I guess we do."

Charity had been so drunk the night before that Lucas had insisted on spending the night to assure that she was OK. There was something about Charity that drew Lucas toward her. She irritated everyone around her, but she captivated Lucas. He had to have her, and if he couldn't have her, he would at least like to get to know her better. She was someone Lucas needed in his corner.

"Lucas, I would like to thank you for being the perfect gentleman last night. I don't want to do anything that's out of the will of God, and you sleeping in the guest room was very noble. You've earned a star on your crown," Charity said.

Lucas chuckled. "Charity, woman, you are amazing. I've only known you for a few hours, but I know I would like to know more. How about we go to dinner tonight? I'll make sure all of the fruit you eat is market fresh."

Charity thought Lucas was moving a bit too fast, but she had a good feeling about him. She decided to mute her mind and listen to her heart. "OK, dinner. I haven't met a man so polite since college. Perhaps we could benefit from getting to know each other. After all, you did take very good care of me last night."

Lucas was ecstatic. "Well, I have to get to my son's football game in a few, so I'm going to leave now. I'll come by tonight around eight and pick you up."

"A son?" Charity asked.

"Yes. Luke. He's four years old," Lucas stated proudly.

"A toddler?" Charity exclaimed. Oh how she wanted a child of her own so badly. She couldn't wait to meet Lucas's son. She knew she was getting far ahead of herself, but she was excited nonetheless.

"Yes. He's playing flag football today, and I have to go and cheer him on."

"How sweet," Charity replied.

Lucas and Charity exchanged phone numbers, and Lucas gave Charity a good-bye hug.

Charity saw Lucas out the front door and sat down to check her e-mail. Surely there would be something from Gabby about the passion group by now. The meeting was tomorrow. Sure enough, there was a message. The message stated that they would be meeting at 12334 Willowfire Lane. Charity wrote the address down and picked the phone up to call Gabby.

"Hello," Gabby answered.

"Well, bless the Lord, saints," Charity answered back.

Gabby loved Charity. Charity was so extra-holy that it was laughable. "Hey there, Ms. Love. How are you this blessed morn?"

"I'm doing just fine. I was calling to get some more information about this group. I am very excited to have received an invitation but was wondering what I should do to prepare for the meeting," Charity explained.

"Well there really isn't much to prepare for tomorrow's meeting. I would just like to bring everyone together for an official meeting, and then we can discuss the direction of the group. So far there are five of us."

"Six," Charity interrupted. "I invited one of my church members who loves children. She said she would be willing to participate."

"Perfect. Six people it is. You already know that I want to get a scholarship fund started, right?" Gabby asked.

"Yes, I believe I was informed of that. What inspired the scholarship?" inquired Charity.

"Well, you know my son Marlin is a senior, and then the rest of them are one year behind each other. I'll need some assistance to send them on their way," explained Gabby.

"I see. Well I know some students that will benefit from this potential scholarship as well. One of my students in particular, Fallon. She's only a junior, but colleges are already scouting her. I love her so much. She's such a bright and talented young lady," Charity said.

"Fallon Jenkins?" asked Gabby.

"Why, yes, Fallon Jenkins. You know her?" Charity asked.

"She and Jalyssa are best friends. They've been best friends since elementary school."

"Oh yeah, that's right. The two of them are always glued to one another. I can't believe I forgot that. Well you know that Fallon is pregnant. Her mother doesn't know about it yet, but I want to make sure Fallon graduates and goes to college. I just don't know the proper way to help her, without revealing her secret," Charity blabbed.

"Fallon is pregnant? Oh no. Charity, I have to go. My boys are getting ready for their football game, and I have to call my daughter. I'll see you tomorrow."

"OK, Gabby, you have a blessed day now. Remember Jesus loves you, and so do I."

Charity looked at her cell phone and saw that she had a voice mail. She pressed the key to check her messages. To her surprise, the message was from Hazel-Ann.

"Good morning, Charity; this is Hay. I was calling because I had some questions about a student you have. Her name is Fallon Jenkins. Please call me back when you get a chance. Thank you."

"Fallon? What could she possibly want with Fallon?" Charity asked herself.

Charity dialed Hay's number and waited for her to answer. She didn't answer the call. Charity pressed End on her cell phone and went to take a shower. There was much too much going on at one time for her to process. She had been drugged with the devil's nectar; rescued by a strange man, who seemed to have what she was looking for in a mate; invited to meet with strange women, whom she knew nothing about; and broken glass all over her nice flooring, all before twenty-four hours had passed.

While in the shower, Charity's thoughts bounced back and forth between the passion group and Lucas. He had such a beautiful smile. His body was molded in all the right places. His hair was cut low, and his beard was trimmed to fit his perfectly round, boyish face. If he was a worshipper of Christ that would be just enough to keep Charity interested.

Charity's thoughts had completely consumed her, until she was suddenly shivering in the shower. She had spent so much time thinking about Lucas that she didn't even notice the temperature change in the water. She quickly hopped out and dressed.

As she walked into her kitchen to slice a grapefruit and eat what would have been lunch by this time, her cell phone started to play "I Give Myself Away."

"Blessings be unto you; this is Charity," she answered.

"Hi, Charity," Hay said.

"Well, hello there. Will you still be joining us tomorrow for the passion-group meeting? I have the time and address for you," said Charity.

"Oh, yes, I'll be there. Give me the information," Hay said as she wrote down the time and address.

"Well what brings you to call me this glorious Saturday morning?" asked Charity.

"I was wondering if you could give me some information on a student that you have by the name of Fallon Jenkins," Hay said.

"Well, yes, ma'am, Miss *Hay*," Charity responded sarcastically, still wondering why she wanted to be called that. "What is it that you want to know?"

"Do you know where she is?" asked Hay.

"No, I guess she's at home with her mother," Charity said.

"No, she's not there. She's been missing since yesterday after school. I believe that she's on the run with her boyfriend," Hay explained.

"You shut your mouth right now, Hazel-Ann Dawson. That child is on nobody's 'run' with anyone. That simply doesn't sound like Fallon. Have you tried to call her mother?"

"Of course I have. Her mother is quite frantic as well. She is the one who told me that Fallon texted her and said she was going with Blessed and would call her later, but she hasn't heard from her since. And Fallon isn't taking any phone calls from anyone."

Charity began to recite the twenty-third psalm. Hay didn't have time for Charity or the circus act she attempted to perform. Hay interrupted Charity just as she was at the part about the "evil shadow of death" or something like that.

"Charity, seriously, we need to find this girl. We find her; we find him. He's wanted for stealing a bus and driving passengers around. So are you going to break into praise and worship, or are you going to get off your ass and help me find them? Excuse me."

"I'm all in. Tell me what you need me to do. I owe Fallon big time," Charity said to Hay.

"Yeah, I know. You really pissed her off with your response to her pregnancy."

"How do you know about that?"

"Fallon told me," said Hay. "You need to be more compassionate toward others, but that's another Sunday-school lesson. Right now, I need you to tell me everything you know about Fallon—her friends, her enemies, her hobbies, her hangouts—anything that could possibly lead to us finding her. She has no idea how much trouble she's in."

"OK." Charity started talking. She told Hay everything she knew about Fallon. She wanted Fallon to come home safely. If she was given a second chance with Fallon, she'd be a much better mentor to her. Who knew, maybe she and Lucas could be godparents to her unborn baby.

For thy loving kindness is before mine eyes; and I have walked in thy truth. (Psalm 26:3)

Did I hear her correctly? Pregnant, I couldn't believe this. Reece couldn't get to this field fast enough. I was about to call Jalyssa but decided that I would talk to her face-to-face when I got home.

The boys had won their game twenty-one to zero. MyReece had scored three touchdowns, just like I told him to, and TyReece was a beast on both defense and offense. He blocked for his brother like no one had ever blocked before. Those boys were bound to end up in the NFL. Everyone at the football field called them the "Dynamic Duo."

It was a shame their parents were never there to see them. They were phenomenal athletes at such a young age. When My and Ty made it to the NFL, chances were they would take extra-good care of their sorry mothers, who never supported them, and their half-sorry dad, who only dropped them off and picked them up — and only because I was with them. The three parents would reap the full benefits from the boys, and I would probably be all forgotten about. Oh well, who cared? These weren't my kids anyway. The only reason I was there was to make sure Reece knew what a good woman I was. Sometimes though, I don't even think he noticed.

"Ms. Gabby, did you see us playing?" My asked.

"I sure did, My. You ran so fast that I don't even think they could see your feet," I replied.

My smiled and showed all of his teeth. He was so proud of himself, and I had to admit I was really proud of him too.

"What about me, Ms. Gabby? Did you see me tackle number thirty-four? He was big too," Ty asked.

"Man, you sacked him so hard I thought he was gonna need an ambulance," I told him.

"Yeah, I hit him real good, huh?" Ty said with a grin on his face.

"Yep, you did. If y'all keep playing like that, we'll be in the play-offs for sure," I told them.

My cell phone rang. I didn't have to look at it. I knew it was Reece, because he had his own ring tone. I answered quickly.

"Hey," I said.

"I'm outside," he replied.

"We're coming," I said and hung up the phone. I was still a little salty about him not staying to see his boys play. Then when Candy came over and aired everybody's dirty laundry, I was even more agitated.

When we got in the car there was a familiar smell. It was the smell of a fresh haircut. I took a double take at Reece. He looked good enough to eat. I always fell weak for him when he got a haircut and his beard trimmed.

"So where do you receive your mail?" I asked, trying to stay focused.

"Huh?" Reece replied.

"Candy says she was looking for you and found you at some trick's house. Talking about she's your girlfriend and that's where you really live," I explained.

"And you believed her? Gabby, who do I come home to every night? If I had a girlfriend, you think I would be able to spend as much time with you as I do? I can't believe you let Candy ghetto ass get you all worked up over nothing." Reece laughed.

He had a point, but I was still pissed. I looked him over again. Damn, he was sexy. He was already a very handsome man, but a fresh haircut made me want to do some things to him.

A second thought crossed my mind. He had a fresh haircut, and these two little superstar football players were in the back seat looking like *wolflettes*; baby wolves.

"Where did you go?" I asked.

"The barbershop," he replied.

"What about your boys?" I questioned.

"What about them?" he answered, looking confused.

"Are you taking them to get their hair cut?" I said, focusing on his face.

"Nah, they're straight," he said to me.

"What? Look at those boys. They look as scruffy as ever. Didn't it occur to you while you were getting your hair cut that you had two little boys that needed their own heads cut as well?" I yelled.

"First of all, calm your ass down. Second of all, I have things to do. *G-Dawg* could only fit me in this morning, so I went when I could. The boys were at the game, and now I have to go up to the store," Reece explained.

"I thought you went to the store already," I said.

"Damn, Gabby, don't you pay attention? I just told you I went to the barbershop and got a cut. I haven't been nowhere but there," he yelled back.

"For three hours, Reece? Get real," I said.

"You don't have to believe me, but I know where I was. I also know that if you want these kids hair cut so bad, you can take them your damn self. I have shit to fucking do," Reece murmured to himself.

"I'm not taking these kids anywhere. I already spent three hours in the blazing sun, cheering for them at their game, which, by the way, you didn't even ask them how it went. I'm over this. Let me drop you off at the store, and I'll come back and get you," I announced.

"That's fine, but don't drive out all my damn gas, like you normally do. And when I call, you need to be on your way back up here quick, fast, and in a hurry," Reece said as he pulled up to the store.

"Give me some money to get them a pizza," I said, ignoring his outrageous demands.

Reece reached in his pockets and gave me two crisp one-hundred-dollar bills. I hated when he made me mad. But what I hated even more was the fact that I couldn't stay mad at him for long. I took the money and stuffed it in my bra.

"Don't snatch from me, Gabrielle. I might just have to take my money back," Reece teased.

"I'd like to see you try," I said with the meanest face I could make.

Reece put his head directly between my breasts and gripped the money with his teeth. He gently pulled it out and looked me in my eyes. Then he opened his mouth, let the money fall, and put his head back down in my chest. His head smelled so good. I was losing this battle between my mind and my emotions.

Reece lifted his head and kissed my forehead. "I love you, Gabrielle," he said.

"You make me sick," I replied.

"That's fine. I can heal whatever ails you later tonight," he said and kissed my lips.

Reece got out of the car and came around to open my door. I got out, walked around to the driver's side, and got inside.

"Mark, you can get up front if you want," I said.

"No, I'll stay back here. The boys are asleep, and I don't want to disturb them," Mark replied.

"Well, I guess I'll be chauffeuring today then." I smiled at Mark and drove off.

I got two pizzas and three two-liter sodas. I went to the house and dropped the boys off. I told Mark to tell Jalyssa to come to the car. She walked outside, and I got out of the car and stood beside the driver's side door.

"What?" she said, looking confused.

"Why didn't you tell me that Fallon was pregnant?"

"Fallon is pregnant?" Jalyssa asked, trying to sound surprised.

"Child, please, I know you know," I said.

"I have no idea what you're talking about," Jalyssa responded.

"So you didn't know that Fallon was pregnant, but you knew all about Blessed, the bus, and the get away?" I questioned.

"OK, OK. I know she's pregnant. She made me pinkie swear not to tell. Her mom doesn't know, and she's trying to figure out her next move," Jalyssa explained.

"Well, I'm trying to get this group together to start a scholarship fund, and I wanted to make sure Marlin and Fallon could be some of our first recipients," I told her.

"Wow, that sounds cool, Mama. But you've got one little problem," Jalyssa said.

"What's that?" I asked.

"Marlin's having a baby too," Jalyssa blurted out.

I was stunned. I thought I had heard him say that last night, but I wasn't sure if I heard right. Now my fears were confirmed.

"What are they going to do? She should get an abortion. Marlin has so much life to live. A baby will mess everything up," I said.

"No way. Marlin said Sade is applying for public housing, and he's going to move in with her and be a family," Jalyssa said.

"I can't deal with this right now. Where is Marlin anyway?"

"He's with Sade. He says he doesn't want to miss anything about this baby. He wants to be with her as much as he can," Jalyssa explained.

"This is too much. I'll be back," I said.

"Where are you going?" Jalyssa asked.

"To Miracle's house. I need her right now," I explained.

"Tell her I said hello. Mama, don't stay gone all night and leave me with double trouble," said Jalyssa.

"I won't. See you in a few," I said and got into the car.

I drove like I was in a high-speed chase, trying to get to Miracle's house. The information I found out just made me sick to my stomach. I didn't even bother calling. At this point, if she wasn't there, I'd sit and wait for her to come. We had so much to talk about. She had to tell me about the dinner, Trevor, and Gerald, and I had to tell her about Fallon and Marlin. My head was spinning. I needed a drink. I wanted something strong, and Miracle always had the best stuff at her house.

Sha' Miracle

After I hugged my godchildren and promised to take them to the movies next week, I headed for my car. I wanted to talk to my dad, but I wasn't in the mood for a lecture about my mother, so I made it a point to avoid the concession stand. I knew I needed to talk to Gerald. I wasn't sure exactly what I was going to say to him.

Candice suggesting that Gerald was in town with a petite Asian woman wasn't surprising. Hell, over the years, thanks to different social-media sites, Gerald had been pictured with plenty of women; however, Gerald Hall was not a womanizer. If he was in a relationship, you could believe he was going to be faithful. That was just the kind of man Ms. Gloria raised him to be.

Even when we were dating in high school, there would be girls all around. I never worried about him being unfaithful, because loyalty was so very important to him. I would always ask him, "What are you doing with me, if you can have any girl in this school?" He would always reply, "I don't want any girl; I only want my Miracle."

I don't know where things went wrong with us. One day I woke up with feelings of insecurity, and I just felt like I didn't measure up. I didn't want to deal with the pressures of being an NFL player's wife. I guess I opted out for normalcy, instead of the life of the rich and famous. I needed my privacy, and I loved working with children. I was sure Gerald would understand that.

The drive out to Lake Nona was long enough that I had plenty of time to think. My navigational system was a blessing, because I never would have found Ms. Gloria's house without it.

When I pulled up to the house, I noticed that there were a few cars parked out front. I had talked with Ms. Gloria briefly before I left the football field. She had assured me that it would be a good idea for me to visit today but Gerald was not his usual, cheerful self. I was a little bit nervous for some reason. I hoped there would be some kind of alcoholic beverage in this house to help me calm down.

Gerald's cousin opened the door to greet me. As I made my way through the house, I was greeted by several of Gerald's family members. They all made me feel very welcome, and so many memories flooded my mind as I spoke to them. I could not believe that Ms. Gloria still displayed so many of my pictures. There were pictures of me. There were pictures of me and Gerald together. It was when I saw our engagement photo that I felt like maybe I should not have come.

I knocked on the door to Gerald's room, and I heard a faint, "Come in."

"Hey, why are you in here all alone?" I asked.

"When my mom said that you were on your way out here, I didn't believe her," Gerald said as he turned the sound down on the television.

"How are you feeling?" I asked as I pulled up a seat next to his bed.

"Pretty good, I guess, for someone with a season-ending injury. I could be rehabbing for the next seven months, minimum. So if this is some kind of sympathy visit, I don't need it. It took me getting hurt just to have a face-to-face conversation with you?" He tossed the remote control onto the floor.

"Of course not, I know you needed your space, so I gave it to you. Gerald Hall, if this is some kind of pity party, you can save the invite!" I yelled.

"Look at my damn knee, Miracle! And as far as space goes, I don't remember asking you for any. I asked you for your hand in marriage, which you turned me down months before our wedding!"

"Gerald, that's ancient history. We have both moved on. I assume you are with some skinny Asian girl."

"I'm with an Asian girl?" He laughed. "Kosame is my happily married assistant. You sound a little jealous."

"Well, if not her, some other tired, skinny girl. I thought you would be married by now. Still sowing your wild oats, I suppose?"

"Miracle, I know you didn't come all the way out here to discuss my sex life. Why have you been avoiding me? What did I do or not do to make you vanish right out of life when I needed you the most?"

He placed his hand on my face. I couldn't even look at him. I looked down at the floor. My heart was beating so fast. He started trying to position himself in an upright fashion. I leaned closer to him to help shift his pillows, but when our faces were directly in front of each other, it just seemed so natural to kiss him.

Whenever we kissed, he would play in my hair. Something about his finger moving slowly through my hair, caressing my neck, made my entire body hot. I wanted to stop him, but I couldn't. He started to gently suck my bottom lip and unbutton my shirt.

"My Miracle, stay with me tonight. I've never wanted anyone like I want you right now."

"Gerald, this is very hard for me."

"Yes, I know this is hard for you; feel this," Gerald said as he started sliding my hand down his perfectly flat stomach. I pulled my hand away just before it reached his penis.

"No, not that. I mean it is difficult for me to be with you like this again," I said as I shook my head.

"What's wrong? Is there someone else?" he asked as his smile turned into a frown.

"Are you looking at me? I'm heavier now than I was in college," I yelled.

"You didn't answer my question. Are you seeing someone right now? If you didn't want me, you wouldn't be here right now," Gerald replied.

"Oh yeah? Cocky or confident?" I started to button my shirt.

"Both! Miracle, what the hell is this about? Why are you trying to play me? If you don't care about the weight, why should I?" Gerald yelled.

"That's just it, Gerald; you seem to have amnesia. I remember you telling me plenty of times to get up and exercise and don't eat this or that."

"Seems to me your memory is a little foggy. Whose father was a PE teacher for thirty years and her mother is a doctor? You helped to train me in high school. How do you go from being captain of the cheerleading squad and a star athlete to a damn couch potato? Please explain that to me!" Gerald yelled.

"I don't have to explain anything to you. I can sit on the couch that I paid for and get as big as I want to, and I don't have to listen to you or my mother complain about it!" I jumped up and slammed the door behind me.

I could hear him calling my name. I knew he couldn't get up to stop me, so I left the house quickly, before he called one of his family members to try to stop me.

As I drove home, all I could think about was how I had probably made a bad situation worse with Gerald. I needed a drink. I wished I hadn't agreed to have this passion-group thing at my house. I was going to go home and make a strong drink. Then I needed to make sure that the house was spotless.

When I got home, the voice-mail button was blinking on my house phone. I listened to several messages; most of them were unimportant. By the time I got to the last two messages, I was so annoyed that I almost didn't listen to them.

"Hey, Miracle, I concluded my business early. If you want to get something to eat later tonight call me. I'll be up late." The sound of Trevor's voice made me weak in the knees. I was so nervous and a little intoxicated last night that I must have given him my home number instead of my cell-phone number. I had to call him immediately. I dialed Trevor's number and waited for him to answer.

"Hi, Trevor, how are you?"

"I'm good now. I called you today. Since you already labeled me a stalker, I knew not to call too many times," Trevor replied with a laugh.

"So, you're back in town? What were you doing?" I asked.

"I wished you could have gone with me last night. I am in the process of having a home built in Mascotte, Florida. I was in Tampa with my family for a short time, and then I spent most of the evening in Mascotte," replied Trevor.

"Wow, Lake County is sort of far from your businesses. I would love to see your home."

"I would love to show it to you. It's almost finished. So, what's up with tonight? I'm in the mood for Chinese food. Can I pick you up, or should I hire a private investigator in order to find out where you live?" Trevor teased.

"I'll text you my address. This is my home-phone number. I can be ready in an hour," I said happily.

"OK, I'll see you in a few," Trevor stated.

I dropped the phone on the bed and went running through the house. Then I realized that there was one more voice-mail message on the phone.

"Miracle, I love you. I'm not going to let you push me away anymore. Call me back so that we can talk this out."

The sound of Gerald's voice stopped me dead in my tracks. I hated to admit it, but I still felt a very strong connection to him. I chalked it up as puppy love. Egypt always said, "The best way to get over one dude is to get under another one." I was going to put her advice to the test.

I pulled into Miracle's driveway, got out, and rang the doorbell. As soon as she opened the door, she knew that something was wrong.

"What's wrong, Gabby?" Miracle asked.

"Vodka, cranberry juice, tall glass, now!" was all I could say.

Miracle rushed to the kitchen and made my drink. I sat at the bar and watched her. Finally, I spoke to her. "Fallon is pregnant."

"What? Oh, no," she replied.

"And so is Marlin's girlfriend, Sade," I added.

"Huh?" Miracle said.

"Yep," was all I could say.

"What is Marlin going to do?" Miracle asked.

"Girl, he has a grand plan. He and Sade are going to move into a public-housing apartment and live happily ever after," I explained.

"Oh yeah? That's their plan? Gabby, you've got to intervene. Marlin is too close to the homestretch to be sucked into mediocrity," Miracle protested.

"I know I do. But I can't say anything right now. He hasn't told me yet."

"Well how did you find out?" Miracle asked.

I looked at her and said, "Jalyssa."

Miracle burst into laughter. "My poor baby can't hold nothing, can she?"

I laughed back with her. The alcohol was kicking in, and I was now much calmer than I had been when I first showed up.

"Enough drama for today, tell me about last night, Miss Thing." I slapped Miracle's arm.

"Trevor, Trevor, Trevor," Miracle sang.

"Trevor? The same Trevor that tried the hell out of you at Subway? This dude must be Billy D. Williams if he has you singing his name in less than twenty-four hours."

"It turns out he's really sweet. He's thoughtful, kind, and very charming. I haven't felt this good about a man since—"

"Gerald," I interrupted.

"Don't remind me. I just came from his house. I just pulled in my garage about five minutes before you did. You almost didn't catch me," Miracle said.

"You went to see Gerald? Well, how is he? Was he glad to see you? How is Ms. Gloria? Talk, lady!"

"Calm down, Gabby. He's doing OK, considering the injury he's had. He acts like he still wants me, but you know I can't be too sure. Maybe it was the pains meds he's on. Things started to get a little heated, and I almost slipped up and gave him some, but I snapped back into reality when he asked me how I went from being the cheerleading captain to a couch potato," Miracle explained.

"No, the hell, he didn't say that."

"Yes, he did, girl. I mean, I can make reference to my weight all I want, but he can't. He doesn't live in this body. He doesn't know what I contend with. So before things got any worse, I hauled ass right up out of that immaculately beautiful home."

"Poor Gerald, all that money and can't even buy a clue. Oh well, I'm glad things went well with you and Trevor last night. So tell me about the dinner party. What did Madison cook?" I asked.

"Oh, we had chicken and waffles. It was really good. But, girl, oh, let me tell you; Tina soaked the fruit in liquor and served it to Madison's nosey neighbor named Charity," Miracle said, laughing.

"Charity? Holy Roller Charity?" I asked.

"Yeah, why?"

"I know, Charity. She's a good friend. I invited her to be a part of the passion group," I said.

"Damn, Gabrielle Sweeny, is there anybody in this city that you *don't* know?"

"Hey, what can I say; it's a small world."

"Now that Charity has been added to the lineup, this should be good," Miracle said.

"OK, I know you're going to think I'm crazy, but did you say Tina soaked the fruit in liquor?"

"Yeah, Tina, Madison's friend. Why? You know her too?"

"She and her cousin Trina are my top clients for buying stamps."

Miracle couldn't take any more surprises. She was laughing uncontrollably. "Stop, Gabby. Don't tell me any more."

"Seriously," I replied. "Damn, I do know everybody, huh?"

"Well, you're the best person to lead this passion group, just because you know everybody in the whole world," Miracle said.

"OK, well, will you have the place ready to entertain by tomorrow? I have Tina picking everything up and coming over to help serve. She and her cousin are like bootlegged caterers, but I don't have to pay them; I just give them a discount on stamps. They change career paths like they change underwear, but the one thing they can do better than anything is cook. They have already gotten all of the food and stored it at their house for tomorrow."

"Sounds good. I'll get some fresh flowers and make this place nice and pretty for you and your many guests," Miracle said.

"Thank you so much, Miracle. I owe you big time for this," I said, hugging her.

"No problem. Just hurry up and leave, because I have to get ready for my date tonight with Trevor," Miracle said.

"Kicking me out? That's a first. This must be serious."

"Shut up, Gabby."

"OK, I'm leaving, but if I were you, I'd have him sweep out some of those cobwebs. It's been a long time, Miracle."

"Good-bye, Gabby," Miracle said.

"Bye, have fun. Don't do anything I wouldn't do, do EVERYTHING!" I laughed and walked out the door.

Talking with Miracle always made me feel better, no matter what I was going through. I chose to table my issues until Monday morning. My primary focus was now the passion group. No one was going to stop me from being successful at this. Not Marlin, Sade, or even that dirty foot Candy, with her false accusations. My friend had found love, and all was well with the world. I chose to focus on all positives and leave all negatives for the birds.

Sha'Miracle

When Trevor showed up, I was feeling really relaxed because of the drinks I shared with Gabby. I invited him in, because truth was told, I needed a few more minutes to get my act together.

"Um, Sha'Miracle, this doesn't look like the house of a S.A.F.E. coordinator," Trevor stated as he glanced around the front of the house.

"What does the house of a S.A.F.E. coordinator look like?" I said. "Please make yourself at home."

"Do you mind if I look around?" Trevor asked.

"No, look around. I will be ready in a minute," I said as I headed down the hall.

"I'm just saying your crib is on point! Who did you hire to decorate this place? I have been talking to a couple of decorators for months now, but none of their work compares to this," Trevor stated as he moved from room to room.

I was in the process of changing my shoes for the fourth time when he made his way into my bedroom. Before I could warn him, Miley came running and barking from out of my closet.

"Miley, stop it!" I said.

"A cocker spaniel? You didn't tell me that you owned a dog. Hi, girl." Trevor bent down and started playing with the dog.

"I don't have a dog. She belongs to my parents. When I get really lonely, I go get her. I can't believe I just told you that. It sounds more pathetic than it really is." I laughed.

"I think that's pathetic and sweet," Trevor joked.

"Shut up, Trevor."

"Give me the name of the decorator."

"Sha'Miracle Morris Incorporated. I don't know if you will be able to afford her." I laughed.

"Are you serious? I know you have a lot going on right now, but I could really use some help with my place," Trevor said as he chased Miley around the room.

"Is that sarcasm? I truly am a very busy young lady."

"I don't doubt that. Between mornings at Subway, work, and dates with Miley, I can see it will be a real task to get you away from all of that." Trevor laughed as he walked up to me.

"Oh, now I remember, you're that jerk from the Subway!" I pushed Trevor's hands off my waist.

"You know we could get some Chinese takeout and kind of chill right here," Trevor said as he started to kiss my neck.

"Thank God, I was never going to make it in these heels. I know of a couple of places that have pretty good Chinese food that will deliver," I said while I kicked my shoes off.

"Good, get your iPad; I want to show you some of the furniture Bobby and my dad think I should buy."

Trevor and I talked for hours about any and everything. We ate very little and ended up watching two movies. I thanked him for enduring the latest chick flick, and in the next breath, I told him I wouldn't be able to sleep for days thanks to his love of horror. Although I didn't want him to leave, I knew I had to get up the next day and be the best hostess in town.

"What is a passion group?" Trevor questioned.

"I'm not really sure. All I know is that a group of people will show up here in a few hours to discuss ways to generate money for kids to go to college."

"Sounds really noble. Will you call me tomorrow, or I mean later today, and tell me all about it?" Trevor put his arms around me and hugged me. His hands moved slowly up and down my spine.

"I sure will. I had fun tonight, Mr. Goodman." I laughed.

"I enjoyed myself immensely." We both laughed together.

"Do not start talking all Ivy League on me." I bent over to give him what I thought was going to be a small kiss, but Trevor turned it into something that took my breath away.

As I stood there in my doorway, panting harder than Miley, I realized that at that moment, my heart, which I had kept guarded for so many years, was finally free. I had given my heart to Trevor, and now I hoped he would do the same.

Hay knew that Luke was tired. The sun had worn him out. After the game she and Lucas had taken him to IHOP for pancakes, and then Lucas left. He asked Luke if he wanted to go with him, but Luke held on to Hay for dear life.

"You know it's because you spoil him, right?" Lucas teased.

"Never that. It's because I'm the coolest parent this kid has. Ain't that right, big man?" Hay said, high-fiving Luke.

"That's right, Ma," Luke replied. "See you later, Daddy."

Hay and Luke pulled out of the parking lot. Luke was mighty quiet. Hay thought he was asleep until he spoke.

"Ma," Luke called.

"Yes, sir, big man," Hay answered.

"I want to stay at your house."

"OK, baby, that's where we're going right now."

Hay had reviewed her notes over and over again. She hit a dead end each time. All she wanted to do was find these children and get them to safety. She rode past the Corner Store on the way home and saw a guy that fit the description of Reece and wanted to stop but couldn't. She wasn't alone. There was no way she would handle a work matter with her godson in the car with her.

When they got back to the house, Hay gave Luke a bath and changed his clothes. Luke jumped into her bed, and before Hay could look twice, Luke was fast asleep. Hay took this opportunity to review each note on her laptop pertaining to Blessed once more.

The police had been on the lookout for Blessed and Fallon all night last night and all day today. The teens had no idea they were being watched. As soon as they were located, Hay would be notified. She just hoped that she could find them before the authorities did. She had made a promise to Nay-Nay, and she intended to keep it.

Blessed walked downstairs to the vending machine. They had been cooped up in the hotel room all night long. Fallon had told him not to leave, but he insisted that he didn't want any of the snacks they had in the room.

"Blessed, please don't leave," Fallon pleaded.

"Boo, I'll be right back. No one knows we're here, so it's OK," Blessed assured her.

"No, I have a bad feeling in my stomach about this," said Fallon.

"Aww, that's just the baby telling you he loves his daddy."

"No, if anything, it's *her* saying she loves her mama."

Blessed kissed Fallon on her forehead and went downstairs. Fallon thought that this would be the best time to turn her phone on and call Jalyssa. As soon as her phone was powered on, her voice-mail indicator rang. She had eighteen voice-mail messages. There was no way she would be able to listen to them all before Blessed came back, so she didn't.

She checked her text messages. Her mom had texted her fifteen times. Fallon quickly read the messages. They started out angry and, toward the end, became sorrowful and worried.

Fallon texted her mom a quick, "I'm sorry, Mom. I'm OK. I'll call when I can." Then she dialed Jalyssa's cell-phone number.

"Hello," Jalyssa whispered.

"Hey, what's up?" Fallon said.

"Don't 'hey, what's up,' me. How are you? Are you OK?"

"I'm fine; Blessed is fine, and so is the baby. We leave on Monday morning. I'm just waiting until then."

"Fallon, I'm scared for you. Why do you have to leave? You didn't do anything. Just let Blessed go." Jalyssa started to cry.

"I'm not leaving him. He wouldn't leave me. We'll be fine, Jalyssa; I promise. Don't cry. Please don't cry." Fallon started to cry.

"Fallon, convince him to turn himself in. Maybe he'll only go to jail for a little while. It's not like he killed anybody; plus you say no one was hurt, right?"

"Yeah."

"What about that police lady that came to the school? Maybe she can help," Jalyssa suggested.

Fallon had forgotten all about Officer Dawson. She was supposed to call her, but she didn't. If Fallon called Officer Dawson now, she was sure the consequences would be worse.

"I don't know, Jalyssa. I'll have to talk to Blessed. Reece made him ditch his cell phone, so I'm the only one with one. Plus if Blessed knows I called anybody, he'll freak. I just wanted to call you to say that I'm OK and I love you."

"I love you too," Jalyssa said to Fallon.

"OK, I have to go now. Tell Jade I said hello," Fallon said.

"OK, bye, Fallon," Jalyssa said.

Fallon ended the call and looked at the screen before she turned her phone back off. There was a text from her mother. The text said, "Baby, please come home. I'm not mad. I just want you back safely. I love you."

Tears filled Fallon's eyes. Her mother had never been so nice to her. It was always do this or do that. She definitely did not tell Fallon she loved her. Each time Fallon had said it to her, she would always reply with "ditto."

Fallon had to get herself together before Blessed came back up to the room. She climbed in the bed and tried to fall asleep. That way she wouldn't have to explain her tearstained eyes.

Blessed walked into the room just as Fallon was drifting off to sleep.

"Boo, I think we're being followed," Blessed announced.

"What?" a sleepy Fallon replied.

"There was a man watching me. He followed me with his eyes the entire time I was downstairs," Blessed explained.

"Blessed, you're paranoid. I told you not to go out that door anyway. You never listen to me though," Fallon lectured.

"Fallon, damn it, I'm telling you. Something is not right. We have to leave. We have to leave right now," Blessed demanded.

"Blessed, the instructions were for us to stay here until checkout time on Monday, check out like a normal couple, get in the rental car, and then drive to Atlanta. If we change things up, we may blow our cover," explained Fallon as calmly as possible.

"You're right. We might. I really need you in my life. I don't know what I would do without you," Blessed said and lay down next to her.

"You know, I was thinking," Fallon started. "The crime you committed wasn't that bad. You didn't kill anyone, and you didn't hurt anyone. Maybe you won't get as much jail time as you think you would. Maybe if you turn yourself in, you'll be in and out before the baby comes."

"Fallon, I do not want to spend one single night in jail. This is not up for discussion," Blessed responded.

"Well, it's just a suggestion. Sleep on it," Fallon said.

"Whatever, I'm too worried to sleep. What's on TV?" asked Blessed, turning on the TV.

He flipped through the channels, purposely skipping the news channels, and found a movie. He and Fallon lay in the bed like a married couple and watched the movie until they both drifted off to sleep.

Laiah went to Hay's house after she got off from work. She didn't need to tell Hay she was coming, because she had her own key to Hay's home. When Laiah entered the home, she went into the room and found both Hay and Luke fast asleep in the bed, with the television on Cartoon Network. Hay's laptop was on the bed and opened.

"Work never stops for her," Laiah said to herself as she took the laptop off the bed and sat it on the nightstand. Laiah kicked her shoes off and climbed on Luke's side of the bed. She stroked the side of his face then relaxed and fell off to sleep herself. The three of them slept for what seemed to Laiah to be an eternity. When Laiah finally opened her eyes, it was dark outside, and she was the only one in the bed.

"What did I tell you about breaking in my house, intruder?" Hay joked.

"Man, I walked in here and saw you two and got jealous," Laiah said, wiping her eyes.

"Mommy." Luke jumped on Laiah.

"Hey, my guy. How was the game?"

"It was awesome. Tell her, Ma. Didn't I show out?" Luke said to Hay.

"Yeah, you showed out all right. He went to sleep on the sideline during the fourth quarter," Hay said.

"Oh, no." Laiah laughed.

"But not before scoring a touchdown for the opponent," Hay added.

"Really?" Laiah gasped. "Well, did you have fun, Luke?"

"I sure did, Mommy," Luke said proudly.

"Well that's all that matters. You my little superstar," Laiah said to Luke.

Luke smiled and hugged his mother.

"What's for dinner?" Laiah asked Hay.

"Um, don't you have a husband to go home to?" Hay answered.

"Don't remind me. I'm too comfortable here," Laiah moaned.

"Get up, hot stuff. Let's get something to eat, so you can go home to your mate," Hay said.

"Speaking of mates, what's going on with Egypt?" Laiah asked.

"I saw her at the football game and tried to make peace with her. She didn't want to hear it. So what was I supposed to do? I left her alone," Hay said.

"Good for you," Laiah replied.

"It's only been a day, and I already miss her though. I hate the way I love that girl."

"I hate the way she treats you. But you already know my take on Ms. Egypt though."

"Yeah, I know," Hay said.

"So tell me about this passion group Ms. Hallelujah Anyhow got you being a part of," Laiah said, changing the subject.

"Well, she said it's going to be something about starting a scholarship fund. That sounds pretty exciting. Maybe I can get some of the guys from the job to be mentors to the kids before they get into trouble. When they're in trouble is when we usually get them, and by then it's too late," Hay explained.

"Who are the people involved?" asked Laiah.

"I'm not sure. Supposedly Charity was invited by one of her students' mother, and everyone was supposed to invite someone, so she chose me."

"Well don't let the Virgin Mary work your nerves too bad. Is she really the same way she was when we were little?"

"Yeah, if not worse. You know her and Brother Sam got divorced some years ago," Hay said.

"I remember that. I heard he had moved out of the state, married another lady, and started traveling all over the world. Charity messed up a good thing," Laiah said.

"I thought so too, but she was already crazy when he met her. I think he thought that she would change, and when she didn't, he had to quit. But people need to realize that you can't change people. What you see is what you get. Crazy, holy, deceiving, or whatever it is, people are who they are," expressed Hay.

"Yeah, you're right about that. How you find them is how they'll be. So how was Lucas looking at the game?" Laiah said, blushing.

"Muffin!" Hay said. "I know you not over here blushing over ole big-head Lucas. Let me call your husband."

"Ha, ha, very funny. I'm not blushing. I'm just saying you know Lucas is always dressed to the tee."

"Yeah, man, once he started dealing, he was Mr. *GQ*. You couldn't tell him nothing." Hay laughed.

"That was a tough time for me. I just knew Lucas and I were going to end up married, but once he got high that one time and flipped out on me, I knew I had to leave," Laiah said quietly.

"Hey, look how far he's come though. He got himself together, stopped using and dealing, and has been walking the straight and narrow for over five years now."

"Yeah, I'm proud of Lucas. I just hope one day he finds love again. He was such a good mate. I could just imagine how great he is now that he's clean and grown up."

"He's all right. I still keep my eyes on him though," Hay said.

"You keep your eyes on everybody," Laiah said while rolling her eyes.

"That's right. I can't be too sure," Hay said.

Laiah's phone rang. She looked at it and said, "It's my husband." She answered, "Hello, husband."

"Hey, love, where are you?"

"Picking up Luke. Pooh is talking my ear off; that's why I haven't left yet," Laiah teased.

"Tell your husband you came and went to sleep like you live here," Hay yelled in the background.

Laiah pushed Hay away from her and held her finger up to her mouth while grinning. "I'm leaving right now. I'll be there in about thirty minutes. OK, bye."

Laiah ended the call and yelled for Luke to gather his things.

"Pooh, you're so silly. My husband says he wants to take Luke and me out to dinner tonight," Laiah said.

"You'd better not let Luke choose the restaurant or else you know where you'll end up," Hay joked.

"IHOP." Laiah laughed. "Leave my baby alone."

Luke came to the front, where, by this time, Hay and Laiah had made their way to, and jumped into Hay's arms.

"Oh, I love you, love you, love you," Hay said while squeezing Luke.

"Ah, boooo! Get a room," Laiah joked.

"See you guys later," Hay said.

"OK, thanks for keeping him, and tell me how the passion group turns out."

"Never a problem, and I will."

"Don't call Egypt. Good night," Laiah said and hurried out the door before Hay could reply.

Hay watched them get into the car and back out of the driveway. She closed the door and went back to her laptop. Egypt was heavy on Hay's mind, but she was going to take her best friend's advice and give Egypt a little space.

After the football game, Avery and I took the kids home to wash up, and then we went out for pizza and bowling. We were a competitive group. A. J. and I agreed to destroy Avery and Mikayla in bowling. Of course, we lost, but it was still a lot of fun.

The kids got money from Avery and headed into the arcade. As I watched Avery walk back to the table with two beers, I couldn't help but smile knowing that he was all mine.

"Hey, I think there is finally an empty pool table. Are you up for another beating?" Avery taunted.

"Avery, please! A. J. is tired from the football game, and I just got my nails nicely French manicured," I said.

"Oh, right! Sounds like excuses to me. This is what the agony of defeat looks like," Avery criticized as he pointed at me.

"After last night and now bowling today, my body is very sore," I alleged.

"How about we skip pool and I take you home and give you a nice, long massage," Avery said as he started to rub my legs.

"Are you gonna take your time? I need it from my head all the way down to my French-manicured toes," I whispered.

"We got all night. I got you." Avery kissed my wedding band.

"Go get the kids; let's go!" I yelled and jumped out of my seat.

"Are you going to take the people's bowling shoes off first, Maddie?" Avery laughed.

"Oh yeah, boy, I can't think when you start talking about rubbing on me," I joked.

When we got home, we sat with the kids and talked about what was going on in their worlds. A. J. was excited about getting ready for the play-offs. Mikayla was still whining about getting a new cell phone, which fell on deaf ears.

Once the kids were in their rooms, Avery and I ran to get into our Jacuzzi. We agreed that we were in need of a vacation. I suggested a couples' retreat. We had been planning to go to Hawaii for the longest time.

"That could be just what Gerald and Miracle need in order to get their relationship back on track," Avery said.

"I don't think Miracle will be vacationing with Gerald anymore."

"What do you mean? Gerald could rehab anywhere in the country, matter of fact, anywhere in the world. He is doing it in Orlando so that he can be close to Miracle."

"Avery, didn't you see the way Trevor and Miracle were looking at each over dinner last night? They left our house and went out for drinks."

"I don't care about that. Gerald made a mistake. Maybe he got cold feet or something. He was under a lot of pressure, trying to go in the first round of the NFL draft."

"Maybe he was so consumed by football that he neglected his fiancée, who, during that time, put on twenty-five pounds. Miracle called the wedding off; it's wasn't Gerald," I said sadly.

"What? I don't understand," Avery said as he shook his head.

"I think Miracle wants to give this thing with Trevor an old college try."

"Trevor, the stranger? I've been to their house a couple of times. Trevor is never there. Bobby insinuated that Trevor had women from Florida all the way up the East Coast."

"Trevor still lives at home?" I asked.

"Bobby and Trevor both live at home with their father. Their mother died from a heart attack about six years ago. Their father took it really hard, so they both moved back into the house to kind of keep an eye on him."

"Wow, Miracle said that they are wealthy."

"Yeah, Mr. Goodman got plenty of bread. He drives a brand-new Aston Martin."

"I'm going to Miracle's house tomorrow for a passion group. I am going to find out just how much she knows about Trevor. If he's just looking for a quick lay, he needs to head back up the East Coast," I replied.

"What the hell is a passion group? You just told me you wanted to do less," Avery questioned.

"This is different. This group is going to help kids pay for college. What is so crazy about the dynamics of the group is that some of the women involved, to my understanding, are Wise University alumni." I laughed.

"Wait a minute; y'all got a group of alumni women from Legacy University and Wise University working together? Nothing is going to get done," Avery commented.

"We're going to have to learn to put our rivalry down for a greater purpose, which is to generate funds to help kids pay for tuition at Legacy U—I meant to say college." I laughed.

"See, that's what I'm talking about right there. OK, good luck, passion group. Let me know what you need me to do," Avery said as he kissed my forehead.

"I love you, Avery Clark."

"I know. Does your ex know that? Every time I see Gavin, I swear, he makes it a point to show off that got-damn tattoo. I want to take him out his misery!" Avery said angrily.

"He has a stupid tattoo; you have my heart, and you always will." I kissed Avery so passionately on the lips.

"The kids should be asleep by now. Mrs. Clark, are you ready for the best massage you have ever had in your life?"

"Yes, Daddy, bring it on.

The Passion Group

The day had finally come. Gabby was more excited than a child at Chuck E Cheese's. This morning, the kids were on their own with breakfast and lunch. Reece was also on his own with his two little boys. Gabby had made the choice that today she would enjoy herself from sunup to sundown.

Just in case Reece needed to go anywhere, she decided that she would get him to drop her off at Miracle's house. She knew if she got to Miracle she would have no problem getting back home.

Gabby shook Reece and woke him up.

"Hey," she said.

"What time is it?" he replied, rubbing his forehead.

"Almost eight o'clock."

"Why are you up so early? And fully dressed? Where have you been all night?"

"Really, Reece? That's you who got all the time in the world to spread yourself to every broad in Orlando. I've been right here.

"Gabby, please don't start, at least not without some love first."

Reece was such a smooth talker. He could talk his way out of almost anything. He was also very charming. Every time there was about to be any little hint of an argument, he somehow managed to change the subject. Most times it was something sweet.

He walked over to Gabby and hugged her tightly. Then he kissed her on her forehead and said, "Seriously, where are you going so early?"

"The meeting for the passion group is today, remember?"

"Oh yeah, that's right. My baby trying to make this money."

Disregarding his comment, Gabby said, "I don't know how long I'll be gone, so I need you to drop me off to Miracle's house."

"OK, when?"

"Uh, now," Gabby said sarcastically.

"OK, let me use the bathroom and brush my teeth."

Gabby drove to Miracle's house while Reece slept in the car. Once they arrived, she got out and started to walk away.

"Hey," Reece called.

"Yeah?" Gabby replied.

"What's wrong with you? You know I need my love."

"Oh, I'm sorry. I'm in a zone." She walked over to Reece, hugged him, and kissed him on the cheek.

"Yeah, you so ready to make this money you forgot to love up on your man."

"Reece, please. This is so much bigger than making money. The money we make goes to students for college. I don't get anything."

"So why do it if it doesn't potentially fatten your pockets?"

"I'm doing it so that children these days know that there's more to life than familiarity, more than mediocrity."

"Alright with your big words. Don't talk to me like I'm dumb. Excuse me, im…com…po…tent," Reece said, frowning.

"It's *in*competent. And that's exactly what I'm talking about. Just like with Blessed and Fallon. He made a fucked-up decision, but what you did made it worse. That boy could deal with his consequences, learn from them, and do better within a year or two. But now, thanks to you, he's a sixteen-year-old fugitive."

Reece had gotten mad and sad at the same time. He felt silly for trying to sound all smart. He felt even worse because his woman had corrected him. Then she insulted him for taking care of his nephew's problems. Reece wasn't about to let her degrade him any more than she had done already.

"Look, Miss Ivy League. I know more about the streets than your frontin' ass will ever know. Blessed is going to be just fine, because I handle mine. Fuck you and your dumb-ass group. That's why you ain't gonna make no money." Reece had gotten the last word, and that was all he wanted. He drove off as quickly as he could.

Gabby sighed a hard sigh then laughed. Reece was stuck in his circumstance, and that's where he was comfortable. Gabby was not trying to change Reece; she was trying to stop new Reeces from forming.

Miracle came out of her door and looked at Gabby. "Hey, what was all that noise?" Miracle asked.

"Oh nothing, just Reece fussing because I'm better than him," Gabby said while walking inside the house.

Miracle shook her head and laughed. She had learned over the years to keep her opinions about Reece to herself, because all Gabby would do was defend him, tolerate him, and go home to him. Miracle chose to keep her breath in her lungs instead of wasting it talking about Reece.

"Reece said 'fuck you' to me." Gabby laughed.

Miracle looked confused. "Why is that funny?"

"It's not, but who cares. I don't like when we fight, so I'm going to smooth this over before it festers." Gabby started texting on her cell phone. She sent the message and laughed some more.

"Gabby, what did you do?" Miracle asked cautiously.

Gabby showed Miracle the text. It read, "Fuck me, huh? You can. You can fuck me all night long when I get home."

Miracle's eyes grew wide. Before she could respond, Gabby's text alert rang. Reece had replied.

"Read it," Gabby said.

Miracle didn't want to. "What if he's upset? I don't want to be in your business."

"Trust me. He's not upset. After six years, I know this man like the back of my hand. Read it."

Miracle's jaw dropped. She handed Gabby the phone and said, "You're right. He's not mad. But, um, I'm done."

Gabby grabbed the phone and read the message. She laughed giddily and put the phone down on the counter. She picked the phone up and read the text from Reece again. It read, "I can't wait that long; go in the bathroom, and make it squirt right now, and send me the video."

"Gabby, come on," Miracle yelled.

Gabby followed Miracle into her room and plopped down on her bed. Miley ran from around the corner and jumped on the bed too.

"Hey, girl," Gabby said, rubbing Miley's fur.

"Miley, no! Get down," Miracle scolded.

Miley jumped off of the bed and sat on the floor. Gabby continued to pet her as she helped Miracle pick out an outfit for the brunch. After saying yes or no to what must have been a thousand outfits, Miracle decided to wear an LU T-shirt and a pair of jean capris. Gabby had on a WU T-shirt and a pair of boot-cut jeans.

The two women went out to the patio and began to set up for the meeting. Gabby's cell phone rang. It was Trina.

"Hello."

"Where the hell have you been?" Trina yelled. "I know your hot, little daughter told you the stamps on the card were short. Do you have any idea how stupid I looked standing there with a cart full of bags and had to leave it all there?"

"Oh yeah, she told me, but something isn't right. I know for sure I left a hundred dollars on there for you."

"No, ma'am," Trina said. "Wait, hold on, Gabby."

Gabby held on for a second; then Trina came back to the phone. "Gabby? My bad. That was Tina on the phone. Apparently she used the card for some last-minute shopping for a dinner party her boss had last night. We're straight, but I cussed her out."

"OK, so what time will you two be here?"

"We'll be on our way in a minute."

"Perfect. See you in a few," Gabby said.

Gabby turned to Miracle and stared into space.

"What's wrong?" Miracle asked.

"Trina said Tina used stamps last night for a last-minute dinner party that her boss had. You said Tina was at Madison's last night. Does Tina work for Madison? This doesn't make sense to me."

Miracle did not respond. She was not the type to tell anyone's business. She would take everyone's secrets to her grave.

The doorbell rang, saving Miracle from having to make up an excuse to give to Gabby.

"Gabby, get the door for me," Miracle yelled.

Gabby opened the door to find two florist trucks. A very handsome man handed her a clipboard with a paper requesting a signature. Gabby gladly signed the paper and wondered what Miracle was up to. To her amazement, she watched the delivery guys come into the house with eighty-three dozens of red roses.

"Um, Miracle, I think you need to see this!" Gabby screamed.

"Oh my God, Gabby, look at all these beautiful roses. Who sent them?" Miracle questioned as she searched for a card. When she read the card, it simply said, "Forever my Miracle."

Miracle's eyes filled with tears. This was one of the sweetest things that had happened to her in a long while. Gerald was her first love, and he didn't have the key to her heart — he owned it. Even years after the engagement was broken, he still had her heart. So many feelings that she thought she had successfully gotten over came rushing back to her like a tidal wave.

Gabby was busy trying to figure out where to put the roses, and Miracle was in a trance that she could not shake. Neither one of them had seen Egypt walk in as the delivery guys were finishing up.

"What the heck is all this?" Egypt yelled.

"Apparently she just received eighty-three dozen roses," Gabby answered.

"Eighty-three? Like Gerald's number? Are you kidding me?" Egypt exclaimed, dropping her Prada bag onto the floor.

Miracle wiped her face and gathered her thoughts. "Hey, Egypt, I didn't see you come in. I'm glad you're here though. You two help me put these things away, so the rest of the people can't see them. I don't want to have to answer any questions.

Together the three of them started picking up the vases. Egypt suggested they put as many as they could into the guest room. Gabby thought they should leave a couple out for decoration.

"Well, at least I don't have to run out and get fresh flowers now," chuckled Miracle nervously.

The three ladies had somehow managed to get seventy dozens of roses into Miracle's guest room. They used one as a centerpiece for the round table where they would dine, six in the formal living room, and the last six in the family room.

Tina and Trina arrived next. Egypt asked if they needed help with anything, but they insisted they had it all under control. The two of them brought everything inside the house and began cooking and setting up. They worked so diligently and so quickly that Miracle understood why Madison had hired Tina.

Madison was the next person to arrive. When she came inside, she found Miracle, Gabby, and Egypt sitting in the family room, sipping Moscato d'Asti.

"Hello, everyone, I see the party has started without me. What's with all the flowers?" Madison remarked.

"Looks like Gerald wants Miracle's attention. This must have cost a fortune," Egypt replied.

"Looks like he wants more than that. Miracle, is there anything you need me to do?" Madison questioned.

Miracle just shook her head. The doorbell rang again, and this time Miracle got up to answer the door. Her parents were at the door. She put on her best "I'm happy" smile only for her mother to ask, "What's wrong, Sha'Miracle?" She explained to her parents that she was simply tired and that she was in the process of having a meeting with a few passionate individuals.

"Something smells great. The flowers are beautiful, honey, but why did you purchase so many?" Scott Morris questioned.

"They're from Gerald." the ladies sang collectively.

"Sha'Miracle, I wish to speak with you at once!" Dr. Morris exclaimed.

Miracle already knew where this was headed, and she was not about to sit through a lecture from her mother about how much she and Gerald belonged together. Let's face it; Mother didn't always know best.

"Mother, I need to finish setting up for the meeting. Miley has already been fed and walked. I'll try to call you later," Miracle said as she turned around and walked off.

"Scott, are you just going to stand there and allow her to be disrespectful? It is because of you allowing her to so-called 'speak her mind' that she has become this impolite little —" Dr. Morris said while pointing her finger at him.

"Little what?" Scott Morris interrupted. "She has become a little thirty-year-old, self-sufficient woman. Elaine, you're blowing this way out of proportion. Let's just get the dog and go. Miracle is too busy to talk right now," Scott Morris said miserably.

"You get the damn dog, and if she doesn't want to come home with us, I'm sure you can make up a perfectly good excuse for that too! Excuses, that your specialty." Dr. Morris turned and stormed out of the house.

Once Mr. Morris was walking out of the house, with Miley happily walking beside him, Miracle reemerged from the back of the house. All the ladies stood up and hugged her and assured her that everything would be OK.

Within the next thirty minutes, Charity Love and Hazel-Ann Dawson walked through the door. Miracle decided that the ladies would partake in some hors d'oeuvres before talking business.

Charity insisted on blessing the food. "Father, in the name of Jesus, we come to you as humble as we know how. We thank you for everyone in the midst today. Now we ask that you bless this food. Lord, please bless the hands that prepared it. Lord, I repeat, please bless the hands that prepared it. Take out all hurt, harm, and danger, and let it nourish our bodies. I rebuke any poison right now. Let there be love and fellowship included with this meal. These and all other blessings we pray in the name of the Father, the Son, and the Holy Spirit. 'The Lord is my shepherd, I shall not want,' amen."

Tina and Trina had put out a mouth-watering starter spread, complete with shrimp nachos, spicy Buffalo-chicken bites, pasta salad, a fruit tray, and a vegetable tray.

"Charity, please help yourself to the food. I really appreciate you blessing us with those kind words," Miracle stated.

"After the other day, I figured I should eat food that I have prepared myself," Charity said as she frowned at Madison.

"I assume you are directing that comment at me. Shame the devil, and tell the truth. What did you plan to gain by meddling in my personal family affairs? You hoped Avery would come home early and catch me doing what? You don't have a man, so I guess you don't want me to have one either!" Madison yelled.

"Wait a minute, Madison; let's not talk your family business at this time," Gabby said as she tried to calm things down.

"Shut up, Gabby! You are the last person to talk about family business. You don't even know what real family is!" Egypt yelled.

"I'm so sick of your ass. Why do you always have something to say to me?" Gabby questioned Egypt.

"Somebody needs to say something to your trifling ass. I can't begin to tell you the numerous times that I have consoled Jade because you weren't around to do it," Egypt yelled.

"Console Jade? The family drama queen? Oh please." Gabby laughed.

"She may very well be a drama queen, but did you know she was also a cutter?" Egypt retorted.

"Egypt, I find it hard to believe that someone as heartless and selfish as you could console anyone!" yelled Hay.

"Don't start with me, Hay. I have no words for you!" Egypt shouted.

"Am I missing something?" Miracle asked, looking confused. "You two know each other?"

"Know each other? We're a couple!" Hay snapped.

"Like hell we are. After the way you dismissed me just days ago, you're a fool to think we're still together," Egypt barked.

"Hmph, but you're so worried about me. Worry about your damn self," Gabby said.

"Bitch, I will fuck your ass up royally if you say one more thing to me," Egypt threatened.

"Oh, I'm extra scared now. Make a move, ho," Gabby said.

"In the name of JESUS, this is too much," Charity said, gathering her things.

"Charity, please. Cut the holy act. That's what cost you your husband. Being too over the top when it's not needed," Hay said.

Charity grimaced, and Miracle spoke up. "Everybody, calm down. Egypt, you are way out of line."

"I'm way out of line? What about your sorry-ass excuse for a mother of a friend, Gabby? No, fuck that; what about you?"

"Me?" Miracle asked in surprise.

"Yeah, you. With so many people out here wanting a decent man, your silly ass has one.

"Two," Madison chimed in.

"Two?" Egypt said. "That makes it even worse. Gerald is doing all the right things and has been for years, and you still blow him off like he's nothing. And who is this other man?

"She just met this guy by the name of—"

"Madison, please shut up!" Miracle interrupted.

"My lips are sealed," Madison said, zipping her lips.

"What makes Gerald a good man? Because he's wealthy and can buy me a houseful of flowers? I guess you think a good man is a man that buys you gifts.

I can buy my own flowers. I need a man that will put Christ first and me second. I need a man that will stop whatever he is doing and come see me, simply because he wants to—not because I asked. All Gerald ever cared about was himself and football. He made a mistake thinking I would play the back to his ego and football! I ended our engagement because I thought that I could never compete with his career. There, I said it," Miracle said as she walked toward Egypt.

"I don't know why you are wasting your time talking to her. It is so obvious that all Egypt is about is a dollar." Gabby scowled.

"Wait a minute! We are going to have to work out our differences before we can even consider trying to come together to do anything. The reason that you showed up to this place at this time is because you want to be a part of something that is bigger than you and me. I suggest we stop yelling, assuming, and accusing each other of things and converse with one another like intelligent women that society can be proud of!" Miracle stated with such passion that she became teary eyed.

Everyone sat quietly. No one said a thing. Gabby's phone rang, breaking the silence.

"Hello, no, why?" Gabby dropped the phone and froze in place.

"What? What is it, Gabby?" Madison yelled.

Miracle picked up the phone. "Hello, who is this?"

"It's Jalyssa; Fallon is dead!"

"Oh, baby, no. Are you sure?" Miracle asked.

"It's on the news right now," Jalyssa replied.

"Who's at home with you?" Miracle said, turning on her television.

"Everybody," Jalyssa answered.

"You find Jade and sit with her until your mom gets home."

"OK." Jalyssa sniffed.

Miracle placed Gabby's phone in her hand. By now the ladies had sat Gabby down. The story was on every local news station. The headline read, "Two teen fugitives killed in high-speed chase."

Everyone watched the news report in silence. When the story repeated, they watched it again. The phone rang.

Miracle got up off the sofa and walked toward the house phone in slow motion.

"Hello." Miracle sobbed.

"Sha'Miracle, baby, are you watching the news? They found the kids, but there has been a terrible fatal accident," Aunt Pearl stated sadly.

"I know, Auntie. I am just sick over this entire thing." Miracle continued to cry.

"I'm so sorry, sweetheart. Let me know if there is anything I can do to help the families. I'll talk at you later." Auntie Pearl ended the call.

Tina walked in and saw everyone sitting. "Dang, who died?" she joked.

"Jalyssa's best friend and her boyfriend," Gabby answered.

Tina gasped. "I'm so sorry; is there anything I can do?"

"No, we'll be OK. We just need a few minutes. You can start preparing the main course if you'd like," Madison said.

Tina scanned each face before she left the room; everyone was crying.

"Everybody, stand up," Charity instructed. The women all stood up.

"Join hands, close your eyes, and set your mind to God." The women did as they were told.

Charity began to pray. "Father God, Father God, we need you right now, Lord. We're asking for strength in this time of sorrow. God, bless the families of Fallon and Blessed. Comfort their hearts as their loved ones have departed from Earth. Lord, bless everyone in this room, for we are all affected by this tragedy. Comfort us, Lord. Strengthen us, Lord, for we know that you are all too wise to make a mistake. God, we know that you won't put more on us than we can bear. Bless Sha'Miracle, Egypt, Gabby, Hay, Madison, Tina, and Trina. Forgive us all for the things we have said and done to offend each other and cover us all in your love. These blessings we ask in your son Jesus's name, amen."

"Amen," everyone said as they all sat down.

"Fallon has been a part of my family for years," said Gabby.

"Blessed was one of my favorite group members. A little rugged but so sweet inside," Egypt said.

"Blessed has gone through so much in his young life. He was finally trying to turn things around for good," Miracle added.

"Fallon was the smartest, most polite child I've ever known." Charity sniffed. "She had a choice between Legacy and Wise. They both wanted her, and she's only a junior. That girl had the voice of an angel."

"I promised Blessed's grandmother no jail time. I promised her," Hay said, tears rolling down her face. "I just met Fallon a few days ago and fell in love with her. She was pregnant."

"That explains why Blessed needed money so bad. Maybe he was trying to pay for an abortion," Miracle assumed out loud.

"That's not it. Fallon was going to have her baby, graduate, and beat the odds. She said so herself. She was always so adamant about not becoming a statistic. She always said, 'Fallon Jenkins is nobody's statistic,'" Charity said, snapping her fingers, imitating Fallon. Charity chuckled and then burst into tears.

"Ladies, our purpose is greater than our problems. Here we are having petty arguments, and these two children are dead." Miracle said. "We have put 'self' aside so that we can indulge in our passion, which is children's education."

"I can't cook," Madison blurted out.

Ten eyes shifted to Madison and did not leave hers.

"I hired Tina to help me with the housework, because I'm so busy with the cleaners, and when I found out that she cooked, she agreed to prepare my meals for me."

"Your husband is gonna kill you," Egypt said, giggling.

"He already knows. I had to come clean when he thought Tina and I were sleeping together," responded Madison.

"Sleeping together?" Charity asked.

"Yes, sleeping together. When you called him to come home early, he walked in and thought we were having an affair," Madison explained.

"But Tina told me she was his sister. I only called Avery because he told me he didn't have a sister, and I wanted to prove to him that I wasn't lying. I'm so sorry. I never meant to cause harm," Charity told Madison.

"It's OK. My marriage is solid. It has to be. I have no one else, just Avery. When my family finally realized that I wasn't leaving him, they stopped speaking to me. They completely cut me off — which is what I was thinking about when you came over, Tina."

"So that's why you looked so sad when I walked in that day," Tina said, walking over to hug Madison. Then Tina went back into the kitchen

"Gabby, I used to like you," Egypt began. "But when I started volunteering at Kennedy, I got to know Mark and Jade. Jade loves you so much. She wants to be like you when she grows up. But she says that all you care about is Reece and his boys. When Reece is not around, you're the best mom in the world; when he is around, Jade feels invisible. She cuts herself to release the pain she feels from being ignored. And Mark, he sticks closely with you, because he wants time. He doesn't care that he shares it with Reece or the boys; he just wants to be in your presence. I wish I had a child to love and have love me back, and you have four that scream for your love and attention, but your boyfriend gets it all. Gabby, you just have to pay attention to your children."

By now Gabby couldn't stop the tears from racing down her face. "No wonder she only wants to wear long-sleeved tops and pants, never shorts or tank tops. I just thought she was being dramatic as usual."

Gabby had to get it together. How could she help children all over the world if she couldn't even help her own? "Thank you, Egypt."

"You're welcome. I apologize for being such a bitch to you," Egypt said.

"And I as well," Gabby replied.

"Egypt, I love you," Hay said. "I really do. But I don't think we're going to work. You're very selfish and so self-absorbed. You don't have any patience, and if things don't go your way exactly when you say, you flip out. Just like Friday when I was working. But don't worry; we can always be friends."

Egypt couldn't believe what she was hearing. She had Hay right where she wanted her, but now Hay was breaking up with her. This wasn't how it was supposed to go. She couldn't deal with Hay in front of everyone; she would do this privately — later. "I can't say that I like what you're saying, but I do respect it."

"Well, I think I met a decent man," Charity announced.

"Say what now, missionary?" Hay teased.

"Yes. After Tina poisoned me the other night, Lucas took really good care of me. Then we went out last night and had a ball," said Charity.

"Aww," said Miracle.

Tina ran from the kitchen. "Lucas? Did you say Lucas, Charity?"

"Yes, he's such a nice man."

"You need to leave him alone while you still have time," Tina said.

"Why?" asked Charity.

"He's the one who got me into drugs. He's a drug dealer. He claimed he's a changed man, but you can never be too sure," Tina assured her.

"We talked about that last night. He told me all about his past, good, bad, and super ugly. He also told me that he was finished with that part of his life, and I believe him. He also has a son. I'd love to meet him. And guess what else? He even went to church with me this morning," Charity said, smiling.

"A man that actually communicates? That's a first," said Egypt.

"OK, but don't say I didn't warn you," Tina said.

"No, Tina, Lucas is telling the truth. He has been on the straight and narrow for some years now. That son Charity is talking about is my godson, Luke. I've known Lucas for years. I'm glad he found a good woman," Hay said.

"OK, let's get down to business," Gabby interjected. "As you all know, we are here to start a scholarship fund for local students. There are eight steps to starting a fund. The first thing we need to do is write a grant or, depending on the amount we wish to put into the funds for distribution, grants. Once we write the grants and generate revenue, we can implement the rest of the steps. We could also benefit from having sponsors. I have everything presented here for you to review."

Gabby passed out folders with information on writing a grant and the steps for starting a scholarship fund. "In light of today's events, I think it's best if we conclude this meeting and meet again at a later date. This will give you all time to review the information and come to the table with ideas."

Gabby waited a few minutes and let the ladies skim the information before she spoke again. "Are there any questions?"

No one had any questions. Miracle spoke, "Well, if that's all for today, we can meet here in one week. Same time."

Charity asked them all to join hands once more and prayed a departing prayer. Sha'Miracle bid her guests good-bye as they left.

Blessed are they that mourn, for they shall be comforted. (Matthew 5:4)

When Hay got into her car and turned on her work phone, she had twelve messages.

"Officer Dawson, this is Sergeant Adams; we need you in the office ASAP."

"Hay, it's Thomas. Did you see the news? It's bad. Call me on my personal cell."

"They killed my boy! They killed my boy! You were supposed to protect him. You gave me your word."

That message was from Nay-Nay. She was screaming hysterically. Hay's emotions were scattered. She felt bad for letting Nay-Nay down. She felt sad for Fallon's and Blessed's families. She felt anxious because she wanted to get the whole story but knew that she couldn't.

Hay continued to listen to messages as she drove home to change into her uniform.

"Officer Dawson, this is Fallon Jenkins. I'm so sorry I didn't call you earlier. Blessed and I are at the Williams Inn on Spring Street. I was just calling to say thank you for being a listening ear and..."

The voice on the other end trailed off. Hay continued to listen. The words sounded muffled at first but then cleared up.

"Boo, we gotta go." That must have been Blessed's voice.

"Why, boo? What's wrong?" said Fallon.

"I swear we're being followed. Fallon, get up; let's go!"

"What about what Reece said?"

"Man, fuck what Reece said. Didn't you hear me? There's muthafuckers clocking our every move. Let's go!"

Hay listened as Fallon scuffled around to gather their things. She must have put the phone in her pocket, because there was lots of movement.

"Where are we going, Blessed?"

"I-4 East to I-95 North, straight up to Georgia. We should be in Atlanta in a few hours."

"What about gas?" asked Fallon.

"We already have a tank full, because we haven't been anywhere but the hotel since Friday. We can fill up later. You just stay calm, relax, and take care of my son. This will all be over soon. I love you, Fallon Jenkins."

"I love you too, Blessed Douglas."

"Boo, Google the location of a 7-Eleven in Atlanta, and then turn on navigation to get there," Blessed instructed.

Fallon removed the phone from her pocket. She must have noticed that she was still connected to Hay.

"Oh shit," Fallon said.

"What?" asked Blessed.

Click, the message was over. Hay saved the message and replayed it three times.

When she got home, Hay ran inside her house, changed her clothes, and sped to the office. The office was filled with people. The sergeant met with Hay, as well as the police involved in the chase.

Sergeant Adams reviewed the details of the events. Hay wrote as the sergeant talked.

"Ever since we left the home of the suspect, we had our officers check hotels for the names of Blessed Douglas, Fallon Jenkins, and Reece Riley. Those were the names you gave us after speaking with the grandmother. However, nothing came up with those names. Our next step was to search all of the small hotels and ask if anyone was there that fit the description of the suspect and his girlfriend.

"There was a positive match at the Williams Inn on Spring Street. We had a few undercover officers in unmarked cars go over and keep watch. They were told not to make any moves until I contacted you. However, in the middle of trying to contact you, the suspects packed the car in a hurry and sped off. Dispatch was alerted that the suspects were on the move. My officers caught up to them and had no choice but to flash their lights to pull them over," Sergeant Adams explained.

"I understand," Hay said as she wrote notes.

"The suspect refused to pull over and instead increased speed and entered the I-4 East on-ramp." Adams continued to explain. "By this time, there were three squad cars following speedily behind. Once on I-4, two of the cars got on each side of the suspect's automobile."

"So they were surrounded?" Hay asked.

"Correct. With nowhere to go, they just kept driving. Somehow the suspect must have lost control of the vehicle, because when he tried to speed up and pass a car in front of him, he swerved to the left side and skinned the rail. He swerved back to the right and then the left again. This time, instead of scraping against the rail, he slammed into it and flipped the car over it and into westbound traffic.

The car went about twenty-five to thirty feet in the air and came down hard. Cars on the other side were thinking fast, because they were all able to avoid accidents themselves and slow down to safe speeds. There was glass everywhere. The paramedics arrived within minutes of being dispatched, due to the live coverage. However, both parties were dead on the scene," explained Sergeant Adams.

Hay wrote and wrote. She didn't look up, because she didn't want her sergeant to see the emotional distress on her face. She was really good about not getting too emotionally attached to her clients, but this case was different. Hay didn't know why this one was different, but it was.

Looking down at her note pad, Hay said, "Were they wearing seat belts?"

"The driver was not; the passenger, however, was. The driver was ejected from the vehicle and landed on a bed of glass. We'll have to wait for the autopsy report, but I'm pretty sure he bled out," Adams said.

"And the girl?" Hay asked.

"Again, her cause of death right now is unknown. We will have to wait on the report from the medical examiner."

"Have the families been notified?" inquired Hay.

"Yes, we contacted Nancy Douglas and Farrah Jenkins," Adams told Hay.

"OK, I think I have everything I need. I'll finish this up and officially close this case," Hay said.

"Very well," Adams replied. As Sergeant Adams began to walk away, Hay stopped him. "Sergeant Adams, I have one question."

"Shoot."

"What do you think he would have gotten had he turned himself in?" asked Hay.

"Probably just probation."

"Really?"

"Sure. No one was hurt, and the bus was safe and sound. Hell, he probably could've gotten hired down at the Saint Bernard bus station when he got his license and turned eighteen," Adams said.

"Thanks, Sarge," Hay said.

Hay felt so bad. She needed to get to Nay-Nay to express her condolences.

Gabby

I hugged everybody and gathered my things. Egypt and I made a lunch date for some time next week. Although her words had cut my heart to the core, I had to admit she had a point. I needed to make some changes. I didn't want my children to resent me when they became adults. I just prayed the damage I had already done wasn't irreparable.

Madison volunteered to give me a ride home. I didn't want to call Reece, because I somewhat blamed him for what had happened to Blessed and Fallon. Charity was going over to Farrah's right now. I would go after I checked on Jalyssa and Jade.

"Gabby, is there anything you need me to do?" asked Madison.

"No, this ride is more than enough. I really appreciate you, Madison," I replied.

"OK, well, if you need me, please don't hesitate to call," Madison said, pulling into my driveway.

"I won't. Thanks so much, Maddie," I said and leaned over to hug Madison.

I walked into the house and marched directly to the girls' room. I found Jalyssa and Jade curled up together, fast asleep. I knelt down on the floor beside them and kissed each one of them. Jade opened her eyes.

"I couldn't get her to stop crying, Mama. She cried until she fell asleep," Jade said.

"Shh…" I said. "You did good, baby girl. You did real good."

Jade smiled at me and pulled her sister closer to her.

"Jade," I said.

"Yes, Mama?"

"I'm sorry."

"For what?"

"For everything. I've been such a fool when it comes to you guys. I had no idea you were hurting like that."

"It's OK, Mama," Jade said.

"No, it's not, and from here on out, I'm going to do better. I'm going to do right by the four pack."

Jade loved when I called them the four pack. "Oh, Mama, it's OK. I love you so much."

"Why didn't you tell me you were cutting yourself?" I asked her.

"I didn't want you to think I was crazy. Plus you wouldn't have believed me anyway. You always call me a drama queen," Jade replied.

"Can I see your legs?"

"No," Jade said and jumped close to the wall.

"Please," I begged. "I promise not to judge or say anything bad."

Jade climbed over a sleeping Jalyssa and pulled her pajama pants down to her knees. I couldn't believe my eyes. My daughter's beautiful mocha-crème-colored thighs were mutilated with cuts. There were about twenty or so there. Out of nowhere, my face was soaked with tears.

"Mama, I'm sorry," Jade said, pulling her pants back up to her waist. She sat down on the floor beside me.

"No, I'm the one who's sorry," I said as I pulled her close to me and rubbed her head. "When was the last time you cut yourself?"

"Friday night before bed."

"OK, from here on out, no more cutting. You're much too beautiful to scar up your body like that. We're gonna fix those pretty thighs up with ointment and cocoa butter. That way the scars will fade faster. From now on, I want you to come to me and tell me how you're feeling," I said.

"You promise you won't get mad?" Jade asked nervously.

"Of course not. Especially if I know you need to express yourself," I said.

"Well, just in case, let's come up with a code word to let you know that it's serious," Jade suggested.

We both thought for a second before Jade snapped her fingers and said, "Mama's girl."

"Mama's girl?" I questioned.

"Yeah, I've never been much of a daddy's girl, and I want to be just like you when I grow up," Jade explained.

"You want to be like me?" I asked, surprised to hear that.

"Yep, flaws and all. Mama, you're so smart and beautiful. You care about people and will do anything to help people. I think you're the best person in the whole world," Jade said.

"I never knew you thought so highly of me," I said.

"You never asked," Jade said.

"Well OK, 'Mama's girl' it is," I said and hugged her tighter.

"Mama's girl what?" Jalyssa said, rubbing her eyes.

"Jalyssa," I said, getting up off the floor and sitting on the bed. "How are you feeling?"

Tears began to flow from Jalyssa's eyes. "Mama, I was on the phone with her the whole time."

I gasped. "Are you serious? Oh my goodness, Jalyssa, I'm sorry."

"I have the audio of my best friend dying etched in my memory forever," Jalyssa said, now beginning to sob.

I rocked Jalyssa in my arms. "I want to know what happened, but I won't ask right now. You can tell me when you get strength enough to talk. Right now, I just want you to rest."

"No, Mama, I want to tell you now. I've been wanting to tell you since I called you, but Aunt Miracle told me to get to Jade."

"OK, if that's what you want, then I'm listening," I said as I held her. Jade sat on the floor and rested her head on my leg. So this was what I'd been missing? I really loved these little girls.

Jalyssa started to talk.

"Fallon called my phone and said she and Blessed were on their way to Atlanta. I said, "Weren't you all supposed to leave tomorrow?"

She said, "Yeah, but Blessed said we were being followed." Then all of a sudden Fallon screamed, "Oh my God."

I said, "What's wrong?" She told me there were three police cars following them. I told her to promise she wouldn't hang up, and she agreed. All the while, Blessed is in the background, screaming for her to hang up the "f-ing" phone. He kept saying, "Hang up, Fallon. Hang up right now."

But Fallon screamed back and said, "No, I don't want Jalyssa to go. I'm scared, Blessed; slow down!" Then Blessed said, "If I slow down, they'll kill me and probably you too."

Mama, Fallon was bawling. She was coughing and stuttering through her sobs. I kept saying, "Calm down, Fallon, It's going to be all right." Then I just heard a loud crash, and Fallon screamed. She screamed so hard and so loud, like she was screaming for her life. Then the call dropped.

I kept trying to call her back, but the phone kept going straight to voice mail. I turned on the news, and it was already playing. Apparently the chase had happened live. They had a helicopter and police cars following them.

Mama, when I saw the car, I knew she was dead. All the glass was out the windows, and the car was flipped upside down. Then the words came across the screen, and I lost it. That's when I called you."

All I could do was rock her and rub her. I couldn't imagine losing my best friend, let alone being on the phone with her at the time of death.

"Jalyssa, baby, do you want to go with me to Farrah's house?" I asked.

"Yes, ma'am," she said sobbing.

I looked down at my leg. "Jade, you want to come too?"

Jade's face lit up like a Christmas tree. "Me? Yes, ma'am; I want to go."

"OK. Let me go and get the keys from Reece. Oh wait; does he know what's going on?" I asked.

"We don't know. Reece has been gone all day. He just got back right before Jalyssa fell asleep. He never asked what was going on. He just came in the house and went in the room," Jade explained.

"He *needs* to get those boys," Jalyssa added.

"Well, we are leaving. The three of us and Mark. My and Ty can stay here with their dad," I announced.

"Really, Mama?" Jalyssa said excitedly.

"Yep, you two get dressed. Tell Mark to get ready too. I'll be back in a few minutes," I said.

I walked toward my room and heard Reece through the door, talking on the phone.

"I know, baby; I know. I'm trying, but you know my situation with her," Reece said. "Of course I love you. It's you who I want to be with. No, Gabby doesn't mean anything to me, but how do I tell her I don't want to be with her?"

I froze and processed everything he was saying. I was much too smart for Reece. I had spent the past six years being comfortable with just existing. I deserved a man that had love only for me. I deserved a man that would be proactive in raising my children — not a man who had my children raising his two boys.

My first thought was to go in and confront him. But then my critical-thinking skills kicked in. Since Reece wanted to be a player, I would become the coach. I had a job now. All that was left to do was get a car. I could get Reece to buy me one, and then I would drop his ass like the garbage he was. I opened my room door. OK, Gab, it's show time, I thought to myself.

"Hey, bae," I said.

"Hey, what's up?" he replied. "Hey, Bruh, let me call you back."

I knew it was a woman he was talking to, but at this point, I didn't even care. "Let me get the keys to go to Farrah's," I said.

"What time you coming back?" he asked.

"I don't know. Blessed and Fallon were killed today, and I need to go be with Farrah."

"Word? What happened?" he asked, sitting straight up in the bed.

"I don't know. Why don't you watch the news?" I replied callously and walked out of the room. "Jalyssa, Jade, Mark, let's go."

"What about us, Ms. Gabby?" Ty said following me to the front door.

"You two are going to stay here and have fun with your daddy," I answered and walked out the door.

We spent the next five hours at Farrah's house. She was walking Charity out to her car when we pulled up. Jalyssa and Jade cleaned her kitchen and cooked a pot of spaghetti. Farrell hadn't eaten anything all day. After eating, Mark and Farrell played video games together.

Farrah had already been down to the morgue to identify the body. I was so sad that she had to do that on her own. Farrah and I went over legal documents, and I made sure the insurance company was made aware of what was going on. Then we contacted the funeral home and made an appointment for Farrah to go down to plan her daughter's funeral.

Jalyssa helped Farrah pick out the best pictures for the obituary and told her that Fallon was pregnant. This made Farrah cry even more.

"I hadn't seen her since Friday morning before school. If she had just come home," Farrah said.

"I know; I know," I told her. "We're always going to be here for you and Farrell. We're not going anywhere."

"Thank you so much, Gabby. Fallon always loved coming to your house with your girls. She said that Jade was like the little sister she never had," Farrah said.

After we finished making sure that everything was ready for Fallon's service, we kissed and hugged Farrah and Farrell and left.

I decided to take my children out to dinner. It had been a long time since we did that. I let Jade pick the restaurant. Being the seafood lover that she was, I just knew that she would pick Red Lobster, but to my surprise, she chose Joe's Crab Shack instead. We went to Joe's and ate until we couldn't breathe. It was a wonderful time. Marlin was always missing because he was with Sade, but now that she was pregnant, I wouldn't complain about him being missing during family time.

As I drove home, I thought. I thought about Reece. I thought about the car I would get him to buy me. I thought about Farrah and how she had just lost her daughter. I thought about how blessed I was to still have my daughters.

Then I thought about the passion group. Maybe we could name the group something to honor the memory of Fallon and Blessed. I would bring that suggestion to the committee. I glanced at each of my children. They were all knocked out, sleeping. Today, although tragic, had turned out to be a pretty good day for the Sweeny family.

Sha'Miracle

The news of Blessed's and Fallon's deaths broke my heart. Once everyone said their good-byes and we agreed to meet at my house again next Sunday, I started to think of how I was going to put the pieces of my life back together.

I immediately picked up the phone to call and apologize to my mother for the way that I had been acting for the past couple of years. My mother knew we had some unresolved issues, but at least she was willing to wait for me to first grieve the loss of the kids.

I got off the phone with her because I knew I had a lot of work to do. It was very important to me to make sure that, come Monday morning, Clinton Middle's faculty and staff would have a grief-and-loss action plan in place. I would need the help of all grade-level counselors, as well as the help from some outside counseling personnel.

I was sitting at my desk, writing down a list of people I needed to contact, when I noticed that my cell phone was ringing. It had been ringing off and on for the past hour, but I decided to ignore it until I had an opportunity to gather my thoughts. There was so much information to reflect on. I was struggling, trying to prioritize which crisis to handle first.

As I sat there looking around the room, the only thing that still seemed beautiful and at peace were the roses. I picked up the phone to call Gerald. As I was dialing Ms. Gloria's number, my cell phone started to ring again.

"Hello," I said.

"Miss Morris, this is Kosame Lu, Mr. Hall's assistant."

"Oh, um, hello."

"Mr. Hall is free on this Thursday and would like to extend an offer of dinner, if you are available."

"I...um...am very busy on this Thursday. Please let Mr. Hall know that I'll be in touch."

"And, Miss Morris, did the flowers arrive to your satisfaction?"

"Yes, please let him know that I was a bit overwhelmed with the excessive amount of flowers, but I do appreciate the gesture," I said as I hit the End button on my cell phone.

Wow, I thought. Let me try to make some sense of what just happened. You, Mr. Gerald Hall, are so "big time" that I need to be scheduled in to have dinner with you? Today is Sunday. I'm supposed to wait until Thursday to see you? I don't think so. I was almost certain now that his assistant sent the flowers. Men!

I needed to call Dr. Beacon, and that's exactly what I did. I spent the next hour talking to some of the guidance counselors at Clinton Middle and Kennedy High. I was in my zone. I wanted to make sure that I crossed every *T* and dotted every *I*.

"Blessed, if you can hear me, I'm so sorry your life ended so abruptly. I will spend the rest of my life advocating for young people like you and Fallon."

It sickened me to think how mental-health issues were not looked upon enough in this country. People loved to talk about how important it was to take care of your physical body, but you'd better not neglect your mental health as well. I had to figure out a way to make legislators aware of what was truly lacking in our schools. There had to be more funding for counseling programs and social-skills courses.

Knock, knock. The sound of banging on the door stopped me from jotting down some quick information from the Internet.

"Who is it?"

"It's me, Trevor."

I opened the door. "Trevor, what are you doing here?"

"I heard a student that attends Clinton was killed today. I've been trying to get you on the phone for two hours. Can I come in?"

"I'm sorry; of course, come in," I said as I made a slight hand gesture.

"Did you know that student?" Trevor asked.

"Yes, and I feel so bad. I didn't protect him. Trevor, I feel somewhat responsible for their deaths."

"Miracle, it's not your fault. You're not responsible for their deaths. It sounds like, to me, these teenagers made a series of bad decisions," Trevor said as he kissed my check.

"I guess, but it hurts. It's just so senseless!"

"I hate to show up over here unannounced, but when I couldn't get you on the phone, I became worried," Trevor replied.

"I've only known you for a few days, but I feel like I've known you forever. Is that crazy?" I asked.

"No, it's not crazy. I have thought of nothing but you since you walked into my life Friday morning," Trevor responded.

"Trevor Goodman, why are you here? What is it that you want from me?"

"What do I want—" He stopped midsentence and scooted closer to me on the sofa. "I want to wake up every morning to see your brown eyes staring back at me. I want to see that beautiful smile and know that I'm the reason you're smiling. I want to change your last name to be the same as mine," Trevor said as he wiped tears from my eyes.

I couldn't believe what he was saying to me. For once in my life, I wasn't going to analyze all the reasons not to love Trevor. I was just simply going to love him. I got up off the sofa so that I could sit on Trevor's lap. I folded my legs behind his waist and pressed my body close to his. I hugged him and started kissing him. He pushed his hands under my shirt and started feeling for the snap to unfasten my bra. I started laughing, because the snap was in the front.

He took my shirt off, and when he looked at my neck, he spotted a beautiful gold ring. I told him I would explain the ring later; right now I needed him to get up and follow me down the hall. As soon as we were about to pass the guest room, Trevor suddenly stopped. Against my wishes, he pushed the door to the guest room completely open.

"Miracle, I noticed all the flowers in the front of the house, but this is ridiculous. What is up with this?" Trevor demanded.

"Nothing is up with this. Gerald's assistant sent me eighty-three-dozen roses." I tried to sound unimpressed.

"This is crazy. Maybe we are moving too fast. Are you still feeling him? It sure as hell looks like he is still checking for you. Is this his way of saying he wants you back? I should have known I couldn't compete with a man you were willing to die for!" Trevor yelled.

"What the hell are you talking about? I almost died from stupidity. I took some medicine to help me lose weight quickly, and my kidneys couldn't take it. Why am I explaining this to you? You know what? Get the hell out my house!"

"Damn it, Sha'Miracle, tell me the truth! Are you still in love with Gerald?"

"No, Trevor, I'm in love with you!"

"I don't believe you. Say it again."

"Trevor, I'm in love with only you. I want you." I kissed him, and this time I followed him to my bedroom. I tried to turn the lights off, but he wanted them on. He got in the bed first. I got on top of him. The ring on my necklace was right in his face. I helped him take his shirt off, and I started kissing him on his chest. He rolled me over on my back and started to unzip my pants. My body suddenly tensed up.

"Miracle, relax. Do you trust me? What's wrong?"

"Nothing is wrong. I love it when you touch me."

"But?" Trevor asked through heavy breathing.

"I've been practicing celibacy for two and half years. The ring in your face reads 'True Love Waits.' I know this may change things between us," I said as I waited for his reaction.

He pulled me closer so that he could get a good look at the ring. He was very quiet. Then he started to laugh.

"Damn, you couldn't have told me about this before I seen you in your sexy bra? I'm going to ask this question, even though I might regret it. Baby, do you still want to wait?" Trevor sounded almost defeated.

"I'm sorry, Trevor. I know I came on to you real strong tonight. My emotions are all over the place because of Blessed's death and the passion group that started out being the not-so-passionate group. I do want to wait. If you want to leave now, I can only respect your decision," I said as I climbed off of him.

Trevor got out of the bed and stared into space. He started talking to himself. He sat down on the edge of the bed and shook his head several times.

"Trevor, you're starting to freak me out!"

"I'm sorry. I'm a little freaked out myself," Trevor replied.

"Just go! I'm sure you can be in another bed in a matter of minutes. Go sleep with Miss Skinny!" I screamed.

"I'm not leaving here and getting into anybody's bed. I'm going to sleep with you, and I mean that literally. I see why your father named you Miracle. It's going to take a miracle for me to keep my hands off you." Trevor laughed.

"So we're good?" I asked, making that smile he loved.

"I admire your commitment. I'm in love with you, so if that means waiting until we get married to make love, then we will have to wait," Trevor said.

I watched as Trevor removed everything he was wearing but his boxers and got under the comforter. I loved a man with muscular arms, and he definitely had that. I guessed it came from all the years of cheerleading; you learned to appreciate a man with strong arms.

The yell leaders were all very strong. They needed to be in order to toss us all around and hold us up in the air the way that they did. I got up and took a cold shower. I couldn't wait to talk with Madison tomorrow. She would probably say that making Trevor wait for sex was just another attempt to sabotage another relationship, but that couldn't be further from the truth. My Auntie Ruby always said, "What God has for me, it is for me." So if Trevor was truly the one for me, I would have to wait and see.

The next morning when Trevor and I walked into the Subway together, holding hands, Bobby seemed shocked.

"Well, look what the cat drug in. Trevor, you look like the cat that swallowed the canary!" Bobby teased.

"Good morning, Bobby. How are you?" I asked.

"Never better! Miss Miracle, can I get your usual this morning?" Bobby asked.

"Um, no, actually I think I will get a BMT with turkey bacon on wheat. Please add a little mustard," I said with a smile.

"Sounds good; I'll have that ready for you in just a few minutes," Bobby stated with a strange look on his face.

"Trevor, I'm going to the restroom," I said.

"T-Dawg! Miracle got a little pep in her step this morning. Any special reason why?" questioned Bobby.

"You're imagining things, because nothing happened last night," Trevor said sadly.

"What? Are you pleading the fifth?" Bobby asked while laughing.

"We've decided to practice *abstinence* until we get married," Trevor said with an unfamiliar tone.

"*ABSTINENCE*? Did you talk that over with your dick? My dick will never be marked absent! He is always present and at attention. You're stupid. Don't you see that this is just another scheme created by black women to try to trap a brother. What about what's her name?" Bobby asked.

"Shut up, fool! Here comes Miracle," Trevor said. "Put your money away, baby; it's no good here," Trevor said to me.

"OK but, Trevor, you still need to pay Bobby for this. He needs his books to look good," I insisted.

"You do realize that I'm the one looking at the books?" Trevor said to me. "Never mind. Keep the change, young blood," Trevor said as he gave Bobby the money. They put their fists together and laughed.

Trevor walked me to my car and gave me words of encouragement, because he knew I was in for a rough day. I kissed him and promised to see him later.

As I got near the school, I could see several news vans. I thought to myself, never a dull day at Clinton.

In spite of the crazy emotional outbursts from the ladies in the group and the devastating news of the death of the children, the meeting had been very eye-opening for Charity. She called Fallon's mother when she left Miracle's house and asked if it were OK if she came over.

Once there, Charity prayed with Farrah and Farrell and sat with them for a while. She let them know that she would be with them every step of the way. As Charity was leaving Farrah's home, she saw Gabby was coming. Charity took the time to console Jalyssa. She hugged Jade, Mark, and Gabby and got into her car to head home.

Charity's cell phone rang. It was Lucas. She smiled as she answered the phone. "Bless the Lord," Charity answered.

"Hello, beautiful. How are you?" Lucas asked.

"OK, I guess."

"Just OK? How was the meeting?"

"The meeting was a roller-coaster ride, but we did get the groundwork laid."

"A roller coaster? Would you like to talk about it?"

"During the meeting we got the news that two students that we knew got into a terrible car accident and died," Charity explained.

"Oh, no. Charity, darling, I'm so sorry to hear that. Would you like for me to come over with you for a while?" Lucas asked.

"That would be nice," replied Charity.

"I'm on my way now."

"OK, I'll be home in a few minutes."

When Lucas arrived, he and Charity talked and talked. They talked for hours. They talked about the children who died. They also talked about the passion group. Charity explained to him how important she thought the purpose of the group was. Lucas suggested that he knew some people who would be willing to invest in such an idea. Charity wrote down some ideas to take back to the group.

Charity often thought about Fallon and the last conversation she had with her. She was so negative and judgmental toward Fallon. She suffered with guilt for many months after Fallon had been laid to rest. However, she finally asked God to forgive her, and she asked Fallon to forgive her also. The last person that had to forgive Charity was Charity. When she did, she thought the scholarship should, in some small way, be dedicated to Fallon's memory.

Charity told the ladies that even though Fallon was pregnant, she always wanted to excel and be successful. In spite of everything that went on with her, she always wanted to excel. Together, the passion group decided to name the scholarship the Excel in Spite of Scholarship. Charity could finally rest at night, knowing that Fallon's legacy was protected by something positive that would support other young people just like her.

Although Charity and Lucas had learned a great deal about each other the night before on their date, they learned even more about each other during the visit on the day of the children's deaths.

Lucas had been through so much in his life. He was ready to settle down and get married. Charity thought that he was talking marriage pretty fast, but he said when a man knew what he wanted, he wasted no time trying to get it.

Charity was flattered but cautious as well. Over the next several months, they continued to court each other. Lucas never missed a Sunday service. He had joined Charity's church three months after they started dating.

Each Sunday, they went to the morning service at eight, so that Charity could make her passion-group meetings. She had grown to love the five ladies involved in the group. They had bonded very quickly, and Charity finally had something she had lacked for so many years — friends. She was finally in her happy place.

Lucas had proven to be a very good mate, and he never pressured her to sleep with him. He told her he respected her to the utmost and that she was worth the wait. He had decided that Charity would be his wife, so he would have the rest of his life to sleep with her when the time was right. Charity had also met Luke and started to spend time with him, and Lucas wanted one thing that Sam never did. Lucas wanted children.

One night as Charity and Lucas were cuddled up, watching a movie as they had done so many times before, Lucas blurted out, "Let's do it."

"Let's do what, honey?" Charity replied.

"Let's take this relationship to the next level."

"What do you mean, Lucas? I don't understand. We've been dating for months now; what more could we possibly do at this point?"

"Let's look at some rings. I want to know what you like. That way, when I'm ready to propose, I'll know exactly what to get."

"Rings?" Charity said. She was so excited. She was happy with Lucas and all, but he was actually trying to elevate their relationship. Charity had fallen for Lucas hard and fast. She never thought she could love a man again after Sam, but Lucas had taught her things she'd never known and shown her things she'd never seen. He never pressured her about missing out on church; he simply went with the flow. When she thought about Lucas, her heart smiled. Her heart had never smiled with Sam.

"Honey?" Lucas said.

"Huh?" Charity answered.

"What are you thinking about?" Lucas asked, gently stroking the side of her face.

"I'm thinking about you and me and how fairy tale-ish this seems. This feels so, so..."

"So right?" Lucas finished her sentence.

"Yes, so right that it scares me. This is all so fast," Charity said.

"Well, I tell you what; pray on it, and when you're ready, we'll look at rings. The last thing I want to do is make you uncomfortable or pressure you. Because the one thing I am certain of is I'm not going anywhere," Lucas explained.

Charity thought. Then she spoke. "OK, honey, we can look at rings, but before we go any further, I would like for us to get blood tests."

"Blood tests?"

"Yes. Not judging but you were on drugs for quite some time in your past. You have also slept with several different women in your lifetime. I just want to make sure you don't have any fatal diseases that will potentially cause me harm, whether physically, mentally, or psychologically," Charity announced.

Lucas wanted to be offended, but she was so sweet with her delivery of words that he couldn't be. She was right. His past *was* tattered, and she had only ever slept with one man before, so he was willing to do anything he had to in order to prove to her that he was genuine with his motives.

"That's fine, honey. A blood test it is, on one condition."

"What's that?"

"You get one too."

"That's only fair. I'll call the doctor tomorrow. Let's finish this movie and go to bed.

And the Lord God said, it is not good for man to be alone; I will make a help meet for him. (Genesis 2:18)

Hay

After the death of the two teenagers, Hay had decided to forget about Egypt and live her life. She had visited with Nay-Nay, who was a total wreck, and helped her through her tough times. Even though it had been months since the kids had died and been buried, the wounds were as fresh as that dreadful Sunday for Nay-Nay. Nay-Nay had become one of Hay's favorite people. She was just like Hay; when she loved, she loved hard.

Hay had been so busy with work that she had stopped visiting her mom so much. After the funeral, she started to visit her mom more. Hay loved her mom, and her mom loved her. Hay's sister, Patrice, had moved to Atlanta to pursue a career in acting. They talked every now and then, but Patrice was busy, and so was Hay. Hay had two women who were filled with love and wisdom that she vowed to never let go. She had Nay-Nay, and she had her mom, Tracey.

Hay wanted to let off some steam after a hard workday. She had been looking for Sashay in school, and Sashay continued to be absent. Tomorrow, Hay would do a home visit to see exactly why Sashay had to do so much baby-sitting and missing out on school.

But tonight, Hay was going to party with her LGBT family. LGBT meant *lesbian, gay, bisexual, transsexual.* Laiah was Hay's best friend, but when Hay wanted to be around people like herself, she went to her other family.

Tonight was jam-session night at the nightclub. There would be a show with the best featured dancers. Miss Sunflower, Rain, and Madam T-Storm were dancing tonight. These three were Hay's favorite trio. T-Storm always got a lot of tips, and boy, could she make it rain.

When Hay got to the club, she greeted her friends with hugs and kisses on the cheek. She hadn't been to the club in months. The last time she was there was the Thursday night before she got Blessed as a new client. Egypt was there with her that night. Tonight, however, Hay was flying solo. She went to the bar to order a drink.

"What can I get you, bruh?" said the bartender.

"Hennessey and Coke," Hay replied.

The bartender fixed the drink and handed it to her. "Eight."

Hay handed the bartender a ten-dollar bill and said, "You good."

"'Preciate it," he replied.

Hay turned around and headed to the dance floor. She had no intentions of dancing. She just wanted to get a good spot for when the show began. The music was loud and bumping—just what Hay needed.

She could smell weed smoke in the air, mixed with cigar and cigarette smoke. The mixtures burned her eyes a little, but the drink was keeping her calm. Before she knew it, her drink was gone. She went back to the bar and got another.

By the time she got back to the dance floor, the DJ had started to play "Back that Ass Up" by Juvenile. No matter how old this song was, it would always get the ladies to jamming. One lady in particular was dancing in front of Hay. Baby was sexy as hell and backing her ass up just right. Hay moved in closer to get just a little bit of contact.

By the end of the song, the lady had turned around, facing Hay, and had placed her arms around Hay's neck. Hay grabbed her butt and squeezed it tightly as the lady ground her hips all up on Hay. Hay thought that when the song was over, baby would move on, but to her surprise, she stayed put.

"My name is Lexi. What's yours?"

"Hay."

"You single?"

"Fa' sho'. What about you?" Hay asked.

"I'm single as a dollar and not looking for change," Lexi said.

"How old are you?"

"Twenty-four," answered Lexi.

"That's what's up," Hay said. She didn't want to start anything either. Her heart was still with Egypt, but there wasn't anything wrong with meeting new friends. "So what's your status? You bi?"

"Oh, no. I'm straight femme. No time for dog-ass dudes," Lexi replied.

"Cool," Hay said, feeling relieved. Dealing with a bisexual woman was not what she wanted. Egypt had taken her through hell and back, not knowing what she wanted. With a femme, there was no guessing.

For the rest of the night, Lexi stuck right under Hay. It was nice to have someone to dance with, someone who showed her all the attention she wanted. The shows were fantastic, as usual. Hay had consumed a total of three drinks, and Lexi was tossing back Patrón shots like they were water. She must have had about three or so.

At the end of the night, Lexi asked to come home with Hay. Under normal circumstances, Hay would have refused, but tonight, for some reason, Hay was horny as hell and wanted some of what Lexi had.

Hay drove them both back to her house, and they went inside. Lexi wasted no time and began taking off her clothes and kissing Hay wildly and zealously. Hay walked Lexi to her room and pulled out her black box. Hay had all kinds of toys and accessories for sex play. Lexi was thankful that she had gone home with Hay. She had the best sex ever that night.

The next morning, Hay woke up early and asked Lexi if she needed to be dropped off.

"No, thanks. I'll call a cab," Lexi said, pulling out her cell phone.

"Are you sure? I don't mind taking you home."

"No, thanks, I'm good."

"If you insist," Hay said.

Lexi's cab arrived in record time. Hay walked Lexi to the door. "Thanks for last night. It was unforgettable," Lexi said to Hay as she got into her cab.

"No, thank you," Hay replied.

This was the first time Hay had ever had a one-night stand. Lexi had said she was single and not looking for change. Hay had not given her a phone number, so she was pretty sure that would be the last she ever heard from Lexi. Oh well, it was a good night. Hay went back inside her house and got ready for work.

"Run, Luke, run!" Charity yelled. She, Lucas, and Luke were at the park. Lucas and Luke were racing, and Luke, with his little legs, was actually beating his father. Charity was certain that Lucas was letting Luke win but when he came to her huffing and puffing, she laughed, because she now wasn't so sure.

Luke ran until he got close to Charity then jumped up in her arms. "I win! I win! Daddy, you're an old man. You can't keep up with me!" Luke put both hands on Charity's cheeks and turned her face to look him directly in his eyes. "Ms. Charity, did you see how I left Daddy eating my dust?"

Charity laughed and hugged Luke. "Luke, your daddy just can't compete with you. I told him not to try, but he wouldn't listen." Charity set Luke down on the ground.

"You trying to turn my woman against me, boy? Huh?" Lucas said, picking Luke up and tickling him.

"No, but she already knows that I'm the winner," Luke said.

"You are both winners. We're all winners in God's eyes," Charity said.

"But who's the winner in *your* eyes?" Luke asked.

Charity smiled and said, "You are, baby boy." She turned to Lucas and said, "Sorry, honey. Luke got you this time."

Lucas laughed and said, "Father in heaven, you see how they're ganging up on me, right? Lord, send down a healing for my aching knees. I need you right now, Father."

Charity laughed and prayed a prayer of her own. "Lord, don't pay this man here no mind. Help him to get up in the mornings and hit those weights at the gym to build up his endurance."

Luke couldn't help but join in the fun. "Lord, thank you for helping me beat my daddy in that race. Now would you please touch my daddy and Ms. Charity's hearts and let them take me to IHOP? Thank you, Lord. Amen."

Charity and Lucas burst into uncontrollable laughter. They ate pancakes all day long when Luke was with them. Today would be no different.

"The Lord has spoken, and the word is IHOP," Lucas said.

"Yes! Thank ya, JESUS!" Luke yelled.

"Let's go, you two," Charity said, gathering their things to put into the car.

When they left IHOP, they went back to Lucas's house to give Luke a bath and take him to Hay. She had called for him while they were out.

"Bye, Daddy, bye, Ms. Charity," Luke called as he stood in the doorway at Hay's house.

"Bye," Charity and Lucas said back in unison.

The two of them headed to Charity's house. When they got there, Charity checked the mail and went inside. There was an envelope from the doctor. Inside the envelope there were two smaller envelopes. It was their blood-test results. Charity opened hers and let Lucas open his.

By the surprised look on Lucas's face when he looked at his results, Charity just knew he had AIDS.

"What is it, Lucas? Is it bad?" Charity asked.

"Well, it's not AIDS," he replied.

"OK, well?" Charity said.

"Let's trade," Lucas said.

Lucas looked at Charity's results, and Charity looked at his. Both of them were disease free. The test had shown that Lucas was allergic to shellfish, but the result that sent her head into a spinning daze was the result that stated Lucas had a trait of sickle cell.

Charity dropped down to the floor and cried.

"Honey, honey, what's wrong? I can't eat seafood, big deal. I'll just eat chicken," Lucas said, dropping to the floor to hold her.

"Lucas, didn't you read the report thoroughly? You have a trait of sickle cell."

"OK, so that's no big deal, right?"

"Yes, it is a big deal."

"What, Charity? Explain this to me."

"I have a trait of sickle cell too," Charity cried.

"OK, so what? Is it like we take some medicine to make sure we don't get sick in the future or something?"

"No, Lucas, honey, you don't understand. If one person has a trait, it's OK, but if two people have a trait, there's a twenty-five percent chance that their child will have full-blown sickle cell," Charity explained.

"Oh no," Lucas said. "So this means—"

"We can't have children, Lucas. We can't have children," Charity said, now sobbing in Lucas's arms.

Lucas didn't know what to say. He didn't know how to comfort her. He didn't know how to make things better. All he knew was that his precious Charity was crushed. All she ever wanted was children. That was all she ever talked about. He also knew that he wanted to have children with his wife, and he knew that his wife would be Charity.

Lucas began to pray. "Lord, we know that you are too wise to make a mistake. Strengthen us as we embrace this abysmal news, and guide us in the direction in which you want us to go. Comfort us, God lead us, God, and help us make the right decisions about our future endeavors. And, Lord, please provide Charity with the assurance that I'm willing to fight right alongside her on whatever battlefield she encounters. In your son Jesus's name I pray, amen."

They sat for a few minutes as Charity continued to sniffle.

"But, honey, what if we're fine? What if we have a child, and he or she isn't born with sickle cell?" Lucas suggested.

"That's not a chance I'm willing to take," Charity answered.

"Well, what does this mean for us?" Lucas asked.

"I don't know, Lucas. I don't know. Maybe you should find you a woman who isn't all screwed up to have your baby for you. No baby deserves to be born sick. And it would be selfish of us to take a chance to bring a sick baby into the world."

"Charity, you're talking crazy. I don't want another woman. I want you," Lucas said.

"Lucas, I want you to leave. I need some time to myself. I have to sort things out. These test results change everything."

"But they don't have to. Charity, I love you. And no matter what, I'm not leaving you. I need you," Lucas said.

"But can you just leave right now? I just need to be alone."

"No, I'm not leaving you by yourself. We need each other right now. This directly affects the both of us."

"Lucas, please!" Charity shouted.

"Charity, no!" Lucas shouted back and pulled her closer and tighter.

Charity cried in his arms. For the next several minutes, they sat on the floor in a tight embrace. No one said a word. Charity cried, and Lucas let her. She knew then that this would be a tough decision for her. He was such a good man, but there was no way she was having children with someone who had the same trait as she did.

Charity closed her eyes and prayed. She asked for strength and guidance as she contemplated whether she would cut her losses with Lucas or stay with him and never have children.

Charity lay in Lucas's arms and felt so comfortable there. Lucas made her feel safe and secure. She felt like, next to God, Lucas was her everything. Charity began kissing Lucas. She felt so sad about the news that she could possibly never have a baby that she just wanted to enjoy the man she loved.

Lucas welcomed her affection and began to kiss her back. Charity had positioned herself in a way that she was lying right beside him. She kissed his lips, then his neck, and then allowed herself to take off his shirt and kiss his chest. Lucas was so fine. She wanted him, to be connected to him; at this very moment, all Charity could think about was becoming one with Lucas.

Lucas was reciprocating Charity's every move. However, he stopped when she removed her sundress and displayed her pink satin matching bra and panties. Charity had the body of an angel. Almost a year of dating and Lucas had never seen this much of it before. He stared at her for a moment then asked her, "Are you sure you're ready for this?"

"Lucas, I love you. I love everything about you. All I want to do is feel you."

"What about waiting for marriage?"

"You plan on leaving me?"

"Hell no. I mean, no, honey, never."

"Well, alright then," Charity said as she straddled Lucas.

Lucas removed his shorts and boxers. Then he spoke again. "You don't want to move this to the bedroom? I always imagined our first time would be special."

"Nothing about our relationship has gone as planned; why should this?" Charity asked, unbuttoning her bra and letting her perfectly sized breast bounce out.

By now, Lucas was salivating. No more conversation, he thought, and he took one breast gently into his mouth and cupped the other. He rotated and gave each breast equal attention, and Charity moaned. As she sat on his waist, he could feel her warmth seeping through her panties. He turned her over on her back and kissed her again. This time he let his hands wander as he kissed her.

Charity arched her back as Lucas made his way from her neck down to her stomach and ended up at her thighs. Her body was so tense that he had to take his time. Lucas carefully parted her legs and planted soft, wet kisses on the insides of each of her thighs. He then took his index finger and moved it up and down the outside of her panties, where her throbbing vagina was. Lucas slowly removed Charity's panties and set them on the floor beside them. Then he kissed her vagina just as he had kissed the lips on her face.

Now totally relaxed, Charity had completely forgotten how good it felt to be touched in such a way. She panted and moaned as Lucas took control of her body with just his tongue. Charity felt a wave of emotions come over her. Her body stiffened; her head began to throb, and she completely lost control of her legs. She had a release so strong that she was wiped out. What she didn't know was that Lucas had just begun.

Lucas came back up to her face, and Charity kissed him like she would never get to kiss him again. He pulled up from her and said, "Condom."

Charity's mind was so blown from both her bad news and her body's good feelings that, at this moment, she chose to live without a care in the world. She replied to him, "Pull out."

Lucas slowly entered Charity's body, and she let out a sigh. He looked at her face to make sure he wasn't hurting her, but the look she gave was one of pure satisfaction. They made love passionately, and Lucas made sure to be as selfless as possible. Charity was his heart, and he wanted to make her happy in any way her could, at all times. When Lucas reached his peak and climaxed, he quickly pulled himself out of her body, jumped up, and ran to the bathroom to wash up.

When Lucas came back, he found Charity still lying on the floor. He had brought a warm washcloth for her to clean herself up. Instead he wiped her body down then picked her up and went to the shower. They showered together and got dressed.

Once in the bed, Lucas said to Charity, "How are you feeling?"

Charity gave him the biggest smile and said, "I'm good."

"Who would have thought it? Missionary Charity is an undercover freak."

Charity punched him in the chest. "Shut up. I thought I would feel extremely guilty when it was over, but surprisingly, I don't—a little guilty, yes, but not extremely. Don't worry; I plan to fully repent, and, oh yeah, we can't let that happen again."

"Hey, you're the one that took advantage of me in my weak hour," Lucas joked.

Charity laughed. "Lucas, I love you, but we still have a very tough decision to make."

"I know we do, honey. I want you to know that no matter what you decide, I will support you."

That made the decision even harder for Charity, because as of right now, Charity wasn't sure if it was Lucas she wanted to be with. She would rather have someone without the trait so that they could have children. She wondered if he would be so supportive if she chose option *B*, another man.

Create in me a clean heart, O God; and renew a right spirit within me. (Psalm 51:10)

Hay went to the office, gathered Sashay's file, and hopped in her company car. She went to Clinton Middle to check and see if Sashay was in school, but once again, she was absent. Hay left the school and headed to Sashay's home. She pulled into the complex and parked her car. Sashay lived on the third floor. Hay hated stairs, especially climbing them in the hot Central Florida heat. Hay knocked on the door.

"Who is it?" a voice called.

"Officer Dawson," Hay replied.

Ms. Baldwin opened the door. "Hi, Officer Dawson. How are you?"

"I'm fine, Ms. Baldwin; how are you?" Hay asked.

"I'm well. Won't you come in?" said Ms. Baldwin.

Once inside, Hay sat down. "Ms. Baldwin, I'm here to discuss Sashay's attendance at school. She's missed more than twenty days this past nine weeks and is about to be recommended for truancy court. I want to prevent that."

"How many days?" Ms. Baldwin asked, surprised to hear this information.

"More than twenty," Hay repeated. "She told me she has a baby sister that's about four months old that she has to baby-sit while you're at work."

"What?" Ms. Baldwin yelled. "I wouldn't leave my baby alone with Sashay if somebody paid me. She goes to day care while I work. I'm off today; otherwise you wouldn't have caught me here today, and guess where my baby is? At day care. As a matter of fact, I haven't seen Sashay in almost forty-eight hours."

"I'm sorry?" Hay said.

"Yes. It's been almost two days since she's been home. I called the police after twenty-four hours, and I've been pacing the floor ever since. None of her friends have seen her, but then again, they're probably lying to cover for her. She called herself running away about six months ago. I caught her at some little boy's house and beat that ass all the way home. She had been pretty good about curfew after that, until now."

"I see," Hay said as she wrote on her note pad.

Ms. Baldwin kept talking. "Sashay just got a job at the Subway close to the school. She started about a month ago. I called up there and asked her manager if he had seen her, and he said she was off for the next three days, so, no, he hasn't."

"What's the manager's name?"

"Bobby Goodman."

"OK, well, I'm going to go up there and see what I can find out. I'll be in touch," Hay assured her.

"Thanks, Officer Dawson."

Hay headed back toward Clinton Middle School and pulled up to the Subway. Once inside, she asked to speak with the manager, Bobby Goodman.

"Hello, I'm Bobby. How may I help you?" Bobby said.

"I'm looking for one of your employees Sashay Baldwin. Have you seen her?"

"I haven't seen her since her last shift," Bobby replied.

"She's been missing for two days. Her mother hasn't seen or heard from her at all."

"Really? I talk to her all the time."

"How so? Do you have a number where I can reach her?"

"I only have her home phone number, but we follow each other on Twitter. We talk a lot on there."

"When was the last time you talked to her on Twitter?"

"Just this morning. I wasn't concerned about not seeing her, because like I said, she wasn't due to come in until tomorrow."

"Can you log on and talk to her now?"

"Sure," Bobby said, taking out his phone. He typed a direct tweet to her that said "hey" and waited for a reply. As soon as he put his phone down, the notification rang. Bobby checked it. Sashay's tweet read, "Hey Bobby" with three smiley faces following. Bobby asked Hay what she wanted him to write back.

"Ask her where she is," Hay said.

Bobby tweeted, "where r u?"

Sashay responded, "chillin y?"

Bobby tweeted, "I need u. Come to the job asap."

Sashay replied, "omw," which Bobby knew meant "on my way."

"Very good," said Hay. "How long do you think it will be before she gets here?"

"A matter of minutes. She's a really hard worker. She does everything I ask with no problem. She always comes early for her shift and often stays late. She's a really good kid."

Hay wrote in her notebook as Bobby talked. Bobby got up to go and check on the employees and switched out the iced tea in the soda machine. He washed his hands and came back to where Hay was sitting. As soon as he sat down Sashay came through the door. She was extremely excited to see Bobby.

"*Hey Bobby,*" Sashay sang.

"Hey, pretty girl," Bobby said and gave Sashay a hug. "I was told that you haven't been home in a couple days. What's up with that?" Bobby said, folding his arms.

Before Sashay could respond, Hay stood up.

Sashay looked like she had seen a ghost. "Um…um…hi, Officer Dawson."

"Hello, Sashay. We need to talk."

"Yes, ma'am," Sashay replied.

Hay and Sashay moved to a table near the back of the restaurant.

"Sashay, what's going on, sweetheart? You haven't been to school and your mom says you haven't been home in almost two days."

"Officer Dawson, you know I have to baby-sit my little sister."

"Your mom said your little sister goes to day care."

"She did?"

"Yes, ma'am. So be straight up. What's going on with you?"

"School isn't really my thing, Officer Dawson. I keep telling my counselor that I want to be put in my right grade, but he keeps telling me that he can't do it unless I pass the test, and the test is too hard. I hate being with those little kids every day. I'm supposed to be in high school, and I'm stuck at stupid Clinton," Sashay complained.

"What if I get you some tutoring so you can pass the test to go to high school?"

"You would do that for me?"

"Sure I would. But you have to do something for me."

"What?"

"You have to go to school and try your best every day. You also have to go home every day and follow your mom's rules."

"I think I can do that. But what about when I spend time with my boyfriend?"

"What boyfriend?"

"Bobby."

"Your boss Bobby?"

"Yes. We've been together for three weeks now. He asked me out the week after I started working here. We've had sex and everything. Officer Dawson, I love him, and he loves me too."

Hay couldn't believe what she was hearing. Sashay was only sixteen years old. Bobby had to be at least twenty-five years old. That was statutory rape. Come to think of it, he *was* pretty caring when she walked in.

Hay finished up with Sashay and prepared to take her home. Sashay hugged Bobby and told him she would see him later.

"You be good now. I'll see you later," Bobby said to Sashay.

"OK. I'll hit you up on Twitter later," Sashay said.

"Cool. Later, sweetie."

"Later." Sashay giggled and got into the car.

Hay turned and talked to Bobby. "So, according to Sashay, you two are dating and have even slept together."

Bobby's eyes stretched as wide as silver dollars. "What?"

"That's what she just told me."

"That's a lie. I haven't done anything but be nice to that little girl. I'm not dating her."

"Well, I still have to notify the parent and file a report."

"You've got to be kidding me. I give the girl a job, compliment her, and show her that all bosses aren't dicks, and this is what I get in return?" Bobby said, heading toward the car.

Hay grabbed him and walked him back inside the restaurant. "Your problem, from what I saw just today, is that you're too friendly. You've crossed too many boundaries. The hugs, the endearing nicknames, the communication via social network—all of that makes you look suspect to her accusations."

"Just because I follow her on Twitter? If I hadn't been following her, you never would have found her."

"That's true, and I thank you for that, but while you see it as being nice, she seems to think otherwise. I would really like to tell you to be careful, but because she has made a claim of sex, I have to report it," Hay explained.

Bobby started walking toward the car again. Hay stopped him. "No, Bobby, let us handle it. Don't make a scene in front of your customers."

Hay got into her car and drove off. When she left the parking lot, a police car pulled up. The officer came in and asked for Bobby Goodman. Bobby told Hannah, the swing manager, that she would have to stay late and to close up the shop. Then he told her to call Trevor and tell him to come down to the county jail.

"This is just a big misunderstanding, and I will explain everything later," Bobby said.

"Don't worry; I got you, Bobby," Hannah said.

Bobby held his head down while he rode to the jail. He couldn't believe Sashay lied on him like this. But as long as his brother was coming, Bobby knew that everything would be OK.

"The first order of business is new sponsors. Does anyone have any?" Gabby asked.

"I do. This company called Alcott International reached out to the Juvenile Justice Department and offered fifty thousand dollars," Hay started. "The owner, John Alcott, asked especially for me, since I was on the board of directors. He viewed our website and said that what we were doing was very noble and he wanted to be a part of our legacy."

Madison, Miracle, and Egypt looked at each other and got ghostly quiet.

"What?" Gabby asked.

"Nothing," Madison quickly replied. "Anybody else?"

"Oh yeah, Lucas has some shareholders in his company, and two of them are interested in sponsoring the scholarship fund," Charity said eagerly.

"How much are we talking?" Gabby asked.

"Ten thousand dollars apiece," responded Charity.

All the ladies applauded. They had started this meeting like they had started all the others. Charity had prayed, and then Gabby asked about sponsors. Madison was the treasurer; Hay was the secretary; Egypt was the parliamentarian; Charity was, of course, the chaplain; Miracle was the vice president; and Gabby was the president. They were their own board of directors.

"What a blessing. Be sure to give their sponsor packets to Madison for processing. Maddie, can you have a grand total by the end of this meeting?" said Gabby.

"Yes, ma'am, I sure can," Madison responded.

"OK, so we have a pretty hefty fund; we have the name of our scholarship—" Gabby started.

"We have the qualifications," Egypt interjected.

"We have the application and the interview process," Miracle added.

"What else do we need?" Gabby asked.

"I think that's it," Hay said. "We just may be ready to rock and roll, ladies."

"Gosh, we have come so far along," Gabby said.

"Yeah, we have. I thought you were all crazy when I first met you. I have to admit; I thought about quitting this group plenty of times," Hay said. "Especially when Egypt and I were on the outs."

"But you stayed. And now you see that it was all worth it," said Egypt.

"It's almost time for our gala," Miracle announced. "The great Dr. Morris will be presenting us with our grand-total check that night."

"Oh yeah, that reminds me; do we still have tickets for sale? I need to take some more to church," Charity asked.

"Hay? Do we?" Gabby asked Hay.

"I believe we do." Hay looked over her documents. "Yes, we still have some. How many do you need?"

"Give me twenty-five more, just to be sure," Charity said.

Hay counted out twenty-five tickets, placed them in an envelope, and handed them to Charity. "That's twenty-five tickets, at fifty dollars per ticket, so your total to report back is one thousand two hundred and fifty dollars."

Charity nodded in agreement.

"Oh yeah, the sheriff's department has agreed to cover all costs for the food and venue for the night," Madison announced.

"Are you serious?" Gabby screamed. "That's wonderful!"

"Yeah, with Hay's connections and my power of persuasion, we convinced them to sponsor."

"That impressive business plan you showed them was the icing on the cake. Thanks for drawing it up, Miracle and Gabby," Egypt said.

Miracle and Gabby smiled at each other, and Gabby spoke again. "It looks like we have everything in order; now all we have to do is get some candidates. Do you all know of anyone?"

"Well, of course, my handsome and intelligent nephew Marlin," Miracle said.

"He's the reason we are all here today. Of course, his high-school guidance counselor will have to help him with the application process, because they'll swear I'm playing favorites," Gabby said.

"They'll probably be right too." Egypt joked.

"No *probably*, they WILL be right," Gabby laughed and said. "Any more people you guys know? Egypt?"

"I haven't been at the school that much lately, because I've been so busy, but I'll go up there tomorrow and see what's going on."

"Madison and Hay, we're ready for full paper work submission," Gabby stated.

"Full paper work will be submitted tomorrow. The Excel in Spite of Scholarship Fund will be nationally recognized in exactly seven days."

"We did it, ladies. We did it!" Gabby said proudly. "Charity, will you close us out with prayer?"

Charity asked everyone to stand and hold hands. She prayed a prayer and dismissed everyone until the next meeting. After everyone said amen, Egypt yelled out, "Sister Time."

Sister Time was the time the six women sat and talked after the business part of the passion group was over. Egypt had thought of it, and it had proven to be very therapeutic.

"I visited Nay-Nay and my mom this week," Hay said.

"How are they doing?" Miracle asked.

"My mom is fine. Nay-Nay has her good days and her bad days. She asked about Jalyssa and Jade. Gabby, make sure you take them over there to visit her. You know, in your new, big-body truck," Hay said to Gabby.

"Jalyssa is just as bad off as Nay-Nay. She still wakes up screaming some nights. Her therapist says this is normal, but I believe her grieving process is taking longer than the average time period," Gabby said.

"Grief knows no time period. You just have to be there and let them do what they need," Egypt said. "Take it from me; as soon as I was over that thing with Brown, it seems like tragedy just kept striking. Sometimes the grieving process takes years, and you don't even know it."

"What about Farrah, Gabby? How is she?" Miracle asked.

"She seems to be doing OK. Mark and Farrell hang out a lot, and Jade and Jalyssa go over once a week to help Farrah with household stuff." Gabby answered.

"See that's what Nay-Nay needs. Maybe Farrell and Mark can go with Jade and Jalyssa to visit her. She's lonely and just needs some company, and she loves children," Hay said.

"OK, I'll make that happen," Gabby said.

"So, Gabby, tell us how it feels to be riding around in a 2012 Cadillac Escalade that's all paid for," Madison said.

"Well, ladies," Gabby said as she stood up and imitated a preacher. "When you have a man, huh, who's doing wrong, huh, and you catch him, huh, and threaten to call the police, huh, you can get anything — hear me now — anything, huh, you want."

All the ladies laughed as Charity said, "Alright now, evangelist. Preach on!"

"No, seriously, I picked out the car I wanted and told Reece I wanted him to buy it for me. He said he wasn't going to spend that much money on a car, so I threatened to leave him. He knows I'm the best woman he's ever had, so he gave in. He bitched about it, but he also gave me that wad. I went down to the bank, got a cashier's check, and the rest is history," Gabby explained.

"So what's going on with you and Reece now?" Hay asked.

"Well, he moved out, and we see each other on occasion, but he no longer spends his nights at my house. My children like it better that way."

"So you haven't been to his new house?" Charity asked.

"Not as of yet. I've been too busy with my new job, this group, and trying to be a better mom for my children," said Gabby.

"I feel you on that," Egypt said. "Jade no longer comes into the office to talk. The only reason she comes by now is to say hello. She's smiling more lately too."

"Well, business has been extremely good for Avery and me. The night of the dinner party, he brought some lawyer over. It seems Lucas talked him into a dry-cleaning and delivering service for the Law Offices of Bailey & Brooks. At first I was totally against it, because my plate was full already, but those lawyers have a lot of dry cleaning, and they tip very well. They love Avery and were always pleased with how we went above and beyond for their dry-cleaning needs. Turns out, I was even able to get the firm to become sponsors for the scholarship," said Madison.

"What about psycho-ass Gavin?" Egypt asked. "Did he ever get that tattoo covered? What's his deal anyway?"

"Gavin's time with me has long gone. He's crazy like that, because number one, I was the best girlfriend he ever had; two, he had never dated outside of his race before, and three, he was a virgin when we slept together. Gavin has been after me for years, and I always pay him no mind. After the robbery, I encouraged him to let go and move on. If he put as much effort into pleasing his girlfriend as he put into trying to win me back, he just might be successful," Madison said.

"That robbery was crazy," Miracle said.

"I couldn't believe that his very own business partner was in on it. You can barely trust anybody these days," Madison said.

"Well, ladies, I think I must go now. Lucas is waiting for me, and we're picking up Luke." Charity looked at her watch. "As a matter of fact, he should already have him by now."

"Tell Luke I'm coming to get him from school tomorrow," Hay said.

"I will. See you all later. Remember Jesus loves you, and so do I." Charity hugged and kissed everybody and started toward the door. Everyone else followed. They said their good-byes, gave out their hugs and kisses, and all made promises to call each other later. Their scholarship gala was just around the corner. They had made so much progress since day one. They all felt excited and ready.

Egypt

I felt good this morning. I'd just gotten home from a five o'clock in the morning boot-camp session. Boot camp was an intense workout regimen I had been participating in for a few months now. The boot camp was not only good for keeping my body in great shape, but it also helped me to declutter my thoughts. For an hour of each day, I allowed my mind to be free of any kind of conflict, whether past or present. I just focused on the instructor and the moves I needed to make in order to get stronger.

Usually I had to wait for Miracle and Madison to show up, but today they arrived before me. I was so proud of Miracle. She looked like her high-school self again. I suspected it must be some man providing the incentive for the weight loss, but she was closed lip about this mystery man she was dating. I couldn't blame her; I hadn't said anything to my crew about Trevor either, and he was growing tired of the late nights and early mornings.

I hurried and showered and put on a nice pantsuit. Today Noah had to appear in child-support court with Candice. It was a modification hearing to determine if the amount of Asia's financial support should increase.

Candice had been giving Noah such a hard time ever since she found out that Elizabeth was pregnant. It certainly didn't help matters when Elizabeth posted her sonogram as her profile picture on Facebook. The situation only grew worse when Noah and Elizabeth got married and had their son. Candice had told Noah that she would not rest until they were back in court.

Well, today was that dreaded day. I promised Noah that I would meet him at the courthouse. Noah always got a little crazy anytime someone mentioned the word court. I knew I needed to be there for him today. I wasn't worried about Candice at all. Candice was pregnant again, and she probably wanted more money out of Noah to take care this new bundle of joy.

When I got to the courthouse, Noah was standing out front, talking with Candice.

"Good morning," I said, trying not to sound to irritated.

"I'm surprised you didn't show up here with Eliza-bitch, since y'all are family now," Candice said to me with such hatred in her voice.

"No, Liz is home taking care of their son. You know, that thing that mothers do when they actually care about their children," I replied and walked off.

I could hear Candice yelling obscenities at me, but I was working on building a better me inside and out, so I just kept walking. I needed to walk the straight and narrow. I got the results of my MCAT the other day. I shared the score with Dr. Morris, and she appeared to be startled. Apparently she scored only three points higher than I did. Dr. Morris was an esteemed alumnus of Johns Hopkins University, and she had agreed to help me with completing the application. I was on pins and needles waiting to see if I would be accepted. Dr. Egypt Moran was starting to have a very nice sound to it.

"Man, I hate being in here. This damn judge is so rude, and he has sent two people to jail already," Noah said.

"You heard the man. It takes money to meet a child's basic needs, so if anybody shows up to court today without any money, off to jail they go," I replied.

"Right, genius, but how can you make money if you are sitting in jail?" Noah asked.

"Really, Noah? These men and women had nine months to figure out how they were going to take care of their kids. These kids didn't ask to come here," I said, rolling my eyes.

Being in child-support court was a draining ordeal on my soul. I was so glad when it was finally Noah and Candice's turn.

The judge stared down at a case file for about three minutes before Candice grew impatient and just started talking about how Noah was self-employed and needed to stop lying about his income.

"Miss Candice Bradley, are you aware that an arrest warrant has been issued for you?" the judge asked.

"Warrant?" Candice sounded confused.

"Yes, that's when a judge orders law-enforcement officers to arrest and bring to jail a person charged with a crime," replied the judge.

"I know what a damn warrant is. I haven't committed any crime!" Candice yelled as the officer was reading the Miranda rights to her.

I sat there in disbelief. The judge told Noah that in lieu of the criminal circumstances with Miss Bradley, this hearing would have to be rescheduled.

Instead of Noah being happy about leaving court, he was ready to go running to her rescue. I explained to him that a criminal case had to go through several steps. She had just been arrested; she still would have a preliminary hearing for the judge to decide if she was even eligible for a bail.

"Egypt, we have to help her," Noah stated.

"We?" I asked.

"Egypt, please call that guy that you know that is a bail bondsman," Noah pleaded.

"Noah, go to Candice's house so that someone is there when the kids get home. I will take care of everything, and I will call you when I know something," I said.

Several hours later, I found out that Candice had been charged with grand theft auto and filing a false tax return. Bail was set at $10,000. I agreed to go and bail her out. I had to use my home as collateral. I also had no idea that I would be filling out papers for almost an hour and a half. I was so tired and hungry, and I just wanted to go home.

Candice did not get out of jail until the next day. I was in line at the Starbucks when the bail bondsman called me and told me that she had been released and was ready to be picked up. I guess I wasn't moving fast enough, because I found her two blocks up from the jail.

"Candice, I'm here to pick you up!" I yelled.

"Just leave me alone, Egypt!" she yelled back at me.

"I'm trying to help you. Please, get in the car," I begged.

"Look, Egypt, I've been through hell in the past twenty-four hours!" Candice said as she cried.

"You have to trust me. Get in the damn car!" I screamed.

"I'm hungry. I need to eat. Can you please take me to get breakfast?" Candice managed to say.

Over breakfast, Candice confided in me about her latest boyfriend. She had only known him for a short time online when they decided that it was a good time to meet in person. She picked him up from the airport in a rental car. She was only supposed to have the car for one week.

After one week of fun and sun, online guy said that he would return the rental car and get on a plane and go back to South Carolina. Well, since online guy was actually from Orlando, he decided to keep the rental car and drive around town in it. A month after the rental car was supposed to be returned, Pebbles saw online guy leaving the movies in it.

"Are you serious?" I asked. "The rental-car people should have contacted you."

"I lost my cell phone," Candice said as she ate another pancake.

"You had no idea that this fool was driving around town in a car that you rented?" I asked, because this was the most irrational thing I had ever heard.

"Nope," she said. "He said he would do me the favor of dropping it off when he boarded his flight. I thought nothing of it. I mean, it wasn't like he could have flown with the car."

"So what did you do when you found out he was driving it?"

"I called and reported the car stolen. After I filed the report, I thought nothing else of it. Little did I know, it had already been reported by the rental-car company, and since the car was in my name, well, you were in court," Candice said.

"Damn, that's messed up," I said.

"Thanks for getting me out. I never thought, in a million years, you would help me," Candice said.

"I love my niece, and she loves you. So that makes me love you by association. But don't get too comfortable." I laughed.

We left the restaurant, and I took Candice home. I wanted to say something about Candice letting Asia move in with Noah, but I figured we had bonded so well today that I didn't want to ruin what little progress we had just made. I told her I would be back on Friday for Asia. She assured me that Asia would have clean clothes packed for the weekend. It wasn't "Kumbaya," but it was progress.

My phone rang as I was driving home. It was Madison. "Hello, friend," I answered.

"Hi, Egypt. Did you remember that today was your day to take the girls to ballet?" Madison responded.

"Actually, I forgot. I was so busy with trying to get Candice out of jail that it slipped my mind. I can pick them up from school and drop them off at ballet, but I can't stay with them today, because I have to meet Trevor later," I explained.

"Trevor?" Madison asked.

"Yes, Trevor Goodman. We've been seeing each other for about a year now. You'll get to meet him soon, but don't tell anyone about him yet. I believe Hay still thinks she has a shot," I said.

Madison was quiet for a long while.

"Hello?" I sang.

"Yeah, OK, sure. Not a word. I'll talk to you later, Egypt, and thanks."

"No problem, Maddie," I said and ended the call. I needed to hurry and get to the girls, because I was anxious to be in Trevor's arms. I craved that man. I think he fully turned me straight again. But because of the passion group, Hay and I would always remain friends, no matter what.

After Avery signed the contract with the Law Offices of
Bailey & Brooks, Clark Dry Cleaners became a part of a very
worthwhile benefits package put together by the senior
partners at the firm. Clark Dry Cleaners would be responsible
for making sure that every attorney looked like a million
dollars. After all, they had just won a half-billion-dollar class-
action suit against a legendary pharmaceutical company.

Avery and I were in agreement with the fact that we
would have to spend money in order to make money. So I had
to purchase a new van and insurance for the van and driver,
not to mention new garment bags, a presser, a washer, and a
dryer. However, the one thing I was truly happy about was
the fact that we were able to hire five new employees. One of
them I was personally training to be what Avery called a
"mini-me."

Lauren Parks was a graduate of Legacy University. She
provided outstanding letters of recommendation. I was
thoroughly impressed with her work ethic.

Thanks to Lauren, I was spending less time at work and more time being passionate about fund raising. I was so proud of our passion group. I knew we were going to exceed our goal of $100,000.

I had made my rounds to all of our cleaners and was now headed to the bank for our last deposit for the day when Lauren called me.

"Mrs. Clark, the delivery driver has already picked up for the last time from Bailey and Brooks, but Attorney Brooks is insisting that we come back again," Lauren said.

"Lauren, just tell Jarrett to go back to the law offices and get the clothing, and we will make the necessary adjustment to his time sheet," I replied.

"I'm sorry, Mrs. Clark, but Jarrett has school tonight," Lauren said regretfully.

"That's right. Call Attorney Brooks back, and tell him that we will be able to accommodate him this time, but in the future, anything that does not make it into Jarrett's last pickup will have to wait until the next business day," I said irritably.

When I got to the bank, the commercial lane was packed. It was almost to the street. I'm going to be here forever, I thought to myself. When I finally made the deposit, I was ready to zoom to the law offices. I hoped not to run into that smug Brooks. Something about him rubbed me the wrong way. I just needed to get the clothing bags, load them in my car, and be on my way.

I was able to leave there without seeing Brooks. I was so far behind schedule that it wasn't even funny. I'd promised the ladies that I would meet them for drinks. I called Lauren and told her to call Miracle and tell her that I was running late and to meet me at Clark Dry Cleaners in the Fairmount Plaza.

It got dark so fast these days. When I turned into the plaza, there were only a few cars around. Once inside the cleaners, I put all the clothing bags from Bailey & Brooks in the proper place, but I wasn't at all satisfied with the way the place looked. The presser wasn't where it should have been, and there were tags all over the floor. Something was not right about this. Jarrett was always very thorough, and he knew that I was not fond of a rushed job.

Knock. Knock. I came from the back of the cleaners to find Miracle at the door. I put the code in the alarm and unlocked the door. Once Miracle was inside, I hugged her and locked the door again. I explained to her that things were not in their proper order and that I needed to fix them before I could leave.

For the sake of time, Miracle started to help me clean. After about twenty minutes, Gabby must have become restless, because she began to knock on the door. I told Miracle to go and open the door for Gabby. Gabby had our full attention, telling us a story about one of her co-workers that she caught sleeping on the job, when all of a sudden we heard the front door of the cleaners slam shut.

"Someone is in here!" Miracle said as she jumped behind me.

"Calm down, Miracle," Gabby said.

"Gabby, when you came in, did you lock the door?" I asked.

"Oh my God, I don't remember! Damn, I don't think I did. I'm so sorry," Gabby said sadly.

"Come on; just follow me. It's probably nothing," I said, trying to sound convincing.

As we slowly made our way to the front of the cleaners, we found Timothy Hook standing in the front entrance. He looked as if he could use a bath, a shave, and maybe an intervention.

"Tim, what's up? The cleaners is closed. I was just here to do some last-minute cleaning," I said.

"I hope you don't try nothing stupid; see what I'm saying? I need to get this money; see what I'm saying? Old boy wasn't listening, so it's whatever," Tim said as he pulled a gun out of his pants.

He pointed the gun straight at me. Miracle screamed so loudly. I thought he was going to shoot her out of sheer annoyance. I tried to convince him that he could have whatever he wanted if he would just put the gun away. I told him that most people paid with a debit or credit card. There would probably be very little cash in here. I was able to find about $1500, which, if I lived, I was going to fuss at Avery about. Tim, of course, was not happy with that amount.

"Look, Tim, you need to take that and get the hell out of here!" Gabby yelled.

"Shut the hell up! I need to think. Madison, we're going to take a little ride to the bank. See what I'm saying? We're going to make a drop, and you can promise them the rest of the money tomorrow. See what I'm saying?" Tim yelled as he grabbed my arm.

"You must be high. Get your filthy hands off me," I said.

"Bitch, does it look like I'm asking? I'll shoot your ass just like your punk-ass delivery boy! See what I'm saying?" Tim replied while he put the gun to my head.

"No, Tim! OK, calm down. Madison, please do something!" Miracle pleaded.

"OK, but it's not like I can get thousands of dollars out of a damn ATM," I said.

"Man, between the three of y'all, I should have plenty of bread to buy some more time. See what I'm saying? I'm going to look out the door to make sure nobody is out there. Get down on the floor, and put your head in your lap," Tim demanded.

As soon as he stuck his head out the door, someone landed a nice jab to Tim's jaw. He fell back into the cleaners, hollering. Gavin came running in like a crazy person. Tim was still holding the gun.

I ran to hit the panic button on the alarm. I yelled for Miracle and Gabby to get out of the cleaners. Gavin was beating Tim senseless. I finally started yelling for Gavin to stop hitting him. He snatched the gun out of Tim's hand. Tim was pretty out of it. He wasn't even moving.

I was so emotional and grateful that Gavin showed up when he did. I hugged him so tightly. I was still shaking when the police arrived. The police were taking our statements when Avery and Trevor got there. I was so happy to see Avery. I just wanted to go home and be with my children.

"Maddie, what happened? Are you alright? Did he hurt you?" Avery asked a million questions at once.

"Avery, I'm fine. I'm just very grateful to Gavin for showing up when he did," I said as I hugged Avery tightly.

"Gavin? As soon as you hit the panic button, the alarm-monitoring center called the police, me, and the ambulance. I have been calling you for two hours. What were you doing here this time of night?" Avery asked.

"Jarrett Fletcher has school tonight, and Brooks was adamant about us coming back to his office and doing one more clothing pickup. I know how important his business is, so I did the pickup myself," I said as I started to cry.

"Damn his business! There is nothing more important than your safety!" Avery exclaimed.

"Avery, I was so scared; things were happening so fast," I said.

"Madison, baby, where is Jarrett? His car is still over there," Avery replied.

I turned to face the parking lot, and Avery was right. Jarrett's car was out there. I pulled away from Avery and ran to look inside of the car. He was not in there. I was so busy rushing into the cleaners that I must have missed seeing it.

As I looked at Gavin's car, I started to think, was it even parked in front of the barbershop? The more I thought about it, I didn't remember seeing Gavin's car. I guess he just happened to pass by the plaza and saw my car. I started feeling sick to my stomach as I heard the sound of the ambulance growing closer and closer. The police and Avery ran over to where I was standing.

"Madison, what is going on?" Avery demanded.

"I think Tim has hurt Jarrett! Tim said he shot him. Officers, please go check the cleaners for Jarrett. Avery, please call his family and see if he made it to school!" I yelled as I started to feel faint.

"Gavin, you're a dead man. You hear me?! You better stop watching Madison and watch your fucking back!" Tim was yelling as he resisted arrest.

"Shut up, Hook! You never were a *real* man! We're done. You are dead to me! I can't wait to spit on your grave!" Gavin yelled as several police officers had to restrain him.

Right before the police put Tim into the squad car, he confessed to shooting Jarrett and said that Jarrett's body was in the barbershop. Gabby and I started yelling for the police to go over to the barbershop and check things out. Gavin became irate and flat-out refused to give the keys to the police. Sure enough, the blood on the door of the barbershop was enough probable cause for the police to go in and investigate.

I was scared, mad, and anxious all at the same time. Avery wanted me to leave with Gabby, Miracle, and Trevor, but I was not going anywhere until I was sure that Jarrett was alive. The police found Jarrett conscious, but he had multiple gunshot wounds. There was a bullet in the midline of his lower back, right thigh, and left buttock.

When the paramedics brought him out of the barbershop, I could visually see that he was alive, so I was able to breathe a sigh of relief. I was so mad at Gavin. Why would he refuse to let the police simply check to see if Jarrett was in there? It just didn't make sense to me. What if Jarrett would have died, I thought to myself.

"Mr. and Mrs. Clark, Detective Jonzon would like to show you something inside the barbershop," the officer stated.

I walked very slowly and held Avery's hand so tightly that he would probably need to put ice on it tomorrow. Inside Gavin's office was a forty-inch flat-screen TV. When the detective turned the TV on, Avery and I could see directly into our cleaners. I thought I was going to vomit. My entire body felt hot, and I started sweating. "What the hell is this? I can see three of our cleaners on the damn screen!" I yelled.

"He must have hidden cameras in your establishments. We are going to need to ask you guys a few more questions. I assume you would like to press charges," Jonzon said as he pointed to some surveillance cameras and other spy listening equipment throughout the office.

Avery pushed past me and ran out of the barbershop. I knew where he was headed. The police had handcuffs on Gavin, but he was still standing outside of the police car. I screamed for the police to get Avery. It took several police officers to restrain Avery. One of the officers pulled out his Taser, and I yelled for Avery to stop with tears running down my face.

"Please, Avery, take me home now." I wept.

"They better hurry up and get that slimy ass —" Avery said as I grabbed his face with both hands.

"Anything else you need from us? We will come downtown tomorrow," I said to the detective.

Avery watched me get into my car. I felt numb. I couldn't believe Gavin would do such a thing. I started to think about how it was no coincidence that he showed up when he did. He saw Tim inside of the cleaners. I wanted to hate Gavin at that moment, but I couldn't help but think that if the cameras had not been in the cleaners, Tim could have possibly hurt us. I wondered if Avery was going to see the situation in that way.

My cell phone buzzed. It was a text message. The message read "BITCH." I looked at the number, and it was some crazy area code. I disregarded it and placed my phone back down. I was in the middle of a new training class. The new employees were taking a test on the software when my phone buzzed.

The phone buzzed again. I looked at the text message. It was the same number but a different message. *"You know he's still fucking other people, right?"*

I replied, "Who is this?" and waited for a reply. Sure enough, I got one.

"The woman you taste every time you kiss Reece lol."

I didn't think one part of this crap was funny. I was ready to curse me a bitch out, but I had to keep my composure at work. I had been doing so well since I started here almost a year ago, and I was not going to let any skank ho Reece was screwing around with mess things up for me. I turned my phone off and finished my day.

As soon as I walked to the parking lot to get into my truck, I called Reece.

"Speak."

"What the hell is going on?" I yelled.

"What you mean?"

"I got some random-ass number texting my phone, trying to check me about you. Who is this chick, Reece?"

"Baby, I don't know."

"How many chicks you screwing right now?"

"None."

"Reece, you're a big-ass liar. For the record, I don't really give a damn who you sleeping with, but it's a different ball game when these hos start harassing me. If you're gonna be a cheater at least teach your hos their place. Nobody is to FUCK with Gabby. Now either you handle this shit, or I do," I said and hung the phone up.

The next thing I did was call the number that was texting me. I was too old to play little high-school games. If a bitch wanted to come for me, she needed to bring her ass.

"Thank you for calling; your party will be notified that you called." *Click.*

Really? A phony number? Who in the hell has time for this? I thought. I dialed Candy's number next.

"Hello," she answered.

"Candy, it's Gabby."

"Hey."

"I need a favor."

"A favor? What?"

"What's the chick's name cross town who Reece messes with?"

"Chanel," Candy answered.

"OK, thanks," I said.

"Wait a minute, Gabby. You really didn't know about Chanel?"

"No, I really didn't know. I had a feeling he was cheating but not exactly with who."

"Gabby, him and Chanel have been together for the past twelve years. They have a ten-year-old daughter and everything. I really thought you knew."

"A daughter?"

"Yep. Chanel is stupid though. She knows about you and the baby mamas, and she says she doesn't care. Rumor has it she has a dude too, so her and Reece just stay together for convenience. It's a fucked-up situation, but, hey, to each its own," Candy explained.

My heart dropped. Tears fell from my eyes. How could I have been so stupid? Twelve years? And here I was thinking I was ride or die at six.

"How do I get in contact with her?"

"My homegirl is her god sister. I'll get her number and call you right back."

"Thanks, Candice."

"No problem."

I drove home and tried to stay calm. Once I got home, I gathered everything Reece still had at my place and boxed it up. Then I spotted My and Ty's football gear. I grabbed that and put it in a separate box. I planned to take all this stuff to the store and drop it right off with Reece. The information I had found out was much too much.

My cell phone buzzed again. It was another text message. *"bitch don't call me now just keep being stupid for Reece he said you adapted to his world and you didn't care that he had three womans besides you. Damn your a idiot lol."*

I couldn't take any more of this. Whoever was texting me had bad grammar skills and was trying me at the same time. Where was Candy with that phone number?

I called Candy back. She answered the phone already talking. "I was just dialing your number. You ready?"

"Shoot," I said.

Candy gave me the number, and I quickly dialed it. "Hello."

"Hello, may I speak with Chanel?" I asked.

"This is she."

"Chanel, this is Gabby."

"Gabby? Oh hell, muthafucking, naw. Bitch, what the fuck is you calling my goddamn phone for?" Chanel yelled at the top of her lungs.

"I'm calling to see why you're texting my phone with bullshit-ass messages," I yelled just as loud.

"I ain't dialed your number, not one time ho. You're the one calling me 'bout Reece dog ass and texting me 'bout him going down on you and coming home to me!" said Chanel.

"I have never called you, *ma'am*. I just got your number a minute ago," I explained.

"Yeah, fucking, right. Well, if you wasn't calling and texting, who the hell was?" Chanel asked.

"Chanel, please calm down. We won't get anywhere yelling back and forth like this," I said lowering my voice.

Chanel chose to listen, because the person who called her earlier hadn't sounded this intelligent. "OK. Say what you gotta say," she said, sounding a bit calmer than before.

"First thing first, I had no idea that Reece and you had been together for so long. Next, I started getting texts from some number today and was trying to get to the bottom of it." I began to explain

"You just started getting texts and calls today? I've been getting them for the past month now. I even went to the authorities and filed a harassing charge against you. When I told Reece about it, he said he'd handle it. But from the looks of it, he hasn't. I've been dealing with Reece for almost thirteen years. He always steps out and comes back. You are no different. Don't be surprised if you find out he has two or three other women besides you. That's how Reece rolls; he's a dirty bastard. The only reason I stay connected to him is because my daughter loves him, and he pays all my bills." Chanel said

"A month? Oh no. This just started for me today. What's the number that's been texting you?"

Chanel told me the number. Turns out, it was the exact same number that was texting me.

"Chanel, I apologize for calling you so irately just now. It seems I still have some investigating to do. However, since you and Reece have been doing this for over a decade now, y'all can continue to do it. I'm done."

"Thank you for calling, Gabby. You must be really special for him to have stayed with you this long. Good luck, and I hope you find out who's harassing you too. If you find her before I do, let her know I'm coming for her, with the police right behind me," Chanel said.

I pressed End on my phone and called Jalyssa and Jade into the room.

"Yes, ma'am?" Jade spoke first.

"I'm going to take Reece the rest of his stuff. I'm officially done with him," I said.

"Really?" Jade said excitedly and hugged me tightly.

"Let go, strong arms. But, yeah, I can't do this anymore. You girls want to ride with me to take him his clothes?"

"Does this mean you won't be going to hang out with him at the store anymore?" Jalyssa asked.

"Yes," I replied.

"What about the boys?" Jade asked.

"Done with that too," I said. "They have moms; they can deal with them."

We got into the car and headed to the Corner Store. Reece was nowhere in sight. I decided to go over to the house where the two babies' mamas lived to drop off the boys' football gear. The boys weren't there right now. It was football practice time.

When I pulled up to the house, Reece's car was there. That was strange. I got out and knocked on the door. No one answered. I twisted the door, and it was unlocked. I walked in the house. There was no sign of anyone in the house, but I knew someone had to be there, because Reece's car was out front.

I heard noise coming from one of the rooms, so I walked toward the room. The door was completely closed, but there were moans and groans seeping from underneath the door. I opened the door and gasped at what I saw. Reece was in bed with, not one of the babies' mamas, but both of them.

He was having sex with one, while she performed oral sex on the other.

"A threesome? Really? So this is what y'all do while I take care of y'all little boys? The three of you are the epitome of nasty and grimy. No time for the boys because y'all too busy screwing each other!" I yelled.

I didn't know whose ass to beat first, so my natural instinct went to him. He was vulnerable due to his nakedness, and the two women had run from the room. I punched and slapped until my hands got tired; then he fell on the floor, and I kicked until my feet were tired. The two babies' mamas had called the police to report a break-in. Neither one of them tried to pull me off of him. I knew I had to hurry up and get the hell out of there. I walked past the both of them and told them they needed to go and help their man off the floor.

Then I said, "Y'all never have to worry about me again. Oh but his main bitch, she's coming for the both of you."

I got in my Escalade, which Reece paid cash for, and drove away.

Egypt

I was pretty proud of myself for convincing Attorney Klein to donate $5,000 to the passion group. I called Madison to share the good news with her. She suggested that we go out to dinner to celebrate. I knew Trevor would be out of town until tomorrow, so our celebration would have to be on hold for one more day, so that way, Trevor would be able to attend.

Trevor had been out of town a lot lately. I knew how much his business meant to him, so I tried to be understanding. I missed him so much. I couldn't wait to see him.

The next day went by so fast. My day was filled with trying to perfect perfection. I was at the salon for hours. Then I had to, of course, get a manicure and pedicure. Last but not least, I had to get an allover body wax. Waxing hurt like hell and was very time-consuming, but the result was so worth it.

I got home and opened a bottle of white wine. I took a nice, hot bath to relax and revive my body and mind. At about seven in the evening, I realized that I had not heard from Trevor. I figured he was probably running a little late because he stopped to buy me roses. About thirty minutes later, he called to say that his business meeting ran late and that he would have to meet me at the restaurant.

I tried to hide my disappointment, because I really wanted to make a grand entrance with him on my arm. I just told him that I missed him and to please hurry.

I looked at myself in the mirror for one last time before I left the house. I was looking gorgeous. I had decided on a designer dress with a slit that stopped at my thigh and the Louis Vuitton red-bottom shoes that Trevor loved to see me in. He was going to flip tonight when he saw me. I was almost to the restaurant when my cell phone rang.

"Hey girl," I said.

"Hello, Egypt. I know you wanted tonight to be a couples' night, so I invited Miracle also," Madison said.

"OK, great, the more the merrier," I said.

Once I got my valet ticket, I decided to try to call Trevor, but his cell phone went straight to his voice mail. When I got inside the restaurant, Madison and Avery were already seated. I tried calling Trevor one more time before I went to the table, to see if he was even in the vicinity. This time he picked up.

"Hello, handsome," I said.

"Hi, darling, I'm so sorry that I'm running late," Trevor replied.

"I just got to the restaurant, so, baby, hurry," I whined.

"Let's just get an appetizer so that way we can hurry back to your place for a real meal," Trevor said.

"Ooh, Trevor, I guess that means that we are not going out for drinks with my friends after dinner."

"Drinks with your friends? I didn't realize that we were going out with your friends. Egypt, I haven't seen you in two weeks; you can't expect me to share you tonight." Trevor sounded disappointed.

"Trevor, your memory is terrible. I told you yesterday that we would be involved in a couples' outing tonight."

"Really, Egypt? I don't remember you saying anything like that. I thought you liked it when it was just the two of us?" Trevor questioned.

"Trevor, I do love it when it is only us, but tonight I want to share some important news with the people I care most about in this world. So I want you to be there with my BFFs." I joked.

"OK, baby, if you insist. I should be there shortly," Trevor replied.

When I got to the table, Madison and Avery were already eating. Avery was almost finished with what looked like a shrimp cocktail. I hugged both of them and showered Madison with compliments.

"Hey, Ethiopia, nice of you to finally show up. I was beginning to wonder if I should order dinner for tonight or breakfast for tomorrow," Avery said.

"Egypt, don't mind him. He's just hungry," Madison said.

"Where is Miracle? Are they still coming to dinner?" I asked.

"I guess the traffic made everybody a little late," Madison said as she looked down at her watch.

For the next thirty minutes, we all made small talk about work, sports, and the latest technology. Avery took it upon himself to order another round of drinks just before Miracle walked in.

"I'm sorry we're so late. We both got off late tonight. How is everybody?" Miracle asked.

"Hungry," replied Avery.

"You look good, girl! You must have been putting in some extra cardio time outside of the gym," I said and high-fived Miracle.

"Hey, don't y'all see me sitting here? Don't start talking that girl crap at the table. Trevor needs to hurry up and get to the table," Avery said irritably.

"He'll be here in a minute," Miracle and I stated at the same time.

"Did I just miss something?" Avery said to Madison with a confused look on his face.

"Hey, baby, I finally made it," Trevor stated as he kissed me on the check.

"Mr. Goodman Sr., it's good to see you. I had no idea we would be dining with you tonight. This is my beautiful wife, Madison," Avery said as he reached across the table to shake his hand.

"I'm glad to finally meet you, Madison. I've heard only fond things about you. I'm afraid I know everyone else here. Miracle, where is my son?" Mr. Goodman asked.

"Here I am. What are you doing here, Dad?" Trevor Jr. asked.

"I have an announcement to make," the elder Mr. Goodman exclaimed.

"No, wait, Trevor. I asked you guys here tonight for me to make an announcement," I interrupted.

"Trevor, please sit down," Miracle remarked to Trevor Jr.

"I did well enough on the MCAT that I will be going off to medical school in the fall. I applied to a few schools, but, of course, I have my heart set on Johns Hopkins. I'm waiting on an acceptance letter!" I stated with such excitement in my voice.

"You can't leave me. I want to marry you!" the elder Mr. Goodman said with such desperation in his tone.

"Daddy, you can't be serious. When we told you to get back out there and start dating again, we didn't mean with someone younger than us! What are you thinking?" Trevor Jr. yelled.

"Egypt, this is the Trevor you have been dating for the past year? You have been dating Mr. Goodman?" Madison asked.

"Miracle, you gave up Gerald for tired little Trevor?" I asked.

"I think we are going to need another round of drinks!" Avery replied.

"Trevor, I'm sorry. For the first time in my life, I want to do something that will benefit someone other than me. I want to be a doctor," I said.

Miracle and Madison jumped up from their seats to hug me. We were all so happy. Trevor Sr. ordered the most expensive champagne in the place.

After dinner we all said our good-byes. I promised Trevor Jr. that the three of us would sit down and have a real adult-like conversation about my intentions with his father, once he and Miracle got back from Las Vegas. I could clearly see that he had some concerns about his father dating a younger woman, but at the end of the day, we were very happy. Well, we were until I told him about medical school. I thought to myself, am I making the right decision leaving Trevor now? Maybe I should stay.

Sha'Miracle

The weather was beautiful as we landed at McCarran International Airport in Nevada. My dad and Trevor went to baggage claim to get our bags, and my mom and I waited patiently in the waiting area nearby. There would be a limousine coming to pick us up and take us to our hotel.

We were in Las Vegas for the annual Brain- and Spinal-Cord-Mapping Convention. This year my mother had been chosen to be the keynote speaker. She had invited Trevor and me along shortly after I introduced the two of them. I had no intention of being in another room with my mother, let alone another state. However, Trevor and his gregarious spirit were happy to accept.

I thought I would die before this day came, but my mother had, surprisingly, taken a liking to Trevor, and our relationship had been mended tremendously as a result. The four of us were always going to dinner, golfing, and even to the football games on Saturdays. My father seemed happier these days as well. Trevor had come in and saved the Morris family from spiraling to the pits of the unknown.

"I believe that's the car. Miracle, darling, see what's keeping your father and Trevor while I check on the car," my mother said.

I walked over to baggage claim. The two men were grabbing the last of the bags just as I walked up. "We thought you guys got lost," I joked.

"Well, if the ladies on this trip hadn't packed their entire rooms, we would have been finished by now," Trevor said, stacking bags on a luggage cart.

"Ha, ha, very funny," I replied sarcastically. "Daddy, Mom is out front waiting. She says the car is here for us."

"OK, Miracle, let's go before she comes back in to get us. Neither of us wants that." My dad laughed as we walked.

Once inside the back of the limousine, my mother opened a bottle of champagne. She poured us all a glass and made a toast. "Here's to a relaxing vacation with family."

"It's only a vacation for us. You have to work," I said.

"When I'm finished with work — believe me — I'll be relaxing. The on-call doctor has my patients, so I shouldn't be disturbed with any emergencies while I'm here," my mother replied.

We pulled into the hotel and got checked in. Once inside our suite, I fell facedown on the bed. Trevor plopped down right beside me and smiled.

I looked up and caught him staring at me. "What?" I asked.

"You're so beautiful," he responded.

I blushed and hid my face again. Trevor was always doing and saying such sweet things to me. I had to make a decision on whether I would give Trevor a try or go back to what was familiar and comfortable with Gerald.

The decision I had thought to be so difficult turned out to be the easiest. Gerald never called me. He would always have his assistant call or e-mail me. Trevor, on the other hand, would come over, send sweet text messages, call to see how my day was going, and was always interested in what I was doing. It didn't matter whether it was school, the passion group, church, or whatever.

It was Trevor who insisted that I try to make amends with my mother. He said he understood that she could be difficult, but I needed to try while she was still here, because he no longer had his mother.

It was for these reasons that I sat at my computer one day and sent Gerald an e-mail. I explained to him that I was in a different place in my life and that I could not see myself being the wife of a football phenomenon. I liked working at Clinton. I liked helping children. I liked my life, no matter how mundane it may have seemed to him. He responded by saying, "I understand. Have a nice life." He didn't try to fight. He didn't try to change. He didn't try to convince me of any changes that could be made to accommodate my feelings.

"Miracle, what are you thinking about?" Trevor asked.

"How tired I am."

"Well, let me see if I can relax you a little more," he said, removing my shoes and massaging my feet. Trevor had the hands of a Greek god. He made any part of my body feel good with just a single touch. I enjoyed my foot massage then took a shower and got ready for dinner. We were meeting my parents in an hour.

For the next few days, while my mother worked, we had the time of our lives. We shopped at the Fashion Show Mall. I picked up something for all the girls. We saw the Michael Jackson Cirque du Soleil show. We took a plethora of pictures and, of course, ate at all the finest restaurants.

On the night before we left, Trevor and I went to dinner alone. My parents were tired and decided to have dinner at the hotel and make it a movie night.

"Sha'Miracle, I have really enjoyed myself these few days. I've had you all to myself, with no distractions," Trevor stated.

"That sounds a little selfish, Mr. Goodman. What's wrong? You don't like sharing?"

"Not when it comes to you. I've never met anyone as wonderful as you. I don't want to go a day without you in my life," Trevor said.

"I love you too, Trevor. You came into my life and showed me what it was like to truly be loved. I don't want that to end."

"It doesn't have to."

"Good," I said.

"Let's seal it," Trevor said.

"Seal it? How?" I asked, feeling confused.

"Let's get married."

"Was that your proposal?" I scowled at him.

"Yes. No. Wait!" Trevor said nervously.

"I'm listening," I said with my arms crossed.

"I mean, let's get married now."

"Now?" I gasped and choked on my bread.

"Yes, now. We can always have a big, pretty reception later. We're in the city of love. I saw a chapel on the way to the restaurant, and I also already have this." Trevor pulled a small Tiffany's box from his pocket. He opened it and revealed a two-carat Tiffany Novo engagement ring. He looked at me, and my eyes were as shiny as the diamond. I blinked one time, and the tears rushed down my face.

"Trevor Goodman, you didn't!" I cried.

"Sha'Miracle Morris, I did." He smiled.

"Where the hell is that chapel? Let's go!" I said.

Trevor laughed, placed the ring on my finger, kissed me, and we left.

As we walked toward the Chapel of the Bells, I looked at Trevor and smiled. "You know my parents are going to freak, right?"

"I don't think so," he replied.

"Why not?"

"Because I won them over with my charm. I'm smooth and debonair. They won't be upset," he said, sounding so sure of himself.

"Oh, well, all I can say is you'd better stay in the kitchen when I catch this heat."

"Oh, I don't plan to ever leave your side," he said. "This is it. We're here. Last chance to back out."

"Back out? Never. Let's do this, Mr. Goodman."

"As you wish, Miss Morris — for the last time."

I smiled again.

When we walked in, everything was already set up for us to go. Trevor had already filled out paper work and prepaid for the ceremony.

"How did you know I would say yes?" I asked.

"I didn't; I only hoped you would."

I smiled, and we walked inside the chapel. When the chapel doors opened, I couldn't believe my eyes. My parents were in the front row, smiling from ear to ear. My mother was holding my bouquet.

"Trevor, you didn't," was all I could say.

"Miracle, you're so special. You deserve nothing less than the best," he replied.

"You didn't think we would miss your big day now, did you?" my mom said.

"When Trevor asked me for your hand in marriage, my only condition was that I would be there, no matter where the wedding took place. So here we are. Congratulations, sweetheart," my dad said.

All I could do was cry. As spontaneous and untraditional as this was, it was the wedding of my dreams. I loved Trevor Goodman, everything about him. He was my soul mate.

On the way back to the hotel, Trevor took my necklace from my neck. He rolled the window down and tossed it out. "The wait is over. I love you, and I can't wait to show you how much!" Trevor then kissed me on my forehead and held me until we arrived at the hotel. Tonight would be the night, and he was definitely worth the wait.

The Passion Group

Today's meeting would be the final meeting before the gala. The ladies had each done so much planning and preparation that they couldn't wait to see the final product. Tina and Trina were in attendance at this meeting. They were going to be hostesses at the gala and needed to know exactly what was expected of them.

In spite of the way they had met, Tina had become one of Avery's favorite people. She could cook like no other. Avery had encouraged Madison to help Tina and Trina construct a business plan. Then the Clarks decided to invest in the two women. As a result, the two ladies had finally been able to start their catering business. It was called T-n-T Catering.

"I have a surprise for you all," Gabby said.

"What?" the ladies all chimed in.

"Listen to the radio, starting tomorrow all the way up until the day of the event. Linda J. has agreed to air a commercial advertising the Excel in Spite of Scholarship."

"Seriously?" cried Madison.

"Yes, and get this; she's going to broadcast live from the gala as well," Gabby added.

"The passion group is on the map, baby," Egypt said.

"Well the programs have been printed; the menus have been decided; the guest list has been updated, and the entertainment is booked," Hay said.

"All that's left to do now is sit back and watch God work," said Charity.

"Thanks again, ladies. I really mean that," Gabby said.

"Oh, Gabby, don't go getting all soft on us now," Miracle said.

"Yeah, because you know you can get crunk," Egypt joked.

"Only if I'm pushed out of my ladylike zone though," Gabby defended.

"I see where this conversation is headed. Let's close on out and open up Sister Time, because I have a few questions anyway," announced Charity.

Everyone stood up and joined hands. They knew the routine. Charity prayed, and everyone sat back down. Charity started talking first. "So, Gabby, did you ever find out who was texting you?"

"Yes, but get this; Chanel found out and called me and told me. I was sure it was one of those tired babies' mamas, but it turns out it was some nineteen-year-old that Reece was messing with," Gabby explained.

"A nineteen-year-old? Reece's old behind needs to be shot. How long had he been with her?" asked Egypt.

"According to her, a year. Apparently he told her that he was leaving me; then when he bought me the truck and she found out, she felt like he needed her assistance in breaking up with me."

"Wow, there are some crazy people in the world," Charity said.

"So what about Chanel and the other two women?" asked Miracle.

"As far as I know, he's still screwing them all. And get this; he's still messing with Lexi too."

"Lexi?" Hay said.

"Yes, that's the girl's name. Chanel says she's bisexual, but I really don't care. I'm just glad I'm out of the situation now."

"She told me she was a femme. And she was twenty-four," Hay said.

"You know her?" Gabby said. "Small world."

"Yeah, I met her at the gay club one night." Hay thought it was best to leave it at that.

"So do you still talk to her?" Egypt inquired.

"No, I never spoke to her after that one night," Hay replied.

Egypt read between the lines. She knew that "one night" meant they slept together. However, she couldn't reveal her jealousy. She decided to let this one go. After all, she was with Trevor now.

"Gabby, did you get tested? You know, for STDs?" Madison asked with concern.

"You know I did. I went to the doctor and told her to take my blood and test me for everything from HIV to chicken pox. I was not playing. Everything came back negative."

"Thank you, Jesus, for that," Egypt said.

"Charity, you're rubbing off on us, girl," Miracle said.

"Well bless the Lord for that," Charity replied.

"So what happened with the cops coming over after you caught them in the bed? Did you get in trouble?" Tina asked.

"Chile, please, Reece didn't want to press charges. Not when I know where every stash is, who every employee is, and where all the money is hidden. He just asked that I keep my mouth shut, and he would leave me alone—fair trade. I'm too smart, too talented, and too good for Reece. I walked around with blinders on for so long. If it weren't for us getting together and Egypt calling me out, who knows when I would've wised up."

"So you know where everything is?" Hay asked.

"Yep," Gabby replied.

"Interesting," said Hay.

"So how is Marlin doing? You know, after everything," Miracle asked.

"He's doing OK. He was sad at first when he and Sade broke up. He said he couldn't believe she betrayed him like that. So now he's focused on graduating and applying for scholarships. He applied to Legacy but hasn't gotten an answer yet," Gabby said.

"He probably hasn't heard from Legacy because he really belongs at Wise," Charity said.

"I know that's right," Hay added.

"Oh here y'all go. He applied to the best college, so just leave it at that." Miracle snapped her fingers in the air. Everyone laughed as they began their college chants. There were two different chants going simultaneously. They laughed again and continued their discussion right where they had left off.

"It's sad that Sade went to such great lengths to trap him like that. He already loved her. She didn't have to lie about being pregnant," Egypt stated.

"I know," Gabby started. "She doesn't want him to leave for college. She started changing when he got back from the college tour. She said she was afraid that he would find someone else and forget about her. I'm happy he's not with her anymore, because he's back to my Marlin, focused on school and being successful. And since he's not with her anymore and Reece is gone, the four pack is stronger than ever. I really thank God for a second chance."

"Hay, what ever happened with Bobby and Sashay?" asked Miracle.

"Sashay admitted to lying. Her stories never stayed the same, so all charges were dropped. I did, however, warn Bobby about being so friendly with children. He was just being nice, but it could quickly turn into something very serious."

"I'm glad that worked out for him. Bobby is a really good guy," Miracle said.

Hay turned to Madison and asked, "What's the latest with you and Avery, since he found out about Gavin's fatal attraction for you?"

"Avery was a little crazy for a couple of months. He hired his own private investigator to find out how long Gavin had actually been watching me. Gavin was sleeping with two different employees of ours at two different locations. That's how he was able to install the cameras without anyone noticing. But get this; the young lady that works for us at the Castle Lake Plaza is filing charges of sexual harassment against him. I guess he was trying to get to her to put cameras there too," Madison said.

"That is crazy and scary at the same time," Miracle interjected.

"What's going to happen to that psychopath?" asked Gabby.

"He has so many charges. Harassment, stalking, breaking and entering, assault on a law-enforcement officer, and resisting arrest are just a few of his charges. Plus, in Florida it is illegal to record someone's conversation without the consent of at least one person involved," explained Madison.

"Wow, that's a lot. I knew he was a little off, but I had no idea he was that crazy," Egypt said.

"Avery and I are waiting for our lawyer to tell us the court date so that I can appear. So I guess we will have to wait and see what happens then," Madison commented.

"Well, guess what I just found out?" Charity said.

"What?" Madison replied while everyone paid attention.

"I'm pregnant."

Everyone gasped.

"What? How? When?" Gabby stuttered.

"It happened the night Lucas and I both found out we had traits of sickle cell. I was feeling so sad and he was being so sweet and supportive. One thing led to another, and we ended up sinning," Charity explained.

"Was it good?" Egypt asked.

"Egypt!" Miracle shouted.

"Well, was it?" Hay asked.

"It was *so* good. That's how I knew it was so wrong. I prayed, asked for forgiveness, and fully repented. We haven't done anything since then. But when my friend didn't come to visit, I took a test. Of course Lucas is ecstatic about it, but I don't know. I don't want a sick baby," Charity said, looking sad.

Everyone crowded around her and assured her that everything would be OK. Charity felt so loved at that very moment. She felt that whether she gave birth to a healthy baby or a baby that was born with sickle cell, everything would work out just fine. She had a support system out of this world, and Lucas had proven to be godsent.

"Well, I think we *all* have something to celebrate. Miss Egypt has applied to medical school, and our goody-two-shoes Miracle went and jumped the broom on us," Gabby announced.

Miracle blushed, and Egypt smiled as widely as she could.

"I still don't know if I'm ready for that change yet," Egypt said. "It's so far away, and I will miss you all so much. And Trevor, oh my Trevor, he hasn't been the same since he found out. He's been pressuring me to stay here with him one minute then being very supportive of the move the next minute," Egypt explained.

"Maybe it's dementia," Madison said.

"Madison! No!" Miracle scolded.

Egypt cut her eyes at Madison then smiled. "I don't know what it is, but I can't figure him out. My mom and brother are very happy though. That's reason enough for me to go for it."

"That's wonderful," Madison smiled.

Egypt pulled an envelope out of her handbag and said, "I wanted to wait until I was here with you all to open this." She opened the envelope and read the letter. Egypt jumped up and screamed at the top of her lungs. "I GOT IN! I GOT IN!"

Everyone screamed and jumped alongside her. Then they all took turns hugging and congratulating her. Now Egypt's decision-making process had to be sped up. At first she was speculating what would happen if she got accepted. Now that it was a reality, Trevor would freak out for sure.

Suddenly Egypt fell to her chair. She realized that if she left, she would be leaving her friends, who had now become the sisters she never had. Getting emotional from this topic, Egypt took the attention from her and turned it toward Miracle. "So, Sha'Miracle Goodman, tell us about this surprise wedding."

Miracle blushed. "I wish you ladies could have been there. That's the only thing that would have made it even more perfect than it already was. I was so shocked to see my parents in the chapel when we arrived. I really thought it was spontaneous, but it turns out Trevor and my parents had been planning it for some time now."

"I have a confession to make," said Gabby.

"What?" Miracle replied.

"We all knew," Gabby said.

"Really?" said Miracle.

"Yes," Hay said. "Trevor contacted Gabby and let her know what he was planning, and Gabby told the rest of us that we had to help."

"Who do you think helped him pick out that fierce ring?" Egypt bragged. "I know you don't think his taste is that exquisite."

"Watch it, Egypt. That's my husband you're talking about," Miracle said, smiling.

"In his defense, though, he was on the right track," Charity chimed in. "He's the one who started at Tiffany's for the ring. He narrowed it down to three that he liked the best, and Egypt helped from there."

"Oh yeah, we have to plan your Orlando ceremony now. I call matron of honor," Madison said.

Everyone laughed. "Madison, you can't call matron of honor; Miracle has to choose," Charity said.

"Well, since none of you are married, I get the position on a technicality," Madison said to Charity and stuck her tongue out.

"We'll talk about all of that later. I'm still getting adjusted to married life right now and finalizing the prenup but a ceremony? Most definitely," Miracle explained.

"Prenup? Say what now?" Egypt yelled.

"We'll talk about that later," Miracle said.

"The next time we meet will be at the gala. I can't wait to see you all there, with your men to escort you," Gabby said.

"Look how far we've come," Hay said then turned to Egypt. "Egypt, I'm happy for you. I also want you to know that whatever you decide, I will support."

"Thanks, Hay, that means the world to me," Egypt said.

The ladies of the passion group laughed and talked into the wee hours of the morning. They talked about how they had one month to get prepared for the gala. They were all so excited about what they had done. The passion group that started out so sour had now become so sweet. People were forgiven; friends had been made, and an unbreakable bond had been formed between the six ladies. It was true passion at its best.

About The Authors

Monica Harper has been an educator for over a decade. She attended Jones High School then Florida A&M University, where she received her undergraduate degree in political science. At Stetson University, she earned a master-of-science degree in school counseling. Later, her commitment to remain relevant in education inspired her to obtain an educational-specialist degree in curriculum and instruction management & administration from Nova Southeastern University. She enjoys spending time with family and friends and is currently working on several different projects.

Adonica Williams is from Orlando, Florida, and has lived there all her life. She has been an educator for more than ten years. She graduated from Jones High School and Bethune-Cookman College (before it was a university). After teaching for two years, she attended Nova Southeastern University and earned a master's degree in management of educational programs. She has always loved to write. Even as a child, she often wrote as a means to express herself as opposed to talking. Adonica's goal is to write as many books as she can and touch as many lives as possible before her time on earth expires. She recently finished her second book, entitled, *These Fools Be Lying: A Compilation of Short Stories*. Her personal credo is, "Excel in spite of." That's what she continues to do.